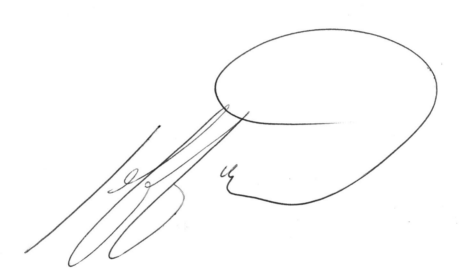

Cover Designer: Laurel Kenny
Chief Editor: Jamie Platte
Story Advisor: Michael Wright

There is no greater love than for one to lay down his life for another.

Jesus Christ

Catherine Knox

A Rose Amongst the Thorns

Throughout the early centuries, the countries of France and Britain fought endlessly. Even though these battles were carried out closer to home, no flag was safe from the other - even on the far side of the earth. This fictional story comes from those days on the high seas when King George III ruled the British Empire and seafaring men toasted their victory to him.

1

It was mid-July in the South Pacific, a place teeming with life, lush tropical islands, and sun-scorched men sailing the high seas; not for riches, but for glory.

On this humid, foggy day, dampened with mist in the air, Thomas Payne, Captain of His Majesty's ship, the HMS York, sat at his desk contemplating which chain of islands they'd be making port in. His brow too showed all the signs of the morning's staleness, as beads of sweat rolled down from his temples while going over his charts.

Hearing a tap on his door, he looked up from his desk. "Come in."
Lieutenant Cole, a stately gentleman in his clean crisp uniform entered. He was a tall man with a proud swagger like the British Flag that fluttered high on the mast.

"Good morning, Captain."
"Morning Lieutenant. How much longer will we be adrift?"
"The men in the pontoon should be finished sealing the waterline within the hour, Sir," he replied. "What are you working on?"
"I'm trying to decide which chain of islands we'll make port and gather more provisions."
"I see, Sir."

As Payne pointed out the nearest ones, they heard the call, "Storm ahead."

"On a day like today there must be a thousand storms ahead," he mused. "Best you get up there, Lieutenant. If it's bad, get those men out of the water. We'll make for clearer skies."

"Aye Captain," he replied, heading for the door.

"Lieutenant."

Cole turned. His expression turned to utter terror. Through the dense fog astern of ship, he saw a large muzzle flash. "Get down!"

Payne pushed his chair back and dropped to the floor.

The hideous sound of a whistling cannon ball splashed forty yards back of the ship.

Before another round was fired, Payne scrambled to his feet. Grabbing his spyglass, he peered out through the haze. Like a giant sea serpent, half hidden within the fog, he observed the square yardarms and sails. "It's a French man-o-war. The bastards have caught us unaware."

Up on the main deck, the beat of the drum resonated throughout the ship, alerting the crew to general quarters. The two heard the heavy pounding of feet, men yelling, while racing to their battle stations.

"Get moving, Lieutenant. Set the pontoon adrift and get those men out of the water, if they haven't already."

"Aye, Captain," said Cole, rushing out.

While quickly strapping on his saber and donning his cover, Payne looked back just in time to see another flash from a forward gun. He quickly hit the deck taking cover. The lead round splashed closer to the stern. When he got up, he glared at the ship like a leopard watching his prey. This time however, he was the prey. No combatant had ever been able to take him by surprise, not even on a wretched morning like this. His mind reeled with anger, mad at himself and the French warship sailing in for the kill. He charged out of his cabin like thunder.

"Captain on deck," said Conning Officer Holbrook.

Payne looked up seeing the main sheet still secured. "Mr. Roberts," he shouted. "Get your crew aloft. I'm needing full sails."

"Aye, Captain."

After gaining the bridge, Payne caught a glimpse of the warship's bow and mast. His situation was dire; his crew was under an assault by a much larger vessel.

Casting his eyes forward he could see the dark menacing clouds ahead; the ocean churning before it.

"I'll take the helm, Lad," he said, grabbing the wheeling and spinning it. The rudder engaged, the York turned - allowing the wind to catch the sails. On other occasions, he would have skirted a hellish storm as this. Today, it was his blessing.

"Midshipmen Meadows, strike below and inform Lieutenant Amsterdam not to pivot the batteries out. I want them perpendicular to the keel. We need to out run this devil fish."

"Aye, Captain."

Holbrook stepped up alongside Payne. "If it's the Nightingale, Sir, we're outgunned four to one."

Payne hastily spun around, studying the ship's outline once again. "If it is the Nightingale - she's three decks high, 24 guns, and her hull is ten inches thick."

"Our batteries won't penetrate that, Captain."

"No," he replied. "Our only chance of surviving is taking the York into that storm. She won't follow, by God, she won't follow."

"Sir, that storm has all the signs of something we dare not want."

Thomas glared at the high rolling clouds building upward and spinning westward. His instincts told him it was the outer edge of a typhoon. Could he slip in then out the side before it was fully upon them?

He glanced back again. With a man-of-war behind and a treacherous storm in front, his odds were bleak facing such threats. Thomas Payne, Captain of the York was not going to bow to either. He'd take on the storm.

Onboard the Nightingale, Captain Leopold, a thinly-laced man with dark beady eyes studied the British flag fluttering in the breeze. He scanned down the mast until his spyglass leveled off at the stern. "It's the York," he bellowed.

"It plundered two of ours and sunk another," said Leftenant La 'foot.

"Mark my word, this day she'll be plundered and sunk herself."

"What about Captain Payne? Will we take him prisoner?" he asked, locking eyes with Leopold. There was no pity within them; just wielding daggers ready to strike.

"No, he'll go down along with his men."

La 'foot smartly clasped his hands behind his back inhaling the fragrance of their soon to be victory. He could already imagine the British sailors along with Payne going down with the York, a death so pleasing for him to see.

"Maintain course and reload the forward battery," ordered Leopold. "We can't allow the York to slip into that storm."

"Ah, but Capitiane – the York will not stand a chance if she continues on her course. That be a typhoon. Best we allow her to enter then come about. That storm will be their doom."

"It may, Leftenant, but Captain Payne is no fool. He may try and trick us thinking he's going to drive the York into that beast, then as he gets near, he'll change course and slip alongside, using her wind to sail the York out of harm's way."

"That he may, that he may."

Ahead of the Nightingale, Payne continued on course through the misty haze. Off the York's bow, three hundred yards out was his destiny. Half way there, he glanced back eyeing the enormous warship with its countless sails.

"You can't out run her, Sir," said Holbrook.

"Let's see if she follows."

As the winds began to howl, rattling the rigging lines, and tossing men about, the

Nightingale advanced on the York through the heavy waves and choppy seas. The men aboard each ship hunkered down ready to battle.

Closing in on his target, Leopold ordered his forward gun to commence firing. "Aim for the rudder, men. With her dead in the water, we'll come alongside and fill her belly full of lead."

The first volley whistled toward the York. The crew heard the blast and then panicked when it slammed into the stern. The bay windows shattered. Payne's desk and chair, along with the lantern, exploded. The flammable oil instantly ignited, setting his cabin ablaze.

"Direct hit, Capitiane," yelled La' foot.

"We've just begun," he spat, facing the helm. "Hard right, take us abreast of her."

After his order, Leopold's fiery eyes locked onto La' foot. "Strike below and inform Leftenant Phillip we're coming alongside. I want half our starboard batteries aimed below her waterline. The other half aimed for her main deck and mast."

"Aye, Capitiane."

Straight way, off the bow of the York, thunderous lightning ripped across the dark sky. With all his strength, Payne spun the wheel then held his course going over the first tremendous wave. If he thought the storm above was bad, the one below was even worse.

Seaman Castaway saw smoke billowing out from underneath Payne's cabin door. He dropped his gear and stumbled toward it. When he opened the door, a burst of flames engulfed him. His screams echoed throughout the second deck.

Hearing the seaman's cry, Amsterdam ordered several battery crewmen to go to his aid and put out the fire.

Out on the violent seas, the bow of the Nightingale passed the York's damaged stern. Payne tried to use the next wave to cut it off. As he did, the Nightingale fired its forward battery. The lead round smashed through the portside rail. Its shrapnel flew across the main deck hitting everything in its wake. The fragmented pieces showed no mercy: cutting men down, destroying rigging lines, and crippling one of the lifeboats.

Leopold waited until the two ships crested a wave and were heading down when his starboard batteries fired. One struck the mast. Two ripped through the sheets. Another drove into the York's midsection like a spear.

The explosion was deafening. The round tore through the ship's belly sending debris in all directions. The men standing at their battery stations never had a chance. Lieutenant Amsterdam was violently thrown off his feet. He flew back, hitting the ship's hull, out cold amongst the dead and dying.

Up on deck, Payne, along with the men left - his ship in ruins, clung to the helm with the last of his strength. He knew the battle was over, the Nightingale would turn for safety. It was now the outer edge of the typhoon he had to fight to survive.

As the crippled York rose up a mighty wave, Payne cried out through the howling winds and torrential rains, "My beloved Catherine, my beautiful rose. May God Almighty save us in our hour of need."

Over the howling winds, La 'Foot shouted, "There is no way they can survive crippled in this storm, Capitiane."

Leopold nodded. He knew the York was finished. "Come about - south by southeast," he ordered. "Let's make for calm water before we go down as well."

When the Nightingale made its turn, Leopold looked back, seeing a monstrous wave lifting the burning York. As it rode up the crest, the ship listed to one side, then was violently sucked down into the bowel of the angry sea. Leopold waited to see her come up the next wave. When the York never did, he knew in his mind, the ocean had swallowed her. Upon his gleeful smile sat sweet victory, sweet revenge. *Come evening, we'll be toasting the death of Captain Payne and his crew.*

2

On a clear September afternoon, with the sun shimmering across the bay, the frigate HMS Bridgeport docked in Port Williams, England - home to his Majesty's third fleet. Captain Steel stood near the gangway while the dockhands secured the mooring lines. Just then, four of the king's royal guards rode down the cobbled pier maneuvering their horses through the crowd of onlookers and merchants.

"You there," called Steel.

The four soldiers halted.

"I have a prisoner that needs to be escorted to the king's prison. Can I place him under your charge?"

"Yes," replied Sergeant William Brandon.

When the gangway was set, Brandon watched the short burly captain with grayish black hair and mustache, along with his lieutenant, disembark.

"Good afternoon, Captain. Who are we escorting?" asked Brandon.

"I have the Captain of the Nightingale inside my brig," he proudly retorted.

"You have Leopold onboard?" repeated Brandon, surprised hearing such news.

"That's right. Our Master at Arms will have him on deck shortly. Now, my Lieutenant and I must hurry to see Admiral Knox."

"I best find you accommodations then," replied Brandon, turning and looking down the pier. "You three - commandeer that wagon," he ordered, pointing to the man standing next to his horse and wagon.

Without arguing, the man escorted Steel and his Lieutenant back to the castle.

As the two entered through the huge wooden doors, they hurried down to Knox's office. The king's court milling about could only guess what news they bring. At the door, a guard stepped forward. "May I help you, Captain?"

"I need to see the Admiral immediately," replied Steel, holding up the ship's ledger. "This cannot wait another moment."

"Wait here."

Ten seconds later, the door opened. "The Admiral will see you."

"Captain Steel," delightfully greeted Admiral Knox, standing and rounding his desk. "I've been waiting for your return. I hope you have good news from the Pacific."

Steel glanced at Lieutenant Warrenton. Knox could tell by the pause and the look in Warrenton's eyes that the news they bring wasn't good. He leaned back on his desk and slowly folded his arms.

"I'm sorry to report, Admiral. During a battle, the HMS York was sunk," said Steel, holding out his ledger.

Knox looked at him, down at the ledger, then rounded his desk. As he took his seat, Steel placed the ledger on his desk.

"I have no idea how you're going to tell your daughter, Sir. Their love affair is widely known throughout the fleet."

Knox leaned back. "With that comment, I suspect your next words to me will be... Captain Payne was not captured, he is dead?"

"I'm sorry to say... the proof of his death is now sitting in the king's prison."

Mystified, Admiral Knox slowly stood.

"The Bridgeport, along with the frigates the Hamilton and Dover, captured the French man-of-war that sunk the York."

Knox locked eyes with him.

"It was the Nightingale, Admiral. We captured Captain Leopold. It's all there in the ship's ledger."

"That bastard. I've wanted his neck hanging from the yardarms for years."

"After the king hears of this news, you may not get that chance."

"You're right. Go home and see to your wives. I'll inform the king of your courageous service in capturing the Nightingale."

Steel and Warrenton stood firm, saluted, then departed. When the door closed, Admiral Knox shook his head dismayed. *Times like this I wish her mother was still around. How am I going to break such news to Catherine? She'll be a wreck for sure.*

With his daughter weighing heavily on his heart, he flooded back to the night she met the flamboyant captain. It was at the Queen's ball, a gala affair with all the trimmings: a night of singing, dancing - the wine flowing freely amongst the guests.

He remembered escorting his daughter into the Great Hall. Heads turned, as they walked through the crowd and proceeded up to the throne.

"My Queen - your Majesty," he said, bowing.

Catherine elegantly curtsied.

King George stood up in his blue velvet outfit with knee-high white socks and polished black shoes. "I'm so glad you could make it," he replied, walking down to them.

"With no ship to sail, where else was I to go?" amused Knox.

"Nowhere, but by my side," replied the king, admiring Catherine with her head bowed low. As he reached out his hand, he inhaled the sweet fragrance of her auburn hair. She took it and stood erect.

"Promise me a dance, Lady Catherine."

"It would be my pleasure, your Majesty," she replied, casting her eyes upon the queen sitting there. Her smile was like the sun, so bright and cheerful.

She could have rightfully called them mother and father, for when her own mother died from a sickness when she was just eight years old, the two over saw her adolescence while her father, Admiral Knox – who, at the time was a captain, was out to sea more often than not.

Some in the king's court loved the idea of Catherine being like a stepdaughter. Others however, envied Catherine with a passion. She had the king and queen's ear and could see them unannounced whenever she wanted. To some, that was worth more than the king's treasure.

"If you don't mind, your Majesty, I'd like a word with my officers before you open the ball," said Knox.

"By all means," replied the king, waving him off.

While the king's servants rushed about filling the tables with wild game and poultry, fruit and baked goods, a group of the queen's court pardoned Catherine from the king's presence and took her aside. They loved cackling like hens at all the fanfare, especially the women in their fancy dresses.

As the guests continued proceeding through the corridor and entering the Great Hall, Queen Charlotte looked back, spotting the charming Captain Payne. She tapped the king's hand. He glanced at his wife nodding her head toward the rear of the hall. His eyes lit up seeing Thomas. "He's done well for a young man," he mused.

"That he has. I'll never forget our first meeting with him."

"Nor shall I, Milady. He certainly has a way with words."

"He has a way with everything."

King George nodded. "After Captain Higgins died at sea, I was thrilled to learn that Thomas was given command of the York."

"It pleased me also. Admiral Knox taught him well," she replied, watching Thomas maneuvering through the crowd of well-wishers.

As he approached the throne, Thomas gave a grand bow. "Your Majesty," he said. Removing his cover, he addressed the queen. "Milady."

"Is that Thomas Payne?" asked Catherine.

"Why, yes," replied Janet, the queen's head maiden. "He's been away for many years."

"I know that, but he's changed," she remarked, keeping her eyes glued on the man.

"We all change, my dear. Look at yourself. Yesterday you were just a young girl. Today you're as beautiful as a rainbow."

Catherine turned, catching the thought. She certainly had changed. The last time she saw Thomas was when his father, Lance, brought him to Windsor Castle and requested her father to take him under his wing in the Royal Navy. Seeing Lance was his boyhood friend and now Lord over Lancaster Shire, he obliged Lance and took Thomas under his wing.

"He sure is dashing, don't you think?" whispered Janet.

"Dashing?" sighed Catherine. *He's more than dashing, he's magnificent. So much taller now, and stunningly handsome.* Her thoughts drifted, while affectionately admiring his deep blue eyes and that adorable cleft in the center of his chin.

As the king spoke with Thomas, Queen Charlotte glanced over at Catherine. She looked as if she was drooling over a well-polished apple. *Well... someone seems to be smitten,* she thought, shifting her eyes back on Thomas. *I wonder,* her thoughts continued, scheming of a way to get the two together.

Before she could come up with a plan, Admiral Knox approached the throne. Thomas stood erect and saluted. "Admiral," he greeted.

"Captain Payne. It's great to see you back."

"It's been a long time, Sir."

"That it has."

Just then, Catherine walked up. The queen raised her brow with delight seeing Knox's daughter not waiting. Her father turned as she came abreast of him. Thomas stepped back taking in her beauty. "This can't be," he gasped.

"You know my daughter, Catherine."

"That I do, Sir, but..." his voice trailed off.

"I've grown," amused Catherine, gracefully lifting her hand. Thomas placed it within his and softly kissed it.

When he stood their eyes met.

Admiral Knox did not like the amorous stare between the two. He quickly stepped in to break up their trance. Just then, the queen walked down and placed her hand on Admiral Knox's arm.

He moved aside.

"If you two don't look like a pair of angels," she gushed. "I think it would be fitting to see Captain Payne and Lady Knox commence the opening of my Ball. Wouldn't you agree, Admiral?"

Admiral Knox smiled, covering his disdain.

The queen saw no sparkle within his eyes to go along with his smile. She had him and he knew it.

"Yes, my Queen, it would be fitting," he reluctantly replied.

"Good," she harped, raising her hand, signaling her musicians to play.

As the music floated over the crowd, the queen gave a simple nod to Catherine and Thomas. They walked out to the center of the floor. There, they took each other's hands.

Catherine curtsied. He slightly bowed, stepped back, and began dancing with her.

Each time she came close, he inhaled every detail of her beauty, from her sensual full lips, her pretty nose, and those gorgeous green eyes: so telling, so mystifying. In that moment, it seemed as if the room disappeared along with the guest. In his mind's eye, they were dancing all alone on a distant shoreline. *She, his fair maiden. He, her knight.*

"Let the ball begin," gleefully shouted Queen Charlotte.

The guests cheered, joining Catherine and Thomas on the dance floor.

Admiral Knox stepped out of his thoughts, still reeling on the queen's involvement of getting his daughter and Thomas together. "What could I have done?" he murmured. "Nothing, that's what," he scolded, getting up and opening his door.

The guard turned, seeing him standing there.

"Summon the captain of the Royal Guard for me."

"Yes, Admiral."

Ten minutes later, William Colfax, a tall, broad shouldered man with dark brown eyes proceeded through the door. "You sent for me, Sir?"

"Yes. I want you to go to Bristol Bay and escort my daughter back to Windsor Castle."

"What shall I tell her the reason, Sir?"

"I need to see her, that's all," he bluntly retorted.

Hearing the cold tone in his voice, William nodded. Without another word, he turned and quickly departed the Admiral's presence.

After the door shut, Admiral Knox waited a moment then hurried out of his office himself. "Where is the King?" he asked the guard.

"I don't know, Admiral."

"Damn," he cursed, running down the corridor. "Does anyone know where the king is?"

People stopped talking and looked at him.

"He's in the West Garden," answered the finance minister.

Knox raced through the castle and out a side exit. The king was sitting with his wife near the fountain.

"Your Majesty," he said, approaching.

"What is it?" replied King George, standing.

Before he told him the news, he looked down at Queen Charlotte. She stood, seeing the panic in his eyes.

"It's Captain Payne."

"Yes, go on," the king ordered.

"His ship was sunk in the South Pacific, your Majesty."

"Oh my God," sighed Charlotte, collapsing back into her seat.

"His ship was sunk, so, where is he?" asked the king.

Knox shook his head.

King George closed his eyes, feeling his heart sinking itself.

"He and his crew are dead, your Majesty."

"And your daughter?"

"I just summoned for her."

King George waved his hand. Two of his royal guards hurried over. "When Lady Knox gets here, I want her to be immediately escorted to the queen's chamber."

"Yes, your Majesty."

When King George faced Admiral Knox, the admiral informed him, "It was the Nightingale. The Bridgeport along with the Hamilton and Dover put her out of commission. They captured Captain Leopold. He's now in your prison, Sir."

The king's jaw locked with anger. He turned toward his wife. "Go to your chamber and wait for Lady Knox."

As her maidens ushered her away, she wept uncontrollably.

"Come," said the king, storming off.

Admiral Knox followed.

3

As the horse-drawn carriage proceeded through the gates of Windsor Castle, inside, Catherine was angry that William would not tell her why her father had summoned her.

When the carriage halted at the entrance, William dismounted and opened the door. Catherine stepped down. A Royal Guard came forward. "You must escort her to the Queen's chamber at once."

Stunned, she looked at William. "What is wrong with the queen?"

"Nothing."

"William Colfax," she retorted. "That's why I've been summoned," she scoffed, running toward the doors.

"Catherine!"

Believing the queen was ill, she did not pause in her stride.

William chased after her up a flight of stairs leading to the East Wing, the Queen's living quarters. When she entered, Queen Charlotte was sitting there. It was evident she had been crying. Her father and King George were standing there as well.

"Milady, Milady," gushed Catherine going to her side. "What's wrong? Are you ill?"

Suddenly, William rushed in. "I'm sorry, your Majesty," he apologized.

King George waved him away.

"I am not ill, Catherine."

She gazed into her eyes. Something was sitting within them. Something terrible. She slowly stood and looked at her father. He too appeared to be heart-stricken.

"What is it? What is it? Why have I been brought here?"

"Lady Catherine, we have bad news," said King George.

"Your Majesty."

The words would not come out.

"I think this news should come from me," said her father.

Queen Charlotte could not contain herself. Tears welled up within her eyes.

"What is it, Father?"

"It's the York, my dear. During a battle, she was sunk in the South Pacific. Captain Payne along with his entire crew did not survive."

His words stung her. They smashed against her heart, shattering it into a million pieces. In that moment, time suddenly stopped. Thomas' sparkling blue eyes, his laughter, flashed before her. Collapsing to her knees, her mind remained adrift in the abyss of darkness. There on the Queen's chamber floor, she wailed like a child, wanting to die herself.

Her father knelt before her. Catherine's pain seared his heart. Tears rolled down his cheeks. Losing her mother was a terrible experience for a young child. *Losing Thomas could cripple her forever.*

"If it brings you any comfort, Lady Catherine," said King George. "We have captured the ship that sank the York. The infamous French Captain Leopold is now in my prison."

Her mind numb, her heart aching, Catherine heard every word but said nothing.

The king nodded to his wife. She reached over, grabbed her bell and rang it. Four of the queen's maidens came hurrying out from an adjoining room.

"Assist Catherine to my room."

Upon entering, Catherine threw herself on top of the bed, and then buried her head into a pillow. Her muffled sobbing brought tears to the women's eyes. They quietly departed; heartbroken.

Catherine lay there motionless. Her life seemed empty. The romantic courtship was over. Thomas was her captain, she... his first mate.

She remembered the beginning of their whirlwind affair. Windsor Castle was abuzz with the news and it spread throughout the land. The only person not happy was her father. Their relationship troubled him due to Thomas being out to sea more so than home. Nevertheless, in the end, he began warming to the idea, seeing her floating in the clouds. That thought drove into her heart. Those beautiful clouds felt as if they had just been yanked from underneath her and she was now free-falling into utter darkness with no escape.

Hearing the door open, footsteps coming toward the bed, she looked up. It was the queen's oldest daughter, Margaret.

"Lady Catherine."

She despairingly gazed at her.

"The Sergeant at Arms is escorting the prisoner into the Great Hall. The king's entire court has assembled."

In her pain and sorrow, the king's words returned. *Captain Leopold... the man who has taken everything away from me.* "I must be there."

"Are you sure?"

"Yes. Leave me now, so I can compose myself."

"As you wish."

When the door shut, Catherine walked over and sat down in front of the big mirror. Her face was a mess from crying. She dipped a cloth into a bowl of water and washed her tears away. When she set the cloth down, she noticed the queen's letter opener lying there.

After combing her hair, she looked back at the closed door then down at the letter opener again. Standing, she fixed her dress then picked up the sharp object. Her eyes drifted upward – catching them in the mirror. Within her remorse, there was a part of her that wanted revenge. She wanted to stab Captain Leopold a thousand times for destroying her world.

With a heavy sigh, she knew that was impossible; not in front of the king. Still gazing upon herself, she dropped the letter opener then hurried out of the room.

Upon entering a side entrance to the Great Hall, she spotted her father standing to the right of the king and queen. As she slowly made her way toward him, an anguished sigh swept through the crowd.

"What are you doing here?" whispered her Father.

"I wanted to be here for Thomas' sake. I also want to see and hear from the man who stole my life," she replied, seeing the king looking at her. She gave a slight nod. The king nodded back.

Just then, the doors to the Great Hall opened. The room fell silent as Leopold was ushered up to the throne in chains.

"On your knees," ordered the Sergeant.

"Your Grace," said Leopold, bowing his head.

King George sat back.

When Leopold looked up at him, within his stare he saw his own death. His time was short. In that dire moment, he begged for mercy.

"Your Majesty, I'm sure King Phillip would gladly trade me for your two spies; the ones that were captured eight months ago."

"Trade you?"

"Yes, your Grace."

"Do you think I had you brought before me, so you can beg for your wretched life?" he blasted. "My intentions of even seeing you at all is to find out what happened to the York. Be warned, however, before you even open your mouth, let it be known there are many ways to die, so I'd strongly advise you to tell me the truth. Did you sink the York?"

"Yes, your Grace."

"Did you see it go down?"

Leopold flashed back to the battle. "We caught up with the York on an overcast afternoon. To the south of our position was a hellish storm. Through the fog, we slipped in behind her. Surprisingly, she seemed to be adrift, unaware of our approach. I ordered my forward battery to fire. I missed two, but wasn't going to miss the third. That round struck her stern.

"In his panic to out run us, Captain Payne drove his ship straight into that storm. The wind picked up, the waves were intense as we slipped alongside her and fired a volley. We crippled the main deck, struck the mast and then put one into her side."

The king's jaw muscles tightened hearing that. "So, you repeatedly struck the York."

"Yes, your Grace."

"Did you physically see the York go under?"

"Not physically, your Grace. After that broadside volley, I ordered the helm about to save my own crew from that violent storm. When I looked back, the York was on fire, her main deck in ruins and she was listing heavily to one side. Then it seemed as if the ocean came alive. It lifted her up and then dragged her down. I thought for sure I'd see her rise up on the next huge crest. She never did."

Hearing Leopold's words, Catherine deeply sighed. In that moment, it seemed as if she was standing there all alone. Then suddenly, like a whisper from heaven, she flashed back to visions and dreams she had months ago. Within her sleep she heard Thomas speak her name. She remembered that it startled her awake several times, as if he were calling out to her - *"I'm alive, Catherine. Can you hear me my beloved rose?"*

Without realizing it, she had rested her head upon her father's shoulder.

"Are you alright?" he asked, caressing her.

Catherine blinked, snapping back to reality. "Yes, yes, Father," she replied, thinking of the king's question, 'Did you see it physically go down'. *Not physically, your Grace.*

Lifting her head off her father's shoulder, she stared at Leopold. *Now I know. Thomas was calling out to me. He was calling out to me within my dreams. My beloved captain is still alive.*

"Sergeant at Arms, escort Captain Leopold to the outer court and have my executioner remove his head," ordered King George. "Your head will hang from the London bridge for all to see."

"Your Grace, I beg you. King Philip will trade me for your spies."

"Your king has already put their necks in the guillotine. Take him away."

The guards stepped forward, seizing him.

Catherine watched them escorting Leopold out then turned to her father. "He's alive, he's still alive."

"Catherine?"

"You heard him. He never physically saw the York go down."

His inconsolable expression told her he believed otherwise.

"Father?"

Before he could speak the king stood up. "I want my ministers to gather in the council chamber; the rest of you are dismissed."

Queen Charlotte took his hand. He turned and faced her.

"I'll see to Lady Catherine."

"Thank you."

When the council had assembled, King George asked, "I want to know the odds of Captain Payne escaping such a storm with a crippled frigate."

All eyes fell on Admiral Knox.

Catherine's intuition washed over him. He dismissed it outright. "It's hard to say, your Majesty. The South Pacific can be a troublesome place to sail. Violent storms seem to appear out of nowhere. Mostly typhoons. If that be the case, Captain Payne's odds of surviving were very slim."

King George sat there a moment then got up and walked over to the windows. "You did say that Captain Steel along with one other frigate searched for the York."

"Yes, your Majesty. They spent two weeks."

The king let out a heavy sigh.

Admiral Knox glanced at the men sitting there. They all knew Thomas and his crew were dead.

King George turned and faced them. "To honor Captain Payne and his crew, I want the flag over Windsor Castle struck at half-mast for a month. I want each of the families paid their rightful due for losing their loved one in battle. I want this done right now, Lord Wilson," he bluntly ordered the castle administrator.

"Yes, your Majesty," he replied, getting up and leaving.

You're all dismissed."

The ministers got up.

"Admiral Knox," said the king.

He stopped at the door.

"Stay."

After the ministers filed out, King George called his servant to fetch some wine. The king and Admiral Knox sat for nearly an hour talking. During that time, Knox spoke of Catherine's thoughts. Sadly, in the end however, they came to the same conclusion - no search party would sail from England.

The argument between Catherine and her father afterward was too much for her to tolerate. She departed the castle like a violent storm herself, knowing somehow, somewhere...Thomas was still alive.

4

When the carriage stopped in front of her house, an elaborate three-story loft home overlooking the bay, Catherine, still emotionally upset, opened the door and stepped down.

Seeing her pale complexion and sad watery eyes, William started to speak.

She waved her hand for him, not to. After opening the small wooden gate and proceeding up to the door, she turned and faced him.

"I'm truly sorry. I really liked Thomas."

His words made her feel even worse. "I want to be left alone. You make sure they all know that," she replied, walking in and closing the door.

He stood there heart-stricken. The last person he ever wanted to see like this was her. Climbing onboard the carriage, he glanced at her door then slapped the reins.

Inside, Catherine kicked off her shoes and headed for the stairs.

Her live-in maid, Beatrice, heard her come in. "Milady, what happened?" she gasped, seeing she had been crying.

"Please, Beatrice," she replied, heading up the stairs.

"You have to tell me."

Catherine stopped and looked down at her. Before she spoke a word, Catherine crumbled in a heap on the staircase.

"Lady Knox," moaned Beatrice, hurrying up to her.

With her hands over her mouth, Catherine sobbed, "I was summoned to Windsor Castle because my father wanted to inform me that the HMS York was sunk." After she told her all that had happened that day, Beatrice, sighed, "Oh Lord of Heaven, tell me this isn't true.

"Beatrice," she sniffled.

"Yes, Milady?" she replied, wiping Catherine's tears.

"I never mentioned this to anyone."

"What?"

"A while back, I heard Thomas calling out to me in my dreams."

"What did he say?"

"I'm here, Catherine."

"Most lovers have dreams. I had my share at your age when being courted by Cornel."

"This is not one of those silly dreams. I truly believe with all my heart he's still alive."

"You truly believe that?"

"Yes. Even though my Father and King George believe otherwise, I can feel him, Beatrice," she replied, caressing her chest.

What love can do to a person. It can make you think and believe things that are not true; for love never wants to give up. She sighed with that thought.

After the heartache she went through as a young child, losing her mother, I was so looking forward to them marrying and having a family of their own.

"I have to find him, Beatrice."

Her words caught Beatrice off guard. "You what?"

"I'll never abandon him. I must," she said, getting up.

"You?"

"Yes."

"Are you thinking of swimming to the South Pacific?"

"Don't be foolish. I know just the man who'll help me."

"Now, Lady Knox..."

"I've already made up my mind," she interrupted. "I'm going to see Captain Flynn."

"Captain Flynn!? That drunken fool. You're going to trust a man that was tossed out of the royal navy for his flagrant drinking?"

"He may be a drunk, but he has a ship and crew. I'm sure for a few bags of gold he'll take me there."

"Take you there!"

"That's right. I'm sure I can catch him down at the Trade Wind tonight."

"Now, Lady Knox," scolded Beatrice. "You can't go in there. That place is full of vulgar men, and wenches who are even worse."

"I can handle that," she replied, heading up the stairs. "Fix me a bowl of soup, please. I want something in my stomach before I go."

"Whatever I fix, surely won't stay down walking inside that pub."

"Just do as I ask, please," she softly replied, taking the stairs up.

Beatrice watched her go then headed to the kitchen.

Inside her bedroom, Catherine took off her dress and opened her wardrobe. She put on a pair of riding pants, button down shirt and high black boots. When she sat in front of her mirror, Beatrice's warning came back to her. "Maybe she's right. I'd hate to get accosted in a place like that," she murmured. Reaching over for her quill, she jotted down a simple note, blew on the ink then folded the parchment. With that, she took the note and her coin pouch and left her room.

"Your soup is ready in the parlor."

"Thank you, Beatrice. I won't be long."

"If you want my advice..."

"Not tonight," she interrupted.

"Have it your way. I'll leave the front door open."

"Thank you," she replied, sitting at the table.

After her meal, Catherine walked out the back door. The wind off the bay was chilly. She pulled up her hood and hurried inside the stable. Her mare neighed seeing her walk in.

"Are you up for a ride in this foul weather, Juliet?"

The horse neighed.

"Good, my dear."

With the saddle on, she mounted the mare and rode out to the small road leading along the high bluffs of Bristol Bay. It was a spectacular view with the rugged cliffs and the rich green valley below. The little town sat in the middle of the valley along the shoreline.

On her way, she spotted several ships in the harbor. Each lit with lanterns at the stern and bow, showing other ships, they were at anchor. The only way from ship to shore was by boat, and she spotted several traveling to and from the anchored vessels.

The town itself was a quaint little village adjacent to the shoreline and pier, made up of rustic timber and stone-built shops. At the corner of Main Street sat the Trade Wind. The dark wooden sign with its weathered white sail and red lettering sat there swinging in the breeze over the door.

Catherine rounded the pub and dismounted. As she tethered her horse to the hitching post, she could hear singing and laughter inside. *This is going to take some nerves,* she thought, heading for the door.

As she walked up, it suddenly opened. Three drunken sailors stumbled out holding on to one another while singing. They never even looked at her, as they crossed the street heading to the pier.

When Catherine opened the door, the stench of the place hit her full on: stale beer, wine, sweaty men; all laced together with a flowery perfume the women were wearing.

She noticed one large wooden candle chandelier hanging from the upper beams bathing the room full of drunken men, and women wearing loosely fitted blouses, dancing and flirting with them.

Standing in the doorway, she could not see Flynn amongst the mayhem before her. *This is no place for a lady,* she thought, heading toward the bar. The bartender walked over seeing her standing there.

"What cha having?" he asked the hooded person.

"I'm not here for a drink. I just wanted to know if Captain Flynn were here."

"Yes, he's in the back with some of his crew."

"Can you give him this, please?" she asked, holding out the folded parchment.

"Do I look like your servant?" he grumbled.

"No," she replied, taking a silver shilling from her pouch. "That's for your troubles."

He cocked his head this way and that trying to see her face.

She wasn't going to give him the pleasure.

"Alright, Ma'am."

Catherine stood there as he walked around the bar and headed toward the back of the room. She stepped sideways to watch him between the people in front of her.

There he is, she thought, seeing the bartender hand Flynn her note and then point toward the door. Flynn took his boots off the table and sat up looking her way. She stood there a moment then quickly turned and left the pub.

Flynn pushed his glass aside and unfolded the paper.

If you would like a second chance, meet me at the old stone bridge in Hillcrest Forest tomorrow at midnight. Come alone. Signed - C. K.

"What's it say?" asked his first mate, Mr. Smith.

"Someone wants to meet me. Do you know anyone with the initials C.K.?" replied Flynn, looking back at the door where Catherine had been standing.

"No."

"Well, whoever it is wants a meeting tomorrow night."

"You think it's trouble?"

"No, I think it's a woman. Let's call it a night, gentlemen," he said, downing the rest of his wine and getting up from the table.

✝

The following night, Catherine paced back and forth in front of her bedroom bay windows. She wished the moon were out, especially with the fog rolling in off the bay. It made her feel apprehensive in meeting Flynn all alone in the middle of the night. However, if she wanted to find Thomas, she had no choice.

Slipping out of her room, she quietly walked down the hallway past Beatrice's bedroom. *If she finds out, I'll never hear the end of it,* she thought, taking the stairs down. At the back door, she pulled her hood up and stepped outside. On her way to the stable, the fog was so thick it settled on her cheeks.

After mounting her mare, she headed westward to a path that would lead her through the forest. When she entered, she could barely see a thing through the misty haze. The giant trees lining the path looked like sentinels with their moss-covered branches hanging overhead, causing her to duck and weave around them.

Twenty-minutes later, Catherine halted near the bridge. As she dismounted, she could hear the small stream. It made her walk up and look over the side. Several feet below, she could see large rocks and deadfall lying in the water. Then suddenly, she heard the sound of a horse coming toward her from the opposite side of the bridge. She quickly hurried and hid behind an old oak tree. Nervously standing there, she heard the horse stop and someone get down.

"Anyone there?" said Flynn, guiding his horse across the bridge.

Catherine sighed stepping away from the tree.

Flynn continued toward her. She pulled off her hood.

"By the hand-written note, I knew it was a woman. I would have never suspected that it would be you, Lady Knox."

"Well, as you can see - it is me."

"By your actions, I suspect your father is unaware of this meeting?"

"You're right. He's unaware."

"Are you after my head too?" he replied dismayed.

That line made her pause.

"Captain Leopold lost his - I surely don't want mine in a basket, meeting you all alone out here. I'd hate to give your father an easy excuse for taking it off my shoulders."

She let that remark go and asked, "I suppose all of England has heard by now?"

"Probably, so what can I do for you?

"Actually... it's... what can we do for each other."

"Alright then, what can we do for each other?"

"I need a captain and a ship. You, I assume, would like to be reinstated in His Majesty's Navy."

Flynn laughed.

"You do, don't you?"

"That would never happen. So... what do you need a ship for?"

"To find Captain Payne."

"Lady Knox..."

"He's alive, Mr. Flynn," she interrupted. "Captain Leopold said he never physically saw the York go down."

"Does one need to physically see a ship go down, especially after being blown to pieces and then having to stay afloat in the storm Leopold described to the king? I wager it was a typhoon."

"By your description of what transpired between His Majesty and that heathen, you must have been there yesterday."

"I don't physically have to be anywhere; I have many ears, Milady," he retorted.

She stood there a moment searching his eyes. The pause was enough for Flynn to know she did not like his remark. "OK," he said, "You want to hire my ship and crew to sail to the South Pacific?"

"That's correct. I'll pay you handsomely for your troubles. Plus, if *we* bring him back, I'm sure the king will have you reinstated."

"Wait a minute, before we go any further - let me explain a few things to you. First off, do you have any idea of how big the South Pacific is?"

"No."

"The South Pacific is a huge body of water. To ask me to sail there to find Captain Payne, is like asking me to find a single blade of grass in the west garden of Windsor Castle."

She went to speak. He raised his hand. "Secondly, how far do you think my crew and I will get with France and England at each other's throats again? These wars are fought all over the world whenever they encounter each other, and... while we're trying to stay out of sight of either country's warships and ports, you want me to be out there searching for that single blade of grass called the York?"

Again, she went to speak; he raised his hand. "Thirdly, *we* - you and I - are not sailing anywhere. I'll have no woman aboard my ship."

After his ranting, Catherine's mind was spinning. It seemed everything he just said went in one ear and out the other, with the exception of - *I'll have no woman aboard my ship.* She felt that statement alone would give her room to argue her position on the matter.

"I understand all the risks, but mind you, Mr. Flynn, I'm part of the deal. I'll pay you half - five hundred pounds, plus this necklace when I'm onboard," she replied, removing it from her neck.

Flynn gazed at the elegant strand of pearls.

"It was a gift from the queen on my eighteenth birthday. It's probably worth more than your ship."

He bypassed that remark and reiterated the risks they would be taking on such a voyage.

"I just told you, Mr. Flynn - I do understand the risks."

He stood there thinking of another angle to change her mind. It came to him quick. "I don't think you do understand. Besides trying to stay out of sight of the French and British fleets, many cutthroat pirates would love to grab you as a prize. You'd make a good slave girl to any Arabian Prince."

That caught her off guard. She slightly looked away thinking about that.

By her expression, Flynn knew that troubled her.

When she slowly looked back at him, there was something in his eyes - something that made her think. *He's trying to scare me into letting go of finding Thomas. It almost worked.* "I'll take that risk, Mr. Flynn," she said. "Now, do we have a deal?"

Flynn dropped his shoulders and sighed. *She's just like her father - the same backbone and determination.* He thought it best to go back to the beginning. "I've never had a woman aboard my ship, well...not while it's sailing."

"Then I will be the first."

"What about my crew?"

Catherine gave that a thought. "We'll tell 'em that I'm on a secret mission for the king."

"Go on," he laughed. "You honestly think they'd believe that?"

"No, I suspect not, but if you don't take me I'll find a captain that will, trust me."

"Lady Knox..."

"My name is Catherine," she interrupted. "I don't mind the title of Lady Knox when I'm mixing with those pompous aristocrats inside Windsor Castle. Beyond those gates, I'm just like you."

"You may think that, but the commoners see you as Royalty, seeing as your father is the Hand of the King and 1st Admiral to his Majesty's Royal Navy."

"Does your crew feel the same way?" she inquired.

"I'm sure they do."

"Well then, go back and speak to your men. Tell 'em they'll be paid handsomely themselves with me going along."

He stood there thinking of another angle to change her mind. "You think you could actually handle a voyage at sea with fifty men?"

"Mr. Flynn," she sternly replied. "My father may have sired a daughter, but he raised me like a son. I've been around military men all my life and even gained some training. So, to answer your question, I'd go with a hundred men if that's what it took to find Captain Payne."

Her words had a bite and he felt them. "Alright, I'll go back and speak with my officers. Meet me here tomorrow night, same time."

Catherine nodded, turned and headed toward her horse. When she mounted, she said goodnight and headed down the path.

Flynn stepped up to his saddle thinking of her offer, *a thousand pounds and that necklace to search for a crippled frigate.* After mounting, he looked back to where she had left. "Crippled or sunk, I'll find it," he said, riding back to Bristol Bay.

When Flynn entered the town, he took the horse to the stables and proceeded on foot to the pier. Mr. Smith and two of his crew were waiting for him.

"Untie the lines; let's get back to the ship," he said, walking down the weathered worn steps to the boat.

"Did they show up?" asked Smith.

"Yes, we'll talk in my cabin."

The two crewmembers said nothing as they rowed across the bay.

Onboard, Flynn requested his Leading Hand, Amos Bishop, and the ship's Master at Arms, Carl Davison, to proceed below with him and Smith.

"Good evening, Captain," the main deck watch greeted.

"Evening, Lad, how is the ship?"

"She's fine, Captain."

"Good," he replied, taking the ladder down.

Inside, Captain Flynn lit a lantern and sat down. The men pulled up chairs waiting to hear what he had to say about the meeting.

"The offer I received tonight was a thousand pounds for each man to sail to the South Pacific to find Captain Payne." He made no mention of the necklace.

"To find Captain Payne," remarked Smith.

"That's right. A thousand pounds each. Anyone here not wanting to go?"

"Do you know how to search the bottom of the ocean, Captain Flynn?" questioned Davison.

"This is ridiculous," added Bishop.

JEFF WRIGHT
CATHERINE KNOX

Flynn could see it himself. It was ridiculous.

"Are you willing to give up a year or more of your life to go searching for a ghost?" asked Smith.

Like hot lead from a musket, Flynn was being pelted with questions he knew they'd ask. He sat there in thought.

"How about telling us *who* made you this offer?" asked Davison.

"It was Catherine Knox," he replied, looking at each man.

"Well, I'll be," mused Bishop. "Of all people... the Admiral's daughter."

"The foolish woman," retorted Smith.

"She said Captain Leopold confessed that he never saw the York go down."

The men laughed.

"And look where it got him," mused Davison.

Flynn sat back, folding his arms.

The three could see he was wanting to go.

"Do you really think Captain Payne slipped that noose?" asked Bishop.

"Seeing it was Payne, I'd wager he could have. He's one of the finest captains I know, besides Admiral Knox," he replied.

"That leads me to ask... does Admiral Knox know of this outlandish adventure his daughter wants us to go on?" asked Smith.

"No."

Davison sat up in his chair. Something was wrong, and he could smell it. "What are you holding back from us?"

Flynn smiled. "That's why I made you my Master at Arms. Well, that's one of the reasons. Your size was the other."

Smith and Bishop had to agree. Davison was six feet five, weighed two hundred and fifty pounds, with not a bit of fat on him.

"Yes, I'm holding something back. Lady Knox is requesting to come with us."

The men's response was quick. Smith stood up. Bishop stood up. Davison leaned back staring at him.

"I haven't said *yes* to Lady Knox's wishes, gentlemen. That's why we're here, so sit down."

The men slowly took their seats.

"If she goes, we're all dead men – you know that?" warned Smith.

"That's right, the king will have his entire navy after us," said Davison.

Flynn thought that too, but he liked the risk, especially after being kicked out of the navy. What better way to get back at the Navy's Royal Commission, the admirals and captains who spoke so dull of him during his inquest.

Especially Admiral Dooly, who sat there as if he had never taken a sip.

The man lived at the Blue Dragon, or more so, inside the Pink Pearl drinking with those floozies. *On those drunken nights, half-dressed, I wonder how his wife felt waiting for him at home?*

"You seem to be drifting, Captain Flynn?" said Smith.

"I am."

"Are you willing to risk your own life taking her with us?" asked Bishop.

"Yes."

Davison tapped his fingers on the desk looking at the captain, who seemed to be somewhere else.

"Mr. Davison, you like your head on your shoulders?" asked Bishop.

"Yes, I like my head on my shoulders, but a thousand pounds is a lot of money."

"If we get caught with her onboard, you'll not see a thousand pounds. You'll see a rope, or the king's executioner," warned Smith.

"True, but she has made it quite clear, she'll find another captain to take her, if we don't," said Flynn.

"You know any captains who'd dare take her up on such a proposition?" asked Bishop.

"Nope, that's why we're taking her," replied Flynn.

The men sat back.

"While you're sitting here in all this doom and gloom of what could happen to us, what if... what if we did bring Captain Payne back?"

The men sat in silence.

Flynn glanced at each one. He could tell they were thinking the same thought – being honored guests at the king's table.

"OK, say we do agree," said Bishop. "What about the crew, you know they'll be up in arms having a woman onboard."

"Well... let me put this to you and tell me what ya think. Lady Knox said something I thought was foolish at the time. Now, however, I think it might just work."

"What's that?" pushed Smith.

"She said to tell the crew that she was on a secret mission for the king."

Smith and Bishop laughed.

Flynn kept a straight face.

The laughter stopped.

"You know," said Davison, twirling the idea in his head. "It just might work if we added a few things."

"And that is?" asked Bishop.

"Many crew members already know Captain Flynn was handed a note at the Trade Wind. We could say the note came from the king himself, requesting Captain Flynn to go on a secret mission. If Flynn here agreed, he would be picking up one of the king's men off of Fletcher's Point. We could then hide her appearance and take her to a cabin. In the morning, while out at sea, she'd walk out. What could they say then?"

"Not bad, not bad at all," replied Flynn. "What do you say, you two?"

"I still say this is ridiculous, but I'll go," said Bishop.

The three looked at Smith. He nodded his head.

"Alright, now that we've decided, I've got one more request from one of you."

"What?"

"We need some information on approximately where the Nightingale sunk the York."

"The crew from the Bridgeport frequents the Blue Dragon in Port Williams," said Davison.

"How about you go there and mingle with the crew. See if you can find out approximately where the Nightingale sunk the York."

"That is something we'll need to know," agreed Bishop, eyeing Davison.

"Alright, I'll head out tomorrow. Be back before we sail."

"Good," replied Flynn. "Now... I'll inform Lady Knox of our idea when I meet her tomorrow. I'll tell her that we'll set sail on the next moonless night, which will be in three days. We'll pick her up off Fletcher's Point."

"How will we know she's there?" asked Bishop.

"Good question."

"How about her waving a lantern," said Smith.

Flynn nodded. "Alright, Mr. Smith and Mr. Bishop, you two will go and pick her up. Once she is safely onboard, we'll hurry her to a cabin without her being seen."

The two nodded.

"Alright, let's get some sleep; we have some busy days ahead preparing this ship for sail."

5

On that moonless night in Bristol Bay, Catherine was excited, and yet, worried sick. Her emotional state clashed as she and Beatrice left the house.

"Hurry, Beatrice, we need to get my things inside the wagon."

"I'm going as fast as I can, Lady Knox," she replied, carrying items herself.

With her suitcases stowed, the two got onboard.

"Now, when you drop me off, are you sure you can handle the horse and wagon?"

"Yes, and I have a right mind to keep going all the way to Ireland."

"Oh now, go on with that notion. When they come for me, just hand them the letter I left on the parlor table."

"I'm so worried, Lady Knox. You know your father will be in a fit when he reads it. Why... he'll have William Colfax drag me all the way back to Windsor Castle to explain – what will I say then?"

"Neither my father nor the king will have you dragged back, trust me. You were just following orders."

"Yes, orders that could have my head."

Catherine sighed, slapping the reins. As the horse took off, she glanced over at her loving housemaid. Beatrice was thirty-years older and acted more like a mother.

Beatrice turned, catching her eye.

"I must go, Beatrice. You understand that. I can't live without him."

She said nothing.

"You think he's dead too, don't you?"

"I never said that."

"You don't have to; it's written all over your face."

"It's not that. It's your father."

What could she say? She was worried about her father as well. The only thing she prayed for was being as far away from England as she could before he sat down and read her letter.

My beloved Father,

Who can understand a woman's heart? Not even God, I suppose. The depth of my love for Thomas and enduring a life without him would be like living with an infertile womb.

I know you will never understand my womanly instincts; I know Thomas is still alive. If I stayed, all my hopes and dreams of becoming a mother, raising children, would never be for me. You see, Thomas is the only man I will ever love. Without him – my world would end.

If I do not return, I have endowed all my earthly possessions to Beatrice. Ensure she's afforded all of my things including the house in Bristol Bay.

Your loving and most gracious daughter –
Catherine.

Onboard the Lara May, Captain Flynn stood near the rail with Davison. Below, Smith and Bishop sat in the lifeboat ready to go.

"You think she's coming?" asked Bishop.

"She'll be here."

"Light off Fletcher's Point," the crow's nest watch shouted down.

Flynn looked toward land. "Hurry, untie the lifeboat," he ordered. "As fast as you're able, gentlemen – let's get the king's servant onboard."

"Aye, aye, Captain."

"Mr. Davison, prepare the crew to haul up anchor."

"Aye, Captain," he replied, heading to the stern.

"I don't see a ship, do you?" asked Beatrice, sitting in the wagon near the bluff.

"No, but it's too dark to tell," replied Catherine, standing there waving her lantern.

"You sure this is the right spot?"

"Yes, Beatrice. He said be at the steps leading down to the small sandy beach before the Point."

Beatrice took in the wooden rail and the steps leading down. From there, her eyes drifted out across the sand to the waves coming ashore. "Look," she gasped, seeing what appeared to be a small boat.

"That's them," beamed Catherine. "C'mon, Beatrice, let's get my gear to the beach."

As the lifeboat neared the shoreline, Bishop got out and pulled it up onto the sand. The two hurried toward Catherine holding the lantern at the bottom of the steps.

"Good evening, Milady. I'm sorry we don't have time for formal greetings. The ship is ready to sail."

Catherine turned toward Beatrice. Beatrice began to cry. She set down the lantern and held her tightly. "If I don't come back, I have written in that letter that you are entitled to my entire estate."

"I don't want your estate," she wept. "I just want you to return."

"I will, trust me," she said, kissing her cheek.

"We must leave, Lady Knox," pushed Smith.

She let go of Beatrice, gave her a slight smile and then took off for the boat. The men stumbled carrying her suitcases through the sand.

Beatrice stood there trembling, watching the three get in. After wading up the steps and looking back at the water's edge, the boat was gone. In that moment of despair, a heartfelt thought came to her, *there is no greater love than to love someone so much that one would be willing to give up everything, even your own life to find them.* With that tender thought pinging on her chest, she climbed into the wagon and cried all the way back to Bristol Bay.

As the two men fought the waves, Catherine sat in the middle of the lifeboat trying to steady herself. The air was mild and tasted of salt. The only thing she could see was the stars above – spread across the night sky like twinkling little lights.

Then suddenly, Smith shouted from the stern, "Hang on."

Catherine looked down just in time to see a giant wave crash alongside the boat. Her whole body jerked backwards. Smith quickly dropped his oar and caught her in his arms.

"Are you alright, Milady?"

"Yes," she replied, sitting up and glancing back at the wave. When she looked forward, she spotted a tall mast and sails flutter in the breeze. In the darkness, the rest of the ship was just an outline.

"There she be, the Lara May," said Bishop.

"The Lara May," she repeated, taking in its size. It was a merchant vessel slightly wider and longer than a frigate. Forward on the main deck were living quarters.

"It would be best if you put your hood up, Milady," requested Bishop.

"Right," she replied, knowing she could not be seen.

"The boat's coming alongside, Captain," a crewman shouted.

Flynn walked over to the portside rail. "Throw up your lines."

The lines were tossed.

"Turn out the J-Davit and get that gear onboard," ordered Flynn.

Two men turned the pulley system outward. The lines dropped. Mr. Bishop tied off Catherine's suitcases. Crewmen quickly hauled them up. The lines were dropped again. This time, Bishop and Smith tied off the boat.

"OK, climb up the ladder," said Bishop to her.

As Catherine took the rope ladder up, Flynn reached down his hand.

"Easy," he cautioned, steadying her on deck.

After letting her go, she stood there watching Smith and Bishop hastily come aboard.

"Get that boat stowed away," barked Flynn. "Mr. Bishop, haul down the jib. The rest of you prepare to sail."

As the crew moved about the ship, Catherine stepped back along the rail giving them room.

"You two there," said Flynn.

"Yes, Captain."

"Take these suitcases down to Mr. Smith's cabin."

"Aye, Captain."

"I'll escort you down."

Catherine said nothing and followed.

The ship's crew stopped their work to watch the hooded man walking behind Captain Flynn. They wondered whom King George was sending on this secret mission – a mission they had not been told.

From under her hood, Catherine glanced at the port and starboard ladders leading to the upper deck of the ship's bow. The forward watch was looking down at her.

Flynn grabbed the small torch from off the wall and proceeded inside the passageway. On her way down, she saw three doors, one on the left, one on the right and one at the end. He stopped at the starboard side door. "This will be your cabin. Mr. Bishop and Mr. Smith will bunk across from you. The forward door is the ship's office. We also use it as our dining facility," he said.

She nodded.

After opening her door and stepping in, he walked over and lit a candle on a desk. "You see, it has everything you need."

"It's cozy enough," she replied, pulling off her hood and taking in the small bunk, table and chair. When she turned and faced him, she noticed he had shaved. She thought Flynn, who was a tall slim man with sharp dark eyes, looked better with it off.

"You can stow some of your items inside that foot locker. Anything you want hung, place in that closet."

"OK."

"Tonight, I think it best you stay in your cabin. I'll bring you on deck tomorrow after breakfast."

"Thank you."

He turned to leave.

"Mr. Flynn."

He turned and faced her.

"What's your name?"

"Richard."

"Please call me Catherine."

He nodded. "Please call me Captain."

"Alright," she laughed. *He's still a Naval Officer.* It pleased her that he was.

"Before I go, I must warn you about leaving candles lit."

"I'm well aware of the danger, Captain."

After he closed the door, she suddenly felt numb. Even though she had been on many ships with her father while they were in port, this felt strangely different. More so, it scared her.

In that hesitant moment, she drifted back on the argument between Beatrice and her. It almost brought her to tears, realizing that her undying love for Thomas had overwhelmed her womanly emotions to the point of her deciding to take a risk such as this.

"A woman's intuition," she whispered, sitting on the bunk. "Beatrice has a mother's intuition and that's far worse," she sighed. "I should have given this much more thought," she continued, getting to her feet.

Without warning, the cabin floor unexpectedly rose up. Then, the cabin listed to one side. "Oh, no..." she panicked, reaching for the table.

Outside, the ship's bow broke over a wave and started free falling into the trough; making Catherine fly back onto the bunk.

"Are yous OK in there?" she heard a small voice say.

"Yes, I'm fine," she replied, hanging onto the bunk.

"Can I come in?"

"Yes."

When the door opened, she was surprised to see it was an African boy with beautiful brown skin and jet-black hair. "What are you doing onboard this ship?" she gasped.

"Me Mobee, Cap's caboon boy."

The ship rose up again. Mobee hung onto the table, secured to the floor. He smiled at her

JEFF WRIGHT
CATHERINE KNOX

as the ship fell back. "In time, you be used to it," he said to her startled expression.

"Where are your parents? I'm sure they would never allow such a young boy like you to venture out to sea like this."

Mobee cast his eyes to the floor. "My parents all dead. Cap Flynn found me living on the streets of Caloon."

"Caloon?" she asked not knowing where that was.

"It's a small village in Nigeria. My father was a fishermon. I knows many knots," he said, turning his frown into a smile. "I show Cap Flynn and he asks if I wanted a jib."

I'll be damn, she thought.

"Cans I ask ya something?"

"Sure," she replied, swaying back and forth from the ship listing.

"What yous a doing here? No sa place for a woman."

She leaned toward him. "I'm on a secret mission for King George."

"Yous a knows him?" he asked in awe.

"Why certainly. My father is Hand of the King and 1st Admiral to His Majesty's Royal Navy."

Mobee quickly fell to his knees and started worshiping her.

"What are you doing?"

"Yous a very import'n person."

"Get off your knees, Mobee. I am not important. My name is Catherine."

He stopped worshipping and knelt up. "Me heard lots of stories about yous father from Cap Flynn. Heard stories about you sa too."

"You have?" she inquisitively asked, wanting to know.

"Yeps. Cap Flynn said yous father smart sailor, and yous..." he replied and then paused, feeling embarrassed to say it.

She looked at him with wide eyes, waiting.

"I hears yous were the most beautiful woman in all of Englon. And, now I sees, it's true."

Catherine could have blushed; instead, she smiled.

There was a knock on the door. She looked up seeing Flynn standing in the open doorway.

"So, you've met my cabin boy."

"Yes," she replied. "He thinks I'm Royalty."

"Get up, Mobee and fetch Catherine something to eat."

"Aye, Caps."

As he walked out, Flynn stood in his way. "No word to the crew that it's Lady Knox."

"Never me hears of her," he replied with a wink.

"Smart boy, now go," he said, rubbing his head.

When Mobee departed, Flynn walked in and shut the door. "We caught some strong winds heading away from the coastline. It should clear when we're further out to sea."

"That would be nice."

"If you find yourself feeling oozy on this voyage, go out onto the main deck. The fresh air will clear your head."

"Thank you for the advice," she replied. "Speaking of ooziness... is there any liquor or wine onboard?" she continued, slightly cocking her head.

"There is, but I'll have none of it."

"No?" she musingly inquired.

"Not with the cargo I now have onboard."

"Cargo?"

"Belay my last. I was speaking of you."

"I see," she replied, allowing his comment to go unanswered. "So, when are you going to tell your crew about me?"

"Tomorrow, after you're properly introduced to my officers. Is there anything else I can do for you before I call it a night?"

"No, I think after dinner, I'll head to bed myself."

He nodded and turned for the door.

"Captain."

"Yes?"

"Mobee's parents, how did they die?"

"It was the Turks. They raided Mobee's village looking for young men to capture and sell off as slaves. Mobee was lucky. Before the Turks came, his parents told him to fetch some water from the well outside the village."

"Such barbarism," she fumed.

"You're right. As we travel further south, it is something we'll have to watch out for. There are many who would love to capture the Lara May and sell the entire crew into slavery, including you and me. Now, try and get some sleep."

After he closed the door, she whispered, "Try and get some sleep. Who can sleep after hearing that?"

6

As the night watches roamed the main deck, deep in the belly of the Lara May, crewmembers huddled together listening to the ol' salt, Johan Bailer, better known as *'The Serpent'*, with his tattooed face and arms. Some thought he was born from a whale. Others thought he had never lived on dry land.

"What do you think of the man who came aboard, and the secret mission he's on?" asked Sailing Master Ludwig.

"Me fear trouble, matey," he whispered, shifting his eyes across the group.

"Trouble?" another one questioned.

"Yarr, me Lad, the All-Seeing Eye sees everything," he replied, showing his gold medallion around his neck. In the center was an eyelid that moved up and down.

"Where'd ya get that from?" asked the floppy blonde-haired boy, Ezekiel. He was the second youngest onboard after Mobee.

"Me obtain this little gem while sailing the high seas on the Phantom with Scar."

"Scar... that evil pirate?" gasped Ezekiel.

"Yarr, I was just a young fry like you. I'll never forget the day I met him. He was trimmed proper, like a royal flush laid out in spades, in his high black boots, brown suede pants – held fast with a silver buckle. His shirt was fastened with pearls, wearing an English Captain's cover with a raven feather tucked in the side. He obtained the name Scar due to a long knife he suffered in battle. The blade went down his left brow and across his cheek.

"After two weeks of sailing, we caught up with a Spanish Galleon unawares in the Arabian Sea. After capturing the vessel, Scar removed it from the captain's neck and tossed it to me. Me never really looked at it until that night while below in me hammock."

"Where did the captain get it from?" asked Ezekiel.

"Why.... buckle me britches, matey. You ask too many questions. One day you might lose your tongue for that," replied Johan, lifting one brow.

"Tell us," pushed Carpenter Mate Hildegard.

"The Spanish captain said he traded three English wenches to the Prince of Baghdad for it. It was his favorite trinket."

"Does it really have magical power?"

"Yarr, that night, while the men around me slept, I pulled it out. I was surprised to see it looked like a closed eye. Me thought it odd at first until I pushed the thin gold lid open, exposing this," he said, lifting the eyelid.

The men gasped seeing a beautiful black gem that looked like an eye.

"As me peered into the stone, me saw two ships in the night pursuing the Phantom. Me thought the eye be warning me of trouble. The following night, before standing me watch, me went down into the stores. There, me gathered some provisions and placed them in a rough sack. When me went up to the stern to be lookout, me tied the sack to the railing and lowered it to the waterline. Me did the same with the small pontoon secured to the rail.

"That's when the crow's nest shouted, *Sails astern*. I casted me spyglass out over the dark waters and spotted them me self. Two English frigates fast approaching. Me quickly slid down the rope and set the pontoon adrift. It wasn't long after, me was spotted and gathered in by one of the English warships. Seeing me was just a small fry, they asked me questions then sent me below.

"From the belly of the frigate, the battle was fiercely fought and over quick. Out maneuvered and out gunned, the Phantom had no chance. Its crew were set adrift in the lifeboats and then sunk."

"What happened to Scar?"

"Sadly, to say, before the Phantom went down, he and his officers were made to walk the plank – each were shot in the back."

"So that's how you became an English sailor?"

"That you be. Me's been sailing the high seas under the English flag ever since."

"So, what kind of trouble does it see on this voyage?" asked Ludwig.

"Sit back, Lads" he replied, rubbing the gem.

They sat there looking at Johan as he stared blindly into the stone.

A hazy mist appeared before him. Like a bird flying through the clouds, the sky opened. Below, he saw an island with high rocky walls like a fortress. Swooping inland the tall dense jungle took over. In front of him were two enormous mountains.

As the vision continued, Johan swayed back and forth. Onward, he flew closer to the mountains. There, he swooped through the ravine then flew downward until he landed.

Johan glanced to his right. He had never seen such menacing looking jungles like that. To his left, beyond the ravine, a valley of high grass, palm and hardwood trees took over.

Looking down before him, were the bones of a prehistoric giant. Johan took in the large human like creature. Then suddenly, the vision disappeared. Johan fell back.

"Johan, Johan," gasped, Ludwig, catching him.

Johan opened his eyes.

"What ya see?" asked Ezekiel worried.

"Me saw land me fear not go," he murmured, staring wildly out into space.

"What land?"

Johan shook his head. "An island the likes you've never seen."

The group looked at one another.

"What else?" asked Hildegard.

"Me saw bones of something," he whispered, shaking his head.

"What bones? C' mon, Johan. Tell us."

"Prehistoric bones of a giant."

"Prehistoric bones?" laughed Ezekiel. "Your medallion surely telling ya fibs."

"Harr, Mates – the eye never lies."

"Where is this place?"

"Me don't know."

"You're just trying to scare us, aren't you?" remarked Ludwig.

Johan looked at him. Stared him right in the eye. "Me's tell you now... whoever came aboard tonight will lead us to a place no ship has ever sailed."

"Who is this man?"

"It's no man, and we are all going to Hell."

Several heads turned in the direction of Mobee's hammock. The group came to the same conclusion; Mobee entered the person's cabin.

"Should we wake him and find out?" whispered Ludwig.

"Me say not," replied Johan. "If Capt'n Flynn wanted us to know, he would have told us. We go waking Mobee, he'll tell Flynn and our necks will be in a noose. Let's get some sleep and see what happens in the morning."

As much as they tried to sleep, Johan's vision haunted them throughout the night.

7

Hearing the sounds of bells: ding, ding – ding, ding, Catherine stirred from her sleep. As she sat up, there was a knock on her door.

"Yes."

"It's me Mobee. I brought yous a bas'n to wash yous self."

"OK," she replied, opening the door seeing his bright smile. "I had the cook warm it up for yous."

"Thank you. Set it over there, please."

"Yous sleep well?"

"Yes, surprisingly."

"Good," he replied. "Cap Flynn will come and get yous when he's ready. Breakfast will be served dur'n the meet'n."

"Thank you, Mobee."

"Yous welcome, Me' lady," he replied, heading for the door.

"Mobee."

"Yea, Me' lady."

"What are the bells I hear throughout the night and this morning?"

"That's the chang'n of the watch."

"I see."

He nodded, walked out and shut her door. *What a polite boy.*

Twenty minutes later, there was another knock on her door. She opened it to find Flynn standing there.

"Good morning. How was your night?" he asked.

"Morning, Captain. I had a peaceful night, except for the bells."

"You'll get used to them. You ready to meet the officers?"

"The sooner, the better."

When she walked into the forward office, everyone stood up.

"Good morning, gentlemen," said Flynn, pulling a chair out for her to sit.

The men sat down.

Smith and Bishop smiled at her. She smiled back then caught the eyes of the two men she hadn't yet been properly introduced to.

"Lady Knox," said Flynn.

"Catherine will do."

There was a knock on the door.

"Enter."

The ship's cook, Lance Woodward and Mobee walked in carrying breakfast. Woodward immediately froze when he saw the woman.

"Did you come in to stare, or serve us breakfast?" barked Flynn.

"Um, serve you breakfast, Sir."

"Well then, serve it, please."

Woodward placed the large silver tray in the middle of the table then took the top off. Mobee placed two jugs of goat's milk down.

"Is there anything else you need, Captain?" asked Woodward.

"No, thank you."

As he went to leave, Flynn called his name.

He turned at the door.

"Not one word," he sternly ordered.

"Not one word, Sir."

When the door shut, Flynn noticed Mobee still standing beside him. He could see a question on his face. "What is it, Mobee?"

Catherine leaned back to listen to the boy. She had fallen in love with him instantly. She could tell the men sitting there loved Mobee too.

"Well, Cap, last night whiles I were try'n to sleep," he started to say, playing with his fingers. "I's overheard the men whisper'n."

"They were," he replied, acting shocked.

"Yea sa, Cap. Now before me tells ya what they were talk'n about, did Johan really sail with Scar?"

"I knew it had to be Johan," chuckled Smith.

Flynn looked at him then focused on Mobee. "Yes, he sailed with Scar on the Phantom."

"Yous know about his medallion, the All-See'n Eye?"

"Yes."

"Well," Mobee replied, glancing down at the floor. "Johan said the All-See'n Eye sees trouble on this voyage."

"Trouble, you don't say, Lad?"

"Yea, Cap."

"What kind of trouble?" he amusingly asked.

"Johan said he seen a land he feared not go."

"The men laughed.

"That might'a sound funny, but what shook me," he continued, looking over at Lady Knox. "Ezekiel asks him about the man that came aboard last night, and what kind of secret mission he were on."

"What did Johan say?"

"He said it was no man and we're all going to Hell," he said and then quickly added, "Pardon me tongue, Lady Knox."

The men at the table shifted their focus on Catherine. It made her feel uncomfortable.

"Mobee, you don't really believe Johan can see into the future?"

"Hear'n that, well... I believe um. I mean, how did he knows it weren't a man that come aboard last night?"

"He could have gotten a glimpse of her before I escorted her into the officer's cabins last night."

"He might."

"Go, now Mobee. I'll talk to Johan."

"OK, Cap."

When the door closed, Flynn rubbed his jaw thinking. He passed it off and concentrated on the meal before them.

As Bishop filled the plates, Flynn started his introductions. "Catherine, I'd like for you to meet our ship's Medical Officer, Doc Ryan and the ship's Master at Arms, Mr. Davison."

"Nice to meet you."

The two politely nodded.

Not so warm and friendly today, she thought, taking in Davison's size. He was a giant of a man, six feet five with broad shoulders and muscular arms. The medical officer looked like a chicken leg Davison could have easily picked up and ate.

"OK, I'll go through the officer's responsibilities first."

Catherine nodded, while picking up her fork and eating her meal.

"Mr. Smith is first mate. He's in charge of the ship's watch bill and oversees the quarterdeck. No one is allowed on the quarterdeck, with the exception of the coxswain and the officer of the deck. If you want to sit out on the poop deck back Aft, you may use the gangway adjacent to the quarterdeck."

Catherine again nodded.

"Mr. Bishop is in charge of all main deck operations with the assistance of Boatswain Mate Cutter and Sailing Master Ludwig. You may walk the deck during normal working hours. Just stay out of everyone's way."

Catherine nodded.

"Mr. Davison is in charge of maintaining good order and discipline throughout the ship. He also runs the brig and armory. In addition, just so you know, I had him mingle with the crew of the Bridgeport down at the Blue Dragon in Port William. He learned that the Bridgeport, Hamilton and the Dover, were the ships that captured the Nightingale near the Fijian Islands."

"Is that so?" she asked, not knowing where that was.

"That's correct, Milady," replied Davison. "We have a long voyage ahead of us."

"How long?" she asked, glancing at Flynn.

"I can't give you a correct time, but we are looking at many months."

She slowly nodded.

"Any more questions?" he asked her.

"No."

"Alright, does anyone here have any questions?"

"If I may," said Doc Ryan. "Not to be rude, Lady Knox, or to put you on the spot."

Catherine placed her silverware down. "Yes, go on."

"I don't know how to say this."

"Speak up, man," grumbled Flynn.

"Alright, everyone here has seen a thousand sunsets, which I do believe they'd all agree that none of them even come close to your beauty."

"Do you want to belay your last?" belted Davison, thinking the doctor was way out of line.

"No. I will not belay my last comment. I'm thinking of the crew."

"Make your point," pushed Flynn.

"I want no harm to come to you, Milady, and I don't want to see a crewmember shackled in chains either. Is there any way you could dampen your beauty?"

Flynn sat back and laughed. The other men followed.

"I don't see anything funny," grunted Doc Ryan.

The only one not laughing was Catherine. She could have blushed; instead, she recognized his worry. "Doc," she said.

The laughter stopped.

"What part of me do you want me to dampen?"

The men held their tongues but could have laughed again.

"Now you have me in a pickle," replied Doc Ryan, embarrassed.

Flynn quickly slapped the table, making the doctor jerk back.

"I want everyone here to know. Catherine is our guest and she will be treated with respect at all times. After we hold muster, Mr. Davison, you make damn sure the crew knows my feelings on the matter."

"Yes, Captain."

As the room fell silent, Catherine was beside herself. One minute the captain was laughing; the next, he was stern and cold in his speech. She wanted no part of his bad side, knowing it could strike at any moment.

When the meal was through, Flynn stood up. "Mr. Bishop, if you will, go out and muster the crew."

"Yes, Captain."

8

After Bishop had left, Flynn glanced over at Catherine staring at the closed door. She may be holding her own, but he knew deep down, she was nervous. As like her father's determination, he wondered if her backbone was like his and would assist her in this new world: a world of rough, seagoing men, whose lives played out on the open ocean. Today, he knew he'd find out just what she was made of.

"The Bos'n will pipe when they're ready," he said.

Catherine looked back at him. "What do you think of Mobee's story?"

"Johan is always telling stories at night. I think he loves scaring the crewmembers."

"It's no man and we are all going to Hell," she repeated Mobee saying.

Flynn shrugged. "Like I said, he may have seen your face."

"That could be true," she started to say. Before she could finish, the boatswain's pipe sounded on deck.

"That's the call to muster. Are you ready?" he asked her.

"Yes."

Alright, let's go."

As Catherine stood, her hands began to shake. She clasped them together walking behind the group. When Davison opened the outer passageway door, over Flynn's shoulder, she took in the white sails, wooden yardarms, ropes, and blue sky. The negative response from the crew was quick as she walked out onto the main deck.

"What is this?" someone shouted.

"This is outlandish. The king would never send a woman on a secret mission!" another yelled.

"We won't sail with her!"

"Hold your tongues," bellowed Davison, shoving several seamen back.

Flynn escorted Catherine past the men and proceeded up the ladder to the quarterdeck. At the rail, he stood there looking down at them. "Gentlemen, I want you to meet the Admiral's daughter, Catherine Knox."

"She's on a secret mission, is she?" questioned seaman Caleb.

"No," replied Flynn.

"We're all dead men, Captain. You have sealed our fate. King George will send ships after us when they discover she's onboard!" shouted someone.

Flynn went to speak. Catherine placed her hand over his. This was her fight, her only chance of finding Thomas. "Hear me," she shouted over the discontented voices.

The crew angrily stared up at her.

She wiped the windblown hair from her face, and continued, "You all know he received a note. I was the one who wrote that note and had the Trade Wind's bartender hand it to him."

"You... foolish woman, your father will have our heads," shouted seaman Jacob.

"I left my father a letter stating my intentions and why," she replied, turning for the ladder.

Davison went to stop her. She nodded for him to step aside. He looked at Flynn.

Seeing she was her father's own: steadfast in her demeanor to settle this herself, Flynn told Davison to let her go.

As Catherine took the ladder down, the crew stared at her with disdain, mistrust, and indignation.

"I hired this ship to sail to the South Pacific to find Captain Payne and his crew if any are alive."

"You're mad. We've all heard that Thomas Payne is dead," seaman Gardener replied.

"And so is his crew," another one yelled.

She held her tongue to those remarks. "What did Captain Flynn tell you the price would be for taking this voyage?"

"One thousand pounds," someone shouted.

She stepped sideways trying to see who said that. As she did, she spotted an old sailor with his face and arms covered in tattoos, leaning against one of the lifeboats. Next to him were Billy Dobbs and Jeremy Lance, two wretched murders.

A day prior to Catherine going to the Trade Wind and handing Flynn her note, the two were traveling across the countryside of Hillsdale. They came upon a farmhouse and asked to stay the night. When the house settled in for the evening, Jeremy killed the husband, then raped and killed the wife. The following morning the two quickly set out for Bristol Bay. When they arrived, they met up with Flynn who was looking for men to go on a voyage. It was the perfect escape. They signed up immediately.

Catherine took her eyes off Johan and continued, "Whoever said that, please step forward."

Sailing Master Ludwig came to the front.

"Captain Flynn had got it wrong," she told him.

Ludwig cocked his head confused.

"I said a thousand pounds for each man."

Whispers resounded throughout the group.

"A thousand pounds we'll never spend," someone shouted.

Catherine glanced up at Flynn. He raised his brow. She quickly turned and faced the crew.

"If the Royal Navy does come after us, I swear before you now that no man here will be dragged before the king."

"I'd like to drag her down to the bilge," whispered Billy Dobbs to Jeremy Lance.

"Make sure you wake me when you do," he snidely replied.

Johan turned, hearing the two whispering. They smiled at him then trained their attention back on the pretty woman.

"How's-ya going to keep that promise?" asked Ezekiel from the front row.

Catherine walked over to the boy standing next to Mobee. Ezekiel looked down as she approached. She bent over, lifting his chin. "Because I have the king and queen's ear," she said into his blue eyes. "I'll tell 'em to march me to the gallows as well, young man."

"What about your father?" he asked.

"I trust he'll be in a fit when he finds out, but I do pray he'll understand," she said,

JEFF WRIGHT
CATHERINE KNOX

standing erect and casting her eyes along the crew. "But hear me now. I will not stop, nor will I ever... until I find Captain Thomas Payne," she continued, walking to the center of the deck.

"You'll go to the gallows with us," asked seaman Davy. "I think not. The king would never put you to death."

"Trust me; I'll go with my last fighting breath," she sternly replied, turning for the ladder. When she walked up to the quarterdeck and looked down at the crew. They were mulling her words over.

Flynn raised his hand. The crew went silent.

"Men, Lady Knox has hired us to sail to the South Pacific to search for Captain Payne. A thousand pounds for each of you. That is more than you'd make in a lifetime."

"How long we gonna be sailing around that vast ocean looking for him?" asked seaman Rosson.

Flynn glanced over at Catherine, then focused on the lad. "Once we get to the area he disappeared in, we'll search for three months, no longer."

Seaman Frits who always made wisecracks, yelled over the group, "Hear me, boys – I guess we're just going on a little adventure, ya see. Gonna be float'n around the ocean until we come across Captain Payne on some God forsaken island. Or maybe we won't.

"But just think, Lads.... Eighteen months from now – we'll all be back in England a thousand pounds richer, drinking and flirting with the floozies at the Blue Dragon. No harm will come to us while searching for a dead man. I'll raise my hand to that."

Cheers erupted.

Flynn waited for the cheering to stop. When it did, he asked, "Anyone else?"

"Yeah, I've got something to say," replied Joshua, the one-eyed jack-of-all-trades. Lost his eye to a marlin spike being struck by a hammer.

"Speak your mind, man," countered Flynn.

"What's the reward if we do find him? I mean... the thousand pounds is for going – bringing him back has to be worth something?"

Flynn glanced over at Lady Knox.

"A seat at the king's table," she shouted. "I know him personally and his pockets are deep. I'm sure he'd be pleased to have one of his finest captains returned to England, and with that, he'll add to the generous offer I just promised each man here."

The men looked from one to another.

"So, what say ye to the South Pacific we go?" shouted Flynn.

"We'll sail," yelled Hildegard.

The crew immediately joined him... "We'll sail."

"Mr. Bishop, Bos'n Cutter – let's get this ship in order."

"Aye, Captain."

Catherine leaned into him. He placed his ear low to hear.

"When is the last time you've gotten close to your men?"

He looked at her confused.

"When's the last time they bathed?"

"When it rains, or when they place a bucket over the side to toss on their heads – why?"

"You know," she said and then paused, "good hygiene and cleanliness goes hand in hand with good order and discipline."

"You don't say?" he chuckled.

"That's right. When have you ever seen the Royal Guard looking like this?"

"Never."

"There's your answer."

"I guess if you don't like the way they smell, it's best you don't strike below to their berthing."

She wasn't sure if he were telling her not to, but it gave her an idea. "I think it best I stayed up on deck."

"That would be wise," he replied, looking over the crew. "Mr. Smith," he said, "report to the bridge."

Smith walked through the crowd and proceeded up the ladder.

"Put us into the wind and let's be on our way."

"Aye, Captain."

"Once Mr. Bishop and Bos'n Cutter get this ship back in order, have Mr. Davison escort Johan to my cabin, please."

"Aye, Sir."

"Lady Knox, if you will," said Flynn, taking the ladder down.

As the two proceeded to the aft end of the ship, Billy Dobbs and Jeremy Lance moved aside. When Catherine walked past, Dobbs nudged Lance to look at her. Lance's eyes drifted down her slender figure. His lustful thoughts ended way below his waistline as he took in her riding pants, showing every detail.

Inside Flynn's cabin, she noticed a finely-crafted desk in front of the rear bay windows. His bunk was upright: chained to the wall, giving more space to the room. Two crossed swords hung on the opposite wall along with several paintings of ships. There was a large world map on the back wall. She walked over looking at it.

"Would you like some coffee?"

"Yes, thank you," she replied, turning and facing him. As he poured two cups, she walked back to the bay windows. "Nothing but water as far as the eye can see," she murmured to herself.

"You like the view?" he asked, handing her a cup.

"I've never seen anything like it."

There was a knock on the door.

"Enter," said Flynn

Davison along with Johan walked in. "You wanted to see him?"

"Yes."

"Am I staying?"

"No, that will be all."

Davison nodded then departed.

"Sit," said Flynn.

"Why me here?" replied Johan, suspiciously eyeing the woman.

"Sit," repeated Flynn.

Johan sat down.

Catherine leaned against the back wall taking in the old sailor covered in tattoos. He was a thin man with scraggly grey hair pulled back into a ponytail. She figured he was Spanish with his dark beady eyes and long nose. *Why anyone would do that to their face is beyond me,* she thought, taking a seat across from him.

"I heard word of your story telling last night. Why don't you tell us the story you told?"

"Whispers from below caught your ear this morning, Capt'n?" he asked, wondering who it could be.

Flynn nodded.

"Me told the young lads what I saw within me' dallion."

"You saw?" remarked Catherine.

"Harr, Melady," he replied, pulling it out. "This little gem has saved me on many occasions. It's the All-Seeing Eye."

"May I see it?" she asked, extending her hand.

"See, Melady?" he sarcastically rebutted. "You don't see at all. This ocean is a monster that sleeps most of the time, but when it's angry, it will swallow you whole," he continued, raising one brow.

"Johan," scolded Flynn.

"Me's just telling her the truth."

"Tell us about the island you saw within your medallion."

Johan looked from one to the other. "Me and you have sailed to many places, Capt'n Flynn, but never to a place like this. It haunts me soul."

Flynn leaned up rubbing his chin. "Jungles?"

"So thick, one could lose themselves."

"Shoreline?"

"High rocky walls like a fortress and mountains reaching to the clouds."

"Anything else?"

"Me saw bones of something me never seen before."

"Animal?" asked Catherine.

"No. They.... they were of a giant."

"Human?" she questioned.

"Yarr, Melady."

"Were they old?" asked Flynn.

"Me told the lads last night they looked prehistoric, but me can't tell, Me's inkling tells me we're all doomed if we continue on this voyage."

Hearing that, Catherine sighed. The ol' salt frightened her.

"Did you see Captain Payne inside that medallion?" asked Flynn.

"Before settling in, me looked into black gem. Me saw nothing of Captain Payne – just a ship listing to one side in a hidden inlet cove. There was a gaping hole at the stern; the main yardarm was busted, its sails hanging over the side."

Catherine quickly flooded back to Captain Leopold's description of the damage done to the York. The hole in the stern crept over her like spiders. She shivered thinking Johan was telling the truth. *But how,* she wondered. *How can a gold medallion see into the future?*

"Any men?" asked Flynn.

"No."

"Where did you get that medallion?" she asked.

"The famous pirate, Scar, removed it from a Spanish captain and tossed it to me. He said he traded three English maidens to the Prince of Bagdad for it."

"The Prince of Bagdad, you don't say?" she mused.

"Surely as me's sitting here."

"That will be all," said Flynn.

Johan got up and proceeded to the door. Before walking out, he turned and faced them. "Just so you know. When me saw you walk out this morn, me thought of jumping overboard, but me fear the sharks more than what's at the end of this voyage." With that, Johan departed.

When the door closed, Catherine stood up and proceeded over to the bay windows. She opened one and inhaled the sea breeze trying to clear her head of what Johan had just said. "Do you believe him?" she asked, keeping her focus on the water astern.

"No," replied Flynn, getting up from his chair.

"I think I should inform you," she continued, slightly turning his way. "Captain Leopold said he took out the stern with his forward gun then sent one round through the York's midsection."

Captain Flynn walked up to her.

"Can you explain how he knew that?"

"Maybe he overheard one of the king's men talking."

"Johan? I think not – none of the king's men frequent the pubs he goes to."

"You'd be surprised."

She caught that as soon as it left his lips, then dropped it just as quick. "I'd sure like to get my hands on that medallion and see for myself," she said, speaking more in thought.

"I can't force him to remove it."

"No, you can't; however," she replied, stepping away from the window and heading for the door.

"However, what?" he asked, suspicious of her thoughts.

"I don't know," she replied, opening the door.

"Where are you going?"

"To find Mobee and Ezekiel."

"Why?"

"This is going to be a long voyage, Captain. I need something to do to occupy my time. I thought I'd give the boys lessons in speaking proper English. They should have some schooling."

"Schooling?"

"That's right. All they hear is poor English onboard this ship."

"Poor English?"

"Yes – Melady. It's MiLady," she mimicked the sailors. "Besides that, Mobee really needs to learn."

Flynn gave that a thought.

"I may not turn them into proper gentlemen, but they will be much better for it. So... with your permission, I'd like to set up a time in the mornings to teach them."

"Permission granted, you can have 'em as soon as they're done with their morning duties."

"Thank you. And while we're on the subject, there are other things I'd like to change, but they can wait," she said, walking out and shutting the door.

"Change?"

Catherine never looked back as she continued to the ladder.

"Lady Knox," he shouted.

She slightly turned, looking back at his door. A smile appeared on her face as she took the ladder up to the main deck.

"Oh, that woman," scolded Flynn, imagining the entire crew sitting around with their noses in books learning proper English.

9

The days rolled by like the temperate waves, as the Lara May continued southward, ever watchful for the British flag, and or, cut-throat pirates that would love to seize her as a prize.

During those long days, which turned into weeks, Catherine was feeling more at ease onboard. Her only problem was staying out of the way of the crew as they moved about the ship, completing their daily tasks.

Just by a nod or pleasant greeting, she knew some of the men had accepted having her onboard. Others however, kept their anger in check, but she knew whom they were and stayed clear of them.

On a bright sunny morning, with whispering clouds overhead, Flynn found her sitting back aft, teaching Mobee and Ezekiel proper English. She glanced over at him talking to the coxswain and Mr. Smith. When he finished, he strolled back to where she was sitting.

"Good morning, Captain," she greeted, gazing up at his sun-tanned face.

"Morning – how is class going?"

"Great," replied Mobee, sitting close to her.

"Yeah," added Ezekiel. "She's teaching us the alphabet today."

By their boyish smiles, he wondered if they were more delighted with sitting with a beautiful woman than learning boring English. If he were a young lad, he would have chosen the later. "I hope you two are getting your morning chores done before class," he said, holding his thoughts.

"I make sure they do," replied Catherine, wiping the hair from her face.

Flynn reached into his pocket and pulled out a clean handkerchief and tore it in two. "You may find this useful," he said, tossing it to her.

"Thank you," she replied, pulling her hair back and tying it into a ponytail.

"I won't take up any more of your time," he said, turning to leave.

"Captain."

"Yes."

"When will we be sailing around the Cape of Good Hope? Mobee said the weather there can get nasty?"

"It can. It's a large peninsula located off the coast of South Africa. We'll just watch the weather as we sail around it. But first we have a port-call to make."

"Port-call?"

"This is an arduous trip, Lady Knox. We'll need more provisions before we venture into the Indian Ocean."

"I understand we need more supplies, but aren't you taking a risk? The British fleet could be sitting there."

"There's a port in Angola the British fleet does not like. Too many of their sailors have simply disappeared."

"That's great.... What about us?"

"I know a wealthy merchant who'll ensure our safety."

"And for me?" she asked, tilting her head.

"I'm not going to risk it; you'll be staying onboard."

"We'll stay onboard with you," said Mobee.

"That's right," Ezekiel agreed.

Catherine wrapped her arms around the boys then looked up at Flynn.

"I'll leave you now," he said, turning and departing their company.

As she sat there leisurely watching him take the ladder down, his authority was apparent, even in his stride. The crew seemed to respect him by halting their work and standing when he spoke to them. *He'll make a fine British captain again one day,* she thought, getting to her feet. "You may go now; class is over."

"Great," said Mobee "First up the mast wins," he beamed.

Ezekiel raced after him.

"Boys," she shouted.

They turned and faced her.

"No crow's nest," she ordered, folding her arms.

"But we's always race to the top," frowned Mobee.

"You heard her," said Smith, standing next to the helm.

"Mr. Smith," moaned Ezekiel.

"How about you two go and find Mr. Bishop. He was looking for someone to make new lines for the lifeboats."

"C'mon, Mobee – that sounds like a fun job," shouted Ezekiel.

"I'll race ya," replied Mobee, turning for the ladder.

After they left, Catherine asked Smith if she could enter the quarterdeck, a place off limits to the crew while the ship was underway.

"You may."

As he gazed at her coming down from the poop deck in her high black boots, brown pants and white shirt, he thought of Doc Ryan's remark; *is there any way to dampen your beauty?* There was no way in his mind she could, not even if she were tossed in a barrel of slop. She'd still come up looking as beautiful as an English garden in bloom.

"A smile held with pride must have a thought behind it," she said, walking past him and leaning on the quarterdeck rail.

Smith turned and leaned next to her. "You're like a rose amongst the thorns," he replied, keeping his eyes forward on the crew.

Catherine glanced over at him, seemingly looking out over the ship. She never suspected him of being a charmer; he was more like a businessman the way he carried himself. "If that was a compliment, thank you. How long have you been sailing?" she then asked.

"All my life."

"You have a wife back home?"

"No."

"Children?"

"No."

That surprised her. Being an older man, he looked very distinguished with his grayish hair and sideburns. Even his brown eyes were appealing. She figured he had many wenches who took care of his needs; everyone has needs, even she did. Her needs however, would have to wait until she found Thomas and took him home.

She lingered on that thought like a new bride anxiously anticipating the night ahead with her husband. Her pause made Smith feel uneasy. He thought he should explain himself. "Being a man of the sea would be a lonely life for a woman having to wait for my return. Many sit idle too long waiting. They go out and pick up suitors to fill that void. I chose not to take a wife for that reason. I never wanted to come home to another man entertaining her in my absence."

Catherine nodded, still floating on her romantic thought. "That might have been a wise choice. I suspect, however – a man of your looks has a woman in every port," she replied with a slight smile.

Smith laughed to that comment.

"I'll take your laughter as a *yes*. I won't keep you any further," she said, turning to leave.

"Lady Knox."

"Yes," she replied, casting her eyes on the coxswain and then back at him.

"Captain Payne is a very lucky man. If we discover his whereabouts, I'm going to strongly advise him to give up this life at sea."

His smile and that telling glint in his eye spoke volumes. "You do that, Mr. Smith. I'd like my man to be home with me," she replied, turning for the ladder.

He stood next to the rail watching her strolling along the main deck. Every man stopped what he was doing to greet her. *For a woman like that, they'd all give up this life at sea,* he figured. He waded out of that thought hearing the main sail flapping in the breeze. "Helmsmen, change course south by southwest."

"Aye, Mr. Smith."

"Mr. Bishop," he then shouted, pointing up at the yardarm.

Bishop noticed a few straps holding the mainsheet needed fixing. "You three, get up there and secure that sail," he ordered several deckhands.

As the men went aloft, Smith spotted Catherine leaning against the ship's outer rail enjoying the view on this warm sunny day.

His eyes then focused on the two men scrubbing the deck behind her. They seemed to be enjoying the view in front of them as well. So much so, they had stopped their work all together. *I didn't like that pair when Flynn hired them at the Trade Wind, and I still don't like them now,* he thought, trying to remember their names. It didn't matter, he was going to keep an eye on them throughout the voyage.

Dobbs and Lance sat there gazing up at the pretty woman hanging onto the ropes. Just her swaying in the breeze was enough to arouse the pair.

"Enticing, isn't she?" whispered Dobbs.

"She is indeed," replied Lance, staring at her sweet curves.

Catherine suddenly turned inward, catching them off guard. They smiled and continued their work. It wasn't the first time she caught men gazing at her. These two, however, made her feel very uneasy. She knew oh so well that behind those smiles were wolves ready to pounce. With a simple nod, she casually departed to the stern of the ship.

There, while looking out over the vast endless sea, she thought of her man. It made her flood back to her dreams and visions. *I know for sure now my darling, that you were calling out to me.* That thought made her close her eyes and whisper in her heart. *Hear me my love – I'm coming for you.*

10

Late that same evening, dark menacing clouds swooped across the night sky. Thunderous lightning broke forth from the heavens, foretelling the approaching storm.

Catherine frantically awoke feeling the ship rocking. As she hurried to get out of her bunk, the ship listed hard sideways, sending her flying across the room. Her body slammed against the wooden hull. In a daze, she moaned from the impact.

Up on deck, the turmoil was even worse. The quarterdeck watch, Sailing Master Ludwig had miscalculated the storm's direction. Instead of ordering the coxswain to go around, he had the seaman sailing straight toward it.

Flynn suddenly awoke feeling the ship sailing through turbulent seas. *What in the hell,* he thought, getting up and dressing. By the time he made it to the ladder, the first storm waves hit. When he reached the main deck, the galling winds and driving rain hit him full on.

"Mr. Bishop," he shouted, holding onto the ladder-well rail.

"Captain," responded Bishop.

"Haul down the mainsail."

"Aye, Sir."

"Where is Mr. Smith?" he then asked.

"I'm up here," shouted Smith from the quarterdeck above. He too knew something was wrong and had raced out of his cabin to the helm. Flynn angrily stared at Ludwig, soaking wet in the driving rain.

"I'm sorry, Captain," he said to his glare.

"It's too late for us to turn back now, Captain," bellowed Smith.

"I know. We'll fight our way through this, but by God, I lose a man," he bellowed, shaking his head. He quickly turned and hurried toward the bow. As he fought his way through the horrific winds, he never spotted Mobee or Ezekiel hiding under the lifeboat. Mobee went to get up. Ezekiel pulled him back. "Where are you going?"

"I want 'a be with Cap Flynn."

"Are you crazy, Mobee? You'll be washed overboard."

As Mobee settled back, he spotted a crewmember crawling along the deck toward the officer's forward cabins. The man got up, hung onto the door handle, then opened it.

Mobee watched the door slam back against the bulkhead. In that moment, he realized Lady Knox was still inside her cabin. "I got to go," he said worried.

Ezekiel tried to pull him back. Mobee shoved him away.

"Mobee," he yelled, watching him crawling along the deck to the door flapping in the breeze.

Inside her cabin, Catherine, fearing the ship was going down, hurried to get out. She frantically made it to the door. When she opened it, there was a man soaking wet standing there. She could not see his face. "Get me out of here," she yelled.

Jeremy Lance was shocked that she was still in her cabin. It almost fouled his deviant plans of stealing some of her coins from her money chest he suspected was there. After her generous offer the day prior, he and Billy Dobbs planned on taking some of her gold and silver and then getting off the ship at its first port-of-call. He quickly thought of an idea.

"I came to get you. Hurry, go down the passageway. Once you're outside, find a place to take shelter."

"Thank you," she replied, holding onto the walls toward the open outer door.

As she left, Lance smiled, walked in, and shut the door.

Catherine got as far as the outer door. The winds and rain pushed her back.

"Lady Knox," said Mobee, crawling along the deck.

"Mobee," she shouted, seeing him. She quickly reached down, grabbed his arm and pulled him inside the passageway.

"Where is the seaman who came in?"

She looked down the passageway. The man was gone. "Maybe he went inside the ship's office."

"C' mon, let's get you to back to your cabin."

"I don't want to die in there," she pleaded.

"We're not going to die. Cap Flynn has it under control."

She peered out into the driving rains and howling wind, seeing the ship listing this way and that, causing the yardarms to breach the huge waves crashing over the rails. It frightened her to the core. "Come, Mobee," she yelled, pulling him down the passageway.

Her door suddenly opened. The man was standing there.

"What are you doing in my cabin!?"

Lance panicked seeing them. "Out of my way," he belted.

As he went to pass, Catherine grabbed him. The coins he stole flew out of his hands, hitting the floor.

"He was in there stealing your money," yelled Mobee, taking hold of the man's arm.

Lance struck Mobee, sending him to the floor.

Catherine grabbed him again. Lance pushed her inside the cabin. When he turned to leave, she latched onto his back. At that moment, the ship rose up a giant wave, sending lance off his feet. With her on his back they fell inside her cabin.

On the floor, Lance fought to get free. She let him go and tried to get up. The ship violently listed, sending Lance and she flying across the room.

Lance got up. She grabbed his leg. He kicked her off.

The ship rose again, sending them lurching backward onto the bunk.

"You... mangy dog, get off me," she cursed, biting his hand.

"You bitch," shouted Lance, slapping her face, cutting her lip.

Mobee jumped on top of him.

Lance let go of her and hit Mobee square in the jaw. Mobee flew back hitting his head on the wooden frame. The lights inside his head went out. He lay there, out cold.

"You're a dead man," she yelled, trying to get free. Lance grabbed her shirt and tore it back. He then pushed her down hard onto the bunk.

Catherine, now exposed, fought desperately to get up. Laying on top, Lance groped her. She bit his ear. He pulled her hair.

Out on deck, Ezekiel saw Davison coming down the portside. He called out to him underneath the lifeboat.

"You stay down there," shouted Davison.

"Lady Knox," he yelled, pointing toward the officer's cabin door now hanging by one hinge. "Mobee went to check on her."

"OK, you stay there."

Inside the cabin, Catherine's strength was draining. Her pleas for help unanswered.

Davison stumbled down the passageway. Her door was open. When he entered, someone was lying on the ground. Then he heard Catherine moaning for help. Like a raging bull, Davison crossed the room, grabbed Lance and drew him off her with both hands. "You bastard," he cursed, throwing Lance against the hull.

Lance felt his body buckle from the impact. The next thing he felt was being picked up and a massive fist hitting him square in the jaw. His head flew back. His legs gave out, dropping to the floor in a thud.

Hanging onto the table as the ship listed, Davison drove his boot heel into Lance's back. Semiconscious, Lance moaned.

"Are you alright, Milady?"

"No, she replied then started to cry.

"Can you walk?"

"Yes."

"Go out and get help."

Without a word, Catherine got up and stumbled out. When she made it to the outer door, she let out a terrifying scream then collapsed in the passageway.

Bos'n Cutter heard her. He rushed over to the open door. "Lady Knox."

"Inside," she gasped, pointing down the passageway.

When Cutter made it to her cabin, someone came flying out. They hit the wall and fell on the floor before him. Davison stepped out seeing him.

"Tie that bastard up in the office. I've got to get Mobee to Doc Ryan quick."

Hearing that, Cutter grabbed Lance by the collar and dragged him down the passageway to the office. By the time he was done with Lance there wasn't much of him to tie up. He severely beat the man for attacking Lady Knox and almost killing Mobee.

The following morning, Catherine awoke feeling weak and unsure of where she was. When she sat up in her bunk, Doc Ryan was sitting there. She looked about trying to remember.

"Morning, Milady," he softly said.

She reached up feeling her face. Her jaw hurt, her lip was cut. The previous night flooded back to her. *Oh my God,* she thought. "Where is Mobee?" she sighed.

"He's fine, he's fine," he reassured her.

"Where is he?"

"He's in the infirmary. He has a concussion from hitting his head."

Catherine closed her eyes and fell back onto the pillow. Tears welled up and she began to cry.

Doc Ryan got up and sat next to her. He wanted to hug her, to tell her everything was going to be alright. Instead, he took her hand within his and let her sob. Sometimes it's best to get all the sorrow out, then when the crying is over, the healing can begin.

There was a tap on her closed door.

"Come in," said Ryan.

It was Flynn. He stood in the doorway looking down at her crying. Ryan raised his hand then nodded for him to sit.

He walked over and took a seat at the table.

Ryan handed her a handkerchief. She wiped her tears and blew her nose.

"Are you alright?" asked Flynn.

She slowly nodded. "What happened?"

"After sailing out of the storm, Bos'n Cutter picked you up and carried you inside. It was Doc Ryan and I who...." his voice trailed off.

She looked down at her nightgown then glanced over at her wet torn shirt and pants hanging over her closet door. It didn't matter that they saw her naked, her mind was too occupied with Mobee.

"I um, I also looked you over," said Ryan. "You're very lucky he broke no bones; however, you do have some very bad bruises on your back and shoulders."

"I can feel each one too," she replied, reaching up and touching her jaw. "I'd like to see Mobee."

"He's still coming in and out. The entire crew want to see him also," said Flynn. "Let's give it a few more days, OK?"

She nodded. "May I speak with the doctor personally?"

"Sure," said Flynn, getting up. "If you're ready for something to eat, I'll have Woodward come down and see you," he continued heading toward the door.

"Thank you, Captain. Oh," she said.

"Flynn stopped at the door.

"Who was it?"

"Jeremy Lance. He's in the brig. Said he was only after your coins and that him and seaman Dobbs were going to get off at the next port-of-call."

"I see."

"You should have told me. We do have a ship's vault."

"I'm sorry. I should have."

"We placed all your valuables there now. Hope you don't mind."

"No, thank you."

Flynn nodded then left.

When the door shut, she focused on the doctor. "Can I ask you a question?"

"Sure."

"When you said, is there any way to dampen my beauty, what were you referring to, or can I make a guess?"

"Why are you asking this now? The men have all accepted you."

She glanced over at her torn shirt. Ryan's eyes followed. He looked at her. "That's what I was pertaining to, Lady Knox," he said to her sad eyes.

"That evil man might have wanted my coins, but when he got a hold of me, well... he wanted more than that," she said. "I never want that to happen again."

"Me neither, Milady. Just so you know, though, the crew all feels bad that this happened to you."

Catherine let that settle over her. "If I may..."

"Yes."

"Being endowed, or blessed the way I am."

"Yes."

"I was foolish in not bringing any corsets. Is there any way I can cover myself so not to insight another man in doing this to me again?"

"I'll have Sailing Master Ludwig come see you. He could make you something out of sailing cloth."

"Have him come to my cabin, please."

"I'll do that. Now, get some rest. I'll check on you later," he replied, getting up and walking out.

When the door closed, Catherine stared at it. The anger within her came to the surface. *Jeremy Lance will pay with his life.*

During the days that followed, Catherine remained within her room. She went out once to visit with Mobee in the infirmary. Even though he smiled when she walked in, it saddened her heart seeing him lying there with a bandage wrapped around his head.

During her time with him, even with his Nigerian accent, she noticed that his English was improving remarkably. It was hard for her not to love him like a mother; Ezekiel too, who stayed by his side in the evenings.

Day of Judgement

During those sad days as Catherine remained alone within her cabin and Mobee laid up, the crew went about their business, keeping mostly to themselves. They all wondered what Captain Flynn was going to do.

Flynn spent those days and nights thinking of the punishment. He and his officers spoke for hours. In the end, with no ruling in the ship's manual for violating a woman, for women were not allowed on vessels, Flynn decided to hang Jeremy Lance. His crimes included: thievery, assault to cause bodily harm, and molesting a female. Not just any female, but the Hand of the King's daughter. He knew for that crime alone; King George would have removed Lance's head from his shoulders.

He called the muster the following morning.

Catherine received word of Lance's hearing the night prior. When she heard the Bos'n pipe, mustering the crew in the morning, it was time.

After walking out of her cabin, she halted; the passageway outer door was still missing. She could see Flynn standing there speaking to his crew in ranks. She stood quietly and listened.

"Today I have a man standing before me guilty of the following. Mr. Smith if you will, read off the charges."

Smith stepped forward and unrolled the parchment. "Jeremy Lance, you are hereby charged with the following crimes: thievery, assault to cause bodily harm to seaman Mobee and physically molesting Lady Knox while onboard the Lara May."

While in ranks, the entire crew's love for Mobee was forthrightly apparent as they glared at Lance in disgust. Each man would have slit his throat from ear to ear if given the chance. If that wasn't enough to grow boils in their stomachs, assaulting Lady Knox was the final nail in Lance's coffin. They could not wait to see him hanging from the yardarms; his dead body then tossed over the side.

"Thank you, Mr. Smith," said Flynn. "As Captain of this ship, I find you guilty of all charges, seaman Lance. Today you'll be hung from the neck until you are dead."

Hearing that, Lance's knees buckled, his life soon to be over.

"Bos'n Cutter, tie a noose and toss the line over the yardarm, if you will."

"Aye, Captain."

"Mr. Davison, escort that mangy dog underneath."

At the rear of the muster, Johan, Ludwig, and Hildegard watched Davison escorting Lance in chains toward the yardarm.

"Have you ever seen a man hung?" whispered Johan.

"No," replied Ludwig.

"It's an awful sight to witness, seeing 'em twisting and turning until their face turns blue."

Hildegard shivered hearing that.

"What about his partner?" asked Ludwig.

"They're land dwellers, both of 'em, matey."

"Land dwellers?"

"Yarr, they've never been to sea."

"How do you know this, Johan?" asked Hildegard.

"One day, me overheard Mr. Bishop telling 'em to go back aft and scrub the portside deck. The two went back and started scrubbing the starboard side."

Before either could speak, the crew in front gasped seeing Lady Knox walking out of the officer's passageway. Some became angry seeing the telltale signs of her ordeal: dark bruises on her face and neck. Angry shouting erupted.

"Get it over with – hang the bastard," someone shouted.

"Yeah - hang that slimy mud worm," another yelled.

Scared out of his mind, Billy Dobbs slowly stepped back further in rank, trying to hide within the group.

Flynn turned seeing Catherine standing there. "I think it best for you to go back to your cabin."

"I think not," she sternly replied.

"Lady Knox?" questioned Flynn.

"This is my fight," she spat. "Mr. Davison, bring me two swords."

Captain Flynn stepped up to her. "What in the hell do you think you're doing?"

"I'm taking my own revenge on this heathen."

"Really - with swords?"

She stepped back looking him dead in the eye. "You watch."

Flynn lifted his chin. "Alright, but if he gets the better of you, I'll shoot the bastard."

"You do that - but believe me, you won't have to."

He quickly spun around. "Mr. Davison - two swords, if you will."

Davison looked at him confused. Murmurs swept through the ranks.

"You heard me."

Davison pushed Lance down on the deck and proceeded below.

"Unshackle him," ordered Flynn.

Bishop stepped up and took off the chains.

"I'm not fighting a woman," Lance grumbled, rubbing his wrist.

"You are today," retorted Catherine.

The crew was now beside itself. Never in all their lives had they witnessed such a spectacle, a woman fighting a man with a sword.

Davison came up from below and handed one to her then tossed the other on the deck in front of Lance.

Lance took hold of his sword and stood up. The crew stepped back, giving them room.

Catherine quickly positioned herself in a parry 3 stance: standing sideways, left arm extended up and behind her head, her right hand holding the sword toward her opponent.

Smith looked over at Flynn with a stunned expression on his face. *This is going to be interesting,* Smith thought, casting his gaze on Catherine.

Catherine cautiously approached Lance, ready to duel. Lance was ready also. The fight commenced with Lance taking the first swipe at her. Catherine blocked his advance, lashed out with her blade, slicing him across the cheek. The pain was instant, the blood flowed freely.

"How does that feel?" she snarled, getting back into her stance.

"You wretched bitch," cursed Lance, touching his face and seeing blood. It made him angry. He charged at her.

She quickly sidestepped his forward advance and sliced him across his back. The red stain on his shirt told she hit the mark.

Lance spun around cursing.

"I'm going to slice you up like a brick of cheese," she taunted him.

The crew began cheering her on.

Lance beaded his eyes on them then quickly trained his focus back on her. "Before I die, I'm going to run you through," he shouted, charging her again.

This time he got the better of Catherine, slamming her against the forward wall. She quickly stomped on his soft shoe with her boot and shoved him back. Lance stumbled and fell on the deck.

"Get up," she shouted.

He slowly got to his feet.

"Your day is about over," she hissed, stepping forward slicing this way and that. Lance tried to fight her off, but his sword was slower than hers was. She cut his left arm then drove her saber into the meaty flesh of his upper right shoulder. Lance fell on his knees moaning. Not done, Catherine twisted her blade inside causing more damage.

"I give up," he cried out in pain.

She slowly pulled it out and introduced the tip to his throat.

The men yelled for her to run him through.

Flynn raised his hand and approached her. "Who taught you how to fight?" he asked amazed at her ability.

"William Colfax, the Captain of his Majesty's Royal Guard," she replied, staring down at Lance.

"I'll be," replied Flynn.

"I'll second that," add Smith.

"Mr. Davison... if you please, escort this scoundrel under the yardarm," ordered Flynn.

"Wait," said Catherine, spotting Billy Dobbs hiding amongst the crew. "You there, step forward."

"Me?" replied Dobbs, pointing at himself.

"That's right, step forward!" she shouted.

Dobbs came to the front.

"Throughout this entire voyage, I've caught both these fools staring at me like a well ripened fruit."

More shouting erupted to hang them both.

"Hold your tongues," ordered Flynn.

The crew went silent.

"They're land dwellers," yelled Hildegard from the rear.

"Who said that?" asked Flynn.

"I did, Captain," shouted Hildegard, raising his hand. "Ask the mud worm which side port is."

That caught Flynn off guard. Both Lance and Dobbs stated they had been to sea before he, Flynn, hired them. "Bos'n Cutter, your marlinspike, please."

Cutter handed it to him.

"What is this used for?" he asked Dobbs.

"I don't know."

"You don't know? How can you not know if you've been to sea?"

"I've never seen one, Captain."

"Mr. Bishop, cut me a strand of line," ordered Flynn.

Bishop handed it to him.

"Put an eye in that line."

"An eye?" replied Dobbs confused.

Flynn grabbed Dobbs by the collar and yanked him up on the balls of his feet. "I'll give you just one more. Tie me a bowline knot in that line, shipmate."

"I don't know how."

"You," he hissed. "Get on your knees," he continued, pulling out his pistol. He placed the barrel to his head. "You've never sailed at all - have you?" he shouted.

"No."

"You lied to me, Lad. WHY!?"

Dobbs glanced over at his friend, Lance, with his hand pressed against his shoulder wound. By Lance's expression, he knew his thoughts, but he, Dobbs, did not want to die. He looked up at Flynn.

"You keep your mouth shut," warned Lance.

"I can't," he replied. "Jeremy murdered a farmer in the countryside of Hillsdale, so he could rape his wife."

"You... lousy pig," cursed Lance. "Tell 'em what you did."

Flynn slowly looked at Lance then back at Dobbs. Dobbs could tell the captain was waiting.

"After he killed the woman, I laid with her."

After the crew heard that vulgar act committed on the dead woman, they began shouting and cursing.

Flynn removed his pistol from Dobbs forehead and stepped back. In a slow, unemotional tone, he said, "A hanging would be too merciful for your foul souls. I sentence you both to being tossed overboard."

"No, please," begged Dobbs.

"Gentlemen, they're all yours," said Flynn to his crew.

Like a pack of wolves, the men charged forward seizing the pair. They manhandled them to the rail.

Flynn, along with Smith, Bishop, and Davison gathered at the side. Billy Dobbs went over first then Jeremy Lance. The two went under then came up like corks in a barrel.

"Please, show us mercy," shouted Lance.

"I'll show you mercy," one seaman yelled back, picking up a large wooden crate and tossing it overboard. "Use that to swim back to England, you murdering bastards."

In a matter of seconds, the ocean swells carried Dobbs and Lance further away. The crew walked along the side of the ship watching them trying desperately to swim to the crate.

Flynn looked back at Catherine. She was gone. He glanced down at her sword lying there then back up at the passageway leading to her cabin. His heart sank like the two now lost at sea. *How can I fix this? How can I mend her broken heart?* Those thoughts gave him an idea.

"I see she left," said Bishop, beside him.

"Yeah," he replied in a tone of regret.

Bishop said nothing to his comment.

"Have Carpenter's Mate Hildegard make us a new door for the officer's passageway. Tonight, after super, I want the entire crew except the watches mustered in front of my cabin below."

"Aye, Captain."

"That'll be all," said Flynn, leaving his company.

Bishop stood there watching the captain making his way back aft. Even his stride conveyed a broken man. He let it go and turned toward Bos'n Cutter. "Get this ship back in order. We have a mission to fulfill."

"Aye, Mr. Bishop."

JEFF WRIGHT
CATHERINE KNOX

11

For three long days, after Dobbs and Lance were thrown overboard, Catherine still wanted to be alone. The assault was more than a violation of her flesh; it was a violation of her innocence. The hardest part for her to endure was she had no one to blame but herself, and thus, she could not bear to see anyone except Woodward, bringing her meals, and Ludwig, who came to measure her for a corset.

During that time, every morning the crew mustered in the berthing below, waiting for her to come out. Each morning was the same. She did not appear.

Finally, on the fourth day, Mr. Smith saw the passageway door open. He walked over to the ship's bell and waited. When Catherine stepped out, he rang the bell to alert the crew below.

When they proceeded up the ladder, there was something strangely different about her. It wasn't the men's clothing she was wearing, or that her facial bruises had turned purple. It was her beautiful flowing auburn hair. It was gone. She looked more like a man.

Hearing the bell and seeing the men filing up from below, Catherine paused in front of the door not knowing what was happening. The men aloft came down as well. Then, they all filed in ranks in front of her. She was startled by all of this.

Even though the men were stunned by her appearance, not a word was spoken within the ranks. Mobee, who was feeling much better, walked up to her with his hands clasped behind his back. She waited to hear what he had to say. He simply smiled and presented her with a beautiful carved rose on a stem with two leafs made from soft pine.

As she took the rose carving, he graciously knelt on one knee before her; the entire crew followed. Their simple gesture brought tears to her eyes.

While thinking what to say, she spotted Captain Flynn, along with Bishop, Davison, and Doc Ryan standing near the ship's aft ladderwell. They slowly removed their covers. Up on the quarterdeck, Smith removed his cover as well.

"Lady Knox," said Mobee.

"Yes."

"The entire crew, along with Captain Flynn, wanted me to tell you that we're sorry, and we promise, with all our hearts, that it will never happen again."

Overwhelmed by his words, she knelt before Mobee and hugged him. The crew cheered.

"Haven't you noticed anything?" she whispered in his ear.

"Noticed? Noticed what?" he musingly replied.

"Now, Mobee," she said, letting him go and standing. "Well?" she pushed.

Mobee looked down at her shoes, and then allowed his eyes to drift up her clothing.

"Are you playing games with me, young man?" she warmly scolded.

"No, I'm not playing games, Lady Knox."

She tilted her head while folding her arms.

Mobee quickly turned toward the crew. "She just asked me if I see anything different about her."

"Mobee," she gasped embarrassed.

"No," the crew shouted.

Mobee turned back and looked up at her. "Lady Knox, may I be honest with you?"

"It would certainly help your situation of lying to me."

"Well..." he said, fiddling with his fingers. "Even if you were bald, you'd still be as beautiful as a sunset in paradise."

His charming little words dispelled her sadness and she laughed; so, did the crew.

As the men gathered around, she looked back where Flynn had been standing. He, along with his officers, were gone. She let it go. She'd speak with him later. Right now, after spending so much time alone, she just wanted to be with the men. Before she could speak, numerous questions were tossed at her.

"Did William Colfax really teach you how to brandish a sword like that?" a crewmember asked.

"Yes, but I never told my father. If I had, I know he'd still be chirping in my ear about it."

Laughter erupted.

"Tell us about King George. What kind of man is he?"

"King George?" she replied. "He's a noble man, a right talented figure. The man you really want to know about is Captain Thomas Payne. Now there's a brilliant captain; a seafaring man, just like yourselves."

"You really think he's still alive?"

"Yes, with all my heart. That man could maneuver his way out of anything. He once weaseled his way out of taking me on a Sunday picnic, so what is a mere storm to that?"

As the men laughed at her witty humor, the ship's bell rang.

"Watches - take your positions. The rest of you, slimy fish heads, get to work, the day's a-wasting," Bos'n Cutter bellowed, winking at Catherine.

As the men departed, Catherine called out to him. "May I have a word with you?"

"Yes, Melady."

"I had Woodward bring me a book on ships. I was wondering if you could teach me everything."

"Everything?" he replied stunned.

"Yes, we can start right after my morning class with Mobee and Ezekiel."

Those little angels, he thought, *they haven't shut up about speaking proper English below since she started her morning classes with them.* He kept that to himself and answered, "I don't think Captain Flynn would mind me taking you about the ship while supervising the deckhands."

"Thank you, when can we start?"

"Today, after your class, if you'd like."

"That would be great. I'll see you then."

Cutter nodded.

After he left, Catherine thought about breakfast. She had told Woodward she'd be eating with Flynn and his officers this morning. *Facing the crew was hard; facing them is going to be even harder,* she thought. With a worried sigh, she turned and headed back to her cabin to wait for Woodward to knock on her door.

It wasn't long after that she heard Flynn and his men walking through the passageway. She knew that knock was coming soon. It made her nervous sitting there, anticipating what they would say to her.

The sudden knock came before she was ready. She slowly stood, ran her fingers through her now short hair and opened it.

"Good morning, Lady Knox. Captain Flynn and the men are inside the office."

"Thank you."

He gave a simple nod and left.

Catherine watched him walk down the passageway then turned and faced the office door. With a heavy sigh, she proceeded to it.

When she entered, the men stood up and greeted her.

"Good morning," she replied, taking a seat.

The men quietly sat down. The anticipation was now killing her for someone to speak.

"I'm glad to see you're looking better, Catherine," said Flynn.

"I feel better."

"You know... this was my greatest fear, and now that it has happened, just saying I'm sorry seems insignificant for what you went through."

She looked at the men sitting there.

"We all concur," they said in unison.

"Your apology is accepted, but it wasn't any of your faults. Besides, Billy Dobbs and Jeremy Lance paid with their lives for what they did."

After she said that, the room fell silent. It appeared none of them wanted to speak on the subject. That was fine with her. "Shall we eat before our meal gets cold?" she said, lifting the top off the lid.

As they sat and ate, Davison knew he had miscalculated her. Sure, she could stand her ground and speak as most women can, but Catherine Knox could back it up. She had the strength and stealth of a leopard. It would certainly boost her standing amongst the crew now that they knew she could brandish a sword and win. He wondered if she was good with a pistol or a bow. One day he thought about asking her.

Sitting there, the silence became unbearable for Catherine. Not one had spoken about her appearance. Maybe it was out of politeness, or maybe it was out of fear that she'd lash out if they did. That was something to ponder, because... fearing something is rightfully respecting something; like respecting a lion out of fear that it could easily rip you apart.

When the meal ended, the men told her they would be glad to see her back on deck. She was pleased to hear that. She was going to be out there more while learning the ropes of sailing a ship with Cutter. Keeping that to herself, she got up.

The men stood.

"I bid you all a good day. I must be off to my morning class."

Flynn wanted to say something. He let it go.

When the door closed, the men sat down.

"I'm surprised you didn't speak more, Captain," said Bishop.

"I wanted to but refrained."

"I think we all did," remarked Smith. "What could we say; she's been through hell."

"Hell," repeated Flynn. "I think it was worse than that - she saw the Devil himself."

"That she did," agreed Ryan.

"Indeed," added Bishop.

"OK, let's get on with the ship's business," said Flynn. "We should make the port of Nambe in two days. Mr. Smith, ensure the watches stay alert as we change course and head toward land."

"Aye, Captain."

"Mr. Davison, pass the word... I want no trouble while in port."

Davison nodded.

"Alright - let's get to work," he said, getting to his feet.

12

That same evening as the bow gently swayed along the calm rolling seas, deep within the belly of the Lara May, Johan and his comrades sat enjoying a nip of port.

Basking in the glow of the candlelight, the subtle sounds of the ship creaking, they waited to hear from the ol' salt.

"Harr, me Lads, I can't believe she changed into a man right before me eyes. Never in me life have me seen such a spectacle."

"She didn't change into a man," sprouted Ezekiel, sitting cross legged on the floor in front of him.

Johan leaned over, raising a brow. "Well, buckle me britches, Lad. What-a-ya... out there swimming, believing there are no sharks? Yesterday she had curves, today she's as flat as a shilling."

"I made her a corset," whispered Ludwig. "I wasn't supposed to tell anyone," he frowned.

"I gave her the clothing," added Woodward.

"Well, shipwrecks - if she gets wind of that scuttlebutt, she may draw a sword on you," remarked Johan.

"You think she would?" questioned Hildegard.

"Yarr, matey.... she's a cat-of-nine-tails, I tell ya. I'd watch me self around her."

"Oh, go on with that nonsense," replied Ezekiel. "She's as harmless as a butterfly."

"Butterfly, you say? More like a yellow striped sea snake. They too look pretty up closely until they lash out and bite ya. Just ask Jeremy

Lance, who faced her poisonous wrath. He, along with Billy Dobbs, have now gone down to the ol place: bottom dwellers - ripe for the pic'ns."

"Ripe for the pic'ns?" repeated Ezekiel, wrinkling his nose.

"He's talking about the crabs," said Ludwig.

"That's right, Mate. As we speak - them, along with those slimy eels, are stripping the flesh from their bones."

Ezekiel imagined such a scene in the dark waters below. It made him feel sick.

"You don't look well," said Johan.

"Let's change the subject, shall we?" he replied. "Has your All-Seeing Eye showed you anything, of late?"

"Me saw a shipwreck in an inlet cove. She appeared as a tomb listing over."

"Inlet cove... where?" asked Woodward.

"On an island we want no part of. It's the island of doom."

"The island of doom?" gasped Ezekiel.

"That be right, Laddy. This place bares all the signs of death. Sadly, me fear Thomas Payne made it there. That be his ship I sees in me vision."

"Have you told Captain Flynn or Lady Knox of your vision?" asked Hildegard.

"The visions and me fears are two different things. An inkling in me guts is just an inkling. I told 'em only what I saw... an impenetrable island, vast thick jungles, mountains reaching to the clouds and them bones of a giant."

"You don't think those giants still live?" asked Ludwig, staring at him.

Within the ol' salt's eyes sat the possibility.

"You said they were prehistoric?" questioned Woodward.

Johan looked at him. "They appeared to be old."

The group looked from one to another.

"Trust me, Lads, this island haunts me dreams."

"I don't want your dreams," murmured Ezekiel, shivering.

"We best call it a night. It's getting late," said Woodward, getting up from the table. He had heard enough; enough to give him nightmares.

When the group got up and quietly slipped off to their hammocks, Mobee rolled over, opening his eyes. Johan's story scared him too. He wondered if he should tell Lady Knox. He'd have to think about it.

13

With gentle seas and a bit of wind, the Lara May sailed onward toward Port Nambe. Flynn and Catherine stood at the bow searching the horizon for the first glimpse of land.

"You think any warships will be there?" she asked.

Flynn lowered his spyglass. "If so, let it be the Portuguese or Spaniards. We have no bicker with them," he replied, turning. "Mr. Bishop, do you have the flags ready?"

"Aye, Captain."

"Flags?" questioned Catherine. "You're not hoisting the British flag, are you?" she continued, seeing a devilish grin appear.

"No, we'll sail in under a different flag. I just need to know which flag to hoist before entering the harbor."

"I see," she replied. "How often have you done this?"

"Every time when sailing this far south. You see, when you're a ship with few turrets, it's best to keep a low profile."

Turrets, she thought, *a name used for cannons.* "Could there be pirates?"

"It's possible, but most often they come in at night. They too like keeping a low profile."

"It's like a witch hunt of sorts out here, isn't it?"

"You could say that, but it's more like a game of cat and mouse, and..." he said, leaning toward her, "you never want to be the mouse."

"Land ho! - off the port bow," the crow's nest called down.

"Mr. Bishop."

"Yes, Captain."

"Have your men prepare for entering port."

"Aye, Aye," he replied, spinning around, "you heard the Captain. Get to your stations."

"Shall we?" said Flynn, waving his hand for her to go aft with him.

The two maneuvered their way through the bustling crew preparing to go ashore. When they walked up the portside ladder to the quarterdeck, Smith greeted them, "Good morning, Captain - Lady Knox. It looks like we picked a great day to make port."

"We did indeed," replied Flynn, seeing Catherine looking skyward.

"Seagulls this far south?" she inquired, spotting a flock overhead.

"Where ever there are fish - you'll see 'em," remarked Smith.

"Small boats ahead," the forward lookout shouted.

"Helmsmen - watch your heading."

"Aye, Mr. Smith."

Nearing the points of the harbor, Catherine observed the rocky shoreline and high sandy bluffs covered with long grass swaying in the breeze. Within the harbor were assortments of small fishing crafts and several ships at anchor.

The port itself was a scene of little brick buildings, mud huts and dirt streets. What caught her attention were the dark-skinned people. She had only seen a few in her lifetime, when the Kings of Africa came to Windsor Castle to speak with His Majesty. They wore the most elaborate clothing adorned with animal skins. Their jewelry: colored beads, long claws and teeth of the beasts that roam the open plains. She waded out of her thoughts when Flynn requested Bishop to hoist the Portuguese flag.

"Aye, Captain."

"Mr. Davison, bring up enough arms for the watches."

"Are you suspecting trouble?" she inquired.

"Always caution on the side of security when safeguarding a ship," he replied, turning toward the helm. "Mr. Smith, steady as she goes."

"Aye, Captain."

"Bos'n Cutter, take a sounding."

"Aye, Captain."

"Eight fathoms," he shouted.

"Mr. Bishop, prepare the anchor detail."

"Aye, Captain."

When Bishop reached the capstan, he waited for Flynn to give the signal. At five fathoms, Flynn lowered his hand; the anchor was released.

Catherine felt the ship lurch forward and then settle back on its chain.

"Set the anchor's pelican hook and haul up all sails," Flynn said, facing her. "Tell me, what holds a ship to the bottom of the sea?"

She smiled with his question. "The chain of course."

"You're learning fast, Milady."

"Bos'n Cutter is a fine teacher."

"That he is," he replied, stepping around her. "Mr. Bishop, prepare the lifeboats. "Bos'n Cutter, ready the J-davits."

"Aye, Captain."

"I bid you a fair day, I must get ready to go ashore," said Flynn, departing her company.

As she stood there watching him swagger down the ladder, the term seamanship washed over her. Captain Flynn was more than inundated with seamanship - he was poetry in motion the way he handled himself on deck. How he took to the bottle like a suckling infant was beyond her thinking. That thought gave her pause. Will he take to the bottle while in port? *If he does - he won't hear the end of it.*

"Lady Knox," said Davison.

"Yes?" she replied, still drifting on Flynn.

"I thought you might want to wear this," he suggested, holding out a sheathed sword.

She glanced at it confused.

"The only ones that will be left onboard will be you, the boys, and the watch detail."

She nodded, taking it from him. "Who'll oversee the first watch?"

"Sailing Master Ludwig - he'll have a team of five crew members.

Again, she nodded, pleased it was Ludwig.

The days in port were long - the nights even longer, as the crew of the Lara May brought shipment upon shipment of supplies onboard. She spent the days with Mobee and Ezekiel, the nights walking the main deck.

The watch detail changed every morning and she was glad Cutter had the last day in port with her. After the men all went ashore, Cutter took her below to show her the ship's internal structure, starting with the keel.

Two steps down the ladder, Catherine plugged her nose; the stench of the men's living quarters was too much for her to bear.

"I can't believe you live in such squalor," she gasped, taking in the filthy hammocks, sweaty clothes hanging everywhere, and the deck. It looked as if it had never been scrubbed.

"You get used to it," he replied, walking through the berthing to the ladder heading down.

They passed the livestock area, which was even worse and continued downward to the bilge. By that time, Catherine had placed a cloth to her nose. The bilge had numerous dead rats floating in the murky water, possibly washed down from the storm.

"Speak quick before I lose my breakfast," she muffled under the cloth.

"That is the keel. It goes the length of the ship. Those are the ribs and the outer boards are called the skin. The internal support structure, the beams and stanchions, carry the weight of each deck."

"Before we go, grab one of those rats and bring it up with you."

"Why?"

"You'll understand when we head back out to sea."

He nodded, reached down and took one by the tail.

Up on the main deck, Catherine sighed inhaling the fresh breeze.

"Where would you like this?" he asked, holding out the dead animal.

"Wrap it in a cloth and place it inside a box next to the bulkhead (wall) up forward."

"As you wish."

Things are about to change around here, she thought, walking over to the rail and staring at the little port town of Nambe.

After those long days and nights at anchor, Captain Flynn and his crew embarked. She stood at the rail watching them climbing the ladder. Some were still drunk, singing and laughing. Surprisingly, Flynn seemed as sober as she was. So were his officers, apart from Bishop, who needed assistance to his bunk.

"Good evening, Milady. You're looking like a real buccaneer with that sword strapped to your waist. This might help also," he said, taking off his newly purchased cover and placing it on her head.

She went to speak.

"Best you get some sleep; we set sail in the morning," continued Flynn, walking past her.

"Wait a minute," she replied, grabbing his arm.

He spun around.

She looked him dead in the eye.

"Not one drop," he grumbled to her stare.

"I can concur; he never had a drink," said Davison.

Catherine stepped back, looking at the two.

"I made you a promise and I'm sticking with it," said Flynn. "Now, we are tired and needing sleep. We have a long day ahead tomorrow."

Catherine nodded allowing him to pass. When he did, she quickly turned and said, "I would like to hold muster once we're out to sea."

Flynn waved over his shoulder and continued toward his cabin.

"After each port call, the ship holds muster to insure all crewmembers are aboard before we set sail," said Davison.

She turned and faced him. "That's fine, but once we're out, I want the crew mustered again. Inform Captain Flynn of my wishes," she scoffed, heading toward her cabin with Flynn's black pirate cover on.

I don't think a Tiger Shark could handle her, he thought.

The following morning, Catherine came out on deck to the crew preparing the ship for sea. All the supplies and provisions had been stowed and the sails unfurled. She walked back aft to where Flynn was standing alongside Bishop. "Morning," she said, staying out of the way.

"Morning, sleep well?" he asked, keeping his eye on the anchor detail.

"I slept like a sailor at sea," she retorted.

He presented her a smile and gave Bishop the order to haul up the anchor.

"Alright, men - put your backs into it," he barked.

Catherine watched them strain, every muscle showing as they walked around the spindle pushing the capstan's bars. Once the anchor was housed, the pelican hook secured,

Flynn ordered Smith to take the ship out of the harbor.

"Did Davison speak to you about holding a muster?" she asked.

"Yes, he did," he replied, waving at Cutter.

"Yes, Captain."

"Pipe the call to muster."

"Aye, Captain."

"Shall we," he said, walking up to the forward deck. "What is this all about?"

"Good order and discipline."

He wasn't sure what she meant by that, but knew he'd be finding out soon enough. The crew moved aside as they proceeded out front. The officer's passageway door then opened. Mobee walked out carrying her sword. She strapped it on.

The crew stepped back fearing her disposition. She seemed unhinged for some reason.

"Gentlemen, I have called you in front of me to talk about good order and discipline, which by all accounts is exceptional aboard the Lara May. However," she said with a long pause. "Cleanliness goes hand-in-hand with good order and discipline. His Majesty, and or, my father, Admiral Knox, would not, for one second, tolerate the living conditions on this ship."

Smith slowly turned, looking at Flynn. Flynn raised his brow to him. *She wanted to learn about ships, well... let's see if she can handle a crew.*

Murmurs sounded throughout the ranks.

"Bear with me gentlemen," she continued. "While you were all having a good time in port, I had the pleasure of walking this entire ship, starting at the keel."

Oh Lord, thought Bishop.

"Bos'n Cutter," she said, in a manner of authority.

He stepped forward.

"Retrieve me that box."

Cutter walked over, picked it up and set it in front of her.

"Open it."

He did as she asked.

Catherine then pulled out her sword and stuck it inside the box. "This.... gentlemen... is an English rat," she said, hoisting it out with the tip. Do you know where rats live?" she then asked, walking along the front row.

The men stepped back holding their noses.

"They live in the filthiest places on earth."

The men looked at the dead creature dangling from her sword.

At the end of the first row, she turned, and walked back to the center. "I can also imagine that you eat and sleep in their droppings."

Bishop caught Flynn's eye. Flynn slowly shook his head, amused by her swaggering demeanor.

"I'm surprised that the sails overhead are not stained with the stench billowing up from the ladder-wells," she continued, pointing her sword toward the mast.

"What would you like us to do?" someone shouted.

Catherine glanced over at Flynn. He gave her a slight nod to proceed.

"This ship is going to be scrubbed from the keel to the crow's nest. I want all hammocks removed; tie 'em together in groups and then toss 'em overboard. The sea will give them a good washing while you're scrubbing every inch of this ship."

"Every inch?" a crewmember cried out.

"Every inch," she repeated. "Inspection will be at fifteen hundred hours," she replied, raising her sword and flinging the dead rat overboard.

Before the crew could whine their disapproval, Cutter stepped forward. "You heard Lady Knox," he shouted. "Carpenter's Mate Hildegard and Sailing Master Ludwig will be in charge. Pick your men and strike below."

"I told you she was a cat-of-nine-tails," whispered Johan. "She uses that tongue just as deadly."

"I'd rather get a tongue lashing than being whipped with a cat-of-nine-tails... which one would you prefer?" asked Woodward.

"I'll take the tongue lashing. Least me ears will get over it sooner."

As the men proceeded down the ladders, one stopped and asked Flynn why he wasn't stepping in.

"She hired this ship, Lad, and now... she wants it cleaned."

"Good riddance," he sighed.

"Lady Knox," said Mobee.
"Yes."

JEFF WRIGHT
CATHERINE KNOX

"Are you holding class this morning?"

"No, I'm afraid not; you and Ezekiel will have to help. Go see Ludwig and Hildegard. I'm sure they can find you both something easy to do," she replied with a wink.

The two smiled and departed her company.

"Well, Milady," said Flynn. "How does it feel to be captain for a day?"

"Not on your life."

"How about taking over as the Master at Arms?" asked Davison, approaching them.

"No, I like my position."

"And what is that?" asked Flynn.

"The only woman onboard," she quipped.

"I just had a sailor say to me - *good riddance.*"

Catherine laughed.

That afternoon, at fifteen hundred hours, the men of the Lara May crawled up from the ladder-wells. Catherine watched them sprawl out on the deck tired and dirty from cleaning all day. Ludwig and Hildegard came up last.

"We're ready for inspection," said Hildegard, tossing his tired derriere on the deck.

Catherine glanced at Flynn. He waved for her to take the ladder down.

Twenty minutes later, they came up.

"Well?" asked Ludwig.

She said nothing, strolling over to the side rail. The men all waited.

"The ship looks great, gentlemen," she said, turning to face them. "Now it's your turn."

"Our turn? To do what?" asked Hildegard.

"To take a bath," she replied. "Bos'n Cutter."

"Yes, Lady Knox."

"Toss the ladder over the side."

Alarmed, Cutter looked at Flynn. Flynn replied by ordering Mr. Smith to come about, releasing the wind from the sails.

When the Lara May sat adrift, the men jumped overboard. The cool refreshing water felt good and it seemed to lighten their spirits as well.

Dripping wet and back onboard, Catherine had a surprise for them.

"Gentlemen, my father always said one good turn follows another. Tonight, Captain Flynn has agreed to give you the night off. Mr. Bishop."

"Yes."

"After tea, please have a few of your men bring up a barrel of port."

The men all cheered.

Catherine raised her hand.

They stopped cheering to hear what she had to say.

"After three days of tolerating this heat, I wouldn't mind a bath myself," she said, unbuckling her sword and walking over to the rail. Without another word, she jumped into the water.

The men quickly rushed to the side seeing her coming up to the surface.

Well done, Lady Knox - well done, Bishop thought, catching Flynn's eye.

Flynn slightly nodded for Bishop to jump in.

Bishop wrinkled his brow.

"Jump," he mouthed.

Reluctantly - Bishop took off his hat, handed it to a crewmember and took the dive.

The men all clapped.

Flynn looked at Davison. Like Catherine - without a word, he dove in.

Now it was his turn. "Hold my cover, Lad," he said to Ezekiel, stepping to the side.

Catherine smiled seeing him leap off the ship.

That night, while the men sang and danced on the high sea, the crew of the Lara May became one in mind and spirit with one goal, one mission - to find Captain Payne.

Unbeknownst to the Lara May, their oneness was going to be challenged. They still had to sail around Cape Hope and then enter an ocean with extreme temperatures and barely enough wind to get through. The Indian Ocean is a body of water without a ripple or a wave. Most often she appears as smooth as glass, glistening in the hot sun.

14

Days after, Captain Flynn could sense a change onboard. The men seemed more cheerful, laughing and talking to one another. Catherine too, seemed happy being a part of the crew now. Today, he spotted her sitting up on the yardarm alongside Bos'n Cutter teaching her the ship's sails, rigging lines and pulleys. She looked down, catching his eye. He smiled, observing the pirate cover he gave her on her head. He tipped his hat. She tipped hers back.

"I see you approve," said Bishop, coming alongside him.

"It gives her something to do."

"That it does," he replied, glancing up at the pair.

"You never know, Mr. Bishop. One day she could take command of her own ship."

"I don't know about that, but what she pulled off a few days ago was short of miraculous."

"Indeed," he replied, thinking back to her jumping into the water. It was a profound statement that she was no better than they were. That thought made him drift back to what she had said during their late-night meeting in the forest: *I don't mind the title of Lady Knox while rubbing shoulders with the pompous aristocrats at Windsor Castle, but outside those gates, I'm just like you.* She certainly proved that.

"One good turn follows another," said Bishop.

"That was brilliant, but what stunned me even more was her saying the captain has given you the night off."

"You didn't?"

"No. Sadly it did not come to mind."

"She's changing right before our eyes?"

"I think she just wants to be accepted."

"You think that's why she cut her hair and is now wearing men's clothing?"

"No. I spoke to Ludwig and Woodward. She wanted to mask her womanhood, so it would never happen again."

"I'm still sick over the assault."

"Me too. I don't think I'll ever forgive myself that it happened on my ship."

"There was nothing you could have done."

"Yeah, there was; I should've said *no* to her coming on this voyage."

"Let it go, Captain, or it will eat you alive," he remarked, walking away.

Flynn kept his eyes on Bishop for a moment. He dropped that thought, turned, and headed aft to his cabin.

As Flynn was charting the Lara May's course, there was a tap on his door. "Enter."

"Afternoon, Captain," greeted Catherine.

"Afternoon, how was your lesson this morning?"

"Great, I'm glad Bos'n Cutter has the patience in teaching me. It seems the more I learn, the more I need to know."

"It takes years, Catherine."

Hmm, he said my name for once. "What are you working on?"

"I'm setting a course to sail around the Cape of Good Hope."

She walked up seeing all the instruments sitting on his chart.

"I suppose you'd like to learn navigation too?"

"It baffles me how you know where we are on this vast ocean."

"It's a matter of plotting a course."

She leaned over staring at the lines, small circles and numbers.

He looked up at her.

She caught his eye. The moment lingered. "I remember an old saying - a penny for your thoughts," she said, breaking the trance.

"Yes, I believe that old saying dates back to the 1500s. I can't remember the gentlemen's name who first penned it though."

"It was Sir Thomas Moore and the year was 1522."

"You're a very smart woman - in many ways."

"Smart enough to have risked everything to find Thomas?"

That line caught him off guard. "Hearts are funny things, Milady."

She stood erect and strolled over to the bay windows.

He turned, seeing her gazing out over the water.

"Do you believe Johan saw the York in the eye of his medallion?" she asked, keeping her gaze forward.

He sighed, thinking of what to say.

She turned looking at him.

"What if I said yes?"

"Then he's alive."

"What if I said no?"

"Then we continue this voyage until we find him."

"Is that your mind, or your heart speaking?"

"My heart," she said and then lightly laughed.

He nodded.

"You're a very smart man yourself, Captain."

"Smart enough to sail this ship, but not smart enough to pull off what you did the other day."

"Well then... it will take the two of us to find Thomas," she replied, walking toward the door.

"Hey."

She turned and faced him.

"I thought you wanted to learn navigation?"

"Later, tomorrow I'm learning the helm."

After she left, Flynn sat down thinking of Johan's medallion. He had to admit, the old salty dog depicted the damage done to the York to a tee. *Was it the York?* he thought. "I think it's time to strike below and sit in on one of those late-night sessions with Johan."

In the pitch black of night, while the watches roamed the main deck and the crew slept below, Flynn opened his cabin door. To his left was the kitchen, to his right the dry food locker. In front of him was the partition that separated his space from the crew berthing. He quietly walked through the kitchen, trying not to hit the pots and pans swinging from the ceiling, to a small opening next to the ship's hull. He stood there listening. Nothing but silence came back to him. He stepped out. The crew berthing was dark, not a candle lit. *I'll try tomorrow night,* he thought, turning for his cabin.

The following night, Flynn heard whispering while standing at the small opening. He quietly knelt looking underneath the hammocks swinging from the gentle seas. There, on the other side of the berthing, he spotted the glow of a candle. The faces were easy to recognize - Woodward, Ludwig, Hildegard, and Ezekiel sitting there listening to Johan.

"What kind of lights are you seeing?" asked Woodward.

"Harr, me see lights from ships."

"Where?" asked Ezekiel.

"On the flat sea ahead, matey," he replied, looking up from the group. "Before that happens, we're all going to the brig," he continued, seeing Flynn leaning against a stanchion in the candlelight.

The group looked back shocked.

Flynn placed a finger to his lips, walked over, and sat down. No one said a word.

"Tell me about the shipwreck you saw within your medallion?"

"Forget the ship, he just saw lights in the All-Seeing Eye," whispered Ezekiel.

Flynn kept his focus on Johan.

"You don't want me dreams, Capt'n."

He glanced down at his medallion. "Open it."

Johan pushed the gold eyelid open.

Flynn was mystified seeing the shimmering black gem. "The ship... did you see the name of it?"

Johan reached up rubbing his grey beard. "It be the York, Sir."

"Where?"

"On the island I described to you."

"Is this island in the Pacific?"

"Can't say, but trust me, Capt'n, the more me peer into the gem, me see things that frightens me soul."

"You talking about the prehistoric bones?"

"It's more than that. There is something hideous about this place. The more me look, the more me want to turn back."

"We're not turning back, so tell me, what else have you seen?"

"Through the misty haze me saw miniature giants that strikes terror in me's heart."

"What kind of miniature giants?"

Johan shook his head. "Can't say for sure, but whoever ventures onto this island faces danger as no man has before."

As he sat there listening to the ol' salt, the man could certainly tell a tale, but within Johan's eyes sat a fear he had never seen before.

"Me also saw a large split in the earth."

"You mean a ravine?" said Flynn, stepping out of his thoughts.

"If that's what you call it. It goes down maybe one hundred meters or more. To cross over was a drawbridge, one like a fortress, but made from bamboo. There were thick jungle vines hanging from branches used to draw it up."

"You think Captain Payne and his crew made it?"

"Me's think not Capt'n."

That caught Flynn. "Then who?"

Johan shook his head.

"Maybe we should turn back, Captain," said Hildegard, scared.

Flynn sat there staring into the candle. The men could tell he was thinking. When he looked up at all the faces sitting there, he sighed. "Alright," he whispered. "Let's keep this to ourselves. Right now, tell me about the lights you saw?"

"When we sail into the flat sea, we must be ever wary. I fear they're pirate ships."

He had never heard the Indian Ocean called the flat sea, but knew Johan was referring to it. "Alright, we'll keep our eyes peeled when we get there. Let's get some sleep, shall we."

"What about Lady Knox; should we tell her about him seeing the York?" asked Ezekiel.

"No, not yet," replied Flynn, standing. "Goodnight, gentlemen," he continued, departing their company.

The four sat there unmoving to get up.

"He came out of nowhere, scared me britches," whispered Johan.

"He scared us all," replied Woodward.

"How did he know we'd be up?" asked Hildegard.

"He knows we talk, because someone told 'em," whispered Ludwig.

"Yarr, and we know who that someone is," replied Johan, glancing at Mobee's hammock.

"If you're thinking of doing something to him, forget it. You'll be tossed overboard like those two murdering misfits," warned Ezekiel.

"Murdering misfits?" repeated Johan. "Those slimy mud worms were worse than that; they were pure evil."

"They got what they deserved; let's get some sleep," said Ludwig, getting up.

When Flynn settled into his bunk, his mind would not shut off.

"It's the York, Captain."

He rolled over, drifting.

"There's something hideous about this place."

He rolled once again.

"Maybe we should turn back, Captain."

Flynn sighed, turning onto his back. He sighed in thought, *a good belt of wine would sit well right now.* That idea led straight to Catherine and the promise he made to her. Disgusted, he rolled onto his side, shoved his pillow underneath his head and closed his eyes. Sleep finally found him in the wee hours of the morning.

15

One whole week had passed, when the Lara May finally sailed along Cape Hope heading into the Indian Ocean. On this bright sunny day, the sky was as blue as the water below.

Catherine was beside herself seeing dolphins by the hundreds leaping out of the water and diving beneath the waves. Here, life thrived for millions of sardines on their coastal run, and those that came to feast on their bounty: the dolphins, sharks, fur seals, and Cape Gannets all partaking in the feast.

The crew took pleasure in feasting themselves, catching Yellow-Fin Tuna, Mackerel, and their favorite - Amber Jack.

It was an exciting day for Catherine as she watched the men hauling 'em to the surface and then using a long wooden pole with a giant barbed hook to snare them onboard.

Flynn along with his officers stood there amused seeing her trying to catch the fish before they escaped. There was no escaping - not with Ezekiel and Mobee, along with Woodward, running around plummeting the fish with wooden mallets before they could flop overboard.

Once there were enough, the men pulled in their lines, and began the job of cleaning the fish. Catherine wanted no part in that task. She walked up alongside Flynn, wiping her slimy hands.

"First time fishing?" he asked.

"Yes. What a charge. I think I had more fun than the crew."

"Wait until the meal; Woodward cooks a delicious fish dinner."

"I'm so looking forward. Now, if you don't mind, I think I'll wash up," she replied, leaving their company.

That evening, as Woodward and his team brought up the meal, the crew gathered on the main deck. Out at sea, you don't get too many opportunities like this, especially with a good slug of port to wash a fine meal down.

The wine sat well for Catherine as she took more than she could handle. When some of the crew got up to sing and dance, she joined in the chorus. The men enjoyed the sweetness of her soft voice floating on the breeze.

Davison, however, was concerned. He walked over to the outer rail, folded his arms, watching her.

Flynn caught the look. "You worried for some reason?"

"Just making sure everyone sees me."

"I don't think one of them would lay a hand on her knowing the punishment would be swiftly dealt."

"That may be true, but wine can do funny things to a man, Captain."

It was a subtle way of voicing his concern and it worked. It got Flynn's attention. Before he could speak, the crow's nest shouted, "Lights aft."

Flynn quickly turned seeing them too. "Douse all lights - silence on the deck. Mr. Davison, Bos'n Cutter - bring up enough arms. All hands quietly to your stations," he ordered, heading toward the helm. After gaining the starboard ladder, he walked back to the aft lookout.

"I'm sorry, Captain, I thought they were stars."

"That's OK, Lad," he replied, taking his spyglass and studying the ship's lights. "Mr. Smith."

"Yes, Captain."

"Change course - southward, if you will."

"Aye, aye Captain."

Catherine came abreast of him. "Who do you think it is?"

"I don't know, but we're not waiting to find out."

"What's your plan?"

"With no lights, we just disappeared. Now all we have to do is slip the noose."

Catherine studied his eyes.

"It could be a long night," he said to her stare.

The minutes seemed like hours watching the lights off in the distance. Flynn could only hope the ship maintained its course and not followed. When the ship finally passed the Lara May's stern, Flynn continued south. Thirty minutes later, he ordered the helmsmen to sail eastward once again.

As the moon gave way to the sun's first rays, Catherine, asleep on deck, awoke to hearing men softly talking. When she opened her eyes, she realized she had fallen asleep against the quarterdeck bulwark, a four-foot high partition. There was a blanket covering her.

Through the light fog, she could see Flynn and Mr. Smith talking next to Cutter who was on the helm. Woodward was standing there filling each man's cup with coffee. The aroma smelled good. She sat up yawning while stretching her arms.

Flynn nodded to Woodward to give her a cup.

"Good morning, Lady Knox," he said, bending over and handing her one.

"Thank you," she replied, getting to her feet and looking about.

She noticed that most of the crew had struck below, only the watches were roaming the ship, carrying muskets.

"I'd ask if you slept well, Milady," said Flynn with a smile. "But I think not, in that position."

"I am a bit stiff," she replied, stretching her back.

"I was going to wake you and send you to your cabin, but knew better."

Smith and Cutter smiled knowing she would have complained.

"Thank you for at least covering me," she replied, amusingly eyeing the two men. "What happened?" she continued, gazing out over the ship. She could barely see a thing.

"I think we lost them, but we'll know when this fog clears. "If you'd like to get some more sleep."

"I don't think I could," she interrupted, "but I wouldn't mind freshening up and changing out of these clothes."

"I'll warm you some water," said Woodward.

"Thank you," she replied. "Gentlemen," she continued, leaving their company.

"When do we ever get warm water?" murmured Cutter under his breath.

Flynn leaned over, looking at him.

"What a great day to be out at sea, Sir."

"I thought that's what you said. Mr. Smith..."

"Yes, Captain."

"Strike below and wake up Mr. Bishop and Carpenter's Mate Hildegard. I'll see you on deck at noon."

"Aye, Captain."

"Bos'n Cutter, go get some sleep too; I'll stand by until they relieve me.

"Aye, Captain."

As he walked away, Flynn called his name.

Cutter turned and faced him.

"You can look forward to warm water when we get back to England."

Cutter laughed then headed for the ladder.

After he left, something washed over Flynn: Johan's vision. *Lights on the flat sea.... Possibly pirates.* "How did I let that slip my mind?" That thought brought him full circle. *If Johan's medallion showed him that, then.... did the All-Seeing Eye really show him the York washed ashore on that island he described?*

16

In the wee hours of the next morning, Flynn crept into the crew berthing and quietly woke Johan. It startled Johan seeing him standing there. Flynn placed a finger to his lips and nodded for him to get up.

The two headed back to Flynn's cabin.

"Your story of how you gained that medallion - is it true?"

"Aye, Capt'n."

"The Prince of Bagdad."

"Yarr, that's what the Spanish captain said; me heard it with me own ears."

Flynn sat there staring at him.

"Are ya tinkering where the Prince may have obtained such a gem?"

"Yeah."

"Me have no mind to knowing."

"May I see it?"

Johan pulled it out of his shirt.

Flynn reached over palm up.

Johan sat back.

"I want to see it up close."

Johan reluctantly handed it to him.

As Flynn sat there studying the round object, he flipped it over shaking his head.

"What be the problem, Capt'n?"

"There is hieroglyphics on the back."

"What be that?"

"It's Egyptian writing. The Prince of Bagdad got it from somebody from Egypt, but who?"

"Maybe it was stolen from one those ancient tombs. Me's heard many tales about such things."

Hearing that, Flynn slowly glanced up from the medallion. "How do you see things?"

"Me closes me eyes, open the eyelid and rub the gem. It then shows me a vision, if there's one to be had."

"The lights you saw - did it show you the flag of the country?"

"No. The last time me saw ships at night in a vision, were the British frigates slipping in unawares on the Phantom. That be a long time ago."

Flynn nodded, returned the medallion to Johan and said, "If you see anything else, you tell me in private."

"Aye, Capt'n - may me go?"

"Yes, that'll be all."

Johan got up and walked out.

Flynn sat there transfixed on the closed door. He could not refute its origins. It was Egyptian, and it looked as old as the Pharaohs themselves. Back then, the Egyptians were into all kinds of black magic and had many Gods. *Was it stolen from an ancient Egyptian tomb? Johan said he had heard many tales. So, have I,* he thought, leaning back in his chair.

Ding, ding - ding, ding - ding, ding. The watches were changing hands.

Flynn dropped his thoughts and walked out.

"Morning, Captain," said Woodward, preparing breakfast.

"Morning, Mr. Woodward. Today I'd like a full report on our dry goods and stores."

"A full report, Sir?"

"Have you ever heard of giving half a report?" he replied, taking the ladder up.

Woodward thought of that. He looked at the ladder Flynn just took. "Half a report," he mumbled.

After breakfast, Flynn invited his officers, along with Catherine, to go back to his cabin to discuss the next phase of their voyage. There, he laid out the charts. The group circled around him.

"As you can see, we have made good time from England to South Africa. Having fair winds and following seas has helped our advance. We cannot rely on that heading into the Indian Ocean."

"How far have we come?" asked Catherine.

"Over a thousand nautical miles and we have many more to go."

The number startled her.

"I told you this voyage was going to take many months, depending on the winds and seas."

"I figured it would. Before you go any further, would you all mind explaining to me the term *abaft the beam*. Bos'n Cutter mentioned it as the most favorable winds, but I'm still a bit confused why they are."

Flynn glanced over at Bishop to explain.

"Well, Milady - when the wind is abaft the beam it means it's blowing directly over the stern or over the quarters. A ship moves faster under those conditions.

"Unfavorable or foul winds are those that blow across the bow. These force a ship to tack or, to be more precise, sail in a zigzag fashion at an eighty-degree angle to the wind, a procedure that is uncomfortable, wearisome, and slow. The vessel heels heavily, the decks are forever wet with spray, and the sails constantly have to be reset. This is the most time-consuming course of all since it forces the ship actually to cover far more distance than a straight line to its destination."

Eyes wide and nodding, Catherine believed she finally understood.

"Any more questions?" asked Flynn.

"No."

"Alright then. I have chosen a course to stay further south than intended. I'm sure you can all agree that it was possibly a French ship we spotted last night, seeing we are close to Union Island, their port-of-call."

"I assume then that is a French island?" questioned Catherine.

"That's correct."

"My thoughts are we stay on a southeasterly course and head to the island of Sumba. The natives there are friendly."

"Sumba?" said Smith. "That's a long way off, Captain."

"That it is. I asked Mr. Woodward to give me a full report on our dry goods and stores."

"And if we run out?" asked Davison.

"We take what we can from the sea," replied Flynn.

They all nodded.

"Mr. Bishop, I want a team on deck fishing at all times no matter our speed."

"Aye, Captain."

"Are there any more questions?"

"Yes," Catherine said. "How far is that island?"

"Farther than what we've sailed already," he replied.

She couldn't fathom the time to get there, but knew they'd be sailing for several more weeks.

"OK, let's get back to work, gentlemen," said Flynn, sitting down.

At the door Catherine turned and faced him. "Thank you."

"For what?"

"For explaining."

"Come see me when you're ready to learn navigation."

"I will," she replied with a smile.

✝

As the Lara May sailed past the country of South Africa, the night watches saw no more signs of ship's lights.

By taking a further southeasterly direction, Flynn invited the Indian Ocean midday sun to beat down on them like a hot branding iron. With no wind, the temperature soared. Shade was now a prize to be had on the flat sea, as Johan so rightly called it. Like glass she was, not a ripple nor a wave.

Bare-backed men laid about the deck wherever they could find shade. The crow's nest was even worse. The watches on high could only stay ten minutes aloft then had to be relieved.

Woodward and his young mates, Mobee and Ezekiel, brought up the livestock and chickens. They were granted the shade; without it, they'd have surely died.

Catherine too would have given all the stars above to get some relief herself. Being a woman, she had no choice but to stay fully clothed. She pleaded with Flynn to let the crew swim, but none was about to. The salt from the sea could shrivel a man's skin in these temperatures. Besides that, were the dark menacing fins coming to investigate an easy meal. A ship's hull appears like a floating dead whale on the surface. Tiger sharks were the main culprit, some reaching five and a half meters - roughly twenty feet - in length.

The first time Catherine saw one up close changed her mind completely about swimming in these waters. She found it even foolish to have jumped in days past, after working the skin off the men's knees scrubbing the ship.

"Have you ever seen anything like it?" asked Bishop, looking down at the creature swimming alongside the ship.

"No..." was her awe reply.

"Harr, Melady. That-ta-be a Tiger shark," replied Johan. "They'll bite you in half and take away the spoils - then they'll come back for the rest."

Catherine slowly looked at him. Their eyes locked for a moment. "You go jumping in these waters there'll be nothing left for us to haul in."

"I wouldn't jump if you put a pistol to my head," she replied, focusing on the shark below.

"They're not bad eating though," said Johan.

"Really?"

"That's right," agreed Davison, walking up behind them.

She turned around.

"Would you like to try a bit of shark?"

She glanced back at Johan. He presented a smile showing off his yellow stained teeth - the two or three he had.

"Alright," she said.

"Bos'n Cutter," Davison shouted.

"Yes."

"Fetch me two muskets," he replied, tossing him the gun locker keys.

"You're going to shoot it?" she questioned.

"No line will hold that beast except a mooring line," said Johan. "One shot to the head and we grapple it with one of these," he continued, picking up a barbed grappling hook attached to a coiled rope. If trouble be had, we use these hooks when commandeering a ship. They work well on sharks too."

Catherine slowly nodded. She was warming to the old salt. Even getting used to his face the way it was - tattooed like a snake's skin. She figured Johan had more wisdom about the ocean than the king's mathematicians had about numbers, and she could learn much from him. The one thing she wanted to learn the most was

JEFF WRIGHT
CATHERINE KNOX

about his gold medallion and seeing things in the future. She dropped that thought when Cutter returned with the muskets.

Flynn heard the commotion on deck and came up from his cabin to investigate. When he saw what was happening, he took the ladder up to the quarterdeck to watch alongside Sailing Master Ludwig standing his watch at the helm.

"Mr. Davison," he called out.

Catherine turned seeing him.

"Aye, Captain."

"Make it safe and orderly."

"That I will, Captain. Alright everyone, stand back, give Bos'n Cutter and I some room. You there, prepare to grapple it in," he said to several sailors. They picked up the hooks attached to the ropes.

Catherine moved over along the rail. Mobee and Ezekiel settled in next to her.

"Let it come back," said Davison, aiming his rifle. "Once it's right below, take the shot."

"Aye," replied Cutter, lining up his rifle.

"Do you really want to see this?" asked Mobee to her.

"Yes," she replied, keeping her eyes glued on the dark shadow and large fin circling.

As the shark swam in along the hull, Cutter pulled the trigger. The blast was deafening; the smoke from the barrel engulfed the crew. Davison then fired. As the shark rolled over, the damage was evident - blood poured out of the gaping wounds, staining the water red.

"Hurry, grapple it in before another comes and takes it from us," ordered Bishop.

The lines were cast and then dragged back toward the shark, hooking into the thick flesh.

"Push out the J-davits and tie off the lines," then ordered Bishop.

Catherine, Mobee, and Ezekiel stepped back as the mammoth shark was hoisted onboard. She was utterly amazed at its size and shivered, looking into the jaws of the beast as Johan, along with two other crew members, pry open the mouth.

"Seeing no man asked for its teeth, me like the front row if me could," requested Johan, pulling out his long blade.

"If you don't mind, I'd like them all," said Flynn, walking up. "It would look good on my cabin wall."

"How about two from the rear? You'll never miss 'em," asked Johan, raising one brow.

"Alright, Johan. Mr. Woodard, let's get this thing cut up and the mess over the side," he replied, looking at Catherine. "I don't think you want to watch this."

"I say not," she replied, feeling a bit sick knowing what they were about to do. "C'mon, you two," she continued, pulling on Mobee and Ezekiel's bare shoulders.

"We'd like to watch," said Mobee.

"Yeah," added Ezekiel.

She raised her brow to Flynn.

"Boys will be boys."

"I'll leave you then," she said, departing their company to the aft poop deck.

While sitting under a bit of shade, she watched the group with their backs to her, carving up the shark. It seemed disgusting, but these were not men with soft hands and safe lives, living behind guarded castle walls. They were by all accounts a ruthless breed who lived on the high seas. Out here, there were no rules except the ship's manual. Other than that, it was each man to his own.

With that thought drifting over her, she looked up at the sails hanging like curtains. Beyond them, the sky was light blue; the sun sitting there like a god. It made her think of the real one; the one who rules all things. *A little wind, my Lord, would surely be a blessing,* she thought, wiping the sweat from her brow.

17

A week had passed before the Lord on High granted Catherine her wish. The winds picked up, bringing dark clouds and rain. It started with single droplets hitting the sails and main deck. The men stood begging, arms extended skyward. When it poured, they all rejoiced, singing seafaring songs while dancing with each other. Catherine too, could have sung and danced herself, but decided to sit back aft and allow the refreshing rain to cool off her fatigue.

The weather stayed that way as the ship sailed onward toward its destination - the island of Sumba, a territory of Indonesia in the Timor Sea.

By the time they arrive, Catherine was dying to walk on dry land again. Standing at the rail with Flynn and his officers, she noticed something different about the ocean. It was turning from a mucky green to deep blue. "Do you notice the color changing?" she asked, pointing down at the water.

"Yes, it lightens my heart to see. We're getting close to the South Pacific," replied Flynn.

"How far from here?"

"Many more miles," he answered, turning around. "Mr. Bishop, haul up the sails."

"Aye, Captain."

"Bos'n Cutter, take a sounding."

"Aye, Captain."

"We have visitors," said Doc Ryan, gazing toward land.

Catherine cast her eyes on the long canoes coming from shore.

"Seven Fathoms," shouted Cutter.

Flynn glanced at Catherine studying the natives. "I assure you they're friendly," he said to her questioning stare.

"They don't wear much, do they?" she replied, keeping her eyes glued on the men rowing.

"No, they don't."

"Five fathoms," shouted Cutter.

"Drop anchor."

"Aye, Captain."

As the Lara May settled on her chain, Flynn ordered the boats over the side, then the metal chest filled with items to barter with the natives. Those going ashore were Davison, Smith, Cutter, and Hildegard in one boat; the second boat would be ferrying Flynn, Catherine, Ludwig, and Johan. Mr. Bishop would remain onboard in command of the ship.

To ensure all was safe, Flynn had Davison and Cutter with pistols. Not to appear intimidating, the pistols were tucked into their belly waist, just the handles showing.

When the natives came abreast of them, Catherine took in their rich sun baked skin, jet-black hair and welcoming smiles. The women were exceptionally beautiful, adorned with flowers around their necks and in their hair. The men appeared as bronze statues with fine sculpted muscles. Their clothing was made of cloth; their headbands made from island plants.

Flynn could not help but admire Catherine's expression as she sat in the boat, taking it all in. "When we come ashore and stand before their king just bow," he said to her.

"Do you know their language?" she asked in return.

"I'll leave that to Johan."

"Johan?" she questioned, casting her eyes upon him.

"Yarr, Melady, been here me self. King Abba knows me well. I think ye be the first English woman they ever set eyes upon."

Catherine drifted on that.

"Mind no fear, Melady," added Johan. "There'll be no trouble here. Once we show 'em our treasure, they'll be pink to barter."

"Treasure?"

"Yarr, we'll be given' 'em our iron for cutting trees and slicing fruit. I convinced Capt'n Flynn to hand over the jaw of the shark we shot. That should lend us well in gaining much provision."

"And what would that be?" she asked, looking from one to the other.

"Mangos, bananas, breadfruit and whatever is available," replied Flynn.

"And other things too," remarked Johan, lifting one brow while presenting a smile only a lusting heart could give.

"You mean native girls?"

"Best trinket for lonely seafaring souls," he confessed.

Seeing Flynn slowly shaking his head, Catherine wanted to comment, but refrained.

As the boats came in, the natives pulled them ashore. The whole village was there to greet 'em. First were the women, who were in awe of the white girl. They touched and poked Catherine as they escorted Flynn's party up to the king, sitting on a bamboo throne; his half-naked guards holding spears, standing to either side.

Johan was surprised to see it was not his friend, Abba, but a much younger man wearing the headdress of the king. "That be his son, me reck'n."

"Let's hope he's friendly," replied Flynn, nodding to Cutter and Davison to put forth the metal chest.

The king stood up. Johan stepped out and started speaking a language Catherine had never heard before.

The young king pointed up to the sun while displaying four fingers.

"He says his father died many months ago - now sleeps with the mermaids. His name is Java."

"Does he remember you?"

"Aye, said he never forget me face."

Flynn nodded while taking in the king.

Johan again began speaking.

"I hope you're telling him we're sorry for his loss," said Catherine.

Johan quickly turned and glared at her. His expression stunned her, then she felt her heart stop, looking up at the king glaring down at her as well.

"Strike me below; you'll be the curse of us all. Women don't speak here," grumbled Johan, facing the king. He politely said something with a bow of his head.

Java walked down to her.

Her eyes took in every detail of his figure, from his almond brown skin, long black hair, and his muscular chest and stomach, his colorful headdress adorned with tropical bird feathers, and the seashells around his neck.

"Don't say a word - just look down at the ground," whispered Flynn from the side of his mouth.

When King Java approached, he lifted her chin. Catherine could not help but to stare back into his mesmerizing gaze. He was as handsome as the day was long.

While feeling her hair, Java spoke some words. He then reached down, took her hands and turned them over to see her peach colored palms.

Catherine froze not knowing what to do.

"Forgive me, she be the captn's daughter," said Johan in the king's language.

The young king looked back at Johan. Words quickly passed between them. "King Java said, daughter of the capt'n should stand behind him and keep mouth shut like clams in the sea."

Flynn quickly grabbed Catherine's arm to pull her back. Java grumbled. Flynn let her go. Java then slapped his hands together. Two beautiful native women stepped up, removed their flower necklaces and placed them over Catherine's head. King Java then waved for her to walk back behind her father.

She never looked at Flynn as she fell in behind him.

Flynn quickly nodded for Johan to open the metal chest and present their gifts.

The situation eased when the young king took in the jaw bone of the shark. He raised it high in the air for all to see. Gasping murmurs expelled forth from his people.

Johan pointed out to sea, then with his hands, showed king Java how they caught the shark.

"Hmmm," he sounded.

Johan presented his two or three yellow teeth while waving down at the chest. Java handed off the jaw and knelt before it. He was intrigued with the Englishmen's tools: hatchets, small saws, and wood mallets. He said words while pulling out the strands of colorful cheap beads, which Catherine suspected, Flynn obtained from the wenches at the Trade Wind. The native women carried on like children as the king tossed them around.

When the chest lay bare, Java stood up and said more words to Johan. He in return asked for the fruits of the island. It was an easy trade. With that, the king requested Flynn and his men to celebrate with him that evening. Flynn agreed with a nod of his head. The king nodded back, turned and walked off with his guards.

A sigh fell over Flynn's group standing there. Catherine wanted to speak, but held her tongue. Johan could see her twisting in her boots, her anger apparent. "Forgive me, Lady Knox, I should've rang the warning bell," he said to her.

"You should have rung something," she spewed between her tight lips.

"Enough, it's my fault," interrupted Flynn. "Mr. Smith, take a party back to the ship and bring forth a barrel of wine. Stand down the men to five, and have the rest come ashore."

"Aye, Captain."

"Tonight, we'll set the village ablaze with wine and laughter. I'm sure the king will have his fill."

The men stood there eyeing one another. Their gleeful smiles were evident of the island fruits they wanted to pick - the native girls.

Flynn caught the looks. There was no need to ask their thinking. This warning bell was something Catherine needed to hear. He explained to her in the subtlest way that the people of the islands openly display their affections.

She caught it instantly what he was trying to say, and it only took her a second to start worrying about her own plight: being a woman.

"Harr, Melady, you being the captn's daughter makes you a treasure, there'll be no harm come to you."

While he spoke, Catherine studied his wise seafaring eyes. She was still upset not being forewarned, but she certainly understood what Johan just did for her. Telling the king that she was Flynn's daughter made her somewhat like royalty. Her anger quickly faded like a setting sun over calm waters. "Your brilliance astounds me, dear Johan," she replied, turning and heading toward the beach.

JEFF WRIGHT
CATHERINE KNOX

Flynn figured if her emotions were a drink, she'd be a glass of sweet bitterness with a twist of anger.

The men stood there watching her taking off her shoes and sitting down in the wet sand. The women of the village quickly gathered around her. She felt like royalty as they gave her shells, pearls, and adorned her head with a woven crown made of plant foliage. She in return gave up her bracelet to the king's daughter.

"She'll fare well, Lads," remarked Johan, "like wind in the sails she is."

"It takes a strong wind to move a ship," said Cutter.

"She be as strong as the chain of an anchor," added Johan.

The evening went well for the crew of the Lara May. Their spirits were high with drink and pleasure. No need to fight; the native women outnumbered the Englishmen four to one and they all clamored for attention.

Catherine sat with Flynn and Johan while Johan spoke to King Java. The king's head was feeling a bit lighter too from the drink and he seemed to be enjoying the singing and dancing around the fire pit. When he reached out his arms and gathered his two wives near, Johan knew it was time to get up. Flynn and Catherine stood as well.

"If you pardon me, King Java, I would like to rid me ills," said Johan.

The king waved his hand for them to depart.

Catherine watched the ol' salt staggering toward the native women dancing to the beat of the drums. "It wrecks my soul to see this, Captain," she said, walking alongside him.

"There are many worlds, Catherine. They too would find the English ways a bit strange."

"I suppose, and I also suppose you're itching to rid your ills, as Johan so politely put it."

"Don't get me wrong, but if the men all left without fraternizing with the women, the king would have taken offense."

"I see," she replied in a bit of shock.

"Out here in the vast expanses of islands, seafaring men have a duty to oblige the natives. It's the one order they don't mind partaking in."

"Well, be on your way, Captain Flynn. I'm heading back to the ship to sleep in a bunk."

Flynn waved to Davison. He staggered over with a native girl by his side.

"See that Lady Knox is put safely aboard."

"Aye, Captain," he replied, "you come along too my beautiful peach," he slurred, wrapping his arms around the beauty with Catherine in tow.

Catherine sighed shaking her head.

At the shoreline, he ordered the boat detail to assist Catherine back to the ship. Once she embarked, she slightly swayed to her cabin.

The wine settled well in Catherine that night. She slept like a sailor at sea. In the morning, she awoke not hearing bells or men talking - just peaceful silence. Getting up, she wondered if Mobee and Ezekiel were aboard. *Probably not,* she reckoned. The last time she saw them, they were using their bows to spear fish and small octopus with the native boys along the rocky shoals. "Thank God they're too young to rid their ills," she said, opening her door.

By the time she gathered herself at the rail, the sun was making its appearance. From her position, she could see men lying on the beach, smoke from the fires billowing up through the palm trees and two sailors, standing watch over the boats. The rest of the village was still sound asleep.

"Would you like for me to call a boat from shore?" said Bishop from behind.

She turned to see him completely sober.

"Mr. Bishop," she replied. "Did you stay onboard all night?"

"Yes, that was my order. Would you like some breakfast?"

The sound of it woke her stomach. "Yes, I would."

By the time Catherine and Bishop finished their meal, Flynn had set the day to gathering provisions.

Still drunk as they were, the men staggered out of huts, clamored out from underneath thick vegetation, and off the beach, while politely brushing aside the women they spent the night with.

They worked all day in the shade of the jungle, gathering what they could from the treasures of the earth. Even within the shade of the dense foliage, the men sweated like English steam pipes, chopping, digging, and cutting the fruits from the trees, then hauling the baskets to the shoreline where it was gathered and set inside the boats.

Catherine came ashore on the third boat heading back to the village. She met Flynn at the water's edge.

"Sleep well?" he asked, assisting her onto dryland.

"Yes, the wine helped," she remarked, bright eyed and wearing a smile.

He nodded with a smile in return.

"How is the work coming along?"

"Good... it took a bit of prodding, but as you can see the men have worked the wine out of their heads."

"More likely they sweated it out in this tropical heat," she replied, wiping her brow.

"I would think," he replied. "How about we take a walk?"

"Alright, is there something on your mind?"

"Walk," he replied, heading down the beach.

They strolled far enough out of earshot when Flynn turned in stride. "It's Johan."

"I'd never suspect," she mused.

"He came to me last night; woke me out of a deep sleep."

"You slept?" she quipped.

He let that comment pass. "Look," he said, stopping in the sand. "I've sat in on one of his little yarns below."

"You have?"

"Yes, and I've also woken him and had him come to my cabin in the wee hours of the night."

"Captain Flynn," she scolded. "What is going on!?"

"Last night, he was seeing things, things he didn't want to speak of, or his hair would turn white."

"It's already white."

"Just a phrase, Catherine."

"Go on."

"I'll start by telling you... the medallion he's wearing."

"Yes."

"It's Egyptian. I suspect, as he does, it was taken from an ancient tomb."

Catherine was surprised to hear that.

"I can't read Hieroglyphics, but the lettering is as old as the Pharaohs themselves."

"So, you believe it has magical power too?"

"We'll soon find out."

"We'll soon find out, what?"

"Johan said last night, he saw an English warship, housing two French scallywags off the Nightingale in the brig."

"Name of the ship?"

"He didn't say."

"OK."

"They know approximately where the York was sunk."

Catherine fell back on her heels, stunned. "Don't keep me waiting, Captain."

"Somewhere passed the Fijian islands."

"Alright."

"There are no islands that far south. I know that myself. When Johan mentioned it, he remembered Scar and his companion, One Eyed Dooley talking of an island no white man has ever seen. I'm wondering if that is the same island Johan said he'd seen within his medallion? You know... the island he spoke to us about."

"Yes, go on."

"I've heard many yarns in my days on the high sea. One comes back to me now. I remember overhearing an old buccaneer by the name of Dagger inside the Trade Wind."

Catherine waved for him to continue.

"Dagger was actually mingling with another seafaring lad. As more men heard him speaking, the bar went silent. Dagger said while sailing with Captain Laramie on a schooner called the Dell, they came upon an island that had mountains reaching to the clouds and jungles so thick one could lose them self."

Catherine instantly thought of Johan speaking those same words. It made her skin crawl. She quickly turned seaward, placed her hand up to cover the sun, seemingly focusing on the horizon.

He paused seeing her hand shaking over her brow.

"Shall I..."

"Yes."

"I remember Dagger saying, at the northern tip of the island, there were huge rock columns hedging out from the point, as if it had been a mountain at one time. Maybe destroyed by an ancient volcano or an earthquake. From the ship's position, they observed a cove, an inlet of sorts through those stone face pillars.

"Captain Laramie ordered a boat over the side to check it out. A party of seven went ashore and were ordered to return by nightfall. Dagger said they started to worry when the boat did not return. The crow's nest watch sighted the boat in the morning. The crew gathered at the rail. It was the boat alright, but nobody was in it."

"No one was in it?" she asked, facing him.

"You sure you're up to hearing the rest?"

"I've come this far, Captain. Hold nothing back from me."

"Alright, that's what the crew thought at first. No one was inside. As it drifted further out to sea, another boat was lowered. Dagger said he never saw the likes of it. After the men in the boat came upon it drifting, they all started shouting. Some even jumped over the side and started swimming back to the ship.

"One man was brave enough to attach a rope and bring it back alongside the Dell. Captain Laramie and Dagger were horrified by what was inside. In the boat was a crewman. He looked as white as ivory with a thick white froth bubbling out from his mouth. Dagger believed that whatever happened to the poor sap, he at least made it back to the boat and shoved off. He must have died in the night. The boat was probably caught up in the swells heading seaward where it was spotted that morning.

"Captain Laramie ordered the boat be torched. Afterward, they hauled up the anchor and sailed away, fearing the island was ripe with disease.

Gazing into Flynn's eyes, Catherine stood there, lifeless like.

"After Johan told me what he saw, I went to the hut and lay down. That's when Dagger's story came back to me. I never did get any sleep last night. That's the reason for our walk. I wanted to tell you."

"Captain Flynn, I do hope you are not trying to put a great fear in me, so I would call this off and head back to England."

Flynn, with a look of seriousness replied, "No, Catherine, I just wanted you to know of the perils we may be facing."

"I thank you for that. Now what is our plan?"

"We're leaving here tonight and sailing onward to New Guinea. I remember a village there. The natives are friendly like here in Sumba. They have deer and other wild game on the island that will sustain us. Once we depart, if Johan's medallion is correct, that British warship will show up somehow."

Catherine strolled down the beach, turned and faced him. He could tell she was reeling in thought.

"I think it best we all sit down and start talking," she said.

"You mean with Mr. Bishop, Smith, and Davison?"

"Yes, their lives are at risk and so is the crew."

"How about we wait and see if we stumble upon the warship?"

She went to speak; he raised his hand. "If the British warship does find us, as Johan believes it will, then we'll sit down with them. It would lend well to our story without them taking us for fools - believing Johan's tales."

His words gave her an idea, one she'd keep to herself.

"OK, we'll wait."
Flynn nodded.

18

In the twilight of the evening, the moon overhead, the men climbed back aboard seemingly still sober. Catherine stood there waiting for one crewmember to embark, Johan Bailer. When he grabbed the top rail, hoisted himself on deck, she caught his eye through the tired happy-go-lucky seamen. She gave a slight nod for him to walk inside the officer's passageway.

Johan pointed to himself, believing it was not him she wanted.

Catherine again nodded.

He strolled through the merriment, the men singing their seafaring songs; *'Fifteen men on the dead man's chest – yo-oh-oh and a bottle of rum'*

"Let's go," she said, turning and opening the door.

After entering her cabin and lighting a candle, Johan stood at the doorway feeling terribly sick all of a sudden.

"Come in and shut the door."

"You're still angry with ol' Johan. Pipe up and tells me."

"I'm not angry with you. Come in."

"If me do - me death wilt be near. I'll be laid waste at the yardarm, me dead body spilt over the side. If me bones don't sink ye fast, the sharks will have me for a feast."

"Mr. Bailer!"

Johan stopped his rambling.

"What are you talking about?"

"If Capt'n Flynn gets a sniff that me were in your berthing, he'll have me neck stretched at the yardarm."

"He'll have to get by me first," she spat, pointing at a chair.

"You curse me," he replied, stepping in; eyes darting this way and that - as if her cabin were overrun with rodents.

"Shut the door!"

"Me feel me hands bound – me neck stretching already sitting here."

"Captain Flynn is not going to hang you. This is between you and I."

"Get on with it before me sees me last days."

"You woke Flynn last night?"

"Melady, me have worries enough looking into the eye of me 'dallion. Seeing yours in a fit, scares me even worse."

"I asked you to be here because I want to know if you saw the name of the British warship in your medallion?"

"Nay, is that it?"

"Oh no... we've just begun this little chat."

"You know the sharks are even bigger in these waters."

While aimlessly staring at him, Catherine allowed her temper to fade.

Johan kept his gaze on her then dropped it to the floor. "OK," he said, keeping his eyes downward. "You say Capt'n Flynn won't hang me for being here."

"No!"

He slowly looked up. "Me 'dallion has become a curse on me poor soul."

She said nothing.

"It was a blessing at first, keeping me ahead of fire and brim, saving me here and there, but now..." his voice trailed off.

She calmly sat back until he finished, then continued, "Tell me, how do you see visions within the eye?"

"Me rub the gold'n eyelid, then me's open it. The visions seem to just appear."

"May I see it?" she asked, extending her hand.

"Harr, Melady, me don't like anyone holding me lucky trinket. If me do, you promise to stay quiet about handling me ancient piece? Me fear every seafaring salt aboard would want to gather it within their paws if you speak a word."

"I promise; it will never leave my lips."

Johan took it off and gave it to her.

It was a dazzling piece, an exceptionally crafted medallion, appearing to look like the sun with a golden eyelid in the center. She slowly flipped it over to see the Egyptian writing. *Flynn was right. It does look as old as the Pharaohs themselves.*

"Me believe it was stolen from the ancient tombs. Who so mindful to steal from the dead must've been a proud fool."

Catherine looked up from the medallion. "I'd have to agree."

Johan sat there fidgeting with his hands. She could tell he was itching to speak. "You have something to say?"

"Yarr, me have something to confess before the mast."

"Go on."

"It was something me should have mentioned long ago. Me saw the York within a vision."

His astonishing words smashed against her heart like the unending waves breaking over the bow. Month upon month she had endured such misery, starting with hearing the York sunk, the king not sending ships to search, then hiring Flynn and risking her own life to find Thomas herself. Besides losing her breath, she could have screamed right then.

"It's there on the island me described to you and Capt'n Flynn."

Her words were there, but nothing came out.

"Sorry for not speaking," he continued, seeing her face now as white as the mainsail.

"After hearing me tell ya, you may want to continue this voyage, but..." his voice broke off.

"You have no idea the pain I've suffered. Now tell me - but what!"

"This island is like none other."

She glared at him.

"There is something terrible about this place."

She sat there thinking of Flynn's story about the Dell. The crewmen in the boat, frothing at the mouth. Before she could speak, there was a tap on her door. "Come in."

Johan froze seeing Flynn standing there holding a candle. Flynn's eyes locked onto him then quickly shifted to Catherine sitting there holding the medallion.

"Come in and shut the door."

"After what I told you on the beach, I should have guessed you'd pull him aside," he said, taking a seat next to her.

"When were you going to tell me about the York?" she scolded.

Flynn looked at Johan.

"Sorry, Capt'n," he said to his stare.

After Catherine handed the medallion back to Johan, Flynn stood up. "Let's continue this conversation in the office; that includes you, Johan."

Catherine stood, feeling the ship swaying. In her state of mind, she never realized the Lara May had pulled anchor and was sailing onward through the Timor Sea.

After entering and sitting down, the door opened. Smith, Bishop, and Davison walked in with a bottle of wine, not knowing they were there.

"Sorry, we thought..." said Smith, turning to leave.

"Stay you three. Mr. Bishop, grab three more glasses.

"Aye, Captain."

"We thought you all hit your racks," said Davison, taking a seat. "What's this all about?"

"Firstly, where are Mobee and Ezekiel?" asked Catherine.

"They're asleep below."

While Bishop filled each glass with port, all eyes were on Flynn. By his pause to speak, Catherine knew he was finding it hard to explain the visions, revelations, and stories. Being a

181

woman, she took it upon herself to break the silence hanging over the group. "We all know about Johan's medallion."

The response was quick. "We also know Johan likes to tell tales," replied Davison, eyeing the old seaman.

"I'm sure you can tell us all kinds of sea tales, Mr. Davison," remarked Flynn in an authoritarian manner.

"True."

"May I see your medallion?" asked Flynn, extending his hand.

Johan glanced at Catherine. She knew he did not like giving up his precious trinket. She nodded with telling eyes that it was OK.

Without a word, he removed it from around his neck and handed it to him.

"Where did you get this from?"

"You know me story, Capt'n."

"I want you to tell these three your story."

As Johan looked at each man, he started at the beginning when he was a young fry like Ezekiel; he met the famous pirate, Scar. He spoke of how Scar took the medallion off a Spanish captain and tossed it to him. He mentioned the Spanish captain obtaining it from the Prince of Bagdad. He continued by telling his vision of the two British warships that slipped in behind the Phantom. That part of his so-called *tale* could not be refuted. It did happen. Scar was killed, his mates too, and the Phantom was sunk. They all knew that. When he finished, Smith spoke up.

"Yes, we all know about Scar. It happened many years ago. And being that it was years ago, you could just be telling a voyager's tale. I mean you're the only one who sees so-called visions within that medallion."

"Harr, me Lad," replied Johan. "Me were on that ship and will confess it before the mast, before the entire crew. Me pipe no lies about that."

As the two squared off eyeing one another, Flynn stepped in. "Alright," he said, "before I get into this deep, Johan told me about the ship lights before we spotted them."

The men looked from one to another.

"Here is the rest of what he's told me." After he said that, Flynn went on telling them everything. The island, seeing the York and Johan's warnings. When he finished, Catherine weighed in.

"Let 'em see the back of the medallion."

Flynn turned it over. The men leaned in to see the ancient writing.

"It comes from the tomb of the dead," whispered Johan.

"You mean the Pharaohs?" questioned Davison.

"Yarr, matey. Me fear now the bones of the ancient dead have been showing me the visions. Warning me of me own doom if me go this way or that."

After he said that, Flynn downed the last of his port, refilled his glass and stood up. They watched him walk over to the bay windows looking out over the dark waters. "If I said I believed him, you'd all think I was crazy," he said, seemingly staring out the window. "But let me tell ya something I told Catherine." He went on and told them Dagger's story he overheard at the Trade Wind. When he finished, Bishop spoke up, "I think it's best we turn this ship around and head for home."

"Me agree," added Johan.

"We are not turning around," interrupted Catherine.

Flynn turned, looking at her.

"We have enough guns and enough men to search this island."

"Are you sure about that?" questioned Davison. "What if Dagger's story is true? How do we fight against a dread disease with guns, or these so-called miniature giants within Johan's vision?"

Dead silence filled the air.

"Gentlemen," said Flynn, sitting down. "Right now, all we have is Dagger's story and Johan's visions."

"But you just said..." Davison started to say.

"I know what I just said," interrupted Flynn. "But I'm with Catherine on this. We stay the course."

Smith sighed. The group trained their attention on him.

"Now that I've seen the ancient writing, forgive me, Johan; I spoke out of turn. That piece of jewelry wasn't made from an Egyptian craft shop. It was probably cast from black magic and hung on the necks of the Pharaohs."

Johan nodded, accepting his apology. "That trinket saved me life many times, but now..."

"NOW.... it's going to save Captain Payne's," spat Catherine, downing her glass and pouring another. "We're going to that island, gentlemen, and I'll be the first to step foot on its shore."

"That's pretty brave talk with a full belly of port," said Davison.

Catherine took another slug, wiped her mouth and viciously replied, "Don't ever dare me, Mr. Davison. I have my father's blood running through my veins. I will be the first to step onto that island. Be sure of that."

After seeing her wielding a sword, Davison couldn't deny her sheer determination in finding Thomas.

"What about the crew?" asked Bishop, bring the two back to the mission.

"We tell them nothing right now," replied Catherine, looking at Flynn for approval.

All eyes fell on him.

"It might be best to hold off on that. I don't need a mutiny right now."

The group agreed.

"So where to now?" asked Bishop.

"Like I said, we stay the course. We'll make port in the village of Dura, New Guinea. There, we'll gather some venison and more game meat. I don't want to spend more than three days there. Afterward, it's onward to the South Pacific.

"You think we can skirt past Port Moresby without being seen by the British fleet?" questioned Smith.

"We'll travel by night. Now... let's get some sleep. We'll have plenty of time to talk before the village of Dura."

"How far is that?" she asked.

Flynn smiled. That wasn't the answer she wanted.

"Roughly two thousand miles. If the wind is in our favor, maybe three weeks or more" said Bishop.

After the meeting, Johan waded down the ladder to the berthing as if he had the anchor strapped to his back."

"Where have you been?" whispered Ludwig.

"Praying."

"Praying?" questioned Hildegard. "When have you ever prayed?"

"Right now, matey. Let's hold hands, our days be numbered."

"Get over there and start talking," said Ludwig, nudging him to the table.

"Me talking is like ringing the dinner bell around here," he mumbled, nodding toward Mobee's hammock.

Mobee opened his eyes hearing whispering.

As Johan sat down, he noticed Mobee's hammock moving. *The fry is up and waiting for words.*

"Alright, we're listening," said Hildegard.

Johan winked and nodded toward Mobee's hammock. The two looked in that direction.

"I saw skeletons walking. They captured a small fry. It looked like Mobee. They roasted him over a fire and then opened him like a melon and enjoyed his inners. Wouldn't you start praying after seeing such a vision like that?"

Mobee cringed hearing his words. He quickly closed his eyes and placed a finger in each ear.

Ludwig and Hildegard held their laughter.

"Say we talk in the morn when no one is near," whispered Johan, getting up.

The two nodded and drifted off to bed.

When the sun slipped up upon the horizon, Mobee stayed clear of Johan. He remained with Catherine after his and Ezekiel's lessons back aft.

"You may go now," she said, prodding him to leave.

"I think I'll stay," he replied, staring at Johan, Hildegard, and Ludwig working on the portside.

Catherine glanced at the three. It was soon apparent that something had happened below that made Mobee want to stay with her. "Did Johan scare you last night?"

"Yes, he said that he saw skeletons capturing a small fry looking like me. He said they roasted him over an open fire and then ate out his inners."

"He did, did he?" she replied, startled by that nonsense.

"True."

"You mean, yes."

"Yes," he repeated.

"Go on now Mobee, let Catherine Knox fight your battle."

"You would?"

"I most certainly will."

Mobee smiled then got up. He drifted past the coxswain and Smith, then took the starboard ladder down.

Catherine stood and strolled down the portside ladder to the three working on the rigging lines.

"Morning, Melady," greeted Hildegard.

"Morning, gentlemen - if I can call you that."

Johan turned, looking at her. Ludwig stood there confused.

"Gentlemen do not scare little boys," she said, folding her arms, "especially at night."

"Mobee," sighed Johan. "He'll be the death of me soon."

She slowly walked up to him, stared him right in the eye. "Mr. Bailer, in the dark of night, one could come to your hammock when you're sleeping," she said, lifting her chin.

"Me sees your point."

"You'll not only sees me point; you may feel it too," she replied, placing her hand down on its handle.

"You speak like a hen protecting her chicks," said Ludwig.

"Let me say it this way. Mobee and Ezekiel are my chicks. Any harm comes to them and you'll feel this hen's wrath."

"Never no harm come to 'em," replied Johan. "Me sorrow would be too much for me poor soul to bear."

"Then why don't you include Mobee in your little group below deck. It may stop his tongue from wagging."

Johan almost said he sees her point, but refrained in saying that. Her point was the tip of her sword, a tip he never wanted to feel. "Let me speak with Mobee. Me tells him me sorry."

"You do that, dear Johan," she replied, departing their company.

"Dear Johan," whispered Ludwig.

"Mind her politeness, she's speaking in anger when using that term to me."

Hildegard and Ludwig looked down the main deck at her, seemingly looking out over the water.

"She holds herself well," said Ludwig.

"She could wrestle a shark and win," added Hildegard.

"She is a shark, even bares the teeth of one," said Johan.

JEFF WRIGHT
CATHERINE KNOX

19

From Sumba to Dura, the Lara May caught the evening trade winds bustling though the eastern section of the Timor Sea. Upon setting anchor, the natives came out to greet the ship. They were friendly, welcoming the Lara May and her crew, especially Captain Flynn, who first arrived there on the HMS Standish many years ago.

King Ulla, a round bellied man with chest muscles that sagged, was a lighthearted old chap. Catherine found his wife, Shoshanna, to be a delightful woman herself.

The crew spent their days hunting within the jungle, escorted by King Ulla's sons - Nimrod and Goshen. Their nights were spent drinking and making merriment with the native women.

On the last night, while celebrating their time together, King Ulla - who wanted to ask Flynn when he first arrived why he was not sailing under the British flag of the Royal Navy - asked him now.

Flynn gave no excuse to his failures of drinking, which cost him his commission, and he ended up as a merchant captain with his own ship and crew. When he told the king that his voyage was to find Captain Payne and bring him back, he thought to ask Ulla if he had ever heard of an island with mountains reaching to the clouds.

Bishop, and Smith were surprised that he'd ask such a question, seeing these people never ventured out that far. However, when Ulla heard the description he called for his cousin,

Tusk, who had sailed with some deviant souls as a young man while living in Port Moresby, an Australian/British port.

Tusk was of old age, his mind fragile, and needed help getting about. They carried him on a bamboo stretcher from his hut to the fire. Catherine felt sorry for the old-timer. He looked like a shriveled-up prune with his arm and leg bones sticking out from his leather-baked skin.

As they set the stretcher down, Ulla informed Flynn that Tusk stopped speaking broken English years back. He figured it was his age, his mind slipping, that he only wanted to speak in his native tongue.

"So, tell me," Ulla said. "Is there anything else you can describe about this island?"

"Besides the tall mountains, on the northern tip there appears to be huge rock face pillars hedging out from the point. Through these rough waters, where the waves and tide can rip a boat apart, there is a cove, or an inlet of sorts."

Ulla tuned toward his cousin and told him what Flynn had said.

After hearing the description, Tusk closed his eyes flashing back in time, a time he thought forgotten. Within his distant memories he saw the terrifying horror his mind had blocked out. *"Basha na ka ie - ahona le Dell."*

Flynn, Bishop, Smith and Catherine froze hearing the ship's name, or thought that's what he said. Flynn knelt by Tusk. "Ask him if he sailed on the Dell with Captain Laramie?"

Ulla asked.

Tusk nodded.

"Ask him if he remembers a man named Dagger," said Flynn, glancing at Catherine. She quickly nodded, thinking if Tusk did sail on the Dell, he'd know that wild buccaneer.

Tusk continued talking for several minutes. When he finished, Ulla translated his words. "He said Dagger was a broad man of iron. Fists like English shields and wore a long knife that had two crossed swords carved in the handle."

The old native's lips quivered as he spoke once again. *"Hyaka me'yana woola se'meno.... island de'ob-lo,"*

His words startled the king. He prodded Tusk to say more. When he finished, Ulla paused in translating to Flynn.

Flynn pushed him for Tusk's words.

"My cousin said when they first arrived, Langley sent a party of seven to go and investigate the island. They were to return that night.

"In the morning, the crow's nest spotted the boat floating offshore with no one in it.

"After retrieving the boat and bringing it abreast the Dell, he saw a crewman inside frothing from the mouth; he noticed a wicked gash on his neck. Captain Langley never saw that and immediately had the boat torched, fearing the man caught some kind of disease.

"Tusk said that he knew the crewman had been bitten by some creature. He then told me to tell you... if that is where you're going, turn back now. Great terror roams the jungles. It's the island of death - *island de' ob-lo.*"

Flynn thanked King Ulla and stood up. Catherine stood, along with Bishop and Smith. In that silent moment with only the crackling of the fire, Flynn looked at her. The two now knew Tusk and Dagger's story was true. What worried her more was Tusk stating the crewman had been bitten by something - something that would cause him to die.

"Captain," said Bishop.

Flynn faced him.

"I fear we are out of our depth continuing this voyage."

"Mr. Bishop, we leave tonight. Tell Mr. Davison to gather the men."

"Aye, Sir."

Catherine looked at Bishop. They stared at one another for a moment, each feeling apprehensive. She turned before speaking and headed to the beach. On her way, she wasn't sure if Flynn meant they were leaving tonight for the island, or back home to England. She waited until she caught Flynn at the boats. Before she could get a word out, Smith and Bishop walked up.

"After hearing that, Milady, are you still eager to set foot onto that island?" asked Bishop.

Catherine glanced at Flynn. Her question sat there - the island or home. By the look in his eye, she knew he was waiting for her to answer Bishop's question; was she still wanting to go?

After all that she heard about this place, damn right she was scared. However, her fear shifted when a thought came to her.

"Gentlemen... after hearing Johan's visions, Dagger's story, and now this," she said, nodding her head back to the fire. "Yes, I am scared, but I know deep in my stomach that the York is shipwrecked on that island along with anyone who may have survived."

The men gave a simple nod, knowing she wasn't finished.

"What if one of you were stranded there?" she quickly asked, catching them off guard.

Their startled expressions made her not wait for a reply. "So, Mr. Bishop... as you are facing all kinds of perils, while trying to survive on that island, what if the angel of mercy came down and whispered, *I had sent a ship to come rescue you, but out of fear for their own lives, they turned and headed back to England. Your fate has now been sealed; your doom is near.*"

Hearing her words, Flynn turned seaward. He stood there a moment thinking. With his back to them, he spoke his thoughts, "If I were on that island and the angel of mercy spoke those words to me, I'd curse you all until my death."

Catherine looked at Bishop.

"I may agree with you on that, but what could cause a man to froth from the mouth? And... what happened to the six men who never returned?"

The four stood there pondering that. In that moment, Doc Ryan walked up.

"Here's someone who may know," said Flynn.

"Know what?" asked Ryan.

"What creatures can bite you, making you froth from the mouth before dying."

"There are many animals and even insects that can do that."

194

"Really?" questioned Catherine.

"Yes. Poisonous snakes being one. Ask Mobee. I'm sure he can tell ya. Africa is full of venomous creatures."

Creatures... As that word rolled off his lips, the group flashed back to Tusk.

In the stillness of the night, the gentle waves lapping along the shoreline, Ryan's thoughts *somewhat* eased their fear.

"It's time to go, Captain Flynn; our mission is at hand," said Catherine, stepping out of her thoughts.

Flynn stood there, seemingly adrift.

"Captain," she again said.

He looked at her, then cast his eyes over the group. "I don't know what awaits us on that island."

"None of us do," said Smith.

"You're right," replied Flynn. "But hear it now from me now. We'll take no chances and prepare for the worst."

"You speak no truer words," agreed Smith. "The men must be told."

"Leave that to me."

20

Five days out of Dura, the crew continued sailing hard at night, hoping to slip past the British fleet anchored at Port Moresby. With France and England still at war, Flynn suspected the British fleet would stay closer to the mainland to protect the port from an assault.

On a warm, muggy night, the Lara May sailed undetected through the Coral Sea and into the South Pacific. Flynn called a meeting the following morning to brief his officers and Catherine about his plans to continue sailing onward toward the Fijian islands. They agreed, but wondered if Johan's vision of coming across a British ship housing the two French sailors would appear to them during their journey.

Flynn said that if they did not come across the ship on their voyage, they'd set anchor in Fiji and ask the villagers about the island: an island just beyond their shores that doesn't exist.

Flynn and his crew, however, never set anchor in Fiji. On a clear, moonlit night, roughly fifty nautical miles away from the islands, the crow's nest reported sails aft.

Upon hearing the commotion on deck, Catherine came out of her cabin. She halted just inside the officer's passageway, gazing up at the bright full moon bathing the ship in soft moonlight. The waters all around glimmered from its effect.

Her pause was brief as crewmembers hurried about, preparing for battle. She herself then ran aft to stand alongside Flynn, Bishop, and Davison who were studying the ship approximately four hundred meters astern.

Flynn lowered his spyglass, turned and ordered the British flag raised along with a small, blue and white flag. That flag was to show the captain of the British frigate that the Lara May was an English merchant vessel. The two flags hoisted at the same time was a secret within the Royal Navy and the English merchant fleet. Most merchant vessels sailed under many flags to escape being taken as a prize. Flynn told Catherine the meaning of both flags.

"So, she's one of ours?"

"Yes, a frigate at that."

"You think it's the ship holding the two French sailors?"

"We won't know until they come alongside," he replied, turning toward the helm. "Mr. Smith, takes us out of the wind, if you will."

"Aye, Captain.

"Mr. Bishop, haul up the mainsail."

"Aye, Sir."

"Lady Knox, after we board, I'll have someone come get you."

She went to speak. He raised his hand. "I think it best the British captain and I speak first inside his cabin. If he sees you, he'll demand answers; answers we don't want to give openly."

She gracefully nodded and departed to her cabin.

Onboard the British frigate Hamilton, Captain Langley lowered his spyglass. "Of all the ships, it's the Lara May," he sighed. "Stand down the crew."

"Aye, Captain," replied Lieutenant Burlap. "Mr. William, if you will, stand down the crew.

"Aye, Sir."

"Why is Captain Flynn so far from home?" questioned Burlap.

"Being three sheets to the wind most times, he probably doesn't know where he is right now," chuckled Langley.

"Yeah, while he was sleeping it off below, that heap of a vessel probably broke anchor and drifted out here all on its own," humorously added Burlap.

As the two ships came alongside, Flynn and his men stood there looking across at the British Captain and his crew. By their posture, Flynn could tell they were amused he was there.

"Ahoy, Captain Flynn," shouted Langley. "What brings you to these waters?"

"Ahoy, Captain Langley, we're on a mission for the king."

"A mission for the king? You don't say."

"That's right; request to tie off and come aboard?"

"Permission granted."

After the lines were tossed, the plank lowered, Flynn, Smith, Bishop, and Davison walked over.

"Evening, Captain - Lieutenants," greeted Flynn, extending his hand.

"So..." said Langley. "King George sent you around the world, for what may I ask?"

"I think we should have this discussion inside your cabin."

"With my officers' present?"

"By all means."

"Follow me," said Langley, turning for the portside ladder.

Inside, the two groups sat on opposite sides of the table. Before they got down to business, Langley offered them coffee. They continued a light conversation until the ship's cook brought in the beverage then departed.

"I find it hard to believe, Captain Flynn, that King George would send you anywhere."

Flynn kept his composure, knowing Langley took him for a foolish drunk. He had sailed with Langley as a midshipman. Back then, he despised the rambunctious old fart. He was heavy handed with his crew and never allowed his officers to lead. His nose had to be in every decision.

"I'm here to find Captain Payne," he calmly replied.

The laughter was instant.

Flynn glanced sideways at his men. None of them saw the humor. Langley stopped laughing, seeing their smug faces looking back at him.

"We searched for three weeks and found nothing. Captain Steel took that information back to England. So why would the king and more so, Admiral Knox, send you out here?"

Flynn could have reached across the table and slapped him. Instead, he laid down his cards. "Alright, the king did not send me. I have a special guest onboard who paid the crew and I a handsome price to sail to the South Pacific to find Captain Payne."

"A special guest," repeated Langley. "Who in their right mind would pay you and your misfits to sail to the South Pacific?"

Angered by that comment, Davison quickly got to his feet.

The officers on the other side stood up.

As Flynn sat there staring at Langley, he said, "Mr. Davison, go back and escort our guest over, if you will."

Davison eyed each man then departed the cabin.

The two groups sat there staring at one another. The tension in the air eased when the door opened and in walked Davison and another person wearing a long-hooded coat.

Langley stood up. Catherine pulled back her cover. The British captain was speechless seeing her standing there looking like a man, her hair cut short and wearing men's clothing.

"Good evening, Captain Langley. I see by your expression that you weren't expecting me."

"Forgive me, Milady, I..." his voice trailed off, gazing down her clothing.

"You're shocked to see me. That is perfectly understandable."

"Shocked doesn't even come close. Do you have any idea the predicament you just placed me in?"

"I've placed you in nothing; now shall we all sit down?" she replied, pulling out a chair.

Langley locked eyes with Flynn. "I could commandeer your ship, your crew and have you all arrested," he bluntly scolded.

"Under what charges?" interrupted Catherine.

"I, um, well."

As he stood there chewing on his tongue thinking of a charge, Catherine placed her hands on her hips. "I'm waiting, Sir."

"Lady Knox, as a Captain of His Majesty's Royal Navy...."

"As the daughter of Admiral Knox, who is the hand of the king, and 1st Admiral to His Majesty's fleet, you have no authority over us," she shrewdly interrupted. "The king is well aware of my being here," she lied.

"The king is? What about your father?"

"Are you going to sit down?"

Langley sighed, taking a seat.

She waited a moment to allow the atmosphere to settle. "I was there in the Great Hall when Captain Leopold was brought before the king in chains. After he stated that he never physically saw the York go down, I went to my father. He would not send out a search party. I then went to King George."

"Who gave you an audience?"

"As you and your officers are well aware, I do not need an invite, or to make a request to see the king or the queen. It was Queen Charlotte herself who brought Thomas and I together, which, soon after, led to a marriage proposal. Now... do you honestly think King George was going to stand in my way of me finding Thomas and bringing him home?"

Langley looked at Flynn, then allowed his eyes to drift over his men. Not one had a smile. He sat back feeling the weight of the world upon his shoulders. He was for all purposes a man of rules; rules that guided him throughout his naval career. Here before him now was the daughter of Admiral Knox, halfway around the world, out of her depth, and out of her league. If that wasn't enough, she had hired Flynn, a washed out naval captain, to assist her in finding Captain Payne - who he knew was dead.

What rule should he apply: commandeer the Lara May and escort it back to England? Take possession of Lady Knox and take her back to England? Or, leave her with Flynn to continue her search? Not one set well with him, for he knew that he'd be standing before King George explaining his actions. He also knew that if he brought Lady Knox back to England, she'd have the king's ear before he, himself, faced him. *She'd abuse me until the king was ripe with anger.*

"Captain Langley," she said, taking him out of his tormenting thoughts. "I also heard word that you have two French sailors off the Nightingale inside your brig?"

"That's correct. When questioning the pair, they seem a bit confused where they sunk the York. However, Lady Knox - we searched for three whole weeks and found nothing, not even an empty barrel."

"I also heard that, but... as you know, it's a big ocean down here, Captain. May I speak with the French sailors?"

Before I grant you that request, answer me this. What if something happens to you and it gets back to your father and the king that I had a chance to save you? Do you think I'd walk out of their presence freely?"

Catherine glanced at the lieutenants sitting alongside Langley.

"Our careers are on the line too," said Lieutenant Burlap.

"Along with our heads," added Lieutenant Madison.

"That may be true. On the other hand, gentlemen. If we do find Captain Payne and return him to England, the king will more than celebrate. He'll honor all those who took part in finding him."

Langley locked eyes with Flynn. "You believe that?"

"If I thought otherwise, I wouldn't be sitting here."

Langley nodded. "Alright, have it your way. Lieutenant Burlap, bring up the prisoners."

"Aye, Captain."

Ten minutes later, the men walked in: filthy, their ankles in chains.

"You wanted to see us, Sir," said one.

"Yes, I have a question, but more so - she does."

The sailors looked at Catherine, stunned that she was there.

"This is Lady Knox. Her father is hand of the king and 1st Admiral to His Majesty's Royal Navy. She was by all accounts betrothed to Captain Payne."

"Speak, speak, please," one nervously replied.

"I want you to show me on a chart where you sunk the York," asked Langley, waving for Madison to retrieve it from the corner.

All stood up. Madison placed the chart on the table. The French sailors studied the map.

"Well?" pushed Langley.

"I don't see it on this chart," one said.

"Don't lie to me. I'll have you gutted and tossed overboard!"

"Please, please, I beg - it was here," the other said, placing his finger on the chart where no body of land stood.

All eyes fell on the position - south of the Fijian Islands.

"Are you sure?"

"Aye, Capitiane."

"Take them away."

Langley sat down. Flynn's men remained standing.

"Well, Captain Langley, we bid you farewell," said Catherine.

"I wish you well, but I fear you're just chasing ghosts."

There was no need for him to explain. The possibilities were there. Thomas could be dead, along with his crew. However, she didn't come this far to turn back now. "If all goes well, Captain Langley, I'll give favorable word to King George on your kind hospitality."

"You do that, Lady Knox."

She nodded, pulling up her hood.

"Lieutenant Madison, ensure the gangplank is cleared before they go across."

"Aye, Captain.

Back onboard, Flynn stood at the rail watching the crew of the Hamilton haul in the wooden plank. When the lines were cast off, he started barking orders. "Unfurl the mainsail, set a course south by southeast."

As he turned to watch the sail drop, he spotted Johan near the lifeboat. He slowly nodded. Johan nodded back, knowing his vision was true.

Catherine caught the looks and nods between the men. She may have been pleased escaping Langley's grip, but deep inside, she was worried; their destination was near.

"Captain Flynn, what happened over there?" a seaman asked.

As soon as the question was raised, the crew gathered to hear.

"Tonight, we sail. In the morning, we'll hold muster. You'll all know then."

The men departed a bit disgruntled.

"All hands who are supposed to be on watch, get to your stations. The rest of you mud-crabs strike below," shouted Bos'n Cutter.

Flynn chuckled under his breath.

Cutter winked, moving past him.

"I guess I'll call it a night, myself," said Catherine.

"Sleep well, Milady," replied Flynn with a nod.

With her mind preoccupied with what lay ahead, Catherine found it hard to sleep. She tossed and turned most of the night. When the sun rose in the morning, she awoke seeing that she had fallen asleep with her clothes and boots still on.

Ding, ding - ding, ding - ding, ding.

"It's the change of the watch," she spat, sitting up.

There was a knock on her door.

"Yes."

"It's Mr. Bishop; we'll be holding quarters soon."

"Thank you, give me a moment to freshen up."

With that, she got up, washed her face in a bowl of water, then put on new clothing. After proceeding out of the passageway, she spotted the crew back aft in ranks. She strolled along the outer rail, took the ladder up and stood alongside Flynn on the quarterdeck.

"You don't look like you slept at all," he whispered.

"I don't think I did. Thank you for waiting for me."

Flynn nodded, then turned his focus on the men standing before him. "Gentlemen, my seafaring mates," he bellowed. "We have traveled for months on end now to find ourselves close at hand to our mission. From the information we gathered onboard the Hamilton, we are setting a new course where the York was taken unawares by the Nightingale."

The crew looked from one to another.

"There is an island, that is not on any chart, we believe the York may be shipwrecked on. That's what we obtained from the two French prisoners aboard the frigate."

"We have heard the whispering below deck of Johan's visions," yelled Seaman Jamison.

Flynn looked down at him. "I've heard those visions myself, and I have also heard tales from a wild buccaneer, that went by the name of Dagger. He too spoke of an island that resembles Johan's vision. So, did King Ulla's cousin, Tusk. As a young man, Tusk sailed with Dagger onboard the Dell. Tusk said he saw the island himself."

"So, you think Johan can see things within that stone?" shouted Seaman Caleb.

All hands looked back at Johan sitting in the shade of the lifeboat.

"Me life is riddled with fleas," whispered Johan to Hildegard and Ludwig.

"Stand up and tell these fleas," replied Hildegard.

Johan nervously stood. "You think me tell stories below to scare the young lads?"

The ship went quiet. They respected the ol' salt.

"Me swear before the mast... even if Capt'n Flynn keelhauled me poor soul, I'd still come up from the depths speaking of our doom."

The wind suddenly picked up, flapping the sails against the yardarms. Stillness settled over the men watching them high above.

Flynn's eyes drifted downward from the sails blowing in the breeze. He took hold of the round wooden rail and shouted, "Gentlemen!"

The crew turned and looked up at him.

"Whatever tales and visions there are of this island, be it in your minds that we are hardened souls born from the sea, once shellbacks of the Royal Navy, rugged merchant sailors and marines.

"Our backbones are as strong as the keel itself - hardened by years of sailing. Each man here has been through the worst the ocean can give; let not these tales and visions scare you now."

"I'm with Captain Flynn," shouted Seaman Jacob.

"I'm with the captain also," yelled Smith. "He has taken us to faraway lands the likes our countrymen have never seen. We've all come back with our limbs intact."

Once again, the crew went silent.

"Hear me now, men," bellowed Flynn. "We have enough muskets and pistols, enough powder and ball. Our swords will be sharpened to their finest edge. Mr. Davison here will teach you how to make hand grenades if we run into trouble. So, what say ye we go in search for Thomas Payne?"

The crew erupted into hollering cheers.

Catherine stood there looking at Flynn.

"You seem to be wanting a job yourself," he said to her expression.

"I have one."

"And what is that?"

"The art of fencing," she replied, focusing on the crew. "I'll train any man willing to learn, how to duel with a sword - even Mobee and Ezekiel."

"I would have thought you'd want them to remain onboard?" whispered Flynn.

"If there is an island out there, the likes we've heard, not even the men remaining onboard will be safe when at anchor."

Flynn slowly nodded.

JEFF WRIGHT
CATHERINE KNOX

Catherine turned toward Mr. Davison, now surrounded by men. She spotted Johan, Hildegard, Ludwig, and Woodward talking. Johan looked depressed. "Will you excuse me," she said, heading for the ladder.

Flynn watched her skirt around the crew, listening to Davison talk about this new weapon of war called the hand grenade. As she approached Johan, he reeled in disgust. "You ruined me soul. Me not worth a tattered rigging line now."

"You all come with me," she said, heading toward the bow.

When they were out of earshot she said, "You all believe Johan?"

"Yes," replied Ludwig.

"We all do," added Woodward.

"Good, so do I, and so does Captain Flynn and his officers now."

"Then if you do believe, then why are we still sailing southeast and not back to England?" asked Johan.

Catherine stepped up to him and took his hands. He looked down, surprised at her action.

"Because, dear Johan, a woman's heart is just as good as that medallion of yours. Trust me, Thomas is alive."

Johan gazed into her eyes.

"I need you," she said to his stare. "I need all of you."

Johan slowly nodded. So, did the rest.

"Then we sail?"

"We sail," replied Johan.

21

As the Lara May sailed onward, the ship was abuzz in activity. Below deck, some of the men were crafting arrows for bows, while others were fitting the muskets and pistols with new flint. Up forward in the belly of the ship, the stone wheel spun as men honed the swords to their finest edge. Back aft, on the poop deck Mr. Davison's group were learning how to make hand grenades.

In front of the officer's cabins, Catherine was teaching the art of fencing to any man wanting to learn. Carpenter's Mate Hildegard created two wooden swords for Mobee and Ezekiel. If they could master the sword, Bos'n Cutter said he'd craft two metal swords to fit their size and then sharpen them on the stone wheel.

In this beehive of sweat and preparation, some men were excited; others thought this whole affair was a waste of time. Captain Payne would not be found, and they'd soon be heading home a thousand pounds richer.

Evening on the third day, there was a tap on Flynn's door.

"Come in."

Davison entered. "You have two crewmembers wanting to speak with you, Captain."

"Sure, sure - who is it?"

"Mobee and Ezekiel."

Flynn leaned back in his chair. "Did they say why?"

"No."

"Alright, send 'em in."

Davison opened the door and nodded for the boys to enter. Before he left, he winked at Flynn. Flynn held his smile as they nervously approached his desk.

"Evening, gentlemen, what can I do for you?"

"Mobee and I want to have a word with you, Sir," replied Ezekiel.

"Well, you're before me now. Go on, speak your minds," he said, taking in their uneasiness.

"We want to go on the island too, Sir," said Mobee.

"I need you onboard."

"There is nothin' onboard that needs looking after, Captain," retorted Mobee. "Besides, Ezekiel and I got to thinking."

Flynn could have chuckled with that statement.

"Years from now, Sir.... when they talk of the voyage of the Lara May, well... we don't want people saying that Mobee and Ezekiel stayed onboard because they were cowards."

"That's right, Captain," added Ezekiel. "A man protects the woman he loves, and well, Sir... Mobee and I are truly fond of Lady Catherine, and we're not going to stand idly by and allow her onto that island without us protecting her. This is something we do not want her or the crew to know."

"Is that right?" replied Flynn, basking in the glow of seeing them coming of age.

"Yes, Sir," said Mobee. "The other thing we wanted to discuss with you, Sir is.... we think it's time that Ezekiel and I are treated like men onboard this ship."

Seeing them standing there holding their own, Flynn was beside himself. "You're done being boys?" he asked, leaning up.

"Yes, Sir," they replied in unison.

"Alright, let me say this to you. One doesn't see the change in themselves when coming of age, becoming a man. Others see it first."

They nodded, unsure of what he meant.

"A good example of that is, why has Lady Knox prohibited you two from racing each other to the crow's nest?"

"We might fall," answered Mobee.

"That's one reason. The other is she sees you as boys who can be reckless at times."

The two again nodded.

"Racing one another to the crow's nest is not a childish thing," he said. "Grown men do that often. It breaks up the monotony while being out at sea."

"Then we'll act like men from now on, Captain," said Ezekiel.

"You want to know something?"

"Yes, Sir."

"When I was a young lad like you two, I watched the sailors. The ones I respected I tried to emulate."

"Emulate, Sir?" questioned Mobee.

"To be and act like them."

They nodded.

While studying their eyes, Flynn asked, "Who do you admire on this ship?"

"You, Captain Flynn," spoke Mobee first.

Flynn nodded suspecting he was going to say that. He waited for Ezekiel to respond.

"Bos'n Cutter, Sir," said Ezekiel.

"Bos'n Cutter... why do you admire him?"

"He knows this ship like the back of his hand and could sail it blindfolded, Sir. When he talks, the crew listens out of respect."

"Then be like Cutter, young man," he replied, looking at Mobee.

"They all listen to you too, Captain Flynn," said Mobee. "My other reason for wanting to be like you is..." his voice broke off.

Flynn and Ezekiel watched Mobee's eyes water. They waited to hear what he had to say.

"You saved my life, Sir," said Mobee, feeling a lump in his throat.

That drove into Flynn like a knife. He kept his composure and replied, "Then become a captain, Mobee."

"Aye, Sir, a fine one at that," he said, wiping his tears.

"Alright, here is my answer. I believe we have many days ahead before we strike gold and find this island. In the meantime, you give this discussion a lot of thought. I'll see the changes before you do."

"What about Lady Knox, Sir?" asked Ezekiel.

"She'll also see the changes. Now go... we have a ship to sail."

"We do at that, Captain," replied Mobee.

Before they opened the door, Flynn called to them.

They turned and faced him.

"I am in awe of your schooling. Lady Knox has done well. Your English has improved remarkably."

"Thank you, Sir," they said then departed his company.

When the door closed, Flynn slowly got up and walked over to the bay windows. Looking out over the vast endless sea, he pondered what Mobee had said. *You saved my life, Sir.* His simple line melted his heart, but deep down inside, he knew the truth.

No, Mobee - you saved my life. My heavy days of drinking were over when I took you in.

As that weighed heavily on his heart, deep within his soul, he chuckled while thinking of a verse from the Good Book - *when I was a child, I spoke as a child, I understood as a child, I thought like a child - but when I became a man, I put away those childish things.*

"Tonight," he said, looking back at his door. "Two boys came in and two men had left. They too have put away their childish things."

22

As the long hot days turned into weeks without any signs of the island, Johan's little group were skeptical of his visions. They sat there listening to him deep in the belly of the Lara May.

"Trust me, Lads – me is true as the point off the bow. Me 'dallion has never lied. All things seen have come to pass. So, believe me now when I say a storm is brewing."

"You've seen a storm up ahead within that black gem of yours?" questioned Ludwig.

"Yarr, matey, it was there before me. Can feel it in me bones too. The sea will rise up like a serpent soon."

"The weather hasn't changed in months down here," said Woodward.

"Take heed, Lad, when you feel the whispering winds coming from the East," he said and then paused seeing Mobee awake. "The ship's ear has awoken," Johan continued, nodding his head.

The group looked back seeing Mobee staring at them.

"You might as well join us."

Mobee got up and tiptoed over. He yawned standing there.

"Tell me young Mobee, did you hear every word ol' Johan said?"

"Harr, matey, me heard every word. Now me's afraid," he mimicked the old salt.

Johan lifted one brow studying the boy. "See'n the Capt'n has taken you in, we'd be hard

JEFF WRIGHT
CATHERINE KNOX

pressed to keel hog ya. So, sit down, Lad and hear me words," he musingly rebutted.

As Mobee took a place at the table, Ezekiel smiled, glad to see him joining the group.

"So, as the Capt'ns boy," Johan continued, leaning his elbows on the table. "Have you ever heard ol Flynn speak of such storms me now see in me 'dallion?"

"I heard him once talking to Mr. Smith about tropical cyclones, whatever they are."

"They're the same as hurricanes," piped Hildegard.

"Harr, they be the beast that lives in the depths of the sea," whispered Johan. "She sleeps most times, but when she rises up, she'll swallow ya whole."

"Worse than the storm we went through months ago?" asked Ezekiel.

"Compared to the monster I speak of now - that were a mere storm in a tea cup, Lad."

"Are you going to tell the captain?" asked Woodward.

Johan looked across at Mobee. "I may be the ears, but you're the eyes of the ship," said Mobee to his stare.

"After the verbal beating me took from those mangy fleas on deck, me rather keep to me self."

"You can tell Lady Knox. She believes you," said Woodward.

"So, does Captain Flynn," added Mobee.

"Let me sleep on it. I do me best thinking with me eyes closed."

"Alright, let's hit our hammocks. Tomorrow is another day," said Hildegard.

"Another day of sweltering heat," said Ezekiel, getting up and heading to his hammock. The rest followed.

23

Four days on, the Lara May sailed across calm rolling seas with clear blue skies overhead. It was another day of wishful thinking that somewhere, somehow, they'd come upon something that would tell 'em Captain Payne was still alive. However, all the lookouts had to report was nothing but clear empty waters as far as the eye could see.

During those warm tropical days, Johan finally got the nerve to speak with Lady Knox. He'd been to her cabin once. That time she asked. Today, he knocked.

"Come in."

When he opened the door, Catherine was surprised to see him standing there. "What is the pleasure of your company today?"

"It's not English lessons that me is here for, Melady. If me may, me would like to speak with you in private."

"Come, come... sit down," she said, charmed by his humor.

"Can me shut the door? Don't want anyone seeing me here."

Catherine held her smile. "Yes, by all means. Close the door."

"Thank you," he replied, taking a seat at her table.

"What's on your mind, dear Johan?"

"It's about me 'dallion."

"Another vision?"

"Yarr, not good."

She sat there listening to his new revelation.

"Whispering winds coming from the east, you say?"

Johan nodded.

"The same direction we're traveling right now?"

Again, he nodded.

"How soon?

"Me 'dallion never gives a time; it just warns me of trouble."

"I'll inform the captain."

Johan stood and walked to the door. He slowly turned and looked at her. His piercing stare was frightening. "I'll see him straight away."

"Be as straight as a navigational line, Melady" he replied then departed her company.

Two days later, up at the bow, Mobee and Ezekiel where enjoying the night searching the starlit sky. While picking out patterns in the heavens, Mobee felt a faint change in the wind. She'd been blowing from the north all day. Now it was coming head-on from the east. "Do you feel that?" he said.

"Feel what?"

"The wind."

"I've been feeling it all day, Mobee."

"The helm has kept the wind to our portside. If we come about, we'll know the wind has changed direction."

Ezekiel looked back at the quarterdeck. Sure enough, the coxswain changed course. "You don't think..." Ezekiel's voice trailed off.

"As sure as I am sitting here."

"Are you going to tell Captain Flynn?"

"Should I?" replied Mobee, thinking. "Let's go below and tell Johan first and see what he says."

"Alright."

Down they went to the berthing below. Johan was humming an old sea song while hanging his wet clothing.

"Harr, me Lads - you look as if ya seen a serpent."

"The wind," gasped Mobee, out of breath.

"We need thee wind, can't live without it," ribbed Johan.

"It's changed," said Ezekiel.

"Eastward, Lad?" replied Johan, lifting one brow.

"Yeah," they said in unison.

"Prepare yourself. The beast is coming."

Suddenly, without warning, the high-pitched call from Cutter's Bos'n pipe sounded, then the ship's bell rang as if a madman were shaking it.

"Hurry mates, get up on deck," shouted Hildegard.

A quagmire of bodies ran for the ladders. In the commotion, Johan stood there rubbing his medallion. "Maybe ol' Johan doesn't need his trinket. This time me bones warned of trouble."

On deck, Catherine raced out of her cabin not knowing what was going on. Upon opening the passageway door, she felt the cold, wet chill: a telling sign of an approaching storm.

"I want securing lines fore and aft," she heard Bishop yelling next the mast.

Her thoughts instantly flashed back to Johan and his vision of a storm. She ran aft toward the quarterdeck. Flynn was already there with Smith on the helm. She could not hear what he was shouting.

"Lady Knox," said Davison, taking hold of her arm. "You need to get back to your cabin. We have a wicked storm in front of us."

"I can't," she yelled. "I'll be sick if I do."

"Alright, but tie yourself off somewhere, fast."

Catherine nodded and continued to the starboard ladder. As she took hold of the rail, the gale force winds rushed past the ship.

"Secure her to the bulkhead," ordered Flynn to Ludwig.

"Wait."

"We're facing a tropical cyclone, Catherine," he shouted, pointing forward.

Her eyes took in the thunderous lightning and wall of dark menacing clouds. "Is this what Captain Payne had sailed the York through?"

"I'd say so," yelled Flynn, lifting his spyglass. He waited until the sky lit up to study the high upper clouds. They were spinning *north*. He dropped his gaze down on the huge waves traveling toward them - *heading straight west*. The white caps frosting at the tips were blowing *northwest*. He immediately calculated the storm was for sure heading north.

"What do you think, Captain?" shouted Smith.

"It's traveling northward."

"Are you sure?"

"Damn it, man... my eyes don't deceive me. Take her hard over right and head south. We'll slip underneath this venomous snake!" he scolded.

Smith gritted his teeth spinning the wheel, hoping the Lara May would sail out of harm's way and not straight into the eye of the storm.

Hearing the anger in Flynn's voice, Catherine waved to Ludwig to secure her to the bulkhead. As they locked eyes, not a word was spoken; both worried about the storm and Flynn's *now* razor- sharp temper.

"Mr. Davison," called Flynn.

He turned, barely hearing him.

"I need you up here."

When he gained the port ladder, Flynn ordered him to assist with the helm. It was going to take two men to weather the southern edge of this blasphemous beast. By sailing underneath, Flynn prayed they'd be only facing severe winds and savage seas being pushed away from its center.

When the first massive wave come rushing toward the bow, Flynn shouted, "Ring the bell, Lad. All hands prepare yourselves."

As she made her turn south, the ship listed heavily to starboard, the wave rolling underneath her. Smith and Davison clung to the wheel desperately trying to keep the rudder at an angle so as not to capsize the ship. A vessel of this size may dip her yardarm but exposing too much of her belly would seal her fate.

Mobee and Ezekiel huddled tightly together underneath one of the lifeboats. Fear had 'em both by the throat.

"We're not going to escape this monstrous storm," moaned Ezekiel.

"I'm not going to the bottom to the deep waters below," shouted Mobee.

"Let me underneath, let me underneath," a drenched, scared crewmember yelled, crawling toward them.

"Hurry," yelled Mobee. "Get under here."

Just as he got to the boys, a huge wave ripped across the ship's midsection. The force lifted the man off his knees and slammed him against the outer rail. As the ship rolled from the impact, the man slid halfway over, his feet dangling in the air.

"Hang onto the lines and pull yourself up," yelled Ezekiel, frantically staring at him.
The man fought hard to regain the deck, but his strength was draining from the powerful winds. He fearfully locked eyes with Mobee and Ezekiel. The moment seemed forever. Then he let go. The terrifying gaze in his eyes ripped out their hearts.

The sea is a monster that sleeps most of the time. But when it awakens, it will swallow you whole.

Through his cupped hands, Mobee shouted, "Man overboard, portside."

Bos'n Cutter rushed over. "Where?" he shouted.

Mobee pointed in front of him.

In his anger, Cutter stumbled to the rail not in fear of the storm while searching the dark waters below. With the torrential rain, sweat, and salt water running down his face, he said a simple prayer.

Behind him, however, was a massive wall of water racing toward the ship. The force of the wave crashing over the ship blew Cutter right off his feet. He tumbled aft down the deck, desperately trying to grab onto anything.

"Bos'n Cutter," screamed Ezekiel, terrified he was going over.

Cutter grabbed a line. It broke. He continued tumbling as the ship listed hard over. Panic set in. He did not want the same fate of the man that just went overboard. Then suddenly... a hand reached out and grabbed him. He looked up to see Bishop holding onto his arm.

"We can't afford to lose you," he shouted, dragging Cutter toward the mast.

There, the two clung together, shielding themselves from the pounding rain.

"We lost one," he said.

"Who?"

"Don't know."

"We're beyond help now, matey. It's each man to his own," shouted Bishop.

Cutter sadly nodded.

"Strike below and see to the pumps."

"Aye."

"Make sure we have enough men down there."

"I will," he replied, crawling toward the ladder.

24

The morning found the Lara May still dealing with the aftermath of the storm: steady winds, wet overcast skies, and four-meter swells. The mood on the ship was as dreary as the day. Men sat about the deck soaking wet and feeling sorry. They lost Seaman Hammerstein last night. He was a good mate, best friend to Seaman Caleb. Their hammocks were below side by side. They were two of Flynn's finest crow's nest lookouts.

As Caleb was going through Hammerstein's footlocker, picking out all his prized possessions to give to his family back home, Mobee and Ezekiel tried to comfort him.

Woodward, the ship's cook, even tried to assist Caleb's utter remorse with a cup of port. Mobee found it odd to give a man a drink so early in the morning, but Caleb had no trouble pounding it down.

Flynn called Hammerstein's service for eight a.m.

Without knowing they had lost a soul, Catherine sat in her cabin preparing for the morning. Last night, after evading the brunt of the cyclone, she waded to her room, stripped out of her wet clothing and laid down. Sleep found her before her head hit the pillow. It wasn't until she was ready to get up and leave when a knock on her door brought her the sad news.

It was Smith. He looked like an English sheep dog that had played in the mud and rain all night. Tired and worn to the bone, he told her what happened. Now wanting to be alone with such sorrow, she excused herself.

Smith gave her a nod and left.

Around seven thirty, she finally walked out onto the main deck. The ship was in tatters. The mainsail torn in three sections, the jib completely gone, and one of the lifeboats lay on its side against the portside rail. Broken rigging lines hung from above, freely swaying in the breeze.

The men looked as tattered as the ship itself, sitting amongst the devastation and mayhem. Not one said a word to her as she made her way to the aft ladder, to Flynn's cabin.

She met Davison on her way down.

"Morning, Milady. Don't be surprised when you walk in," he said in a tone of sadness.

Confused, she looked at Flynn's cabin door. Her knock was gentle.

"Come in."

When she entered, Davison's words weren't so confusing after all. Flynn was seemingly looking out the stern bay window dressed in his British naval uniform, his well-polished saber at his side. Her eyes took in his Captain's cover sitting on his desk.

Who would disapprove in a time like this - a time of such sorrow - that a washed out naval captain could not don his uniform, a uniform he surely wasn't entitled to wear to conduct the service? *No one.*

Besides that, to her, Flynn was not the same man she had met in the forest. He just saved the Lara May along with forty-nine crewmembers. That is seamanship. That is a British Captain of His Majesty's Royal Navy; one her father would rightly toast.

She lingered on her thoughts while closing the door and walking over to him. "Morning, Captain."

He said not a word, just kept his eyes forward.

"I'm sorry we lost Seaman Hammerstein last night."

"Me too. He was one of my finest," he replied, turning to look at her.

With compassionate eyes she slowly nodded, knowing every captain considered each man his son. To lose one in battle was heart wrenching; to lose one at sea would cripple a man's soul.

"I heard word that Mobee and Ezekiel are below comforting Seaman Caleb," she softly said.

"That's good to hear. I was just thinking of what to say to the men," he replied, walking over to his desk.

She watched him pick up the Good Book with its well-worn cover. "On such sad occasions as this, there are many wonderful things you can read from that book. I've always been drawn to Romans 8 - 35 through 39."

He flipped through the pages to that verse. After reading it, he looked up and thanked her.

"Shall we?" she said, heading for the door.

When they gained the main deck, all hands slowly stood, surprised seeing Flynn in his naval uniform and carrying a bible. Without a word, they sullenly followed him aft to the quarterdeck.

"Mr. Bishop, strike below and gather those pumping out the bilge."

His order was subtle, soft to the ear - like a father who had lost a son.

"Aye, Captain."

Smith and Davison took the ladder up with him and Catherine.

Flynn stood there a moment, waiting for the rest of the crew. When they all assembled, he started his mournful speech.

"My heart is a swamp of sadness for losing Seaman Hammerstein last night. There was nothing anyone could have done to save him," he said and then paused.

"If I may lighten your own hearts with a simple prayer," he continued, taking off his cover and opening the book.

All hands bowed their heads.

"Who shall separate us from the love of Christ? Shall trouble or hardship or persecution, or famine, nakedness, or even the danger of a sword?

"As it is written, for your sake, we face death all day long; we are considered sheep to be slaughtered.

"No, shipmates," he said, glancing up, and then quickly looking down at the verse. "In all these things we are more than conquerors through Him who loved us.

"For I am convinced that neither death nor life, neither angels nor demons, neither the present nor the future nor any powers – high or low, nor anything else in all creation will be able to separate us from the love of God that is in Christ Jesus our Lord."

Upon finishing, he closed the book.

All heads lifted, gazing up at him.

Flynn looked down at his wet, dirty crew and then outward across his ship in ruins. In that still moment, a flock of birds flew by heading east.

Flynn looked up.

Catherine looked up.

The whole crew looked up seeing them.

"May Seaman Hammerstein lie in the comfort of the Lord," he said, donning his cover. "Men," he then billowed, feeling rejuvenated seeing the birds. "Our hearts may be saddened by the loss of a fine crewmember, but even Hammerstein would not allow us to waver from our mission. As we have just witnessed from the heavens above, land is near," he joyfully beamed. "I ask you now my seafaring mates, for Seaman Hammerstein we go... what say ye?"

All saluted Hammerstein with an arousing cheer.

Flynn briskly turned toward the helm. "Come left... put us on a course with those birds," he ordered.

"Aye Captain."

"Sailing Master Ludwig, get our sheets in order."

"Aye, Captain."

"Mr. Bishop, tidy the deck and see to the lifeboat."

"Aye, Captain."

"I'll take the crow's watch," shouted Mobee, heading for the rigging lines heading up."

"Mobee," yelled Catherine.

Flynn placed his hand over hers on the rail. "Climb, Mobee, climb... Keep your eyes peeled on our feathered friends," he countered her disapproval.

Catherine stared into his eyes.

"We don't have boys on this ship anymore, Lady Knox - only men."

His voice was stern, his expression stone cold. She let it go with a slight nod of her head.

While the crew set about getting the ship in order, and Mobee high on the mast keeping his eyes trained on the birds, Flynn had one more thing to do. Speak with Seaman Caleb. "Mr. Davison."

"Yes, Captain."

"When Caleb is ready I want to speak with him in private. He'll not be put to work for three days, not even stand a watch."

"Aye, Sir," he replied then left.

Flynn stood there a moment watching his crew removing the tattered sails, cleaning the deck and securing the lifeboat back in its place. *These are men born from the sea; hardened, yet brittle. The loss of one man is like losing a link in the chain - each one just as important as the other.*

He dropped that thought seeing Catherine now on the main deck removing a tattered rigging line from one of the pulleys and Ludwig showing her how to weave a new line back in. *She too has become a link in the chain,* he thought, heading to his cabin below.

On his way down, he had to admit the verbal reality of loving her just as much as Mobee and Ezekiel. He surmised the entire crew loved her as well.

The knock on his door came sooner than expected. "Come in."

It was Davison.

"Is he ready?"

"Yes, Captain."

"Send him in."

Davison opened the door. Seaman Caleb entered. Davison quietly shut the door and left.

"Have a seat young man."

Caleb sat down.

"Coffee?"

"Thank you, Sir."

As he reached over and poured him a cup, he pondered on what to say. "In times like these, Seaman Caleb, when you lose your best mate, it's hard sitting there listening to what others have to say; for how would they know how you're feeling, right?"

"Yes, Sir."

"With that, I'd like to start off by saying I know you've lost your best friend, and I... well... I feel as if I had lost a son," he said, gazing at him with heartfelt eyes.

The captain's words surprised him. They felt like a touch from God. "I thank you for that. Hammerstein was like a brother I never had."

Flynn sighed sitting up. "To lose a man that way rips out my heart. It rips out my guts. He was a fine seaman and I trusted his eye."

"He was at that, Sir."

"Put this in your heart, Seaman Caleb. Even though Hammerstein wasn't chummy with everyone onboard, he was highly respected and loved for his abilities. Let the crew mourn with you."

"I will, Sir."

"I have advised Mr. Davison, who'll report to Mr. Smith and Mr. Bishop, that you'll not work for three days, or stand a watch."

Caleb nodded.

"Take your time, drink your coffee - I'm going to see to my ship," he said, getting up and leaving.

When the door closed, Caleb sat there all alone. With mournful tears rolling down his cheeks, he drank his coffee.

Below deck, Flynn walked through the berthing. Several men were cleaning it up. He continued onward to the next set of ladders. Down he went hearing men talking. Seeing his feet, then his legs, the men stopped chatting when he entered the storage deck.

"How is it going?" he asked them, pumping the seawater out.

"We'll have her dry by noon, Captain," replied Hildegard.

"I thank ye for your brawn and sweat. The Lara May will soon rise to her full potential and we'll find where those birds nest. As you well know, birds and land go hand in hand," boosted Flynn with a smile.

"They do at that, Sir," he agreed.

25

Throughout the day and into the night, the Lara May skimmed across choppy seas with the same foul grey weather overhead. In the morning, the crew awoke to a damp hazy fog.

With his new assignment as crow's nest lookout, Mobee got up early to stand his watch. On high, where the mist lay thin, he observed the sun rising northeast of their location. Below, where the fog lay thick, he could scarcely see twenty meters outward from the ship.

With his eye glued to the spyglass, he turned in every direction, searching. It wasn't until the sun had burned the mist around him that he could see... and see he did. "Land ho, off the starboard beam."

"How far, Lad?" Smith called up.

"A quarter mile, maybe less."

"Bos'n Cutter, pipe all-hands on deck. Send someone to inform the captain."

"Aye, Mr. Smith."

When Flynn hurried on deck, Cutter and several seamen were preparing to taking soundings. Mr. Bishop had his men in place to drop anchor. On his way to the quarterdeck, Flynn finally saw the island coming into view. He raced up the portside ladder. Sailing Master Ludwig was standing helm watch.

"Come left," ordered Flynn.

"Coming left, Sir," replied the Coxswain.

"Sailing Master Ludwig, as we approach, place the ship perpendicular to the island."

"Aye, Sir."

Catherine walked out seeing nothing but fog and men moving about the ship. A seaman stopped and excitedly said, "We're coming upon an island."

"Where?" she beamed, searching through the fog.

"There, Lady Catherine," he said, pointing off the starboard bow.

"Thank you," she replied, heading aft to the quarter deck.

As she met Flynn near the helm, he reported that it was Mobee who sighted the island.

She looked up at him with his eye glued to his spyglass. "How far?"

"Close," he replied, turning. "Mr. Bishop haul up the mainsail. Steady the helm on same course."

"Aye, Captain."

"Why are we stopping?" she asked.

"In order to get our bearing, we'll drift a spell until this fog clears."

Catherine placed her hand over his on the rail, her telling elation easily seen. He only hoped for her sake and his that this was the island they were looking for.

"Thank the Good Lord for the birds," she quipped.

"You're right, without sighting them, we could have sailed right past it in this foul weather."

She agreed with a nod.

"Let's pray that your betrothed is here, Catherine."

She presented a pleasant smile.

"You may remain here on the quarterdeck while Mr. Bishop and I walk the rails," he said, taking the ladder down.

She stood there watching he and Bishop walking along while looking down into the water.

"Would you like for us to drop the boats and pull us in closer, Sir?" asked Bishop, wishing to make landfall soon.

"No, not yet. I think it's best we stay hidden until this foul weather clears. We haven't a clue what or who may be on this island."

"Aye, Sir."

Within the heavy fog, the crew on deck stood idly by; each man wanting to see the island, a place some begged to see, some never thought possible... then there was Johan Bailer, who cursed the very thought of it.

"Look," a seaman shouted aft, "debris in the water."

Cutter spotted the vines, broken tree limbs and branches adorned with white flowers. "Hurry, gather that branch."

Two seamen uncoiled the barbed hook and tossed it out. Once on deck, Cutter removed a flower and handed it to Ezekiel. "Give that to Lady Knox."

He ran down the deck, up the ladder and stood before her with a smile as bright as the sun. "This is from the entire crew, Milady."

"Why, thank you," she fussed, glancing at Cutter. With a delightful smile, she closed her eyes and inhaled the sweet fragrance. When she opened them, everything suddenly seemed to be moving in slow motion. Cutter wasn't looking at her anymore. He was gazing out over the water... so were the crew.

She slowly turned, and from the pit of her stomach, she exhaled in awe. One moment the fog was there and then, it was gone. In its place, the island appeared. She slowly walked over to the rail. Without a thought, her fingers let go of the flower. The velvet petals and stem landed in the water. It drifted away on the gentle swells before her mind reengaged.

Like Gods rising up from the deep blue sea, sheer granite cliffs stood before her. At the top, tropical trees and lush green foliage made up the crown. Hanging over the cliffs were thick jungle vines; ever so begging for the rocky shoals and water below.

Large mantels jetting out from the granite face gave home to shrubs, trees and vines. At the base, where the turquoise water met land, was a sandy beach. To the left of her, large rock formations pressed against the granite cliffs. To the right, where the cliffs dropped off, was a vast landscape of dense jungle protected by mountains piercing the sky.

In her trance-like state, she proceeded down the ladder and stood alongside Flynn. "Have you ever seen anything like this?"

"No," he replied, mystified by the island's sheer ruggedness and beauty. "But that looks familiar," hc continued, pointing northward out to the point.

A chill ran up her spine taking in the huge rock columns hedging out to sea. She had seen them in a thousand dreams, dreams that awoke her in the night. When she looked into Flynn's eyes, she spoke not a word. It was all there in her wandering gaze; Johan's description of the island.

Before he could speak, Seaman Belford, a tall scrappy lad who went by the nickname of Carrot due to his reddish hair and the patch of freckles splashed across his face, shouted with excitement, "I see something, Captain. Looks like wreckage from a ship."

"Where?" yelled Flynn, hurrying aft.

"There, Sir, wedged within that shoal."

"Your spyglass, son."

Flynn homed in on the beach and immediately saw the objects. "It's from a ship, alright."

The entire crew gathered around.

"Is it from the York?" asked Catherine, wishing beyond hope that it was.

"It could be," he replied, keeping the spyglass trained on the beach.

"Maybe we go ashore and see if it is," suggested Davison.

Flynn lowered the instrument. All eyes were on him, more so Catherine; her eyes were glaring for answers.

"Bos'n Cutter."

"Yes, Captain."

"Pick two for boat detail while Mr. Davison, Mr. Bishop, along with seaman Belford and you, search the area."

"Yes, Sir."

"Since we know nothing of this island, or if there are natives, I want the party armed with pistols, muskets, and grenades. If you find any evidence of the York, wave your hands."

"Aye, Captain," they all said in unison.

The section of shoreline where Belford spotted the items was a rocky shoal jetting out to sea. They decided to make landfall further down on the sandy beach.

Upon reaching the water's edge and hauling the boat ashore, Davison set the crew in order. "I know it feels good to be on dry land again, but keep your wits about-cha while we search."

"We will," replied Jamison.

"Alright... Seaman Belford, you spotted the items; lead on."

Excited, he ran northward toward the shoal. Davison, Bishop, and Cutter watched him set his rifle down and carefully wade into the water. There, he untangled a moss-covered length of rope and tossed it onto the beach. Further out, he bent over and grabbed an iron ring with three long slat boards attached. He carried it out as the three approached.

"That's part of a rigging line and a ship's barrel," said Bishop.

"You're right, but it doesn't mean it's from the York. Let's keep searching, there may be more," replied Davison.

The four men continued onward through the rocky shoal and shallow water. When they came upon a huge boulder and went around it, they froze. Before them, half buried in the sand, was a portion of a lifeboat. All that remained were a bit of the hull and a quarter section of the side.

Not far from that were an old black shoe and a torn section of a shirt.

Bishop walked over, picked up the shoe and tossed it to Davison. "It looks like an English sailor's shoe."

"You think," questioned Davison, checking it out. When he went to toss it back behind him, he gasped, "Will you look at that?"

Bishop, Belford and Cutter turned. At the base of the granite cliff, twenty meters down from them, was a small passage between the cluster of large boulders and the base of the granite wall.

"We didn't even notice that when he came around the boulder," said Cutter.

"No, but we do now. Let's see where it leads," replied Davison.

"You sure?" asked Belford.

"I didn't come all this way to frolic in the sand, Laddy," grunted Davison, heading over.

Belford followed the three inside. The further he walked, the moist air turned hot and muggy; vines clung to the sides and hung down from the rock ceiling. Forty feet down, sunlight was bathing the exit.

"Halt," whispered Davison.

"What is it?" asked Bishop, worried.

"Look down, straight ahead."

"Human remains," gasped Belford.

"Remains," repeated Cutter, pushing past the men. His eyes took in the skeletal portions – an old skull and rib cage lying against the rock face wall.

Click...

The sound of Davison pulling back his musket hammer brought the three out of their trance. "Prepare your weapons, we haven't a clue to what we're walking into out there," he said, continuing onward through the pass.

They locked their hammers back and followed.

Before exiting, Davison raised his hand. The three stopped, seeing him just standing there listening. From the side of his mouth he gave another warning. "Be ready for anything."

They nodded, training their barrels forward then slowly walked out into a hidden cove filled with a tapestry of lush green foliage, tall palm trees and overhanging cliffs with spots of sunlight streaming down on the moss-covered ground.

"Were not in England anymore," murmured Davison, taking in the sheer beauty with glimpses of blue water out toward the point.

"That's for sure," said Belford, walking out further through the thick vegetation. As he turned to see how far the cove went inland, he fell to his knees.

Davison, Bishop and Cutter walked out to see what caught his eye. Like statues, they stood in awe. Laying half on her side, covered in moss and vines, with her keel and a portion of her side buried, was the HMS YORK.

Davison lifted his musket over his shoulder then wiped the sweat off his brow. "We've sailed for months on end, to the far side of the world for this single moment, Lads. That adventure has ended, and now a new adventure will start. If Captain Payne be still alive, we'll strike out from here and find him."

"We will at that," said Bishop, keeping his eyes glued on the crippled frigate.

"Let's be off. Captain Flynn will want this news fast," said Davison, turning for the passage.

As they went to enter, Belford stopped. "Did you hear that?"

"Hear what?" asked Cutter.

"It sounded like hissing."

"Hissing?" questioned Davison.

"It must have been the wind," suggested Bishop.

"Maybe you're right," replied Belford, looking back at the York.

"C'mon, let's go," pushed Cutter.

Deep in the bowels of the rotting ship, a miniature giant sat there watching over her babies. She was a formidable predator that would lash out at anything to protect them. Today, she only hissed a warning.

"There they are," someone shouted.

Flynn lifted his spyglass. The four men were waving their hands while running toward the boat. Once they got there, the men at the landing quickly shoved off and rowed hard toward the ship.

"What did you find?" asked Flynn.

"Let us come aboard," replied Davison, climbing the ladder.

Anxious to hear, the entire crew gathered around.

Davison waited until they had all gained the main deck before telling 'em.

"Captain, Lady Knox... men... the York is there; she's on that island," boosted Davison.

The crew cheered, elated to have come this far to actually find it.

As the men celebrated, Catherine stood there stunned. "Is it true?" she asked.

Davison couldn't tell if she were happy or upset. "Yes, we found her."

She looked at Bishop. "We did," he assured her.

She looked at Belford and Cutter.

"We wouldn't lie to you," said Cutter.

As if someone had let all the air out of the balloon, her expression went slack. She stepped up and kissed each one on the cheek. After she did, her knees gave way and she completely broke down. crumbling to the deck sobbing.

Cutter went to bend down. Flynn halted him while waving at Doc Ryan. He knelt beside her and gently placed his hand on her shoulder. "It's OK. You can let it all out," he whispered, feeling tears welling up into his own eyes.

He then looked up and asked for a clean handkerchief. The crew never saw Woodward move so fast. He ran down the ladder and was back in seconds.

"Here," said Ryan, handing it to her.

Catherine took the cloth and cried even more. The entire crew standing there felt the emotional weight she had been carrying all this time. A moment ago, there were 49 crewmembers. In an instant, there were 49 knights standing around her - each willing to sacrifice their lives to find Thomas Payne, *her* captain.

Flynn waved Bishop and Davison to the side. "Where is she?" he asked, keeping his focus on Catherine sitting there.

"She's on the other side of the point," replied Bishop. "Out there between those rock columns is a hidden cove."

"Any signs of the crew?"

"We came upon one poor soul. His remains were lying in a passageway we discovered."

"Would it be wise to go forth from here or sail around?"

"I'd sail around to the point and see if there is a better advantage. If not, we can always return, Captain," replied Davison.

"Alright," he said. "Bos'n Cutter, have several men secure that boat and leave her in the water. Sailing Master Ludwig, put our sheets into the wind."

"Aye, Sir."

"Mr. Bishop, muster the crew."

"Aye, Captain."

Flynn walked over to Catherine. "Here, let me help you up."

She raised her hand for him to take it. On her feet, the two walked over to the rail. Catherine wiped her tears then blew her nose.

"It sure is a beautiful day, isn't it?" he said, seemingly gazing up at the blue sky overhead.

His words were off keel. They were something one would not say in a moment like this. It caught her off guard and made her laugh. "Yes, it is a beautiful day, Richard," she sniffled.

"Today, for some odd reason, I'll let that slide," he mused with a pleasant smile.

"Good," she laughed.

"The York is here Milady; it's time to find your captain."

"That's right, for I didn't come all this way to call you Richard, Captain Flynn."

Flynn chuckled. "You want to know something?"

"What's that?"

"Thomas Payne is a very lucky man."

"You tell him that when you see him."

"I will... Shall we?" he replied, escorting her aft.

Up on the quarterdeck, Flynn waited a moment to speak to his crew in ranks.

"Men, as you just heard, we are within a yardarm length of the York. After all that we have gone through, all that we have endured is now standing before us. Leave it to the crew of the Lara May to come up with the bounty."

The crew cheered.

"Now, a year ago, when I met with Catherine, and she said that she wanted to hire my ship and crew to take on such a task as this, I thought it insane: insane to travel to the far side of the world in search of a captain that had lost a battle - his ship sunk and reported dead.

"In the passing days, after our second meeting together, my thoughts had changed. I could go on with my meager life, my meager way of making a living onboard the Lara May until I was too old to sail, or... I could do something that would resurrect my life. For honest purpose, gentlemen.... I was already a dead man who had given up."

His words stunned the crew.

"It's not in each man to seek honor, glory, or fame. Some of you may want to keep yourself safe, as like a turtle that can safely stow away inside his shell when danger approaches. Nevertheless, I say this to you all. You can decide to be a turtle or a shark.

"Neither I, nor any man here will despise, or think one a coward for staying back. I only seek volunteers to go with me onto this island in search of Thomas Payne."

As the crew whispered amongst themselves, Catherine stood there in awe. In her lifetime, she had heard the king speak, her father speak, and many high-ranking officials, but she had never heard anything like that. His heartfelt words even gave her the courage to strike forth from this floating world called the Lara May and go onto the island.

"Captain, Flynn," shouted Cutter.

Flynn, along with his officers, looked down at him standing in the middle.

"The men and I did not come all this way for nothing."

"Go on with your words."

"Not one man here thinks of himself as a stinking sea turtle. We are all sharks seeking honor, glory, and fame."

"Fair enough, but understand one thing: even sharks can be killed. I lay that at your feet... for some of us here may not return - including myself."

"We've all decided to go, Captain," someone shouted.

"I bid you well in that, but as you know, not everyone can go. Those ordered to stay behind will have our backs. That too has honor and glory, for without the protection of this ship, those going ashore will be counted as dead men."

"How will you decide?" asked Hildegard.

"Leave that with me," replied Flynn. "While we set out around the point, I'll sit with my officers... for some of them are staying back as well."

The crew agreed.

"Shall we, Lady Knox?" he then said, waving his hand toward the ladder.

She stood there a second studying his eyes.

He could see a question within them. "Yes, what is it?"

"I was just wondering how long you'll give us to search for Thomas and his crew."

"That depends on the ship's provisions. The men staying will have to eat. Ourselves, we'll take enough for each man to live on for a week. After that, we'll gather what we can from the island."

Catherine nodded, knowing both sides; those staying back and those going would have to fend for themselves. She was hoping they'd stay until they found Thomas, or found any signs that he and his crew had actually survived. The latter, she thought, of finding such signs would convince Flynn of continuing their search - no matter how long it took. The men left on the Lara May could fish and hunt near the shoreline, keeping an ever-watchful presence on the ship.

Inside his cabin, Flynn sat with his officers and Catherine. To pick a crew would not be easy, for seafaring experts had to remain onboard.

That was Flynn's first assignment. He picked Smith and Sailing Master Ludwig to stay back and take charge. The helmsmen would be Seamen Gilchrest and Ferret. Those four alone could make their way to the Fijian islands, and from there - back to England if his search party was not back in time. His only order to Mr. Smith was he had to circle the island and fire flares before departing. If any flares were returned, he would know they were still alive.

The next conversation was on who was going. Doc Ryan, Davison, Bishop, Cutter, Hildegard and Johan would be his primary men, along with Ezekiel and Mobee.

He knew Catherine was going to fight his decision on bringing the boys. When she made her case for them staying behind, he stood up and walked over to the bay windows.

"In your world, Lady Knox, boys grow up under the guidance of their parents. In my world, boys come aboard and become men. You know in your heart of hearts that Mobee and Ezekiel have done just that: become men."

Catherine sat there looking across at Flynn's officers. Not one was going to rise to her defense.

"Your fond love for them is apparent," continued Flynn. "However, Mobee became my son when I took him in. Ezekiel, on the other hand, lost his parents to the plague; are you aware of that?"

"He did mention it to me."

"His love for ships and sailing were first recognized by his aunt and uncle. They'd always find Ezekiel down at the pier talking to sailors. One night, his uncle Ben came to the Trade Wind to see if I would take him aboard. I was just a young lad like him when I caught the dreadful bug to live out my life at sea. I would not refuse the boy a chance to see if he could make it."

"And he has," she interrupted.

Flynn slowly turned from the window and looked at her sitting there. "They'll be in good hands, won't they gentlemen?"

"They will at that," replied Davison.

"Alright," Flynn said, taking his seat. "Besides the ones I picked, I want ten good men. Now I know they all raised their hands to volunteer, but not everyone is suited for a mission like this. Therefore, Mr. Davison and Mr. Bishop, get with Bos'n Cutter and pick out those who *you* believe have the experience for such a task. The rest will stay back."

"Aye, Captain," they said and departed.

Mysterious Island

"In all me days, in all me life, the sea has brought me good faith. I feel harpooned now: cursed by me 'dallion. What lies within, will strike and forever more me bones will lie in the murky depths below.

"Those who seek fame and fortune, who seek honor and glory, will soon realize they come with a price. A tally is on each man's head that goes blindly onto this island. Mark me words, some will never sing a seafaring song, or drink a toast at the Blue Dragon. Their names may not be forgotten, but their souls will forever more be lost."

"Quit your moaning, or I'll harpoon ya," spat Cutter, walking up behind him in the berthing below.

Johan turned seeing him standing there with his hands on his waist. He had that Cutter's look, the one that said - get to work, or I'll lay ya over the side.

"You want to scare 'em before they've even stepped foot onto this island?" he whispered.

"Why... I..."

"Captain Flynn will have your hide he hears ya speaking like that," he interrupted.

Johan lowered his eyes to the floor.

"I'm going to give you a mission."

Johan slowly looked up from the floor while lifting one brow.

"Mobee and Ezekiel - I want you to stay close to 'em, you hear me?"

"Yarr, me Lad. Ol' Johan has already sought fit to keep them abreast. If ever harm came to either one, I'd surely beg to be tossed overboard."

"Good," replied Cutter, turning and facing the crew. "Those chosen, get what you're taking on deck. Mr. Davison will be handing out the weapons, I'll be handing out your supplies, and Woodward will issue your provisions," he continued, heading for the ladder.

Hildegard walked over to Johan.

"Don't tell me you have words?"

"I don't. Just a warning."

"I've been warned."

"I heard Cutter. It's not Flynn you'd have to worry about; it's Mr. Davison. If he hears ya speaking like that, he'll have you by the throat."

Johan could already feel the big man's grip. "If it came to that, I'd harpoon me self."

"Hurry up... pack your things, they're waiting for us," grumbled Hildegard, heading for the ladder.

Johan shoved the few items he was taking inside his gunny sack, then headed for the ladder. On his way up, he whispered, "If me ever had a wish, I'd wish I'd be singing a seafaring song while toasting our success at the Blue Dragon."

As he gained the main deck, Cutter was barking orders. "Alright, fall in line to get your weapons, supplies and provisions."

The ten men chosen got in line. Johan waited in the back. As he stood there, he watched Lady Knox showing Mobee and Ezekiel the proper grip on their swords. They looked like pint-sized warriors with their bows and spears crossed over their shoulders, their arrows stowed neatly inside their quivers and packing a pistol in each of their belts.

Not that he worried they couldn't defend themselves. He witnessed their skill with the bow on the Island of Sumba, shooting fish and octopus in the shallow water alongside the native boys.

"What cha taking, Johan?" asked Davison.

"I'll be taking a musket, pistol, machete, sword, and toss in a pouch of them explosives you made."

"Mr. Bishop and Bos'n Cutter will be carrying the hand grenades. You'll get the rest along with some rope. Each man will carry four meters."

"Harr, me Lad, I hope you're beside me at the Blue Dragon," he replied, moving over toward Cutter and Woodward.

Davison stood back with that comment. He dropped it when Flynn walked over. "That's the last man, Sir."

Flynn nodded and turned toward his party. "Take a place on deck until Ludwig brings us in close off the point."

Up at the bow, Catherine leaned against the rail watching the ship slowly make her way around the tip. The crew felt she wanted to be alone. Doc Ryan thought no one should be alone at a time like this. He walked up the ladder and stood alongside her. She gave him a slight glance and then focused back on the island.

One would think she was worried to just discover that only the ship had made it this far, or they'd find only skeletal remains nearby. You cannot comfort those kind of thoughts, so he just stood there gazing at the formidable landscape.

"He's here, Doc," she whispered, keeping her eyes forward.

Ryan said nothing.

"Do you believe in a woman's intuition?"

"My wife has it," he replied. "Does yours tell ya that Thomas is still alive?"

"Mine senses his heartbeat."

"You should work with me. I could use a person who can tell what's wrong with a man as soon as they enter my office."

Catherine laughed.

Ryan turned, placed his hand over hers on the rail. "If he is on this island, we'll find him."

"I'm worried about Captain Flynn," she replied, looking over Ryan's shoulder at the crew preparing the one remaining lifeboat on deck. The other boat was still in the water, tied alongside the ship.

"Worried about what?"

She set her eyes upon him and answered, "Calling off the search before we do find him."

"Leave that to me."

Catherine looked at him confused.

"I may be just a medical doctor who hasn't a clue about sailing, but I've known Captain Flynn longer than any man aboard this ship. We have been friends from our youth."

"All this time, and I'm now finding this out?"

"It's something we don't discuss. As young men, I took to the injured; he took to the sea. We've had our time apart, but trust me, Captain Flynn and I are still the best of friends."

She went to speak. He raised his hand.

"So long as we don't find ourselves in dire hardship, Flynn will remain. I don't think he wants to return to England without Captain Payne. He knows there is a price on his head."

"But I have the king's ear."

Ryan nodded. "Let's just find him and bring him home, shall we?" he replied, departing her company.

"Alright, get that boat ready," shouted Cutter. "You four climb down in the other and be ready to shove off. I want soundings done once we round the point."

Catherine turned seaward, catching the waves crashing against the massive rocks. *This looks dangerous.* Before her thoughts continued, she heard Flynn barking aft.

"Come right; bring her to half-sails."

"Aye, Captain," replied Smith, waving to the men sitting up on the yardarms.

"Mr. Bishop, as soon as we have a sounding, drop the anchor."

"Aye, Sir."

"Bos'n Cutter, have your men in the boats call out as we make our turn."

"Aye, Captain," he replied, looking down at the boats - one tied off at the stern, one at the bow. "Keep at it men."

"No bottom yet," one shouted up.

As the sails were hoisted and the Lara May made her turn, the cove came into view. All hands stood at the rail anxiously waiting to see; and see they did. Way in the back, where the tide settled and then went back out to sea, there was the York: sitting there, listing on her side.

"Eight fathoms," a crewmember called up from the boat.

Flynn ordered the anchor dropped. The first sound was the splash of the anchor. The second sound was moans, gasps and wails from the crew seeing the crippled ship.

The death of a vessel is hard to experience, even harder seeing the jungle taking her as a prize. Her stern was gone. She had a gaping hole in her side. Moss and vines hung from everything, along her yardarms, rails, and mast. The only remnants of her sails were the parts tied heavily to the arms. They are the lungs of a ship; they're what makes or breaks her. The tattered pieces of cloth hanging there looked like draped flags over a rotting wooden coffin.

When Catherine took the ladder down and waded alongside Flynn, it was apparent in her stride and expression that she was utterly distressed seeing the York in such conditions.

"For all I see, it pains me how she gained the island there. I'm surprised she wasn't busted up along thcsc brcakcrs and eddies," he said.

She looked into his eyes, watched his lips moving, then stared at the York.

"It's a terrible death to witness, Catherine, but there she be, still in one piece."

She nodded, keeping her eyes forward.

It pained him to see her so depressed. "We did not come this far to throw wreaths and say farewell. We came to find Thomas, and that is what we intend to do."

"That we will," she replied, slowly looking at him.

With that comment, Flynn turned toward his crew. "All hands going ashore, grab your gear. Bos'n Cutter, form up the beach guard. As soon as we land, I want the beach secured."

"Aye, Captain."

"Mr. Smith."

"Yes, Sir.

"Now remember. If we find any evidence, we'll report it to the boat crew. During our time searching the island, we'll fire off flares, pinpointing our location. Keep the Lara May abreast of our flares."

"Aye, Captain."

Those going ashore were:

Captain Flynn, Catherine Knox, Doc Ryan, Mr. Davison, Mr. Bishop, Cutter, Hildegard, Johan Bailer, Ezekiel and Mobee, and 10 ex royal navy sailors, merchants and Marines - all hardened crewmembers, skilled in the art of war.

They climbed down with their muskets, swords, and pistols. They climbed down with their machetes, bows and arrows. They climbed down carrying enough gunpowder and ball, along with their personal items and provisions. The last thing lowered was torches made from hardwood railing wrapped with sailing cloth dipped in oil used for sealing the ship's waterline.

Flynn looked up at the crew from the lifeboat.

"If you do find any evidence that some have survived, permission to move the ship to the leeward side of the island and wait," requested Smith.

"Best you do. We don't know what low tide looks like here."

"Good luck and Godspeed," said Smith with a salute.

"Take us ashore," ordered Flynn.

With his eyes remaining on Smith, the two boats rowed ashore.

27

As the tidal seas swept against the massive columns and washed out again, the boat crew strained, rowing through the turbulent water. Upon reaching shore, Flynn assisted Catherine onto dry land.

"You six, secure the beach. The rest of you, grab the gear. Once we're ready, the security detail will go in first."

As the men with muskets guarded the group, and the boats were unloaded, Catherine did not wait. She drew her sword and headed inland toward the York's final resting spot: an inlet deluged with shallow water, mud and plants.

While slicing a path through the foliage, nothing seemed to matter. Not the men, her father, nor the king or queen.

"Lady Knox," shouted Mobee.

She did not waver in her stride; her thoughts were somewhere else.

"Lady Knox," yelled Ezekiel.

Flynn looked back seeing her walking toward the ship. "Damn," he spat. "Catherine... wait."

As if in a trance, her eyes slowly drifted off the York, taking in her surroundings. One hundred meters back, a mesa of granite fifty feet high went completely across the northern section of the island. Over the centuries, parts of the wall had given way, leaving piles of rocks, boulders and hanging cliffs.

At the top of the mesa, the jungle took over once again. In front of the wall was a lush tropical landscape of various plants, palm trees, deadfall and rocks. The ground was moist, the air very humid. The sounds of birds and insects drifted throughout the inlet.

When Catherine reached the York's midsection, she stopped. Glancing up at the mast, along the yardarms and then down at the main deck from bow to stern, she thought for all purposes - no one, not one soul, could have survived on this wreckage of a ship.

The gaping hole in her side seemed bigger now than when a cannon ball drove through it. The stern and rudder were completely gone, along with her sails.

In that quiet moment, in the midst of the inlet cove, Catherine's emotions welled up within her eyes. *My darling Captain, the love of my life... in the deepest part of my soul, I knew your ship had survived the horror of war and storm. My heart senses that somewhere on this God forsaken island you are here; you have survived.*

"Catherine," shouted Flynn, hurrying to catch up.

She drew in the moist air, then exhaled while glancing back at him.

"I ordered the security detail to come in first."

She seemingly gazed at him, determined he would not see her emotionally upset again. *Why* the York's lifeboats came to her suddenly, she did not know, but used them as an excuse for her unsettledness.

"Catherine," again said Flynn.

"Do you see this?" she harped.

Flynn took in the York. "Yes, what be your troubles."

"Where are the lifeboats?"

"We found a part of one buried in the sand, along with a boot and torn shirt," said Davison, walking up.

"There were two."

"You think whoever survived used it to leave this island?" questioned Flynn.

"They could have."

"Hey, over here," someone shouted.

They turned, seeing a group searching an area full of ship debris. The three headed over.

Along a clear section of vegetation, next to a huge downed tree, stood four wooden crosses. Catherine read the names; Murray, Holder, Larkin, and Rose.

"Check this out," said Hildegard, removing the overgrowth away from the rotting trunk.

Hidden within the plants, moss, and vines was a wooden plank. Carved in the middle was an arrow pointing toward the granite wall.

"There's your answer, Catherine. Whoever survived, headed inland," said Flynn.

She rubbed her jaw looking in that direction. *My intuitions are right - he is here.*

"There must be numerous passages at the base," commented Bishop.

"Will you look at that?" interrupted Seaman Jones, pointing at an eight-inch dragonfly sitting on a large leaf.

"I've never seen one so big, have you Captain?" asked Seaman Jamison.

Flynn took in the large insect. "Doc Ryan," he said, wanting advice from the bookworm.

"Why ask Doc Ryan? You should be asking Johan," snapped Catherine. "He said he saw the island within his medallion."

"Harr, Melady. Me heart shrinks seeing the dragonfly. Me warned long ago that we should turn back. Me now fear we may come across things we don't want to encounter."

"Mr. Bailer," she spat, feeling prickles up her arm.

"Catherine," scolded Flynn.

She rubbed her arms, staring at the Captain.

In the silence, Bishop turned in every direction. "What else could be here that big?" he questioned, facing Flynn.

Flynn shook his head watching Doc Ryan studying the insect. "Let's just hope only these are big," he said, standing erect and locking eyes with Flynn.

He could sense the jitteriness within the men. "Bos'n Cutter, go back and report to the boat crew our finding of the crosses and arrows pointing inland."

"Aye Sir,"

"No matter what we encounter, big or small, we'll be on our own from here on out. Just keep your wits about ya, gentlemen."

"What's your plan, Captain?" asked Davison.

Surrounded by his party, he laid it out. "We'll stay together, but in groups. You five and Mr. Davison are *group one*. You five and Mr. Bishop are *group two*. Catherine, Hildegard,

Cutter, Johan and those two," he said, pointing to Mobee and Ezekiel standing near the York, are with me, along with Doc Ryan - *group 3*. Even as we move out together, you stay close to the officer I just placed you with, understand? Don't let them out of your sight."

The men nodded.

Catherine glanced back at Mobee and Ezekiel climbing the York's tattered rope ladder to what was left of the main deck. "What in God's name..." her voice broke off.

The men turned to see.

"Mobee, Ezekiel," shouted Flynn.

"Someone has to search the ship," hollered Mobee.

"It's now stable, Lad," he replied, waving for them to climb down.

When they came abreast, Catherine said not a word, but raised one brow - a sign of her disapproval.

"Alright," said Flynn, "let's split up and search for a way through."

Ten minutes later, Bishop called out.

The men gathered.

"I'd say it's up there, Captain."

Flynn spotted another wooden plank with an arrow carved in the middle on a rock ledge just above 'em. "Climb up and see, Hildegard."

When he reached the top, just below him, on the other side, was a flat section that lead into a pass. He quickly called down his finding.

"Be careful going up," cautioned Flynn.

As the search party proceeded onward, a terrifying beast nesting in the belly of the York peered out through a hole in the side. All six eyes glared at the prey climbing the rocks. The creature hissed, turned, and headed for the opening in the rear.

Down it went to the shallow, muddy water below. There, it crawled along the ol' dead ship toward the granite wall.

When it reached the top of the ridge, it arched its grayish black thorax and lifted its front hairy legs. With its fangs dripping, it let out a call. Those of its kind crept out of their lairs.

After jumping down, Flynn stepped forward studying the pass. The flooring was four meters wide. The jagged walls, five meters high. On top, on either side of the walls, large leafed plants and vines hung down from dead trees crossing over.

By any stretch of imagination, Flynn knew this wasn't going to be easy. How far the pass went was beyond him, but there she be: a way into the interior of the island.

Resting often due to the humid heat, they traveled for most of the day. By evening, they came upon a large opening that had another pass heading west. They were traveling south.

"Should we check it out?" asked Cutter, anxious to investigate.

"No, we'll stay here for the night. Group two, climb up and gather some wood," replied Flynn.

Catherine came alongside him.

"Find yourself a spot to settle in. We have a long day ahead of us tomorrow," he said.

She nodded and walked over to Mobee and Ezekiel getting comfortable against the wall.

"Alright," said Flynn, "keep your weapons near ya tonight. Be ready for anything."

As the evening waned, slipping into darkness, several men sat near the fire pits talking about the day. Sleep overcame some, while others continued chatting.

Through the lush canopy above, the stars were fully out. The moon, it seemed, wanted to stay away. Maybe it feared the eight-legged predators crawling across the jungle mesa toward the pass below.

"I've gotta relieve myself," said Seaman Jones, getting up.

"Don't be long," replied Davison, tossing another log on the fire.

Jones waved and continued onward into the western pass. When he went in a way, he stepped behind a boulder and set his musket down. As he stood there, silently overhead, long hairy legs appeared, followed by a hideous head with four menacing eyes and fangs. It was a large rock spider the size of a melon.

The spider's front leg tapped Jones' head. Jones quickly brushed his hair thinking it was a bug.

The spider crawled down closer then gave a wicked hiss. Jones quickly looked up. Before he could scream, the thing slightly turned, lifted its abdomen and sprayed a thick silky webbing all over his face.

Petrified, Jones stumbled backward, frantically trying to remove the substance. The spider then leaped upon him. With a powerful bite, it drove its fangs deep into the side of his cheek and neck. The effect was immediate; the poison raced to Jones' heart. His eyes glazed over, a white bubbly froth oozed from his mouth.

Two more spiders quickly jumped on, sinking their fangs into his flesh. As he laid there dead, they spun poor Jones in webbing and dragged him down the dark western pass to enjoy their meal in peace.

"What is taking Jones so long?" asked Davison, getting up from the fire.

Chit-chit, chit-chit...

"What is that?" questioned Bishop, standing and looking about.

"I don't know, but I don't like the sound of it," whispered Davison, picking up his musket.

Before Bishop could speak, a group of menacing spiders crawled up to the ridge above their heads on either side.

"Get up, get up!!" shouted Davison.

The frantic tone in his voice brought everyone to their feet. Not knowing what was happening, some grabbed their muskets, while others drew their pistols. It wasn't until Catherine let out a death-defying scream that everyone looked up. From out of the darkness, the horrifying eight-legged creatures started crawling down the walls.

Flynn placed his hand on Catherine's shoulder. She screamed, quickly turned, almost striking him with her sword. Within his eyes sat a fear she had never seen before.

"Grab your gear and move back," he shouted.

"Torches, light the torches," yelled Cutter.

Several lit torches, swinging them this way and that, keeping the spiders at bay. Overhead, the spiders began spraying their webbing down upon the party. It clung to their clothing, their hair and faces.

In the frenzy, shots rang out. Mobee and Ezekiel took to their bows, catching those crawling down the walls toward them. Others wielded swords and machetes at the ones on the ground. Spiders coiled and screeched, dying of their wounds.

Suddenly, two leaped upon Seaman Hill, sinking their fangs deep into his shoulder and back. Johan cursed, driving his sword through one's abdomen. The thing wailed, falling off. Mobee quickly put an arrow through the other spider.

Davison reached down and started dragging Hill. Hill never moved.

"Leave him," shouted Doc Ryan. "He's dead."

As the group continued down the southern pass, the spiders converged onto Hill, spinning him in a thick white cocoon.

"We can't let them get behind us from above," shouted Flynn. "As we keep moving, toss grenades up and over the wall."

Davison and Bishop quickly began throwing the grenades. The explosions were deafening, sending spider parts down upon them.

As the passage turned and a few looked back to see where they were going, someone shouted. Flynn glanced back. The pass was covered in webbing, blocking their way. "Torches to the rear," he yelled.

Some in the front raced back.

"Burn it," shouted Flynn.

In the mayhem and confusion, one spider slowly crept up to the ridge, peering down at its prey. It leaped onto Ezekiel, making him fall. Before he could wrestle it off, it sunk its fangs into his shoulder. The pain was instant. He let out a cry.

Catherine turned, seeing the wretched thing. She quickly drove her sword through its abdomen. The spider wailed and hissed. Catherine twisted the blade and then cut upward and through the beast. It fell off Ezekiel, dead.

"Doc Ryan," she yelled.

Ryan glanced over. It was Ezekiel. He rushed over. "Captain," he shouted.

Flynn stepped back from the fight, seeing the boy. "Mr. Davison, pick him up and let's go. The rest of you keep moving back."

After fighting their way through the trap and continuing down the pass, they stepped out onto a flat section, the southern edge of the mesa. Right below, seven meters down, was a mantel of rocks jutting out from the granite wall. On one side, Bishop spotted an old rope tied off hanging over the ridge. "Captain Payne went this way," he shouted.

"Hurry, secure some more ropes and lower Ezekiel," ordered Flynn. "You four keep them at bay with your torches as we head down."

When the party was below, Seaman Adams tossed his torch and quickly took hold of the ropes. The others guarding the flat section did the same until all were standing with Flynn on the large mantel.

As the spiders crawled down the wall after them, Flynn's men and Catherine moved back - ready to fight. Then suddenly, the spiders stopped.

"Why aren't they coming?" asked Davison, half out of breath.

"I don't know," replied Bishop.

Flynn turned, looking down the mantel at a bluff below. From there, the thick dense jungle took over. He slowly looked up at the spiders sitting there hissing. "They're not coming because they're afraid of something down here."

"What could they be afraid of?" asked Catherine.

"I don't know."

"Captain," shouted Doc Ryan.

Flynn and Catherine walked over. Ryan had cut Ezekiel's shirt open, exposing the wound.

"Mr. Davison, have your party stand guard; the rest of you bring your torches over here," said Flynn.

Mobee knelt. His dear friend looked bad, pale white. "You hang in there, you hear me?" he pleaded.

"Mobee," whispered Ezekiel.

"I'm right here."

"I'm sorry, Mobee."

"There's nothing to be sorry about."

"I don't want to die."

"You're not going to die. Right, Doc?" asked Mobee, staring at him.

The telling look in Ryan's eyes said he was.

"Do something, Doc, or I'll shoot you," yelled Mobee, drawing his pistol.

"Mobee," said Catherine, kneeling next to him. She slowly removed the pistol from his grip.

"Don't worried, Mobee. It's not the doctor's fault," gasped Ezekiel.

Tears welled up in Mobee eyes watching his friend dying right before him. "I love you, Ezekiel," he whispered, taking his hand.

"I love you too, Mobee," he whispered back, squeezing it tight.

With that, Mobee looked on as Ezekiel's eyes glazed over and he stopped breathing. It was instant. Mobee crumbled to the ground sobbing like a child.

Catherine gathered him into her arms. Her face was a mess from crying too.

The men standing there felt the same crushing blow. They loved Ezekiel as well.

Ryan stood up looking at Flynn. The captain's face was a ball of pain.

"Their poison is worse than the venom of a snake," he said.

"Worse than the black plague," added Johan, glancing down at Ezekiel lying there dead. In that dreadful moment, his words to Hildegard washed over him. *I'd harpoon me self if anything happened to either one of them.* That thought turned ol' Johan inside out. His heart was broken, smashed against the remorseful shoal.

28

At daybreak the following morning, the men, along with Catherine, sat there completely spent. In the stillness, the spiders gone, they realized three were missing. Besides Ezekiel and Hill, Jones, Davenport, and Butterfield were not there.

During the terrifying night, no one knew those three were taken. The loss of five men sat in Flynn's eyes; his face drawn, he hardly spoke.

Catherine didn't know what to say; neither did the men. It wasn't until Davison got up and stretched his legs that Catherine got up as well.

Flynn glanced at the pair.

"Captain," said Davison. "It's time to move on.

Flynn nodded, getting to his feet.

Filled with remorse, they proceeded down off the jagged ridge to the grassy bluff below. Upon reaching it, the entire group took in the vast jungle with two towering mountains in the center of the island. Just over the green canopy, the blue water with its endless waves seemed to touch the sky on the horizon.

Anywhere else, one would have said it was paradise, but this was no paradise. It was, however, a splendid spot to bury Ezekiel, overlooking such stunning beauty.

Flynn called Mobee over.

His head down, shoulders sagging, Mobee came abreast of him.

"I think this is a fine place to bury Ezekiel, don't cha think?"

Mobee lifted his head gazing out over the landscape, then cast his eyes further out at the sparkling blue sea. "I think so too, Captain," his words sounding shaky.

Flynn deeply inhaled, feeling his pain. "Bos'n Cutter, form a burial detail," his voice cracked.

"Aye, Sir."

"I'd like to help," said Mobee.

"You don't have to."

"Yes, I do."

"A man has to do what a man has to do. Go on now," replied Flynn, patting his back.

He walked over, took a small shovel from Cutter, then looked about.

"You see a place?"

"Over there next to that tree."

"Alright," replied Cutter, "we'll bury him there."

With Ezekiel wrapped in his blanket, each man walked up to pay his respects. Mobee was last - it's the way he wanted it.

Kneeling, Mobee placed his hand on Ezekiel wrapped inside. "What words can I use to tell ya how dear you were to me? Like a brother I never had. You were my best friend and comrade. I thought we'd be together forever," he sniffled, "but it didn't turn out that way." With that, his tears flowed freely down his cheeks.

Through his sobbing pain, the entire group emotionally looked on. Johan was the worse. He was riddled with sorrow.

With a mound of dirt and nice wooden cross over the young lad, the men and Catherine sat there in mourning: mourning for Ezekiel, and... in mourning for the other four they had lost last night.

Johan looked over at Mobee, grief-stricken, sitting there. He picked up a stick and started carving the end. Without looking up from his knife, he spoke from his heart. "You, Lad, have the spirit of a lion," he said, then paused.

Mobee glanced up.

"I've been nagging and kneeing the whole way... me sorry soul should be laid to waste at the yardarms, me neck dangling from a rope. Maybe even keelhauled for fearing me bones would never see another day."

Catherine shifted her eyes on Flynn. He gave her a look to let him go on.

"We lost good men last night, but losing Ezekiel is just too hard for ol' Johan to bear. I've sailed with the finest. I've sailed with criminals, and even with Scar, but never have me sailed with the likes of you and Ezekiel.

"You came to us as young lads, and right before me eyes, you turned into men. Everyone here can surely attest to that."

Nods and yeas went out from the group. Even Catherine agreed.

"Whatever we face from here on out, ol' Johan will be as sharp as the tip of me sword; I swear. Just like you Mobee; just like you."

As the group sat there drifting on Johan's words, Catherine felt herself adrift. She placed her finger upon her cheek, catching the tears.

"Ol' Johan," replied Mobee. "You are the keel, the ribs and the planks. You are the mast and sails. The blue water belongs to you, my dear friend."

"I thank thee, Lad, for your reassurance."

"Reassurance," repeated Mobee. "One day I'll teach you how to spell that word. Maybe even teach you proper English," he replied, looking at Catherine with a faint, teary-eyed smile.

It made her smile. It made everyone smile; some even laughed.

"Oh now, Mobee.... you want ol' Johan barred from the Blue Dragon? Worse, they'd hog tie me to the rafters if I waltzed in speaking like the king."

"No, we can't have that, can we?" Mobee lightheartedly chuckled.

Sometimes in remorse, the heart finds a way to set itself free from the sorrow it feels. Everyone was surprised that it came from Mobee - the one whose heart was completely shattered - losing his best friend.

"No, we can't," Flynn weighed in. "What we can have is group *one* - go down the bluff and find us a path."

"Aye, Captain," said Bishop.

"The rest of you gather your gear."

Cutter walked over to him. "We've been up all night, Sir. I think the men would like to rest a bit more."

"We will, but not here."

Cutter understood what he meant with those eight-legged creatures nearby.

"Captain, I believe we found the way," Bishop called up.

"Great, let us be off."

Through the thick vegetation, Bishop showed him a small trail.

"That be the way, Capt'n," agreed Johan. "I'll take point with Bos'n Cutter," he continued, raising one brow to the strong, burly seaman.

Cutter nodded, stepping up to the front.

While moving out in single file, Mobee stopped and looked back at the bluff. His heart felt like a sinking ship leaving Ezekiel behind, thousands of miles away from home. With tears rolling down his cheek, he said his last farewell. "I'll never forget you for the rest of my life," he sniffled. "I can promise you that my friend. I never will."

Catherine glanced back at Mobee.

Flynn placed his hand on her shoulder. "He'll catch up."

She nodded knowing Mobee needed that moment alone. "I'm going to miss Ezekiel."

"So am I. I loved him dearly."

As they proceeded onward through the hot, humid interior, each step they took, each stride they made, their eyes and ears were keen to the sights and sounds all around them. The wild bird calls, hoots from tree dwelling animals and the buzzing insects kept their nerves on end.

By noon, the men had had enough. They hunkered down next to a stream, sheltered by enormous hardwood trees. On the other side, a thick grove of bamboo took root in the moss-covered ground, taking its nourishment from the rich soil and slow-moving current.

Mobee, it seemed, wanted to stay close to Johan and Cutter, both of whom had taken off their boots and were soothing their tired feet in the water.

Flynn, Catherine, and Doc Ryan settled next to a tree, its roots protruding up from the ground. The cool moist soil and shade felt good as they rested.

29

Onboard the Lara May, Smith called the remaining crew to quarters.

"Lads," he said, "as you can see, that storm has caused us much pain. We now find ourselves in a fitful place with only half a crew to get this lady sea worthy again. Nevertheless, we will - with sweat and blood if need be.

"My first order is to have all decks scrubbed, the livestock and chickens brought up on deck. Then, we'll set about replacing every broken board, mend all the tattered sails and wash 'em over the side. When completed, the entire crew, including myself, will paint this ol' gal."

Seaman Drake raised his hand.

"Yes, what it be?"

"We haven't been on dry land for months, Mr. Smith."

That was a good question. "I suppose you're right, Lad. Today, we'll pull anchor and find us a safe harbor on the eastern side of the island to get the Lara May repaired. I'll give the crew this day off, but tomorrow, we start. Fair enough?"

A resounding cheer went out from the group.

"Mr. Ludwig, see to the anchor detail."

"Aye, Mr. Smith."

"Mr. Woodward."

"Yes, Sir."

"I want my bedding brought up and laid out on the poop deck."

"What if it rains, Sir?"

"So, let it rain. I'll not lie in comfort, gentlemen... not with half our crew and Lady Knox sleeping on the jungle floor every night."

They all nodded.

"Alright... haul up anchor, drop sails and prepare us to swing about."

With a good ocean breeze, the Lara May made her turn and sailed around the northern tip to the eastern side of the island. Passing the granite mesa, Smith spotted a tiny harbor with an inlet stream; its water flowing back into the ocean. Above the stream in the back, a beautiful waterfall cascaded down from the rugged cliffs. It was a good place to repair the ship for when Flynn's party returned.

After dropping anchor, Smith once again mustered the crew. They all drew straws to see who would go ashore first.

The first ten men rowed to the sandy beach and got out. Some stayed to swim, while others walked inland toward the waterfall.

With muskets and pistols in hand, they navigated along the bank of the stream. Nearing the sheltered pool, Seaman Coleman halted, putting his hand up. Those behind froze. He slowly turned and whispered, "Wild boar."

Within the eyes of each man sat the pleasant smile of a fabulous meal.

Coleman waved for two men to step forward. "There they be... drinking at the edge of the pool."

"I'll take the one on the right," whispered Seaman Johnson.

"I'll take the one in the middle," said Seaman Tuttle.

"That leaves me the one to the left," murmured Coleman, aiming his musket. "One, two - fire..."

The lead balls found their mark. All three boars dropped right there.

The men on the beach and the men on the ship heard the shots. Their first instinct was to panic. All was well though, when the four carried the dead boar out and lifted them high in the air.

Smith sighed, seeing them and then went back to his position - sitting on the poop deck back aft. With his feet up, a cup of coffee in hand, his mind began to drift.

"What be on your mind, Mr. Smith?" asked Ludwig, walking up.

"I was just thinking that two weeks is not a lot of time to find someone on this island. One could spend months searching and not find Thomas - even though he is here."

"What else?" he asked, sitting alongside him.

"What if they don't return?"

"I guess we'd had to live out the rest of our lives on some island like this," replied Ludwig, turning and studying his eyes. He could see Smith thinking about that.

"I suppose you're right. There's no way we could go back and tell the king we left Catherine."

"The king," Ludwig amusingly chuckled. "I'd be more worried about her father. He'd have all our heads on spikes."

"I trust Captain Flynn will find Thomas. I've been with that man for several years now. He's no fool."

"No, he is not."

"I want someone in the crow's nest every night."

"Aye."

"Now remember... if we see a flare, we fire one back."

"Correct."

"If another flare is fired by Flynn, we move the ship up or back to stay parallel to his position. If he fires two after the first volley - we go and get him."

"That we will, Sir. Oh... before I forget."

"What?"

"All the men are sleeping out on the main deck."

"And if it rains?" he mused.

"I think someone said - so it rains."

Smith laughed. "Go see to the men. Make sure you give the next party enough time on the beach."

"Aye, aye, Sir."

When he left, Smith looked toward the beach at the men swimming. *May the Good Lord be with us, for I'll surely not leave this island without Lady Knox.* That thought made him wonder how she was faring out there in that vast jungle.

30

Flynn opened his eyes, leaning against the tree. He didn't know how long he had dozed off, but when he caught Catherine's eye, she smiled, or somewhat smiled, upon that drawn expression of hers.

"You may want to wash that stuff off," he said, nodding toward the stream.

She glanced down, not realizing she was covered in splotches of gooey webbing, spider guts and blood. It made her feel nauseous. She quickly stood up.

"Mobee, Bos'n Cutter, and Johan," said Flynn.

They walked over. "See to it that she's looked after."

"Aye, Captain."

The three escorted her down to a secluded section where the stream opened into a pool. There, she pulled off her boots, removed her pants and shirt and waded into the water with her filthy clothing. When she turned, the men were sitting with their backs to her.

"Are you coming in?"

The three looked at one another thinking she was nude.

"I have my undergarments on, gentlemen."

"C'mon, Johan, you're getting to smell like a rott'n tomato," remarked Mobee.

"Ol' Johan likes smelling like a rott'n tomato."

"Go on you two. I can't stand the smell of either one of ya," barked Cutter. "I'll watch our backs."

The three swam for a bit, then Johan got out, so Cutter could clean off. When he came up next to Mobee treading water, Mobee turned and smiled. After the heartache of losing Ezekiel, he thought he'd never see that rainbow of happiness splashed across his face, so bright and cheerful.

When he looked at Catherine, he knew why Mobee somewhat forgot his sorrow. She could wash away a man's heartache with just a tender gaze, or just spending a relaxing moment together.

When the four reentered the camp, Flynn noticed they had all gone swimming. Mobee seemed in brighter spirits; so, did Johan. When he caught Cutter's eye, he was relieved. He knew the Bos'n remained in charge; Catherine's safety was everyone's responsibility now. With that, he sent the men in groups to bathe; he was the last to go.

The following morning, before striking out, Flynn gathered the men and gave a hearty speech on the trauma they had endured.

"Gentlemen, as you well know... each man here has gone to war; each man has seen death in all its horror. We have all seen the wickedness of the sea and survived her wrath. And now," he said then paused, "we are seeing things for the very first time. Be it what it may, we'll overcome this too. Whatever is out there, in any shape, form or size, we'll defeat it. We have the weapons and most importantly, we have the intelligence to overcome what tries to kill us from here on out."

Catherine watched the men sit up. His speech seemingly giving them new hope and pride.

"Does any man here have anything to say? If so, say it now," asked Flynn.

Seaman Kettle stood up.

"Yes, Lad - what be on your mind?"

Kettle glanced at Johan and then focused on Flynn. "I thank thee, Sir for your words. I also want to thank the great serpent for his. I think we all have been nagging, whiny, and wheezing to some extent during this entire voyage. Johan was right when he said - from here on out I'll be as sharp as the tip of me sword. I think each man here will be just that, Sir - as sharp as the tip of me sword."

"Alright," said Flynn. "As sharp as the tip of me sword we go then."

The men stood up. "We're ready, Captain," said Cutter.

"Good, while you and Johan find that trail, I want you all to reorganize your pack and count your supplies."

Once the group was ready, Johan and Cutter walked across the stream, looking for the way Captain Payne and his men had traveled through the jungle.

Johan found the trail right away, heading straight for the western mountain. With the fires kicked over, they set out once again.

It was a nightmare navigating through the dense jungle. At times, the vegetation was so thick they could scarcely see the sky. If that wasn't bad enough, the buzzing large insects and heat was getting unbearable.

By mid-morning, with the temperature already soaring, they came across a clearing next to the base of the mountain. At the base, was an old landslide that met the green grass.

Catherine picked up the eerie stillness right away. "You hear that?" she asked, looking about.

"Hear what?" replied Flynn, confused.

"That's what I mean. It's too quiet. Sort of scary, don't cha think?"

He turned, looking at her.

"Captain Flynn," shouted Hildegard, breaking the spell between 'em.

"What is it?"

"Look over there."

The entire group spotted what appeared to be a cave with a rock ledge jutting out over the entrance.

"If that's a cave, it might be a bit cooler inside to rest awhile," stated Flynn.

As they neared the entrance, Seamen Jamison and Hitchcock volunteered to go in and check it out. The rest of the men dropped their packs and rested.

With a torch in one hand and a pistol in the other, the two went down a bit then stopped when the tunnel opened into a dome that had three dark passageways. The air was moist, coupled with an acidic odor.

JEFF WRIGHT
CATHERINE KNOX

"What is that awful smell?" gasped Jamison.

"I don't know, but it's worse than a bilge on a prisoner ship," remarked Hitchcock.

"Let's go back and tell 'em we ain't staying here."

As the men walked out, Hitchcock stopped and looked back. "Shh... you hear that?"

Jamison stood there listening. "It sounds like something scurrying back there."

They both held their torches high to see what was coming. "Mice you think?" questioned Hitchcock.

"It could be," said Jamison, and then... he screamed.

Out of the darkness, coming towards them, were giant black ants, one-foot long.

"Run..." shouted Hitchcock, racing toward the entrance.

Hearing the commotion, the men and Catherine quickly stood up. As the two ran out, they were shouting, "Run for your lives... ants."

Baffled, the group could not grasp the word *ants*. It made no sense, but they kept running toward the trees, then started climbing the nearest ones.

Flynn instantly thought of the spiders. He knew they did not come down for a reason. He knew what that reason was now. "Hurry, get up there," he yelled, climbing the rocks to the jagged rim over the cave.

Catherine, Bishop, and Johan made it to the ledge just in time as hordes of big black ants came pouring out from the opening.

The men scattered in every direction. Hildegard and Caleb were the last to take off. The ants homed in on both men; Hildegard kept running while Caleb took to a tree. The ants climbed up after him; the others mobbed Hildegard. He fell. They viciously piled on, biting and stinging him.

"Help me... somebody help me," Caleb shouted, kicking at the ants. When he reached the top and nowhere to go, the ants took a hold of him. They cut into his ankles, his legs with their mandibles. He viciously fought back until they were all over him.

The group below watched in horror; the screaming and yelling then seeing Caleb let go and fall through the tree - taking the ants with him. On the ground more came, stinging and biting him.

Off in the distance, someone shouted, "FREEZE... DON'T MOVE."

In the grip of panic, no one knew who was shouting.

Davison and Mobee, along with everyone on the ground, stopped in their tracks.

"I can't take this, I can't stand here and watch Hildegard down there," spat Catherine.

"IT WOULD BE WISE TO SHOOT THAT MAN. HE'S NOT GOING TO SURVIVE."

Flynn knew the moment was desperate; Hildegard and Caleb were not going to make it. "Johan," he said, nodding for him to shoot Hildegard.

With a heavy heart, Johan lifted his crossbow and aimed it at Hildegard fighting for his life. "May the Good Lord forgive me," he whispered, pulling the lever. The arrow found its mark, slamming into Hildegard's chest. He stopped moving. Johan then placed another arrow on the string and aimed it at Caleb. There was no need for him to fire. The ants had already decapitated poor Caleb.

The scene before Catherine shook her to the core, almost faint like. Johan dropped the crossbow and took her into his arms.

The sound of the bow hitting the ground, brought the ants up onto the ledge, searching for movement. Johan quickly covered Catherine's mouth. Flynn and Bishop froze, dead like. The ants crawled over Bishop's leg, up and over Flynn.

Panic sat within Catherine's eyes. She dared not move, not even breathe.

Just above them, a giant three-foot centipede was crawling down. The creature was unaware of the danger. The ants tore into it, slicing it apart. Soldier ants stood by while others took the pieces down from the ledge.

Catherine closed her eyes, trembling. She wanted to scream; she wanted to let out the sheer terror in her heart. Johan held onto her tightly until the last ant had left the ledge. "Easy now," he whispered, letting her go.

"I think I'm going to be sick," she murmured.

"Hold fast, Lady Knox."

The man on the bluff watched the awful scene before him. There was nothing worse than taking someone's life to save 'em from such horrendous pain and suffering. He shouted a warning to those on the ground, so they would not end up like that. "ALL YOU ON THE GROUND... STAY STANDING SILL. THEY ONLY ATTACK SOMETHING MOVING."

As the ants began dismembering Hildegard and Caleb, each man held his breath, watching the largest ones, *the soldiers*, standing there as if guarding the bloodshed.

Mobee cringed, hearing the sounds of chomping. He dared not look back as the ants were cutting through Hildegard's tendons and bones. Then suddenly, he felt a large ant crawling up his leg. He tried not to tremble as it continued up his back and then perched on his shoulder.

"Don't move," whispered Davison alongside him.

Mobee rolled his eyes toward the thing. In all his born days, he had never seen anything so wicked. Not even the spiders compared to these creatures with their long antennas, large mandibles and big black eyes.

It has to see me, it has to see me, his thoughts shattered, and then... he felt the burning sensation of his own urine running down his leg.

As the ant climbed off Mobee, he moaned, "I just pissed myself."

"It's alright, Lad. Just remain still," said Davison.

Up on the ledge, Bishop's anger turned to a boil. "That's seven men we've lost!"

"And we'll lose no more," scolded Flynn, looking at him.

The fire within his eyes bore into Bishop, but he could not look away.

"The men hear that tongue, it will cause a mutiny. I'll not have that here, Mr. Bishop, especially from you," he spewed between his gritted teeth.

Bishop looked at the ground, then cast his eyes upon Catherine and Johan.

"Harr, me Lad," whispered Johan. "You speak that way again, me cut your tongue out," he continued, drawing his long blade.

"Gentlemen," Catherine calmly weighed in.

"Speak your mind, Lady Knox," grumbled Bishop.

She looked at him, stared him dead in the eye. "You have been warned, Mr. Bishop. I'd take that advice most seriously."

Bishop placed his back against the rock wall and regrettably sighed. What he just said was not in his heart. It came from his anger.

The sun was at noon when the last giant ant returned to the cave. The men in the trees climbed down, some still weakened from witnessing the horrendous scene.

As Flynn and Johan assisted Catherine off the ledge, she was in no better shape. Her whole body shook as she slowly made her way past the only remnant of the wonderful sailor she came to love - Hildegard's head. She glanced over at Caleb, or what they left of him - his boots. It made her stomach wrench and then she bent over and puked.

Flynn waited. When she stood up, he handed her his hankie. Her face was pale white. What could he say.

"I'll be OK."

Flynn nodded and escorted her toward the bluff.

Up at the top, Flynn was beside himself seeing the man standing there.

"I'm Captain Albright from the York."

"Lance Albright," gasped Catherine, removing her hat.

Albright was stunned seeing her. "What in the..." he started to say.

"I have no time for speeches, Mr. Albright. I need to know about Thomas."

"Excuse me," interrupted Flynn.

The two stopped talking and looked at him.

"Captain Albright, please give us a moment," he said, turning toward his crew. "Is there anyone brave enough to retrieve the last remains of Hildegard and Caleb?"

The men's stomach churned, looking down at what was left.

"I'll go," said Davison.

"Thank you, Mr. Davison. You three, dig two holes. Bos'n Cutter... make us two crosses."

"Aye, Sir."

With the small holes covered, the wooden cross over each, Flynn remorsefully spoke. "We just lost two good men, fine seamen they were. Bow your heads as I say a prayer."

Mobee slipped up alongside him. With his head bowed, Flynn continued. "In the hour of their death, may the Good Lord be with Hildegard and Caleb. May He take them from the blue waters here on earth and set their feet on dry land in Heaven forever and ever, amen."

"Amen," the group said in unison.

With the short vigil over, the men and Catherine lifted their heads staring at Albright: his face and arms covered in mud, wearing nothing but a pair of tattered pants, and his boots with palm leaves sticking out as socks. His only weapons, a spear and machete strapped to his back, along with a deerskin pouch hanging off his shoulder.

Even though Albright was more thrilled than Flynn was - knowing his days on the island were ending, his heart felt the utter sadness each of them carried. "I'm truly sorry for your loss."

In her mixed emotions - happy to see him and sickened by Hildegard and Caleb's death, Catherine quickly retorted, "Mr. Albright, I'm thrilled to see you, as everyone here is, but forgive me in my hour. I stand here tormented, devastated at the horrors we have witnessed on this island. We have traveled many miles, months on end to find Thomas Payne. As you can see, we have lost good men for our troubles - seven thus far."

"As I heard Captain Flynn say, we'll lose no more," replied Albright.

"Can you guarantee that?" questioned Davison.

"I can't guarantee anything, but I've survived this long."

"Fair enough."

Albright nodded and focused on Catherine. "Does your father and King George know you're here?"

"They do."

"They do?"

"After learning that the king nor my father would not send ships to look for the York, I left my father a note explaining what I had done. As you can see, I hired Captain Flynn and his crew, so please... tell me now: is Thomas still alive?"

The men stepped forward to hear.

"I believe he is."

"You believe he is?" she spat.

"Yes, but it is hard to say. I see signs of him everywhere. Footprints, machete cuts, but no Thomas. Then again..." he said as if drifting, "all those could have been my doing."

"Have you lost your mind, Mr. Albright?" she angrily questioned.

"I don't know," he replied, shaking his head. "When I see footprints or machete cuts on branches, I think they were made by Thomas."

Catherine went to speak. Flynn touched her arm. She let it go.

"You've been here a long time, Captain Albright. I'm sure, after a while, we'd all start seeing things as well."

"You're right," he replied. "Besides locating Thomas' whereabouts, there is much more you need to know."

"About what?"

"Lots of things, but I'll say them in order. One, that wasn't the only ant nest. They're crawling all over this place. If you see one, stop, and let it go on its way. One by itself is a scout searching. If you see more than one... freeze as you did today."

Nods went out from the group.

"Two, the spiders fear the ants. I wish we had known that when we headed inland. We lost four good men fighting them bastards for days."

"We figured the spiders feared something down here, Captain Albright. They stopped chasing us when we came down from the granite mesa," replied Flynn.

Albright nodded then continued. "Number three... the island's inhabitants."

"Inhabitants?" repeated Catherine.

"Yes, the only species that walks upright."

She stood back; so did Flynn.

"If I say it... you won't believe me, so, come, I'll show ya," he said, turning and leaving.

As the group marched down from the bluff, the silence was deafening. Each man periodically looked back with deep remorse, leaving more crewmembers behind.

How many of us will die before this is all over? By the somber stillness, Flynn knew that thought was on each man's heart. He, too, had no answer, but remained fixed on losing no more. *If the Marine Captain could survive, the rest of us will survive as well.* It was just how Albright survived all these months that Flynn wanted to know.

The men walked for several miles down trails, crossing swamps to a gorge between the mountains.

"Up there on the flat section you'll see it," said Albright.

Cutter, Bishop, and Johan went up the rocks. Lying on the ground were the bones of a very large humanoid like creature.

"Captain Flynn," Cutter called down.

Flynn looked at Albright.

"Go on up," said Albright to his stare.

When Flynn got there, he stood dumbfounded. "Doc Ryan," he shouted.

"I'm coming."

When Ryan came up to see, his eyes went wide. "What in the hell..." he gasped, walking around the skeletal remains, not believing what he was seeing. "Are you telling us that this human like creature lives on this island?"

"C'mon, Doc," mused Catherine. "That skeleton has to be as old as the dinosaurs."

Albright glanced at her, then focused on Ryan.

"In the Good Book, there are many passages that referred to what we are looking at. One group I remember was called Anakims - a race of giants. The most famous one, I believe you all know, was called Goliath."

"That was thousands of years ago, Doc," said Flynn. "How old is this one?"

Ryan knelt alongside the thing, ran his finger across the skull's forehead then picked up the bones of the arm. "My guess is... this humanoid has been dead for six months, maybe more."

As the men stood there in disbelief, Catherine sat down. Mobee sat next to her.

"You only hear their drums at night, further south," said Albright, gazing in that direction.

The group slowly turned, looking through the gorge. At the end of the passage, the landscape changed into a valley. After that, the jungle continued.

"Have you seen one?" asked Davison.

"Yes, the one you're looking at now."

With her head spinning, Catherine glanced up at Albright as he continued.

"I was hiding over there behind those rocks when the giant came running through the gorge. I almost lost my mind seeing a... a large reptile - a lizard I guess, chasing after him. The thing attacked the giant. He speared it through the head. The wound on his leg was bad. I really don't know why he climbed up here, but as you can see, he laid down and never got up again."

Mobee shook his head, hearing all this. "Did you say a large lizard?"

"Yes."

"Are there any other creatures we should know about that just might want to make a meal out of us? Just thought I'd ask."

"I just told you of the ones that will eat you if caught," he replied to the brown-skinned boy.

Johan stepped through the group. "Harr, me Lads, these are the bones I saw in me 'dallion. Me feared looking into the eye since me coming ashore."

The tattooed man puzzled Albright. *He must have been a wild buccaneer in his day.*

"Look now," belted Flynn.

Johan raised one brow at his captain.

"As sharp as the tip of me sword, remember," countered Flynn to his stare.

"Aye, Capt'n, me never forget me promises," he grunted, taking a seat on a rock.

Catherine sat there watching Johan open the golden eyelid and peer into the black gem.

Through the misty fog, within the eye of the medallion, Johan saw a large split in the earth with a wooden drawbridge going across. From there, the landscape changed. The ground proceeded upward, somewhat like a mountain, but more so, like the sides of an ancient volcano in the shape of a horseshoe, jutting out to sea.

In the middle of the enclave was a large dome like structure made of wood and bamboo. The large doors opened. The floor was sand; the internal beams tree trunks. The roof was constructed of woven grass.

There were torches leading up to what appeared to be a throne. Sitting on the seat was a light brown-skinned man. He looked ten, maybe twelve feet tall with a well-defined chest, shoulders and arms. His head was huge. He had a square jaw and flat nose. Adorned on his head was a crown of colorful bird feathers. Around his neck sat the biggest diamond he had ever seen. Palm sized, it was.

The image quickly disappeared. In its place, Johan saw a woman standing on the shoreline with her back to him, looking out over the ocean. She had long black hair, probably eight feet tall. Her clothing was made of deerskin with one shoulder bare. As she turned toward him, Johan took in her features. She was very beautiful. Her eyes were strikingly blue, with a long nose and supple lips. The deerskin pelt hung down over her large breasts and opened in the middle exposing her stomach, then continued over her thighs.

She suddenly glanced down the beach. Johan looked to see what caught her attention. It was a group of men all ten feet tall or more. One was carrying a white man over his shoulder. He appeared to be unconscious.

When they reached the woman, she ordered them to drop the man. She then knelt beside him, admiring his handsome face. Johan was surprised. The man was Thomas Payne.

She lifted Thomas' head, ran her fingers down his brow and nose, then touched his lips. "Uta me'yana," she said in her native tongue.

One of the men stepped forward. "Be' tuna loc a' tee," he replied, pointing toward the large dome structure.

Within the swirling haze, Johan flashed back to the island of Sera. The native dialect was very similar.

"I want him," the woman said.

"Go ask your father, the king," the man replied.

As the image disappeared, Johan fell off the rock and laid there on the ground.

"Johan, Johan," gasped Catherine, getting up and rushing over to him.

Johan opened his eyes.

"What did you see?"

"The giants have him."

"What!?"

"Thomas now belongs to the king's daughter."

Catherine fell back against Flynn kneeling there. He held her as she sighed.

"If I may be so inclined," said Albright. "What did I just witness?"

Flynn looked at Catherine, who looked up at Albright. "He sees visions within that medallion of his. Don't ask us how, but he has seen visions throughout this voyage and every one of them has come true."

Still confused, Albright slowly nodded. "OK, right now... we need to go. My hut is several miles from here, and we don't want to be out at night."

"Is there anywhere to shoot off a flare from your hut that my ship would see it?" asked Flynn.

"Yes, there's a ridge. Come, I'll show you."

JEFF WRIGHT
CATHERINE KNOX

31

The walk through the jungle was bitter pain; uneven terrain, thick vegetation and swamps - exhausting. Through it all, they stopped several times while scout ants wandered by, searching.

After proceeding up an isolated ridge, Albright swung one way and then another, clipping along the base of the eastern mountain. At a split in the trail, he halted. The crew gathered around him.

"This mountain breathes smoke and ash every ten days. It's the reason Thomas and I chose to settle here. The native hunting parties stay clear; out of fear, I guess."

All eyes drew up at the peak. At the summit, steam rose out, fanning over the top, giving it a majestic appearance.

"How long has it been doing that?" asked Doc Ryan.

"Six months, I guess."

The crew focused on Ryan, waiting to hear more.

"I'm not a geologist, I'm a doctor," he said to their stares.

"Did you see any warnings within your vision?" Flynn asked Johan.

"No, Capt'n, just Thomas captured."

"Let's keep moving. We need to get to the hut and start planning his rescue," said Catherine in a serious tone.

As they continued onward, Mobee stopped in the rear. Johan came up alongside him. "What is it?" he asked, looking about.

"That smell - you smell it?"

"Yarr, me smell it. What could it be?"

Catherine glanced back at the two talking.

"It smells like the tar pits in Botswana."

"Tar pits, you don't say."

"Yeah... my uncle, Libby, he once took me there when he worked in the diamond mines. There were tar pits all around that smelled just like that odor."

"Really now, Lad," he replied, glancing at Catherine walking toward them. "C'mon, Mobee - we'll talk later."

"What's going on back here? We must keep moving."

"Nothing, just resting a bit," answered Johan.

From the twinkle in his eye, Catherine knew he was keeping something from her. *I'll find out later*, she thought, waving for them to move out.

As the three caught up, the party had exited the jungle and were standing in a clearing next to the base of the mountain. Catherine was amazed seeing a natural looking barrier constructed of thorn bushes butted against the rock formations. It circled outward across the clearing and then butted against a massive rock column on the other side. The opening was twenty feet wide. The ground within the sheltered area was grass. A massive tree stood in the middle, its branches extending outward touching both the base of the mountain and column.

"Home sweet home," announced Albright, removing a section of bush.

As the crew followed, they spotted a rope ladder hanging down from one of the tree's limbs.

Catherine cast her eyes upward. Within the branches was an elaborate tree house made of hardwood and bamboo; its roof constructed of long dry grass woven tightly together. There were openings on all sides that could be drawn and secured to let the breeze in, or kept shut during storms. On the outside was a walkway or balcony with bamboo railing.

What made the place so spectacular: just past the tree was a beautiful waterfall cascading down from the mountain. The men and she walked over to see. A hanging ladder extended over the edge to a shimmering deep pool below. At the side of the pool, the water overflowed and continued to a river below. Standing high above, they could see the river weaving its way through the ravine's lush jungle vegetation, ending at the mouth where it emptied into the sparkling blue sea.

"You've done well, Mr. Albright," said Flynn, impressed with his skills.

"Constructing this over the many months kept both me and Thomas physically and mentally fit."

"What about the ants?" questioned Catherine, walking up.

"They don't like the black tar I put on the thorn bushes."

Mobee and Johan looked at one another, each thinking of diamonds.

"That's the odor I smell?" she questioned.

"Yes, there are several tar pits nearby. I also use it on my torches. It lasts a long time."

"Where is the nearest pit?" asked Flynn, waving at Cutter.

"Not far, just past the clearing heading east."

"Take four men and dip all our torches in tar."

"Aye, Captain."

"The rest of you find a place to settle in."

"The tree house can bunk three comfortably, Captain," suggested Albright.

"Then you, Catherine, and Mobee will sleep up there."

"Not me, Sir. I'm sleeping down here," interrupted Mobee, smiling at Johan.

Catherine caught the grin. *These two are concealing something.*

"OK, Lad - it's your choice."

As nightfall crept over the mountain, the crew sitting about the fire, Catherine asked Albright how they had survived the battle and storm.

Albright gazed into the fire. He seemed to be somewhere else - somewhere on the high seas when he spoke. "I've never seen anything like it," he started. "On a foggy morning, the French Nightingale caught us unaware. How a ship of that size can catch anyone unaware is beyond me, but she did.

"Throughout the morning, Thomas tried desperately to stay clear of her guns. Once we sailed out of the haze, off on the horizon a turbulent storm was brewing. It was a long shot, but Thomas thought it was our best chance of survival. He ordered the helm to head straight for the storm. We'd take shelter within, knowing the Nightingale would not follow.

"As we closed our distance, I'll never forget the black thunderous clouds, the gale force winds and heavy seas. Before we could make it, the Nightingale fired a volley from her forward gun.

"They splashed two behind us and then one hit its mark, right through the upper stern. With the stern now hit and the York on fire, Thomas took over the helm and sailed that ship straight into the jaws of death: waves forty, fifty feet high.

"Right before a mighty wave tossed the crew and vessel, the Nightingale came abreast. She sent one through our midsection and another across the main deck, aiming for our mast.

"The screaming, hollering, watching men being blown apart - some going over the side," he murmured, reliving the nightmare.

"All I can remember is... when I looked back... the Nightingale had pulled her bow to port and was sailing out of harm's way. When I faced forward, Thomas sailed over the crest of a huge wave and then he turned the York broadside before the next monstrous wave was upon us.

"I believe a man hung at the yardarm would have had a better chance of surviving than what we faced. As sailors, we all know it's a death sentence for any ship to expose her vulnerable side to an angry sea.

"I closed my eyes and braced myself, waiting for the tremendous wall of water to hit. When it didn't, I opened my eyes seeing Thomas sailing that wave broadside, the roaring crest crashing right behind the York.

"Don't ask me how. No Captain had ever pulled off a stunt like that and survived, but we did. When the wave spat us out the side of the storm, we tossed and turned like a cork in a barrel. Badly listing and taking on water as she was, I thought for sure we'd be laid to rest with the deep blue sea as our coffin," he said, looking about the men sitting there spellbound.

"How did you come about this island?" asked Mobee.

Albright shook his head - flashing back once again. "After we cleared the storm, we drifted crippled for days. Then through the misty haze one morning, the crow's nest lookout shouted, land ho. I thought it impossible but there she be.

"In the York's battered condition, each man knowing she'd never sail us home, Thomas drove the bow right into that inlet cove. When the tide went out, she sat there like a tomb.

"We buried our dead, collected what we could from the wreckage, and eight of us that had survived headed inland through the mesa.

"The spiders came that night. With only spears, bows, and machetes, we were no match for those horrid things. I've re-lived that nightmare a thousand times: seeing the last of our men attacked so viciously and then dragged away. Every time we tried to save one, others came. Those glaring evil eyes, that hideous hiss, while exposing their deadly fangs - made my skin crawl right off my bones," he sighed, shaking his head.

"Only four of us made it to the ledge. There, Thomas quickly secured a rope and dropped it over while we kept them bastards at bay. I hated being the last man down trying to keep them away from me.

"You know where that one tree sits on that bluff? Thomas halted right there. He said... 'we'll stand and fight or, we'll die together.' When your captain gives you an order like that, what can you do... you fight."

Catherine sat there numb, imagining Thomas ready to fight or die. Was he a fool, or one brave soul? She knew in her heart that it was the later. She stepped out of her thoughts as Albright continued.

"As they came down hissing, trying to spray us with their webbing, a strange noise came from within the deep jungle below. It sounded like a thousand rodents on the march.

"The spiders stopped attacking and reared up as if they were listening too.

"When I looked back to see what it was, my mind seemed to shut down. Everything began to move in slow motion. Coming out of the jungle was a horde of those large black ants heading straight for the bluff. They were everywhere. I would have run, but Thomas shouted - *don't move*. I thank the Good Lord I listened.

304

'Standing there frozen, the ants rushed right past us and started viciously attacking the spiders. The terrifying sound still rings in my ears: spiders hissing while being torn apart by hundreds of ants. When it was over, we watched the ants carrying away their prize: body parts - legs, heads, and abdomens.

"For days after, we stayed in the trees and only foraged at night when the ants were gone. One month on, two of our friends became deathly sick. Malaria I think, Doc."

"Were they always cold, but sweated like pigs?"

"Yes."

"It sounds like the dreaded sickness," spoke the doctor.

"Well, they only lasted a week, leaving Thomas and I on our own."

"What about the giants?" asked Bishop.

"The giants," he repeated, gazing once again into the fire. "Our first encounter was near a slow-moving river. Halfway across, we heard noises, then people speaking a native language coming toward us. Thomas quickly waded to the bank, yanked a hollow reed and stuck it in his mouth. Then he went under. I hurried and did the same.

"I couldn't believe my eyes seeing 'em walk right past us. They had long poles, each carrying dead spiders and deer.

"When they were gone, Thomas and I slowly lifted our heads out of the water and stared at one another. The moment seemed so surreal. Bare chested men, ten feet tall with legs like tree trunks, muscles like iron; we were beside ourselves.

"How were the two of us going to survive on this island? It came to us as soon as we crawled out onto the muddy bank and through the undergrowth to a boulder. Thomas looked at me; I looked at him. We both looked like crap - covered from head to toe in thick mud, vines, and leaves.

"I went to wipe the stuff off. Thomas stopped me and whispered - *we are now the jungle.* I hadn't a clue to what he was talking about. Thought the man plum lost his mind. Then, as I glanced down myself, I realized what he was saying. Covered in jungle debris, we naturally blended into our surroundings. That's how we traveled from there on out.

"We got so good at creeping up and spying on the hunters that we could sit right under their noses and they hadn't a clue we were there. That's how we found out about the ants. Stop moving and they won't attack. The other thing we learned about the giants is they never ventured near the eastern mountain. They'd always point upward at the smoke and ash, say some gibberish words and move off.

"Thomas and I searched for days around the mountain until we found this place. It was well hidden, had water and one nice tree. The tar pits came in handy too. At first, we thought the thorn bushes would protect us from the ants. That wasn't the case. We killed many, ate their abdomens and then discovered the pits."

"You ate their abdomens?" spewed Seaman Kettle, feeling his stomach turn.

"The natives were eating 'em, so we tried it. Surprisingly, they tasted like chicken stewed in lemons. That's why I was at the bluff today."

"What happened to Thomas? How'd you two get separated?" asked Davison, intrigued with his story.

"It was getting late. Thomas wanted to follow the giants through the valley. Unaware of what was out there, we found ourselves surrounded by reptiles as big as a lifeboat. As the giants moved on, we took to the trees and stayed there the night.

"After coming down the following morning, Thomas wanted to continue south. We happened upon a river. Not suspecting it had an undertow, we started to cross. Thomas went under and never came up. I searched for him for days. When I came upon a waterfall, I figured he went over. Thought I'd find him on the bank somewhere down further, but that wasn't the case.

"I ended up going back to the tree house hoping somehow he'd just show up. Today, however, after hearing Johan's vision - the natives found Thomas before I could."

Catherine sat back. Hearing his story was painful, but not as painful as what sat in her heart: *the king's daughter now has Thomas.* Was he her slave or a toy she could show off to the other women? It made her sick thinking that maybe, just maybe - she was having her way with him. She had to know, and she asked. "What about the females. Have you seen any?"

Flynn cast his eyes upon her. *Only a female would ask about another female.*

"Sometimes they too join the hunting parties."

"And what do they look like?"

"They're also big - seven, maybe eight feet tall."

"Are they pretty?"

"Yarr, Melady," interrupted Johan, raising one brow.

"I'll give you yarr... Melady," she spat. "Lance Albright!" she continued.

"Some are fair, but most wouldn't be dancing at the Blue Dragon, if that's what you wanted to hear."

"The Blue Dragon, why..."

"Catherine," grumbled Flynn.

She sat back and sighed. All she wanted was to find Thomas. To wrap him in her loving embrace and tell 'em his nightmare was over - that he was going home with her. They'd get married, have children and give up this awful life at sea.

Albright looked at her seemingly drifting on the wind. "If it would gladden your heart to know, Lady Knox... Thomas Payne is the greatest captain I've ever sailed with, and... we're not leaving without him. You can be sure of that. We now have the firepower to overtake these natives."

She stepped out of her thoughts, hoping beyond hope it would be true: that they'd get him back. "What's your plan?"

"The first thing we need to know is the layout of their village and where they're keeping him."

"Who's going, Sir?" asked Davison, standing up.

"I want you, Johan, and Mr. Albright to go to their village and report back your findings. I want Mr. Bishop, Bos'n Cutter along with three men to scout out this area. We need food."

"What about me?" asked Doc Ryan.

"You're staying put, Doc."

"You know, Captain," said Bishop. "If trouble be had in the valley, those that are going cannot use their guns or grenades. The giants will hear 'em. This party must only use their spears, standard bows, and crossbows to kill anything that may want to attack them."

"As true as the point off the bow, Mr. Bishop," remarked Johan.

Flynn nodded, thinking. He looked at Mobee. "I need your skill with that bow, Lad."

"As sharp as the tip of me sword, Captain, I swear I'll kill anything that comes near us," he replied, taking his bow, placing an arrow on the string and lining up a shot.

Catherine stared at him aiming his bow. *He is not the boy that came to my cabin anymore. This savage voyage and the hardship we've faced has turned him into a man.*

"Alright - it's getting late. Where can we fire off a flare?" asked Flynn.

"Right up there," replied Albright, pointing to a ridge above them.

"Bos'n Cutter, climb up and light off a flare. When you see the Lara May, fire a flare in

return to mark her position. If she is behind us -
light off another one. I want the ship and crew
right alongside us as we head south to rescue
Thomas Payne."

"Aye, Captain."

After the flare went up, the Lara May gave
one in return. She was behind their location.
Cutter shot off another flare. Mr. Smith marked
the position; pulled anchor and set sail two miles
southward down the coast.

32

Before the morn's light swept across the pale sky, Albright and his team were up. They said their goodbyes knowing this expedition was not for the faint at heart; it was going to be a long, arduous affair.

With packs, standard bows, crossbows and spears; with their rifles, pistols and a bag of grenades, they set out through the thorn bush barrier.

Flynn's crew, along with Catherine, watched them disappear down a path into the deep jungle.

"I don't think I'll get any sleep until they return," she said.

"We'll stay busy," replied Flynn. "There's a lot to do while they're gone."

She turned, seemingly searching his eyes.

"Those are the finest men we have, Catherine. They'll be alright."

She knew that; however, having such skills doesn't mean you're able to use them against the odds they now faced. Before she could reply, Flynn called out to Bishop.

"With no luck of wild game yesterday, take a party hunting. We need food."

"Aye, Captain."

"Bring back some fruit," added Catherine.

Bishop nodded then rounded up the men.

After the group departed, Albright headed south toward a stream. With the trail unnoticeable, the men just followed. At the water's edge, the current was slowly moving around and over rocks and debris. Dead trees lay everywhere, their bark covered in green moss.

On the bank, the men plastered their faces and arms with mud and then covered themselves with plant leaves and vines.

Mobee, having brown skin, never said a word as he covered himself. When he finished and got off his knees, he asked, "Before we strike out, do you know if these natives are cannibals?"

Johan, Cutter, and Davison looked at Albright.

"Good question. I wouldn't know. Thomas and I are the only other humans on this island."

"It's something we need to consider," answered Mobee. "The last place I want to find myself is tied to a pole while being roasted over an open pit. It gives me shivers just thinking of my flesh being peeled from the bone and eaten."

That bit of ill talk caught Johan. "You listen hear, Laddy," he started with a lift of one brow. "We have enough firepower to defend ourselves. Why... as sharp as you be with that bow, and Marine Captain Albright sharp with them pistols and muskets, and Davison and ol' Johan here with grenades in each hand, we'll turn the tables on these natives. Why... me face death before... me never wavered. No man here has."

Mobee looked at each one.

"You satisfied?" asked Albright.

"Yes."

"OK, with a steady pace, we should reach the gorge by noon. From there, we'll take it slow through the valley."

"You got it; lead on," said Davison.

Albright followed the stream further down and then climbed up onto flat land. There was nothing but shades of green, hanging vines, with a bit of blue overhead.

"Keep your eyes peeled for ants. They're always here," he warned.

The men looked about. The jungle was so dense they could barely see the ground beneath their feet, much less, ten meters away.

"Ahya naka ne'sum-ba," a native voice came from up ahead.

Albright quickly dropped and hid within the foliage. The rest followed.

As the natives moved through, Johan listened to their conversation. He nudged Albright. The ol' salt pointed toward the northern mesa. "They're going after the spiders."

Mobee, Davison, and Cutter peered out through the undergrowth. The giants were like sculptured statues: extremely tall and very muscular. Some wearing Mohawks, others with ponytails; their faces and chests painted with white powder. Their weapons were primitive: bows and spears with sharp stone tips.

As Davison glanced back at Mobee, he panicked. Mobee wrinkled his brow then slowly turned, looking behind. Two meters away, a large ant was coming. He slowly tapped Cutter's leg. Cutter glanced at him. Mobee nodded toward the rear. Cutter cringed seeing the thing.

The large ant crawled alongside Mobee, then up and over Cutter's leg.

Johan instantly froze seeing it.

Albright never saw the danger and went to get up. The ant viciously attacked him. Johan drew his machete and cut the ant in half then pulled the sharp mandibles out of his thigh.

The pain was instant. Albright cringed.

Johan quickly shoved him over and covered his mouth. "You swallow that pain, or we're dead men."

With watery eyes, Albright tried to speak.

Johan slowly released his grip.

"We have to get out of here. More ants will come."

"What cha mean?"

"That bastard sent out a signal. I don't know how, but once an ant attacks, more come. I've seen it."

"OK, bandage that leg and let's get moving," said Davison.

Camouflaged like plants, they crept out of the area. The trek to the gorge was a relentless battle; hacking through the thick vegetation and hanging vines. Albright with his leg badly cut made the hike even worse.

When they came to a clearing with several large trees, they rested, feeling as if their muscles had melted away.

"We could easily die out here," said Cutter, wiping the sweat from his brow.

"I thought I would," murmured Albright. "I thought many times to just hang myself and get it over with."

The men stared at him.

"You've only been here for a while. Try staying alive for over a year on this God forsaken island."

"After the life me lived, me not dying in this God-awful place. Me going to die in the arms of a pretty island girl," said Johan.

"What cha talking about?" questioned Mobee.

"If me get out of here in one piece, me sailing days are over. Me ol' bones are brittle; me back feels like a twig."

"You'll never give up the sea," said Davison.

"Mark me words, if she's as pretty as a sea pearl, me will stay in her arms until me last breath. I swear on me ol' soul, I will."

"Go on with that talk," spat Mobee, getting up.

The rest stood, stretched their aching limbs, ready to continue onward.

"Shh, you hear that?" said Cutter.

The men stopped and listened. A crack of thunder sounded in the distance.

"We might as well sit down and wait it out," he grumbled.

"No, we're going to keep moving," replied Albright, checking his leg.

"You know what's coming?" asked Cutter.

"That's right, a storm. Do you want to hunker down like the giants and ants whom I know will be taking shelter from the wet weather?"

"No, we're not. Get up, Bos'n Cutter, we're leaving," spat Davison.

The telltale signs of foul weather swooped in. The wind picked up, the temperature dropped; rain soon followed. Like a river in the sky, it poured so hard it buckled the palms and foliage.

They tromped onward, cold and wet, until they came to the gorge. It, too, looked like a river with all the water coming down from the mountains.

Through the driving rain, Cutter shouted, "There's no way we're getting through. We must seek shelter."

"OK, I know where there's a small cave," replied Albright.

"How big?" asked Johan, not wanting to step one foot inside a cave after seeing Hildegard and Caleb torn to pieces.

"There's enough room for all of us."

It was nothing but a hollow hole at the base of the mountain. The men sat there dripping wet.

"Storms like these can last for days," said Mobee, peering out.

"We don't have days," remarked Albright.

"No, we don't. Get some rest. We leave in an hour, regardless of the weather," said Davison.

The men picked a spot and settled in.

It wasn't an hour before the sun broke through the clouds. With it, came the blistering heat. Outside appeared like a foggy day; the heat burning the moisture away.

Through the misty hazy, the men were once again on the move. The pass was a mere half mile. At the end, they took in the valley from sea to sea. Each man with a spyglass studied the southern tip; the ancient volcanic rim stood there like a fortress. Its molten black rock appeared menacing.

"There she be," said Johan, "our destination."

"Yes, but first we must cross this place," said Albright.

"Prepare ye weapons then and let's be off," replied Johan, heading down into the valley.

"Nothing, not a sound," said Cutter, walking through the high green grass.

"Nothing moves in this tormenting heat," replied Albright.

"We should take a break ourselves," suggested Mobee.

"I'll take you to the river where I lost Thomas. It's shady and much cooler."

"Lead on," said Davison.

It was a thirty-minute trek around rocky outcrops, tall trees, then down into a large flat gully. There, along the fast-moving current, they took shelter within a layer of uprooted trees.

"We'll stay here tonight. Just watch yourself if you go in. The undertow is dangerous."

The men walked up to the water's edge.

"How deep?" asked Cutter.

"Waist high, but in some places, it will go up to your shoulders."

Cutter took off his boots and waded in. The water felt good.

Mobee followed, then Davison; each man staying near the bank.

"How's your leg?" asked Davison bending and washing his face.

"OK, but it hurts like hell."

"I can imagine," said Cutter. "I'll never get over hearing Hildegard and Caleb screaming before you ended his pain," he continued, glancing at Johan sitting there. "You coming in?"

"Yes, he's coming in," interrupted Mobee.

"You don't like the smell of rott'n tomatoes," countered Johan with a gleaming smile. After he said that, something caught his nose. "What is that smell?" he questioned, looking about.

Albright sensed the odor. "We're being hunted. The dragons are near. They always hunt in packs."

"Dragons, the ones that killed that giant up in the gorge?" asked Davison, getting out of the water.

"That's right. Grab your bows and spears. Our guns will draw the natives."

Downriver from them, a fifteen-foot dragon slowly crept out of the brush. Its long flickering tongue darted this way and that - smelling its prey. A thick white drool hung from its jowl.

Another beast crawled out toward the group: its tail in the air, ready to strike.

"We're in for a fight, Mates," spat Johan.

"Spread out... try to get a heart or lung shot," said Albright.

"Me will shoot one right between the eyes, me will," replied Johan, aiming his crossbow.

As Davison backed up, behind him, a third dragon appeared, creeping out of the vegetation. With its powerful jaws, it grabbed Davison's thigh and began shaking him like a leaf. Davison screamed trying to pry its mouth open. Its sharp teeth tore into him, ripping a large chunk of flesh from his leg. Blood poured out from the gaping wound.

Davison's wailing cry echoed through the jungle.

Albright lined up a shot to kill the beast. Before he could fire, spears and arrows came whistling through the trees all around them. One spear sunk deep into the side of the dragon. The animal let go of Davison and rolled over onto its back. The other dragons took off, back into the jungle.

Knowing what was coming, the men froze. Six giant natives walked out of the foliage. From behind, another five came out aiming their bows and spears.

Mobee glanced down at Davison. He looked at the ghastly wound on his leg and the white froth oozing from his mouth. Scared, he quickly dove under the water.

His comrades turned, seeing the current taking him downriver.

"Mobee," shouted Johan, getting up and diving in.

"*Hy-ana me - solo,*" go after them, one giant shouted, walking over to Davison. He looked down into the white man's eyes. They were yellow, so was his facial skin. *"Bo la be cu 'ta,"*

319

he's already dying from the poison, he said, lifting his spear and driving it deep into Davison's chest. Davison's body jerked from the blow; blood quickly oozed from his lips, mixing with the white froth. Davison's last words were a gurgling gasp - then he was dead.

Helpless now, Cutter and Albright crumbled to the ground. Death was near, and they knew it.

In the fast-moving river, the current was too fast for the giants to catch up to Mobee and Johan.

Mobee's small frame was like a twig through the rapids. The white water dragged him around huge rocks, down slippery gullies until he came upon a waterfall and went over.

Johan tumbled through the water. When his head popped up, he frantically looked for Mobee. He was nowhere in sight. Fighting for his own life, Johan continued downriver, until he too went over the falls.

After twisting through the air, he plunged into the water forty feet below. Six feet, ten feet, he kept going down; then finally he stopped. With barely enough strength, he swam to the surface and made it to the bank. Bruised and battered, he lay there gasping, feeling half-alive.

Before Johan could gather a thought, he heard a big splash. Fearfully looking back, he saw a giant leaping over the falls. One, he knew, already had hit the water behind him.

Quickly scrambled off the bank, he dove under the foliage, covering himself with mud and debris.

When the second giant came to the surface, they both waded downriver searching for him.

Further downstream, Johan heard a desperate cry. "Johan," yelled Mobee, fighting his captives.

Johan cringed. *The bastards have Mobee.* Blinded by hate and utter sorrow, all he could do was remain hidden as the two giants walked up through the shallows and then stopped in front of him. Peering out, he could only see their legs.

"He has to be here," one said.

"I don't think he survived that fall; if he did, the long tongues will get him. It sounds as if Rua and his group have the boy."

"Where do they come from?"

"We'll soon find out. Let's continue and meet up with the king's son."

Feeling sick, Johan thought to himself. *Me life is ruined, me ol' soul bound to the depths. With no harpoon to end me here, as me promised Hildegard, me could hang me self for allowing Mobee to be captured.*

The others me fear will be roasted over an open fire, just like Mobee said, just like Mobee said, his thoughts sat there tormenting him.

As the natives surrounded Albright and Cutter, they remained lying on the ground.

With their bows and spears pointing at them, Suena, the fierce looking one, spoke with threatening gestures for them to get up onto their knees. He then ordered his men to collect all their weapons and belongings.

"Where do they come from?" asked Fetu to Suena.

"They sure didn't come from the busted long float we discovered some time back," replied Suena, picking up a stick and walking over to them. Beside the two white men, he drew an outline of the island then placed an X where the York was located and then another X where they were now standing. Looking over the two men kneeling, he stared at Albright, who appeared to have been in the jungle longer than the other had.

"La ka tee, ne mina," he ordered one warrior.

The warrior walked over, grabbed Albright by the hair and yanked him to his feet. The immense power in his arms was staggering.

Suena handed him the stick, pointed at the map and grumbled, *"To la neu isha ma keya?"* where are the rest of your men?

"What do you think he wants?" asked Cutter.

"I imagine he wants to know where the rest are hiding," replied Albright from the side of his mouth, staring down at the X markings.

As Albright hesitated, Suena called out, *"Mo nana be cula."*

A mighty warrior walked up behind Cutter, pulled back his head and started driving his massive fingers deep into Cutter's eye sockets.

Cutter cried out from the immense pain.

"Okay, Okay," yelled Albright.

The warrior stopped, but hung onto Cutter; just in case he was ordered to do it again.

"Tell him where the others are. If you don't, they'll kill us and continue to search," moaned Cutter.

Albright stared at him thinking.

"As long as we're still alive and together, we'll have a better chance of getting off this island, Mr. Albright, so make an X, damn you!"

Albright reluctantly made an X on the map.

Suena immediately sent two of his warriors to go and spy out the location of where Flynn and his party were hiding. With that, he spoke and made gestures for the men to get up and start walking through the jungle.

As Cutter and Albright got to their feet, they turned and looked down at Davison lying there. His face was a horrible mess. His eyes were now sagging out of their sockets; his facial-skin a ghoulish yellow from the dragon's poisonous bite.

"La-ka ty ee," get moving, ordered Suena.

Sickened, the two walked away knowing the dragons would be back to finish Davison off.

"Ish nana, Fetu - com'ula ke mona." if they try anything, Fetu, take care of them as you do the spiders," ordered Suena.

The other giants laughed.

"I'm wondering what King Loma will do with them," questioned a warrior, guarding the rear.

"Maybe one of those long floats came to our island," replied another.

Suena looked back at the two. "The king will know what to do with them."

33

Hanging over one giant's shoulder, Mobee fought desperately to get down.

"The sapling has courage," the king's son, Rua remarked, walking alongside Lotto, carrying the boy through the jungle.

"He'll make good slave."

I wish I knew what they were saying, thought Mobee.

When they came to the huge gap in the earth, one native reached up and untied the rope to the drawbridge. The heavy bamboo structure dropped before them.

As they crossed, Mobee took in the large opening. It was deep, probably seventy feet down. There were boulders and deadfall scattered about the dirt flooring.

At the other side, a native pulled on a rope lifting the drawbridge and then secured the rope to a branch.

Rua nudged Mobee. He turned and looked up at him. *"To bon na pin sho,"* the bridge protects us from the long tongues.

Not knowing what he said, Mobee just stared into his eyes. They were as black as Johan's All-Seeing Eye. That thought made him think of his comrades. Did they escape, or had they been captured like him?

As they carried Mobee around the ancient volcano, he could smell the sea before hearing the waves coming ashore. Out of the jungle and onto the sand, the hunting party walked down the beach toward the village.

The natives came to see what Lotto was carrying.

As they gathered, they began chanting and laughing. Some poked Mobee with sticks; others slapped his face.

"Leave him be," grumbled Rua.

The natives bowed then ran back to the village.

The commotion brought King Loma and Queen Se'fina out of their hut.

The king's daughter, Tu-la-lay came around the back to see what was happening. When her eyes landed on Mobee, she beamed, "Look, Father - another one."

"I suppose you want him too?"

"I do, Father," she replied, running toward her brother.

King Loma glanced at his wife.

"He's got brown skin like us," she said.

"He must come from one of the islands. We'll know when he speaks," replied King Loma, heading toward the dome.

As the crowd gathered, Rua and his hunting party walked through the doors and up to the throne. His father and mother were sitting there.

Lotto set the boy down on the sand. Mobee was amazed at the bamboo structure, its artistry beyond belief.

When he turned toward the king, he froze. Beside him on his carved hardwood throne were two large dragons, secured with chains around their necks - chains he suspected were taken from the York.

King Loma tossed each a deer leg then focused on the boy. *"Bu ta sha nee?"* Where do you come from?

Mobee stared at the menacing creatures.
Suena slapped Mobee's head. Mobee looked at the king. He was an older man, maybe in his fifties. Around his neck was a huge diamond.

"Tasha kee," said the king, touching his lips.

Mobee knew the gesture: speak. "My name is Mobee. I come from Africa - the land of many animals."

"He speaks like Tu-la-lay's slave," remarked Queen Se'fina.

"Fetch him," replied King Loma.

Two guards left. One minute later, they escorted Captain Payne out front.

Mobee lost his breath seeing him. Thomas himself was stunned, taking in the boy. It gave him hope that a ship was nearby.

"Do you know him?"

"No."

"He wasn't on that long float you call ship?"

"No."

Mobee was surprised hearing Captain Payne speaking their language.

"There were more," interrupted his son Rua. Cora here said they had captured four more above the waterfall. This one and another tried to escape down river. They went over the falls. We captured him, but could not find the other."

"More?" spat his father. "You come from ship?"

Mobee looked at Captain Payne.

Thomas asked the question in English.

"Yes."

"Where is ship?" asked King Loma, leaning up.

"I don't know; we got lost looking for supplies to continue our voyage," he lied.

Thomas could tell he was lying. He relayed Mobee's answer.

King Loma walked down to the boy. He touched his hair, felt his skin - then looked at Thomas. "He speaks your tongue and yet he is brown like us."

Thomas told him that he comes from Africa, a place of brown people just like them.

Just then, the doors to the dome opened. The gathering turned. It was Suena and his hunting party escorting more white men into the dome.

Suena made them kneel before the king. His warriors tossed their belongings and weapons down beside them.

Mobee was happy seeing Cutter and Albright; worried however, that Johan and Davison were not there.

King Loma picked up one of the muskets. "What is this?" he asked Thomas.

Thomas glanced at Albright kneeling there. The look between the two was of relief - they were both still alive.

"You gonna tell him?" spoke Albright.

"You think I have a choice?"

Albright glanced up at the king waiting for an answer. "No."

"Bo wa ka," fire stick, answered Thomas, pointing toward the wall as if he had a musket in his hand.

The king stood there confused.

Rua stepped up, took the musket and placed his hand over the barrel. "It's not hot?"

Thomas shook his head then turned and looked at Albright. "Is it loaded?"

"Yes," answered Cutter.

Thomas gestured for the musket. Rua handed it to him. He pointed it at the wall and pulled the trigger. The loud explosion and smoke scared the villagers. Some ran out of the dome screaming.

One warrior walked over studying the damage. "Look," he gasped.

King Loma stepped over to the wall. He turned toward Thomas. "Your kind has unspeakable power."

Another warrior picked up their swords, machetes, and knives; weapons they had never seen. "King Loma, see here."

He touched the blades. It was the same substance as the chains around his pets.

"These are the men I spoke about, Father," said Rua.

"I killed one. He was bitten by a dragon. I know where the rest are," Suena spoke up.

"Where?" demanded King Loma.

"I sent two of your warriors to spy on them and bring back report."

King Loma turned toward his men. "When they return and we know where they are, you'll bring them all back."

His warriors bowed then departed the dome.

"Once they return and tell us, Father, we'll capture them all before the sun rises and falls," promised Rua.

"Can you defend against such weapons?"

"Yes."

"Good, I want all their weapons safely guarded."

Rua nodded.

"Go."

When Rua left, Tu-la-lay stepped up to her father. "Can I keep this one?" she asked, pointing at Mobee.

Mobee took in her features. Besides the rest of the females, she was the tallest woman he had ever seen. Her eyes were deep blue. The same color of the ocean at sunset. They were very striking against her light brown skin and long black, wavy hair.

"You keep for now while I think," he grunted. "Take those two away. Pin them to the ground in the sun," he spat, heading to his throne. When he turned, he ordered the guards to have them remain there until the moon appeared, then shackle 'em to the trees.

While guards escorted Cutter and Albright through the front door, two guards escorted Thomas and Mobee around the back to a large bamboo cage. Tu-la-lay followed. When they shut the door, she walked up and looked down at Mobee.

"Ho na, na kee lay way," she said with a smile then left.

"What did she say?"

"She said... you belong to me now. You do as I say, or my father will kill you."

Mobee took his eyes off the woman and looked at him.

"Her name is Tu-la-lay, which means, princess of the sea."

"Princess."

"They're a merciless breed. Now tell me, who are you, and how did you get here?"

"I'm Mobee; I come on the Lara May."

"Captain Flynn's Lara May?"

"Yes, Sir," he said, looking out of the cage at their surroundings. Feeling trapped, he sighed, "SHE'S HERE."

"The Lara May?" assumed Thomas.

"No... Lady Knox, Sir. She is here on this island with us."

Hearing her name was like a bolt of lightning piercing his heart.

Mobee saw the color in his face wash out. Without waiting for him to regain himself, Mobee spent the next thirty minutes telling Thomas everything, the entire story of the long voyage in search of him.

With his head spinning, his emotional state ajar, Thomas just sat there staring at the sand between his feet.

A thousand nightmares of never seeing her again crawled up from the depth of his soul. He was beyond reason, beyond reality - lost in a world of love and hate: his immense love for her, hate for his situation.

The very thought that she was here on the island almost drove him insane; insane enough to want to chew through the thick bamboo bars holding him captive to get to her.

"Captain Payne."

His eyes stayed fixed on the sand.

"Captain Payne, don't lose it now."

Thomas slowly glanced up.

"We have to figure a way off this island."

Thomas sat in thought.

"They took all our weapons. Inside one of our bags are ten grenades."

The two stared at one another, both thinking the possibilities of escaping.

"If I cannot escape and retrieve that bag, our only hope is Mr. Smith and the remaining crew onboard the Lara May. Our last signal to and from ship was days ago."

Thomas weighed that over.

"My other worry is Johan and Mr. Davison."

"Johan and Davison?"

"Yes, the last time I saw Johan, he jumped into the river after me. It appears they never found him. Davison should be with Albright and Cutter."

"They mentioned killing one due to him being bitten by a dragon. They did not say his name, but I'd suspect it was Davison, since he is not with the other two."

Mobee seemingly looked out through the bars – he knew it was Davison. *Another now dead.*

34

After the natives had left, Johan lay there exhausted. When he finally crawled out from the undergrowth, he stood there listening. It was an eerie stillness. A stillness that crawls up your neck and whispers: *you're all alone.*

The chilling effects made him more aware of his surroundings. Even the plants and trees seemed to be watching him. With his mind alert, Johan traveled down river hoping to discover footprints or signs on the foliage where the giants had captured Mobee.

With no weapons except his dagger, he continued onward until the rich river mud presented a clue: footprints - lots of them, heading south. Before leaving the water's edge, he searched for a sturdy limb to craft into a spear.

With the tip sharpened, he fastened a length of vine around the end for gripping.

He may be emotionally weak from age, but ol' Johan was as clever as a fox. His life at sea and the many months he spent on the islands had given him an advantage. Not that he had ever encountered such menacing creatures, or giants like on this island; he was still determined to make it to the native's stronghold and then report back to Flynn his findings.

Throughout the day, the humidity and uneven terrain sapped his strength, making him rest often. From shade to scorching sun, he tromped onward until he came upon the gap in the earth; the same large split he saw within his medallion.

At the edge, it appeared the deep ravine cut the island in two - possibly from the ancient volcano on the other side.

Johan slowly gazed up at the molten rock ledge and then allowed his eyes to follow it as it curved back toward the sea. *Just beyond that is where Mobee and Captain Payne are being held.*

With no equipment, no rope, nothing, Johan knew he was not getting across. The drawbridge was up, secured to a limb on the other side.

Before departing, he glared at the ancient formation. "Be it in your minds... I'll be returning with aid, with weapons and men to get you out of there, as sure as me still alive."

As nightfall approached, during his journey back, Johan took to the trees, staying clear of the dragons. He heard 'em throughout the evening, scurrying around looking for something to eat. When he finally made it back to the mountains, through the gorge and up into the clearing, he stopped - and so did his heart.

The thorn bush fencing was scattered about, signs of large footprints were everywhere, *but no dead giants.* That thought made him glance up at the ledge where the lookout stood. The seaman was dead, one of his legs hung over the side. He could not tell who it was, but with him gone, he knew the giants could have easily slipped in, catching Flynn and the crew unaware. *It would have been as easy as snatching a wee one from a crib.*

The thirty or so feet to the concave opening was hard to face - *are they all dead?*

With each step he took, Catherine's charming smile, her laughter washed over him. Finding Flynn and the rest dead would have been hard taking, but to see her lying there would have crushed his soul completely.

Inside, hanging from the tree, was a man. He was relieved there were no other bodies. Walking through the ruins of the tree house, busted and tossed about, Johan gazed up at the poor soul. It was Mr. Bishop. His face was blue, his tongue was hanging out; he'd been dead for more than a day.

What upset Johan even more were the arrows sticking out of Bishop's back and chest. *They probably hung the bastard first then made sport of him. Maybe to intimidate the others or,* he thought, *Bishop refused to do as they said.* That was Bishop, never minding the consequences of shooting off his mouth at the wrong time.

With his dagger, Johan cut the line, allowing Bishop's dead body to fall. After dragging him out, he went up onto the ledge. The dead lookout was Seaman Kettle. He had an arrow sticking through his neck.

Lying next to him was his backpack. Inside, Johan found the flare gun, three flares, and two grenades. *Be it me luck, they never came up to check on the lad,* he thought, gathering the pack and then pushing Kettle off the ledge. When his lifeless body hit the ground, Johan shook his head. "Sorry ol' chap... me back too brittle to have carried ya down."

With no shovel, he covered each with rocks. After a simple prayer, Johan walked back and sat down amongst the ruins.

It seemed like hours that he just sat there in a minefield of thoughts. Those now dead, he could see their faces and the good times they had.

In his heart-stricken mood, the noonday sun shone down upon his medallion. It seemed he hadn't considered gazing into the All-Seeing Eye for days. Upon peering into the object that had carried them this far, Johan went into a trance. When the vision disappeared, he awakened with a different outlook. *Was it possible*? He wouldn't know sitting there.

With that, he headed up into the mountains. Finding what he saw within the black gem, Johan gazed out over the island wondering where Mr. Smith had anchored.

Without knowing, Johan faced south as if he were a ship. He fired off one flare to his left, *mid-port*, then *two lengths* ahead of mid-port, and then the last one, he fired straight in front of him - *due South* toward the native's stronghold. All he could hope for was Smith reading the flares correctly: *haul up anchor and sail the Lara May to the southern tip of the island.*

As that thought drifted over him, Johan set his face like a flint and headed down the mountain, back into the jungle.

Within the overgrowth, the sun's rays barely met the ground. "Pay it no mind," he whispered. "Just find them," he continued, cautiously looking about.

Further on, he knelt by a clearing and waited. Soon after, a scout ant appeared. Cautiously reaching inside Kettle's pack, Johan grabbed a handful of blackberries, the ones he had gathered up in the mountains. The sweet, alluring treasure he saw within his medallion.

They were more than sweet; the red filling was like a drug. It had an intoxicating effect. The more one ate, the more docile they became. Thereafter, the subject became hooked – they could not live without 'em.

With a handful of berries, Johan picked up a stick and began scraping the ground. The scout ant hurried over to investigate the movement. Johan dropped the berries in front of the thing.

It was instant. Once eaten, the ant harbored no malice against Johan. Besides that, it looked upon him as the source and wanted more.

Johan tossed a few on the ground. The ant consumed the berries, then surprisingly, it wiggled its abdomen, shooting out a fine mist. *That's the signal Albright had mentioned.*

Two large soldier ants quickly appeared. They raced over to Johan. As they fed, he slowly stood up. The scout ant then climbed his leg, up his back and rested on his shoulder. From the corner of his eye, Johan gazed at the menacing creature. Just one was intimidating. A hundred; terrifying. He witnessed firsthand what they could do to a man.

With the three ants, Johan quickly headed to the river where Albright had taken them. He knew more ants would come. He hoped he had time.

Nearing the place where he had leaped into the water, he froze seeing something lying on the ground. The two soldier ants crawled over to it, but would not eat. Johan's stomached turned, knowing what it was. With his spear, he flipped it over. It was Davison's head. Most of his face was gone. Not far from that was one of Davison's boots with a chewed leg bone sticking out.

Looking southward across the river, Johan's anger churned within. *The giants could have killed Davison and then left the poor sap for the dragons.* As that bore into his soul, he slowly lowered his eyes upon the two soldier ants. In that moment, ol' Johan wasn't Johan anymore – he was... as sharp as the tip of his sword; no longer fearing the dragons or the giants. He feared nothing.

"We'll cross below the waterfall and pick up the trail south," he said to his formidable companions. With three soft clicks, they were on the move.

Down the side of the fall they went. When he came upon the place where he discovered the footprints, he crossed over with the scout and two soldiers.

Before heading down the trail, he knelt at the river's edge scooping up chunks of soft white mud mixed with clay. He covered his legs, his chest, and then he smeared it all over his face.

As he slowly stood, he said, "Be it in your minds, ol' Johan is coming, coming with an army. I can hear them not far back."

35

The band of warriors, thirty in all, escorted their captives around the ancient volcano. When Flynn and his crew walked out onto the shoreline, it felt like freedom; freedom at least from the horrendous march through the jungle. No one thought they'd get this far; they'd all be killed like Bishop and Kettle.

Through it all, Catherine prayed to the Heavens they would not discover that she was a woman. She was lucky. Some took a beating, even Flynn, but they never touched her.

It was agonizing to watch, but deep within her soul, she knew she was risking her own life. She knew that before boarding the Lara May on that moonless night off Fletcher's Point.

As she walked down the beach toward the village, to see Thomas one more time, she'd suffer her fate of dying, if it came to that. While gazing out over the vast blue ocean, that painful thought sent her heart on the wind.

Tears welled up within her eyes thinking of her Father, King George, Queen Charlotte, and her loyal and most trusted friend, Beatrice. As she caught each tear, she heard the village natives whooping and hollering.

Rua's warriors returned the calls while beating their chests.

Underneath the brim of her hat, Catherine took in the women and children. She was amazed to see the women almost as tall as the men were. Most with long black hair, wearing colorful seashells around their necks; some with flowers in their hair and beads around their wrists.

They gathered shouting in their native language.

"Whooka ta - nana be'noka," Go tell my Father we're back with the rest," said Rua.

While the women and children hurried off, Flynn glanced over at her. Catherine, in turn, gazed at him. All their fears sat within their eyes.

With a slight motion of her lips, Flynn read her word, *Mobee*. He slowly shook his head. She wasn't sure if he was saying, I don't know, or he's probably dead. Either way, it saddened her broken heart even more.

With a disheartening sigh, she closed her eyes, feeling the gentle breeze caressing her face. It felt good, but it would not remove the guilt she now felt deep within. All those who had perished, had done it for her. Yes, for her. She's the one who set this in motion. It was all her fault. So far, nine men had died so she could be with Thomas. The price was too high. It made her feel even worse.

When the drums sounded, Catherine stepped out of her torment. The village appeared like the villages she had seen on the voyage with two exceptions: this village had a large circular dome in the middle, and the natives were giants that hated their presence.

Rua and Suena shoved several men down. The rest got on their knees in the sand. When their eyes landed on Albright and Cutter tied to the trees, their hearts rejoiced. Their thoughts however, were now on Mobee, Davison, and Johan. *Where were they?*

Then suddenly, the village witch, Ma' loon, the king's spiritual advisor, an old hunchback woman with grey straggly hair appeared from one of the huts. She was ghastly looking. *"Woo ka taaa, se la me no. Say sha lee,"* The skulls of our ancestors speak to me. There is someone watching over these white men, she spewed between her rotted teeth.

"What be your vision?" asked Rua.

"From the misty haze, I see a man with immense power. He is not alone. He brings death to us all."

Before Rua could reply, the dome's outer guards lifted their conch shells and blew into them. The doors of the dome quickly opened.

Bare-chested giants walked out escorting the king's dragons with chains around their necks.

Catherine and the men were beside themselves seeing the sight.

As King Loma appeared in the archway, the natives all bowed in honor and respect. He was a tall elderly man with long greyish hair wearing colorful bird feathers on his head, claws of a dragon wrapped around his biceps and something sparkling hanging from his neck. Flynn picked up the shiny object right away. It was a diamond; a diamond the likes he had never seen before.

"Is this all of them?" asked the king.

"Yes, Father," replied Rua, walking up and bowing. "This one seems to be their leader," he continued, pointing down at Flynn.

"Bring him here."

Rua nodded. Two warriors yanked Flynn off his knees and ushered him before the king.

"*Moo noc,*" kneel, spat Rua, shoving Flynn down in front of his father.

"*Woo sha cu na yuk a,*" where do you come from?

Flynn looked up. The king's dark eyes bore into him. Flynn felt the nap of his neck go cold. "I don't speak your language."

"*Bo toc ka, Thumos,*" go get Thomas, ordered King Loma, nodding.

Catherine heard his name. Flynn heard his name, and so did the rest. She could have screamed right then, but caught the stern look from Doc Ryan.

It seemed like forever before they escorted Thomas out front. When they did, she let out a dreadful sigh, seeing him wearing nothing but a white cloth around his waist. He was much slimmer than when she saw him last, and he appeared weak from the year or so of being a captive slave.

Thomas wanted so much to look at her, but faced the king out of respect.

"*Who osha cu na yuk a,*" King Loma repeated his question.

"They come from my country, England," Thomas replied in their native tongue."

"*Ogland,*" repeated King Loma; not able to say the English word - England. "They come on ship like yours?"

"Ya na," yes.

"You think more will come?"

"Ya na."

King Loma grumbled, kicking the sand.

"How many ships does your island have?" asked Rua.

"More than the stars above," replied Thomas, pointing upward.

Murmurs went out from the warriors.

The women suddenly began chanting.

The crowd turned.

Catherine lifted her head to see what was happening. Two women were walking up to the king. She suspected the elder was the queen, the younger, her daughter - the one who now owned Thomas. She gazed upon the young thing, taking in her finer details: tall, blues eyes, jet-black hair and splendid curves. Her jaw muscles tightened; her stomach went into knots. *I could get up and... and what?* her thoughts angrily twisted.

"Greeting," said King Loma to his wife.

"My King," replied Se' fina, casting her eyes down on the white men. As she did, something caught her eye. One appeared to have been crying. There were tear stains on his cheek. What caught her attention even more was the man's fair complexion, the only one not wearing facial hair. She let it go and asked, "What will you do with them?

"I will have council with the village elders."

Se' fina nodded then departed with Tu-la-lay.

As they left, Catherine cast her eyes on Thomas just meters away. She felt her heart pounding so hard she thought all could hear it.

"Tie 'em to the trees like the others," ordered King Loma, turning for the dome.

Rua and the village elders fell in behind the king. Before being escorted away, Thomas looked back at the group. When his eyes landed on Catherine, she could see the heart-wrenching agony etched in his shallow face. All that he'd been through, all that he had endured for over a year sat painfully within his expression. As her eyes watered, Thomas' entire body went tense - he was then quickly shoved to follow the guards back to the cage.

Catherine and the men were taken alongside Albright and Cutter and tied to the palm trees. When the warriors left, Catherine asked about Mobee and the others.

"They have Mobee. They're keeping him with Thomas. I don't know about the others," whispered Albright.

Catherine thanked the heavens hearing Mobee was still alive.

Inside the dome, King Loma took his place. The elders, his top warriors and the wretched old hag sat down before him.

"Before I start, what say you?" the king asked Ma' loon.

"I say we kill them all," interrupted Suena.

Startled, the elders turned and looked at him. King Loma sat back.

"My King," said Suena, standing. "I spoke out of line."

"You spoke your heart," replied the king.

Suena nodded.

"Sit," the king ordered.

Suena looked about. The faces drew in on him.

"What say you, Ma' loon?" repeated King Loma.

"I hear from our ancestors," she replied, pointing up at the skulls perched on the inner poles. "Something is coming; something we cannot defeat."

That caught King Loma off guard. He looked at Bou'nod, his oldest and wisest servant. "I can see in your eyes you have words for the king?"

"Yes, my King. Suena speaks like a long tongue. He wears his feelings on his forehead where they do not belong. Now that Ma' loon hears from our ancestors, warning us.... you, Suena, should have never killed those two. More white men will come from Thumos' island with hardened hearts, seeking revenge."

The elders nodded in agreement.

"You asked Bou'nod to speak."

King Loma waved for him to continue.

"My words to you King Loma is... we discovered that ruined long float in the northern cove; then we captured one. Now, we have more. They too must have come from a long float, but we've not seen it yet. My worries," he said and then paused, "we have witnessed their fire sticks. Their power is greater than ours. If more come, I fear we'll not be able to defend our way of life."

"Those are wise words, Bou'nod," replied King Loma. "I too feel the sky going grey over our village," he continued, casting his eyes on Ma' loon. "You hear from our ancestors," he said, pointing up.

The elders and young warriors turned and looked at the skulls sitting there.

"Yes, my King," she replied. "Their voices come to me in the night. I can only repeat what they tell me."

"Then we must prepare," replied the king.

While King Loma spoke with those in the dome, a young native girl by the name of Tea-lee crept around the back side of the village. She walked up to Mobee and Thomas inside the bamboo cage. Mobee had seen her before and liked the pleasantry within her gaze; a look that said – I like you.

"La tun a coo noc," take this and leave, she whispered, handing him a sharpened seashell.

Mystified by her gesture, Mobee took the item. She smiled then hurried off.

"Go, Mobee, find the grenades," said Thomas, looking out toward the front of the village.

Mobee hesitated.

Thomas looked back at him. "Go, that's an order."

Mobee quickly cut the cage lashings, pried the bamboo apart and eased himself out of the cage.

"Hurry, run," said Thomas.

Moments later, two warriors walked back to check on them. When they saw the boy was gone, they manhandled Thomas out of the cage and rushed him to the front of the dome.

"The boy has escaped," shouted one.

The entire village went into an uproar.

The doors to the dome opened. King Loma, along with his council stood. A warrior belted the news. "The boy has escaped."

"Seal off the volcanic wall and the bridge," ordered King Loma.

As Mobee ran across the back side of the village, he noticed all the huts were built up, off the ground to allow the breeze to flow underneath. He quickly tossed himself under one. He lay there shaking, scared to death. Terrified of being caught paralyzed his ambition to get up and search for the grenades. *How stupid of me,* he thought. *Even with a handful of grenades, how can I defeat so many?*

Three natives ran past. He watched them run toward the ancient wall. *They're sealing off my escape. The bridge will be guarded too.*

With that, Mobee crawled to the other side of the hut, looking out toward the ocean. He could see the king standing with a group shouting and pointing. *I'll wait until nightfall. By then, they'll think I've slipped by their guards.*

It was the longest day in Mobee's life. He crawled to the center of the hut. There, he buried himself in the soft sand. When the moon finally appeared over the ocean - its rays gleaming across the calm seas, he slowly made his way to the rear of the hut.

He could smell the scent of wood burning; see the dim light from the fire pits out front. There were no drums, no dancing – nothing. He knew the mood in the village was utter torment.

That word settled over him like hot coals. *Tormented.... you've tormented me enough, you bastards,* he thought, slipping out and hurrying across the sand toward the back of the dome.

There, he quietly cut through the lashing and pried the bamboo wall apart. With just enough space to slide through, he knelt on the floor inside. The dome was dark and still - just two torches lighting the center. The skulls sitting just below the torches gave him the creeps.

Up near the throne, the king's dragons were asleep. On the ground below them, were all their supplies: muskets and pistols, crossbows and standard bows, their machetes and swords. When he spotted the pouch with the grenades, he glared at it.

Slowly, cautiously, he crept toward their weapons, all the while eyeing the dragons and the pouch. When one of the dragons stirred, he instantly froze, anticipating that it would open its eyes and see him. The moment crawled across the nap of his neck, watching the dragon's tail go up and then slowly go down. A heavy sigh washed over him when it drifted back into a deep sleep once again.

Two steps, three steps: the pouch sat near his feet. He looked at the dragons just meters away, then slowly reached down and picked up the cloth bag.

When he made it back to the wall, he looked at the dragons. *That was close.* Without another thought, he slipped out and ran toward the thick vegetation and hid.

Two natives walked past carrying torches. He waited, then headed deeper into the foliage toward the ancient volcanic wall.

Out front, Rua walked over to Thomas, now tied to the trees with the others. "Call for the boy and tell him to come out or we'll start killing you all, one at a time."

"Mobee," shouted Thomas.

Mobee stopped.

"They're going to kill us one at a time if you don't come back. Run..."

"What in the flaming madness are you saying?" scolded Flynn.

Thomas glared at him. "They're going to kill us anyways. Our only chance is Mobee finding those grenades and us getting the hell off this island."

Flynn stared at him then his expression changed. *By the Grace of God, I hope he does find them.*

"You no kill 'em," scolded Tu-la-lay, shoving her brother.

Rua glared at her.

"Tell him, Father," she grumbled.

"We not kill them. Need 'em to cut our trees and gather our fruit."

Tu-la-lay smiled at Rua. She then smiled at Thomas.

After hearing Captain Payne shout run, Mobee dashed up the rocks as fast as he could. At the top, he looked back. Through the palm leaf canopy, he saw the king, his son, and daughter standing next to Captain Payne. Within his anger, the Captain's words came back to him, *run...* "Run to where? Run to what?"

He sat there numb, not knowing what to do, then it hit him. "I must find the Lara May. It's our only chance."

36

Daybreak found Mobee lying in a dense fog sweeping across the island. He slowly sat up amongst the molten rocks and wiped the dew from his face.

Still in a haze, he could hear two giants talking. Peering over the rock ledge, they were right below, guarding the bridge. He realized then, while sitting there listening to them last night, he had fallen asleep. *Now what am I going to do?*

That thought made him look down at the pouch containing the grenades. *It might be my only chance - kill 'em both and make it to the coast.* Taking one out, he stood. The giants quickly spotted him above.

Before Mobee tossed the grenade, something caught his eye.

The giants saw him staring out past the drawbridge. They turned to see what he was looking at, and then they immediately froze.

Within the fog appeared to be someone walking toward the bridge. Something was perched on the strange looking man's shoulder.

The closer he got, it was apparent what it was: a flesh eater. Behind him, not far back, were two more much larger ants.

Caked in white mud from head to foot, with an ant symbol on his chest and wearing a shiny gold object around his forehead, his appearance frightened them. He looked as of a God.

It rattled one so that he shouted, *"Hy 'a na-ca to akin,"* it's the king of the flesh eaters.

"You down there," said Mobee from above.

They frantically glanced up.

"Here, catch," he said, tossing the grenade.

One caught the object not knowing what it was. The powerful explosion was deafening. One second, the giant was standing there; the next, pieces of him were scattered about. The other giant was overtaken by shrapnel. He lay there moaning in his own blood.

As Johan walked up to the bridge, Mobee was beyond himself seeing the ants as if they were his pets.

"Before the rest come, lower the bridge, Mobee."

Mobee instantly picked up the scurrying sound of something coming. It sounded wicked: the clicking and clattering of legs, hundreds of them, marching toward the bridge.

"We don't have much time, Mobee."

Mobee hurried to the ground, stepped over pieces of human remains and scrambled up the tree. When the drawbridge dropped, Johan told Mobee to run – run to the coast and find the Lara May.

"Johan, how can this be?" he said, startled, seeing the horde of ants.

The ol' salt gave no answer just an order. "Go now, Mobee - find the Lara May; our hour is near to leaving this island."

Mobee quickly ran along the edge of the gap until he came upon a formation of rocks. On the other side, he could hear the waves pounding the shoreline. Climbing up, he made his way through crevices and then came out onto a large flat rock, overlooking the sea. Below him was a sandy beach and more rock pillars sitting just off shore.

"Where could she be?" he said, peering through the heavy fog out past the breakers. *I won't be able to see her if she is on the move. Get to the beach and head north,* his thoughts raced, climbing down.

At the water's edge, he ran across the hard-wet sand until he rounded an inlet. There, along the shore, he spotted two boats and men walking toward them.

"Hey, I'm here," he yelled, stumbling toward the group.

Ludwig turned, seeing him. His eyes lit up. "Mobee," he bellowed.

Overwhelmed, Mobee collapsed in the sand; his nightmare now over.

Twenty minutes later, they assisted him up the ship's ladder. Upon gaining the main deck, he fell to his knees, his whole body shaking.

"Hurry, carry him over to the mast," ordered Smith.

In a daze, Mobee just sat there staring up at the crew.

"Where is Flynn, Catherine, and the rest?" questioned Smith.

Emotionally unable to speak, Mobee just shook his head.

"Come now, Lad, tell us what happened. Where is everyone?" asked Woodward, the ship's cook.

"Ants... spiders.... dragons," dribbled from his mouth.

JEFF WRIGHT
CATHERINE KNOX

"Quit your rambling," spoke a seaman.

"Yes, go on with you. Give us the news. Are you the only one left?" asked Smith, kneeling before him.

Mobee stared into his eyes. "The spiders got Ezekiel and a few others... the ants took Hildegard... and... the giants captured Flynn, Catherine, and the rest."

Smith looked up at Ludwig. They thought the kid had plumb lost his mind. Ludwig quickly nodded for a crewman to douse Mobee with water. A seaman picked up a bucket and splashed it upon him.

Mobee jerked, awakening his senses.

"Go on now, Mobee, tell us straight... what happened?" again asked Smith.

Trembling, Mobee sat there telling them most of it. When he came to Johan and the ants, he looked down at the deck and said, "I don't know how he got them to follow him, but there were hundreds following him at the bridge. If they get to the village, no one will survive."

Smith lifted his chin. "Are you telling me that the ants are following Johan?"

"Yes. He... he has... he has somehow tamed the ants and is now leading them to the giants' village."

Smith stood up, took off his cover and sighed.

"Haul up anchor," shouted Ludwig. "Mr. Smith," he continued, watching him walk over to the rail. "Mr. Smith," he repeated, coming alongside.

"It's beyond my imagination that such things exist," he murmured to himself, staring out over the water.

Ludwig stood there looking at him.

"Spiders the size of melons, ants a foot long, reptiles bigger than a lifeboat..."

"And Goliath-sized giants," added Ludwig.

Smith slowly turned, seemingly gazing at him.

"It's Mobee, Mr. Smith. Have you ever seen him in this condition?"

Smith glanced over at the lad sitting there, looking like a shipwreck himself.

"They have Flynn, Catherine, and Captain Payne, Sir. We did not come all this way..."

"You're right," barked Smith. "We did not come all this way for nothing," he bellowed.

With a swaggering turn, he walked back to the crew. "I want all weapons on deck. Prepare the fore and aft guns. We set sail for the southern tip. Now go on with you all... we're about to go to war."

The crew erupted in cheers and then set about their tasks.

37

Within the misty haze, several natives turned seeing someone coming down the beach. Horrified, their minds could not engage the spectacle: a man with a flesh eater on his shoulder and two larger ones following.

"It's the God of the flesh eaters," shouted one.

The group ran off screaming toward the village.

Hearing the terrifying noise, King Loma rushed out of his hut. His wife hurried to his side. "They say it's the God of the flesh eaters," she panicked.

"The grey skies have come," sighed the king.

"My King, I worried it was not true."

Suddenly, Rua ran up. "The man is covered in white mud with a symbol of a flesh eater on his chest. He is wearing some golden object on his forehead."

The old hag walked up to the king. "I can feel his power already. Our ancestors have spoken the truth to me."

Johan walked up before the village. The children and young adults took to the trees in fear of being eaten by the ants. The warriors all lined up before their king. The dome guards brought out the dragons.

King Loma stared at the man, then took in the flesh eaters. Something was different about them. He had seen many, but none more feared than these. On their abdomens was a shimmering blue streak.

"Hooka ta - la me. Shin bow ne ky ya," I am Johan, seer of all things," he bellowed, lifting his arms skyward. As he brought them down, he looked upon the ant on his shoulder. With just the sound of a click, the ant crawled down and stood in front of Johan; its antennas searching for movement. The two large soldier ants moved up alongside the one.

The natives were mystified at his ability to control the flesh eaters. They were even more stunned when he reached into his pouch and pulled out a soft white stone and pointed at Ma' loon.

"The All-Seeing Eye seeks you, old woman. Your power is useless," hissed Johan, crushing the stone and then blowing the fine particles toward her.

The old hag fainted, falling on the ground as if dead.

The natives stepped back in fear.

King Loma was not pleased with that. He broadened his shoulders and with a slight lift of his chin, threatened Johan. "Your three flesh eaters are no match for my dragons."

Johan eyed the king then, glanced down along the king's warriors standing in front of him. "You see three before you, but I have brought many more," he replied, pointing up along the volcanic cliff edge.

The natives turned and looked up. Their minds reeled in fear seeing the horde looking down upon them.

"You set your dragons free and my flesh eaters will destroy your village and devour your people."

Se'fina grabbed her husband's arm. King Loma looked down upon her.

"Your only choice now is to let them go," warned Johan, pointing at the white men tied to the trees.

"He's the one who jumped into the river after the young one," said Fute.

"How can that be, fool? spat the king, "No man has ever walked in peace with the flesh eaters."

"He went over the falls and never came up. Maybe he found a passage to the flesh eaters' lair?"

"Then what... he convinced them to follow him?" shouted the king.

"Let them go, Father, or we'll be eaten alive," pleaded Tu-la-lay.

King Loma glanced at his daughter.

Before he could answer, his son, Rua shouted, "Look."

The natives howled, seeing the Lara May in full sail rounding the southern tip.

Onboard the Lara May, the men clamored along the rail, stunned seeing the giants.

"Is that Johan?" gasped Ludwig, looking through his spyglass.

"My eyes have forsaken me. It is Johan with large black ants as Mobee described," replied Smith, studying the village. Off to the side, he spotted Catherine, Flynn, Cutter, Doc Ryan and Captain Payne tied to trees.

Just then, Johan slowly turned toward the ship. All aboard focused in on him. Johan lifted his hands and placed them into a cross. He then slowly turned, facing the natives.

"Prepare the fore and aft guns," shouted Smith, knowing the sign Johan just gave.

While staring at the king, Johan pointed left at the boulders at the base of the bluff.

Smith ordered the forward gun to fire.

The blast was deafening. The hot lead ball whistled through the air, hitting its target. The boulders were reduced to rubble.

The sound of the mighty gun echoed throughout the village. The power of the ship and the flesh eaters evaporated the warrior's pride. Fear now set in amongst them.

King Loma and Johan stared at one another. Two powerful men and one must give way and accept defeat. Johan was assured it wasn't going to be him.

Disheartened, King Loma tossed his staff on the ground. His warriors tossed their spears and bows down.

Johan nodded, turned toward the Lara May, and waved his hand.

"Lower the lifeboats," ordered Smith. "We'll go ashore with musket and pistols. The crew remaining, keep your positions on the ship's guns."

Catherine sighed, seeing the king surrender. She turned and looked at Johan standing there as if he were a God.

"Free them," said Johan.

King Loma nodded to his son. Rua and several warriors walked over and untied the men.

"Johan," shouted Flynn, rubbing his wrists.

Johan cast his eyes upon him. "Mind me now, Captain, and do as I say, so we may leave this island in peace."

Flynn waited to hear what he had to say.

"Kneel before me, all of you."

"What?"

"Shut up and do as he said," spat Catherine, kneeling.

Flynn grumbled, falling to the ground. The rest followed.

King Loma took in the white men kneeling before the man wearing the gold medallion around his head. "You speak our language – how?"

"I know many languages. You are from the Tonkinese people."

"Did you hear that, Father?" gasped Rua, surprised.

"I heard him."

"There is the young one who escaped, Father!" shouted Tu-la-lay, pointing at the long floats coming ashore.

Catherine stood in shock seeing Mobee standing at the bow of one of the lifeboats with musket at the ready.

"I shall return, King Loma. We'll talk then," said Johan, waving toward the cliff line.

King Loma looked back. The flesh eaters were leaving.

Johan then let out several clicks. The three ants turned and followed him down the beach.

The natives sighed in awe of Johan. He was a man with immense power. King Loma was in awe himself. He wrapped his arms around his wife. "We'll make peace with the white men."

"So, we shall, My King. So, we shall."

Thomas and Flynn walked past the warriors and stood before the king.

In their native language, Thomas spoke. "I never came here to take your island or possessions. I spoke of a terrible storm that brought me and my crew here so many months ago. Your warriors saw my ship. It would never sail again. We had no other choice but to stay. But now," said Thomas, gathering Flynn next to him. "Our countrymen have come to take us home."

King Loma looked at Flynn. *"Be yana hy coshin ee."* is that your ship?

Flynn wanted to chastise the king for his warriors killing Bishop and Kettle. "Tell the king we make peace, but there is a price for this peace."

Thomas looked at him.

"I've lost nine men. Two by the hands of his warriors. Shall we just let them get away with that?"

Thomas glanced at King Loma. He was waiting to hear what Flynn just said. To Thomas, the death of nine men was painful; however, he lost his ship, his entire crew and then was captured and made a slave for over a year. He'd lay all that at the feet of peace just to go home. He told Flynn his feelings on the matter.

Flynn swallowed his pride and nodded.

"Your words to the king?"

"He can have our machetes to cut their trees and fruit, our swords and crossbows to defend themselves against the dragons for the stone he wears around his neck."

Thomas stood back hearing that. "Your words to the king?" again he asked, knowing that would not sit well with King Loma.

"You know this island is ripe with diamonds, Captain Payne."

"Are you planning on staying to search for them?"

Flynn gave that a thought. "No. Tell him we'll trade our possessions for provisions to restock the ship for our long journey home."

Thomas slightly smiled and then informed the king.

King Loma nodded. He then raised his hands and clapped. "We celebrate tonight. Go out and find much food and fruit. We shall feast."

As Thomas turned to go to Catherine, Tu-la-lay rushed over to him. "You stay with Tu-la-lay, Thumos?"

Catherine saw Thomas coming toward her then be stopped by the king's daughter. She went to walk over. Doc Ryan quickly grabbed her arm. She turned and glared at him.

"Not here, not now," said Ryan, looking about. "You'll have him as soon as we're back aboard the Lara May."

Catherine sighed, knowing he was right. "OK, there is someone I want to see anyway," she replied, heading toward the beach to greet Mobee coming ashore.

"I wish I could stay with you Tu-la-lay, but I must return home. My king is waiting for me."

"But Tu-la-lay wants you."

Thomas gazed up into her eyes.

"Say no more, Thumos. We celebrate. Two people at peace. Afterward, you tell Tu-la-lay you stay with her. We make life together on our island."

"I'll speak with the Captain. He'll give the answer.

Tu-la-lay smiled.

Unbeknownst to her, Thomas just found himself an out. Flynn would tell her during the festivities that he must return to England.

38

After setting the white men free, the mood in the village was a mixture of relief and animosity. It was truly visible that some of the king's warriors were upset now that they could walk amongst them. Those that kept an upper chin glared at the wooden craft sitting in the bay; its white clothes now stowed, men walking about - ever watchful.

Se 'fina, on the other hand, was one of those relieved. Even though her husband, King Loma, now overwhelmed by surrendering to a much smaller people, knew he'd come around.

Off to the side, however, there was one who groaned even more. It was the old hag; the hunchbacked woman, Ma' loon. She had been reduced to ashes. Her power now seen as useless.

"Your frown gives you away," said Bou'nod, approaching her.

"I hear the bones of our ancestors rattling under the ground."

"Not one has lifted a firestick or their metal spears against us, and yet they could for Suena killing two of theirs."

The old hag allowed her eyes to roam over the long floats coming and going from the ship, the white men standing at the shoreline with their firesticks; their metal spears attached to their waist. "Where is the God of the flesh eaters?" she asked.

"He is no God, but a white man with great power. He and they have left, but said he'd return to speak with King Loma."

Ma' loon studied his eyes. "His power comes from a faraway place, the land of the dead; ancestors greater than ours."

As her thoughts washed over him, Bou'nod reflected on Johan's words to the king. Johan spoke many languages, a traveler – *where is this land of the dead?*

That same evening, when the sun finally set, and the moon took over, its shimmering light cascading upon the calm water, Smith was at the rail overseeing the items Flynn was going to trade for the much-needed provisions: their machetes, axes, and crossbows.

With the crates secured in the lifeboats, Smith looked toward the village. The beachhead was completely visible from the fires and torches burning brightly in the night.

Lifting his spyglass, he took in the giants preparing for the festive evening ahead. When his eye landed on King Loma standing on the steps of the dome, he gazed upon his wife, daughter, and son. They seemed to be happy. Flynn thought otherwise. To ensure the crew's safety, his order this afternoon was to have the fore and aft guns manned and the beach guards with muskets at the ready near the lifeboats.

"You coming ashore, Mr. Smith?" called Ludwig up to him.

Smith stepped out of his thoughts. "That I am. Those staying aboard, keep your eye ever present on the beach guard. If they signal with their hands, prepare the fore and aft guns."

"You think there'll be trouble?" asked a seaman.

"One can never tell in these situations."
"You can count on us, Mr. Smith."
With a nod, he took the ladder down.

When the boats arrived on shore, Flynn ordered the crates brought up to the steps. There, they were opened before King Loma. The pleasantry in his eyes told Flynn the King was happy. The King then ordered his people to fetch whatever Flynn wanted in the morning.

Smith walked over to the men milling about before the celebrations commenced. "My Lady, Captain," he greeted Thomas and Catherine.

Before either could speak, the haunting sound of conch shells reverberated in the night. They all turned, seeing native women coming out in single file carrying all kinds of baskets to the tables.

"I think we should take our places," said Thomas.

King Loma, his wife, and daughter, proceeded to their seats at the center of the main table. Thomas and Flynn walked over and sat beside them.

The sight of Thomas sitting next to Tu-la-lay did not sit well with Catherine. She understood: as leaders, Flynn and Thomas needed to be near the king and his wife. She took her place at the end of the main table with Doc Ryan, Mobee, and Cutter. The natives sat on one side, the white men on the other. The rest of the villagers took their places at tables set apart from the main.

Across from Catherine sat Suena, the mean looking one who killed Kettle and then hung Bishop and then filled him with arrows. They stared at one another. She dropped her gaze when King Loma stood up. She did not know what he was saying, but knew he was opening the festivities.

After clapping his hands, the servants brought out the meat from around the dome. The aroma was evident; they had been cooking all day. The first thing was a full headless deer, its legs tied to a pole. The next item was a wild boar. After that, Catherine's eyes went wide when ten strong warriors proceeded to the table carrying an eight-foot dragon. *Who in their right mind would eat a God-awful thing like that?* she thought, watching them set the beast before the king.

King Loma handed his son one of the machetes from the crate. When he reached over to cut the bamboo stitching holding the stomach closed, Catherine could have puked.

"Eat whatever they put in front of you," whispered Doc Ryan to her.

With her stomach turning, she looked at him then sheepishly smiled catching Suena's eyes.

After the last cord was cut, two giants pried open the belly. To the crew's surprise, one reached in and pulled out a roasted spider.

They sat there stunned, watching the giant rip the spider in parts and hand the pieces across to them. Albright and Mobee took what was offered.

"Eat up, gentlemen, you don't want to upset the king," said Mobee, biting into the meaty portion of a leg. "Mm... it tastes like monkey; a bit greasy but good."

The crew just sat there, staring at Mobee smiling at the King. They wondered if he was lying or telling the truth. Then again, they had never eaten a monkey.

"Eat," ordered Flynn, taking a bite of his portion. As they ate, more roasted spiders were pulled from the dragon's belly and passed down the table.

Catherine watched Suena take the creature in his bare hands, its long, cooked legs dangling before her. The sight of the horrid thing made her flood back to that terrifying night. Seeing Ezekiel being attacked flashed before her, and with her sword, she ran the spider through. The hideous screeching, the thrashing about as its guts oozed from the gaping wound.

Reliving the nightmare, Catherine began to shake, then she lost it and let out a horrifying scream.

Alarmed by the man's reaction, Suena fell off his seat in the sand.

Thomas, hearing her desperate cry, rushed to her side. She stood trembling, her eyes filled with fear.

"Catherine, Catherine," he pleaded.

The beach guard ran up. Flynn stood up, so did King Loma. Silence overcame the village.

Tu-la-lay slowly got to her feet, locking her eyes on Thomas holding the man. Then, it clicked. *"Be noka hy a kee,"* what do we have here, she bellowed, walking toward them.

Murmuring whispers drifted through the natives. The crew stood ready, waiting to see what was going to happen.

As Tu-la-lay approached, Thomas faced her.

"That is no man, Thumos."

"No, she was afraid to give herself away."

"Who is she?" she asked, brushing past him to see the girl.

The tense moment brought Se' fina to her feet.

"She is like you: royalty. The King of England's favorite daughter," he somewhat lied.

Tu-la-lay took her eyes off Catherine and stared at him. "Is she your woman?"

Thomas could see the anger within her stare.

"Yes, she is my woman."

It was immediate; Tu-la-lay spun around and went to hit Catherine.

Thomas caught her hand and held it tight.

Catherine glared up at Tu-la-lay. In that moment, all her emotions, the long agonizing voyage, seeing men she came to love dying came rushing up from the pit of her stomach and she exploded. "I have traveled through hell.... waded through gut wrenching torment and much pain to finally be here," she shouted, reaching out her hand toward the beach guard. "Bare me a sword and I'll run this mindless creature through, for I swear... I'll not be denied in taking Thomas home with me."

"Stop!!" shouted Se'fina.

As all eyes fell upon the queen, her order halting the tense moment.

"We all heard Thumos. This is his woman, one of royalty. His king's daughter."

All eyes fell on Catherine.

"But you, Father... you gave Thumos to me. How can you break your promise?"

Thomas waited to hear what her father had to say. Before he could speak, Cutter stepped out of the group. He did not need to know the language to understand what was being said. Tu-la-lay wasn't going to give up Thomas.

A time comes in every seafarer's journey when he knows his days are numbered. Bos'n Cutter knew his day had come.

"Who be naca," speak, said the king.

"Captain Payne, even though we are free men, free to go home, you inform the king that I will take your place. Not as a slave, but as Tu-la-lay's mate."

"Bos'n Cutter, do you know what you are saying?" Flynn weighed in.

"I do, Captain."

"You'll never leave this island if you continue."

Cutter looked upon his friends. Within their eyes sat the same undeniable thought.

"I know what I'm doing, Captain Flynn. Go ahead, Thomas, tell the king."

Thomas conveyed Cutter's proposal.

Tu-la-lay gazed upon the big burly man.

King Loma looked at him. Cutter pushed the issue even further. "Tell the king if she marries me, I'll build them long floats like the Lara May."

Thomas conveyed that to the king.

King Loma nodded. "I'll sit with my council," he said, turning toward the dome.

As the procession of elders followed King Loma, Catherine whispered.

"Bos'n Cutter, you don't have to do this."

"I know I don't. I'm laying down my life for your destiny," he replied, casting his eyes upon Thomas and then back at her.

"My destiny?"

"That's right. In all my days of sailing, I have never seen such bravery, such determination that you'd risk your very life to find Thomas and bring him home."

"You'd stay here, never to return to England?" questioned Thomas.

"After hearing Johan say he was ready to give up this life at sea, I too have been mulling it over, and I've decided I'm done traveling the world. I've had enough of what the sea offers, and besides, she is not bad looking."

Catherine slowly turned, taking in Tu-la-lay's features.

"As you can see, Milady... there are parts of her the sun never sets."

His words floated in her ear like sweet notes from a violin. She slowly turned studying his eyes. "Smitten, are we?"

"She's the finest pearl I've ever seen. I'd be the luckiest man on earth."

"You better pray you're lucky," said Thomas. "These people are a wretched brew."

"They were a day ago, but now..." his voice trailed off.

They waited to hear what he had to say.

"Captain Payne, if you want to make me happy, take Catherine home and raise a family together," he said.

Thomas gazed at her. It was all she wanted. She fell into his arms and wept.

"The God of the flesh eaters has returned," a native shouted.

Tu-la-lay stepped back from the two hugging one another. She hurried to her mother's side.

As the natives bowed, Flynn took in Johan - the ol' salt he had known for years. It was apparent that his time on the island had changed him... or maybe, over time... it was the medallion. The visions he saw seemed to be more powerful now. How he got the ants to follow was beyond him.

His thoughts abruptly halted when he saw his own men now bowing to Johan.

"It appears I've missed something," said Johan, looking at Thomas and Catherine.

"You have," replied Catherine, wiping her tears, then curtsying to him.

Johan faced the natives. *"Hy yaka be nod who sho ta be na na."* I come in peace, and peace we shall have between our people.

The natives rejoiced. King Loma and his council appeared in the archway, seeing him standing there.

Bou' nod relayed what Johan had just said.

King Loma stood there a moment reflecting on what to say in return.

Casting his eyes over his village, he spoke truth to them. "We are a people isolated from the world, a world we know nothing of except here on our island.

"As a people, we have never been defeated. I don't think we were defeated."

Murmurs went forth from the village. Many were confused by that.

"Instead, we were given wisdom. Wisdom from another land, another people," continued the king.

The warriors looked upon one another.

During the silence, Thomas turned toward Flynn and his men and restated what King Loma had just said.

All heads nodded. They too had learned much from these natives. Wisdom was gained on both sides. Thomas conveyed that to King Loma and his people.

The two sides eyed each other. Flynn reached out his hand toward Rua. He looked down at it, then took it within his.

King Loma clapped. All looked up at him. He and his wife then spoke with their daughter in private. On their return, King Loma announced, "My daughter will marry the maker of long floats."

As Cutter walked up the steps of the dome, the crew of the Lara May cheered.

By that time, Catherine had seen enough. She walked off alone toward the beach. The calming sound of the waves, the night sky ablaze in stars washed over her. Closing her eyes, she allowed the gentle breeze to settle her heart.

"Catherine," said Thomas.

Hearing his voice, she slowly turned and faced him. Tears welled up within her eyes.

Thomas could not only see her anguish, he could feel it deep within his soul. She was frail, exhausted and bitterly angry. He took her hands, kissed her forehead, her cheeks; nose to nose. Her soft complexion, his warm breath on her ignited their passion - their eternal flame for one another.

"Come," he whispered, pulling her hand.

"Where?" she replied, glancing up at the village then following him down the beach.

Alone for the first time in over a year, they walked in silence along the shoreline. Her heart was on fire; his heart was pounding to hold her. Minutes had gone by before he stopped and looked back. The village was just a twinkling dot.

When he turned to face her, he melted into her wanting gaze. A look that said kiss me, kiss me passionately. As he took her within his arms, his sweet sensual kiss aroused her hunger. She replied by allowing his tongue to explore her burning desires.

Within the heat of their passion, she gasped, "Thomas, oh Thomas."

He felt her knees buckle. He eased her gently to the sand. There, they lay kissing and caressing one another. Then he stopped. She looked into his eyes. Their breathing was heavy, staring at one another. They had never gone any farther than this and he knew they would have continued until they were completely spent.

It dawned on her why he stopped. Her heart sank like wreckage.

"My beloved angel, you know how much I want to."

"Yes, I do," she whispered. "So, do I."

He closed his eyes and sighed, feeling his manliness wane. When he opened them, she was staring into his face, searching... searching his thoughts.

"This situation we find ourselves in brings me to a place which I never thought possible. I thought of a million wonderful ways to ask you, but this moment gives me no choice."

His words confused her.

"Catherine, will you marry me and be my beloved wife forever and ever?"

Her heart burst with joy. They were the words she had wanted to hear from the moment she laid eyes on him at the Queen's Ball. It wouldn't have mattered if he asked her in a pit of mud, in a horse stall, she would have said yes, and her answer was that quick. "Yes, yes, I'll marry you, Thomas Payne."

After she said that, something washed over her. They had a long voyage ahead. There would be no way she'd wait that long to make love to him. "I don't know how we're going to manage being so close to one another aboard that ship and not being able to..."

"What are you talking about?"

"You honor me and my family's good name wanting to marry me before we make love to one another."

"I'd have it no other way, Catherine."

"Well then, how are we going to get married?"

"We'll get married by Captain Flynn."

JEFF WRIGHT
CATHERINE KNOX

She laughed.

"Maritime law states that a captain at sea has the authority to marry two people."

"No?"

He smiled at her.

"Captain Payne."

"Yes?"

"You mean we could be husband and wife in a matter of days?"

"Yes, Milady."

It was instant. She grabbed him, kissed him deeply. The moment seemed forever, then she released her grip. As they melted into one another's eyes, within hers was a question.

"Yes?"

"I only want one wedding present from you."

"Anything."

"I want for *you* to give up this life at sea. I want to live in the country; never to see water again."

His face remained slack and then he laughed.

"Is that funny?"

"No... I was just going to tell you that upon our return, I'll be resigning my commission. After hearing Bos'n Cutter's remarks, I've decided to give up the sea as well"

"You mean that?"

"Yes... and if you want to live in the country, so we shall."

"Oh, Thomas... you'd make me the happiest woman in the world."

"That's all I want you to be."

After he said that, the two melted together, entwined as one, on that distant shoreline, so far from home.

39

Ding, ding – ding, ding, Catherine arose hearing what she thought was the ship's bell. Opening her eyes, she saw whispering pink clouds splashed against a light blue sky. The break of morning had come. "Thomas," she said, nudging him.

He stirred, leaning against the palm tree, her head resting against his shoulder.

Ding, ding – ding, ding.

Fully awake, he saw crewmen and villagers carrying items to the lifeboats.

"Flynn doesn't waste any time, does he?"

She stood, shook the sand from her clothing, then walked out toward the beach with him.

"Morning, Captain," she greeted.

The pair looked filthy, but happy. "Morning you two.

"How soon are we leaving?" asked Thomas.

"As soon as the ship's cook stows away these provisions.

"I need a favor, Captain Flynn," said Thomas.

"What can I do for you?"

"For us," interjected Catherine.

Flynn shifted his eyes between the pair. It was obvious. He waited.

"We want you to marry us," they both said in unison.

A gallant smile appeared across his dirty face. "Your father, Admiral Knox would have me laid to waste at the yardarms for this, but seeing we have a long voyage ahead, it would be my honor."

Catherine stepped up and hugged him.

Suddenly, the conch shells sounded. Catherine let go of Flynn and turned seeing the doors of the dome opening. King Loma and Johan walked out.

"Have we missed something?" she questioned.

"He's been in there for over an hour with the king."

"Really?" she suspiciously mused.

We'll find out soon enough," replied Flynn, walking over to the lifeboats. "Be careful with those baskets."

Thomas and Catherine stood there watching the king and Johan coming down the steps. The dome guards raised their shells and blew into them once again. This time Queen Se'fina, Tu-la-lay, and Cutter appeared in the doorway.

The entire village lined up and bowed as they proceeded down to the shoreline.

The farewell was pleasant - coupled with utter sadness, as each crewman stepped up, said goodbye to Cutter and returned to the ship.

When it was Catherine's turn to speak to the Bos'n, tears welled up within her eyes. "You've become like a brother to me. And as a brother, I must ask you, are you happy in your decision in staying here?"

"I take that as an honor, Milady, and... yes, I am happy," he replied, taking Tu-la-lay's hand.

Catherine looked up at the tall beauty. The anger between them was over, each now satisfied with the outcome. When she focused on Cutter, she said her goodbyes. "You're a fine man, Mr. Cutter. If you ever return to England..." she said and then paused, "There'll always be a seat at our table for you."

"I thank thee, Lady Knox. You never know who'll show up at your door," he replied with a wink.

She turned, bowed to the king and queen and was just about to walk toward the lifeboat when Se' fina reached out her hand. Catherine stopped and looked at it.

Thomas stepped up to hear the queen's words.

The two women gazed at one another for a moment.

"Thumos, tell her that the king and I are sorry for upsetting her last night."

"It wasn't you who upset her."

"The spiders, Thumos. We didn't know until afterwards."

Thomas nodded, then conveyed the queen's message.

Catherine smiled, bowed her head and let go of her hand. "Tell the queen that it's OK. I'm fine now. And also tell her - we shall always have peace between our people." With that, she turned and stepped into the lifeboat alongside the other crewmembers.

Thomas and the boat's detail shoved it off. He stood there watching her heading toward the ship. He then turned, seeing Flynn walk up to Cutter.

"I've never been speechless, but today I find no words, Bos'n."

"There's really no words that need to be said, Captain."

Flynn nodded in thought. "I suppose you're right. I wish you a long and happy life, Bos'n Cutter," he replied, extending his hand.

Cutter took it within his. "Give me a year and they'll be as British as British can be, Sir."

Flynn smiled, letting go of his hand. He stepped up to King Loma and Queen Se'fina. "Take care of him for he is a good man. He'll teach you much about the ways of the sea."

Thomas conveyed his message.

"Ho nana be kata lim too," he'll become a son to us when he marries my daughter.

Flynn bowed and headed toward the last remaining boat.

Thomas stood before the king and queen – before the entire village. "I'll give word to my king of this peace we have made. No ship will come in anger against you."

King Loma extended his hand. "I'll miss you, Thumos, so will my wife."

He looked at her. She smiled.

With that, he turned toward Cutter. "Even though you did not have to remain, I am like Flynn, there are no words that can express my gratitude."

"There is no need to. I would have followed Catherine to the end of the world in search of you. I've never witnessed such...." he said, shaking his head.

"She is her father's daughter."

"That she is, Sir. That she is. Take good care of her."

"You can count on it."

With the morning sun breaking over the horizon, Cutter stood in silence watching the Lara May pull anchor and haul down her sails.

As the bow turned seaward, a lump caught in his throat. He made his choice; it was his decision to remain and marry Tu-la-lay. He looked up at her. She in turn glanced down at him. Within her beautiful blue eyes sat his new ocean; one he'd contentedly sail upon for the rest of his life.

✝

Those that had gone ashore in search of Thomas, were like the rope lines they had just climbed: tattered, frail, completely spent. Without a word, Smith walked up the portside steps and took over the helm. The rest of the crew found a place on deck and sat down. Flynn walked up to the mast and stood before them. He, too, looking tattered and frail.

The crew looked upon his weary face in need of a shave.

"Before we started this journey, I said that it was possible that some would not be returning. No one here really thought that was a possibility, but here we are, less nine men."

The crew nodded.

"Mr. Albright."

He stood.

"I want you to ring the bell for each name I mention."

"Aye, Captain."

"Seaman Butterfield."

Ding, ding....

"Seaman Davenport."

Ding, ding....

"Seaman Kettle."

Ding, ding....

"Seaman Hill."

Ding, ding....

"Seaman Ezekiel," sighed Flynn, shaking his head.

Ding, ding....

Seaman Caleb."

Ding, ding....

Seaman Jones."

Ding, ding....

"Carpenter's Mate, Hildegard."

Ding, ding....

"Mr. Davison - Master at Arms."

Ding, ding....

"Mr. Bishop - Second Mate."

Ding, ding....

"May they be within the arms of Him who created us, sailing the blue waters of Heaven for all eternity."

With each ring of the bell, the tears flowed freely. Flynn's simple prayer even made Catherine cry.

As the men looked upon her being held in Thomas' arms, some cried themselves. Mobee was one of them, so did Ludwig - both losing their best friends.

Flynn swallowed the dry lump in his throat and continued. "We are down nine men, but we will sail onward and make Port Williams and home with what we have left. I don't think we need a Master at Arms, but Mr. Albright will take that position. Mr. Smith will be overseeing the main deck with Sailing Master Ludwig. Captain Payne will take the duties of the helm and overseeing the watches." As he looked upon each man, one was missing. "Where is Johan?"

"Back aft, Sir," replied Ludwig, nodding.

Flynn glanced back. Johan was leaning on the rail looking toward the island.

"May I, Captain?" said Mobee, getting up.

Flynn nodded. He wasn't ready to speak to him.

Mobee strolled up, leaned against the rail alongside the ol' salt. Johan kept his eyes forward. Without a word, Mobee just stood there studying the island - now just a dot.

Johan glanced sideways, catching the lad seemingly looking out over the water. He noticed the tear stains on his cheek. "The Captain's words were a pleasant one," he said.

"Yes, they were."

They stood in silence for a moment, each man keeping company with his own thoughts. Then Mobee asked, "How did you do that, Johan?"

The sea legend smiled. He knew that was coming. He knew every man onboard wanted to know the answer, more so, Captain Flynn.

"Me 'dallion is more powerful than me ever imagined, Mobee."

He waited to hear more. Johan left it at that. It didn't matter. Mobee knew they had days, weeks and many months ahead. In that time, everyone would know each man's story: stories no Englishmen back home would ever believe.

"After this is all over, Mobee – you come see ol' Johan."

"I will. You can count on that."

Mobee was right, the days turned into weeks, the weeks into months before they rounded the coast of South Africa and into the blue Atlantic - the last stretch before *home.*

40

After the Lara May skirted around the coast of South Africa, Thomas, who oversaw the helm and watches, sailed her out into the unpredictable, Atlantic. There, he believed they'd catch the trade winds and following seas.

Flynn gave no objections, seeing first hand Thomas' remarkable ability in navigating a ship. The man, as Albright said so long ago, was the greatest sea captain he had ever sailed with. Flynn penned that in the ship's ledger. He, too, learned much from Captain Payne in their days together sailing homeward.

Three weeks out in the Atlantic, Thomas ordered the helm landward toward Spain and then up the coast and home.

Ten nautical miles out from Port Williams, the crow's nest shouted, 'sails off the portside'.

Catherine ran to the rail, studying the ship. She was elated seeing the British flag fluttering high in the breeze.

"That's a schooner, sharp, sleek and fast," said Thomas, coming alongside her.

"She's coming about, Captain," the crow's nest called down.

"Helmsmen, steady your course. Mr. Smith, slack the jib and haul up the mainsail."

"Aye, Captain."

"Sailing Master Ludwig, hoist the British flag."

"Aye, Sir."

As the HMS Brisbane made her turn, Captain Wellington, through his spyglass, studied the cargo ship. "I'll be damned, it's the Lara May."

"Captain Flynn's Lara May?" asked Lieutenant Davenport.

"There is only one Lara May and it belongs to the man now under arrest for kidnapping."

"Kidnapping, Sir?"

"That's what Admiral Knox ordered."

"But Lady Knox went on her own accord."

"We have our orders, Lieutenant."

"Do you want general quarters, Sir?"

"No, as you can see, Flynn has hauled up his sails. We'll come abreast and board."

When the ships came together, the securing lines tossed, Captain Wellington and his Marines boarded the Lara May with all intentions of placing Flynn and his crew in irons. Upon seeing Thomas, more so, the fiery beauty standing beside him, all bets were off; her father's order was tossed over the side.

"It sure be a fine afternoon, seeing you alive, Captain Payne," boasted the tall lengthy British Captain with greyish wide sideburns. "We thought you were dead."

"If it weren't for Captain Flynn, my wife, Catherine, and his crew... Mr. Albright and I would still be shipwrecked on that God forsaken island."

"Did you say, my wife?" he asked, gazing at Lady Knox.

"Do you need a chart to understand, Captain Wellington?" she retorted.

"Oh, no, Milady. As surely as the tides come and go, I do understand. Your voyage must have been long. However, let it be known here and now, we were under orders to arrest Flynn and his crew for kidnapping you."

"Kidnapping," barked Flynn.

"That came straight from Admiral Knox, Captain Flynn."

The crew looked at Catherine. She gave no reply to their questioning stare. "Will you be escorting us into port, Captain Wellington?" she asked.

"Yes, Milady," he replied, nodding to his Marines to return to the Brisbane. "I give you fair warning though. You'll not be received on the pier as you have been here. I bid you all farewell," he continued with a slight nod and then departed back to his ship.

As the Lara May sat adrift, Johan stood there rubbing his hands. "Harr, me Lads."

Everyone turned.

"Upon making port, me fear.... we'll all be abused."

"We'll all be bottom dwellers, ripe for the pic'ns, is that right Mr. Bailer?" Catherine amusingly replied.

He raised a brow to her comment.

"My Father hasn't seen me in over a year, dear Johan. He'll be elated when I go ashore. I'm sure of it."

"Let's pray he does," remarked Flynn, turning toward his crew. "Haul down the mainsail, set the jib. Helmsman, follow the Brisbane into port."

High over Port Williams, the sentry manning the fort wall peered into his spyglass seeing a naval ship escorting a cargo ship into port. "What be the reason?" he murmured, studying the ship's structure. His jaw dropped. It was the Lara May. "Corporal Hummel!"

"Yes, Lad, what is it?"

"Take a look."

"I'll be," he gasped. "We need to get word to Admiral Knox, quick."

It was a mundane afternoon at Windsor Castle when Admiral Knox heard a frantic knock on his door. "Come in."

William Colfax entered. "As I speak, Sir... the Lara May is being escorted into Port Williams by a British naval ship."

It took but a second for the Admiral to stand. Ten minutes later, the entire castle exploded with the news.

Admiral Knox, the king, along with his Royal Guard rushed to Port Williams.

As the pier hands caught the lines and were securing the Lara May, thundering hooves and the heavy sound of wagons came racing down the pier. The Royal Guard ushered people away and then locked down the entire area. Admiral Knox dismounted his horse. Two sentries opened the king's carriage door.

Flynn and his crew watched the admiral storm across the cobble stones toward the gangway.

"You, Captain Flynn, and your entire crew are under arrest," he shouted. "I'd have you keelhauled myself...." he continued and then abruptly stopped yelling, seeing his daughter and Thomas Payne walk up to the rail and look down at him.

"Did I hear you say keelhauled?" amusingly questioned King George, eyeing Catherine and Thomas.

"Father," she beamed, running down the gangway. She collapsed within his arms like a child. He held her tight, relieved she was home safe.

"I'm so sorry, Father. I was such a fool for doing what I did, but as you can see, Thomas was still alive when I begged you to go in search of him."

Now an emotional wreck, his eyes watered. "Catherine, hush. You're home now. That's all that matters to me."

As Thomas made his way down the gangway, another carriage entered the pier. The guards on all sides halted their horses. The door was quickly opened. Queen Charlotte stepped down.

"Out of my way, out of my way," she scolded, briskly walking up. When her eyes landed upon Catherine and Thomas, she held her hands to her face and wept with joy.

"My Queen, my dear Lady," fussed Catherine, letting go of her father and hugging her.

The fanciful King George stood there delighted in the moment. Charlotte loved her like a daughter; loved Thomas as well. It was she who pushed them together and... her heart shattered like a glass chalice when she was informed that Catherine had sailed off with Captain Flynn to find him.

For days, weeks and months afterward, she punished herself, and now... her heart rejoiced seeing them safely home.

Flynn and his crew stood there amazed at Catherine's reception with the king and queen. They felt they had skirted death and would live another day.

"Your Majesty – Admiral Knox," said Thomas, feeling a lump in his throat.

All eyes fell upon him.

"I have to report... apart from Mr. Albright, I lost my ship, my entire crew. The both of us would have been lost forever, if it wasn't for Lady Knox and Captain Flynn."

King George nodded, eyeing the two.

Admiral Knox stared at Flynn. A moment ago, he could have lopped off his head for allowing his daughter to talk him into taking her to the South Pacific. Now, he was too overwhelmed to take revenge.

"I only have two requests, actually three," continued Thomas.

"Speak up, Captain," said King George

"I would like to see Captain Flynn reinstated in the Royal Navy. His sheer determination in rescuing us was undeniably remarkable. He lost ten men, but continued onward through the jungles in search of Mr. Albright and me. Without him, your Majesty..." his voice trailed off.

Caught off guard by Thomas' request, Flynn was beside himself. It was a request, he figured... would be denied.

The king glanced at Admiral Knox, who appeared to be wanting to say something. As King of England, this was his choice, and he alone was going to make it. "Your request is granted, Captain," he replied, looking upon Flynn. "I'll go even further than that." he said, stepping forward. "Captain Flynn, I am awarding you and your entire crew with the king's silver medal for gallantry in your unwavering persistence to find Captain Payne. You also, Lady Knox. As far as those who perished, I'll have my finance minister get with those families and see they are taken care of."

"Your Majesty," said Catherine. "My pledge to each man was one thousand pounds to go."

"A thousand pounds?"

"Yes."

"I'll add four thousand more to each man."

Catherine curtsied. Flynn's crew sighed with joy hearing that.

"Now, after this is over," King George continued, "I'd like an audience with you and your crew, Captain Flynn. Tonight, we'll celebrate."

"Yes, your Majesty," replied Flynn, bowing his head.

His crew bowed their heads as well.

At the back of the group, Johan cringed hearing the king wanting an audience. The last thing he wanted was telling the king about his mystical medallion, the one he gained so long ago from the famous pirate, Scar.

"What is your next request?"

"This is two-fold, Your Majesty. Firstly, I'd like to resign my commission in the Royal Navy."

Queen Charlotte stepped up to the king, eyeing Thomas.

"After living a nightmare, I thought would never end, I'd like to bid farewell to the sea."

"Not knowing what you went through, Thomas," said Queen Charlotte, "within your eyes it is evident that you have gone through much pain and sorrow."

"Yes, my Queen."

"I hate losing a fine captain, but your request is granted," said the king.

"Thank you, your Majesty. My next request is to you, Admiral Knox."

The Admiral had an inkling of what that request would be. He stood on the balls of his feet waiting to hear.

"I would like your permission, Sir, to marry your daughter."

That went over like an anchor hitting bottom. "Up to this moment, Captain Payne," sharply replied Admiral Knox, "I have never put in question your integrity. But seeing you have been with my daughter in such proximity onboard a ship for so many months at sea, you never took the liberty..."

"I married them, Admiral," interrupted Flynn.

"You married them!" he blasted.

"Yes. It was Captain Payne's idea. We had a long voyage ahead. Thomas made it clear to me that he would not dishonor her or her family's name, Sir. So, I married them."

Like harps on the wind, Flynn's words floated into the queen's ear.

"If you have already married my daughter, then why are you asking me, Captain Payne?"

"Admiral Knox," scolded Queen Charlotte. "The Captain just did an honorable thing in asking for her hand."

"But they are already married, Milady."

"That doesn't matter. Your daughter deserves a proper wedding and I'll see fit that she does."

Admiral Knox felt all eyes on him, more so – his daughter. Her eyes were filled with immense love for the man now asking for her hand. There was only one answer he could give. Long winded, but it was given. "Seeing such love and joy within my daughter's eyes, gladdens my heart. I would be honored to call you my son-in-law. You may marry my daughter, Captain Payne."

"Oh, Father, you just made me the happiest woman in the whole world," beamed Catherine.

"Is there any other request?" asked the king.

"Yes, your Majesty," replied Mobee.

"Come forward, young man."

Mobee walked through the group.

"What can I do for you?"

"It's not for me, Sir. It's for someone else."

"Go on."

"We lost ten good men, your Majesty."

"Yes, and I'm sorry for that."

"Well, your Majesty... one of those men was my best friend. He died fighting the most horrid things on that island while searching for Captain Payne."

"Horrid?"

"Spiders the size of melons, Sir."

King George stood back. He looked at Thomas. Thomas slightly nodded.

"Go on."

"In tribute to his unwavering love for country and king, I'd like that island to be named after him, your Majesty," said Mobee, bowing his head.

King George felt his words deeply. It saddened his heart that, so many had perished: Thomas' whole crew, Flynn's men, one being this lad. "What is his name?"

"Ezekiel, Your Majesty."

"Admiral Knox," said King George in a tone of anguish.

"Yes, My Lord."

"I want all naval charts updated depicting Ezekiel Island."

"Yes, your Majesty."

"How's that?" the king replied, leaning over to Mobee.

"I thank you, Sir."

In the midst of this heart rendering moment, Johan saw his chance. He slowly turned, excused himself through the Royal Guard and proceeded down the pier. Strolling along, he thought, *I'll catch up with the men at the Blue Dragon, or maybe at the Trade Winds in Bristol Bay. There, they can tell me how their meeting went with the king.*

"Mr. Bailer."

Johan cringed hearing her voice. He slowly turned and faced Catherine.

"Where are you off too, may I ask?" she said, clasping her hands to her waist.

"Why, Melady... am off to see a man who specializes in stones."

"Stones?" she questioned, eyeing his gunny sack.

"Why yes, Melady."

"What kind of stones?" she suspiciously inquired.

"One actually."

"One? From where?"

"You ask a lot of questions to ol' Johan."

She amusingly cocked her head staring at the him. "I've got an inkling in me guts that it is not just any stone, but one that sparkles. Am I correct?"

"As true as the point off the bow, you are. As true as the point."

"King Loma's diamond?"

"You should have been a mind reader."

"How?"

"Me gave him the secret to taming the ants, Melady."

"You gave him the blackberries for the diamond?"

"Why, yes."

"I see," she replied. "And what will you do with such wealth?"

"Once I know the stones worth, I was going to see Miss Becky at the Pink Pearl."

"The boarding house""

"Yes. Ol' Johan is going to ask her to marry me."

"A harlot!"

"She owns the place."

"She's still..."

"No, she never was. Me tried on many occasions to rid me ills with her. She wouldn't have a bar of it."

Catherine stood back, amused in his way of explaining a man's desire in having a woman.

"You see, Melady, Miss Becky has always kept a chair for me at her table and... and me figured.... if me asked her polite like, she'd say yes."

"Then what, you'd take her out to sea with you?"

"Why no, Melady. After hearing you and Thomas speaking of a country life, me thought me try living on an ocean of green instead of blue."

"You... living in the country?"

"Yes, me thinking of purchasing the Klondike Castle, if she still be for sale."

"Mr. Bailer," she started, feeling her heart going weak. "You are the salt of the sea, a man I deeply admire. I want you to know from the bottom of my heart that there will always be a seat at our table for you, and... I want to see you sitting in it one day. With Miss Becky, if all goes well with your proposal."

"I'd be so grateful to oblige you, Melady."

"Good."

"Before me depart your presence, me'd like to say...."

"Yes," she interrupted, staring into his eyes.

"Thomas Payne is wealthier than me. You, Melady, are worth more than all the gems on earth – worth more than all the pearls in the sea."

Without a word, Catherine stepped up and kissed his cheek. "I miss you already, dear Johan." With that, she slowly turned and headed back to the group.

Johan gazed upon her leaving. *Never in me life have me seen such....* his thoughts delightfully drifted. With a warm tender smile, he left the pier and headed to the Lea Burrow Inn to see a man who specialized in precious stones.

Epilogue

It was twilight on a far-off sea. With the night sky ablaze in stars, the HMS Hornbeak sailed across the calm still waters. Way below in the officer's dining facility, the men sat there enjoying their wine while listening to a story. When it was finished, some leaned back, mystified.

"Now I know some of you here find it hard to believe, but that is the entire story – the tale of the voyage of the Lara May."

"It's truly hard to fathom, Sir." said Lieutenant Nobble.

"Every bit of it is true."

"After Flynn reentered the Royal Navy, what did he do with the Lara May?" asked Mr. Roberts.

"He turned the cargo ship over to Mr. Smith and Sailing Master Ludwig."

"What about Bos'n Cutter, Sir. Did he ever return to England?" asked Ensign Storm.

"No."

As the officers drifted on Cutter remaining on the island with Tu-la-lay, there was a knock on the door.

"Enter."

"Sorry to disturb you, Sir," said the ship's Master at Arms.

"What is it?"

"Our two young lads would like to speak with you."

"Alright.... drink up men, I have business at hand."

The officers quickly drank their wine then filed out.

"Let 'em in."

"Yes, Sir."

Young Daniel and Collins entered. As the door closed behind 'em, they hesitantly looked back.

"Come forward."

The two cautiously proceeded up to the table.

"You have my ear. What can I do for you?"

"Well, Sir..." replied Daniel, nervously glancing at his friend. "We'd like to have a word with you.... Captain Mobee."

"What be on your minds?"

"We want to be treated like men onboard this fine vessel, Sir."

Slowly leaning back in his chair, deep within his heart, Captain Mobee remembered a time long ago when Ezekiel and he were just boys: *we thought like boys, spoke like boys, played like boys, but when we became men, we put away our childish things.*

The End

Novels by Jeff Wright

Mr. Bones Trilogy;
1. From Out of the Darkness
2. Goldie Locks
3. Den of Scorpions

The Ghost of Sage Grey

The Mysterious Abigail Rose

Yeti
Yeti II

Whiskers

You can follow Jeff - at
www.facebook.com/jeffwrightbooks

91200714R00222

Made in the USA
Columbia, SC
18 March 2018